Behind the Gate

By

Brenda Lynn

Dedication

To my husband, Mike, who has never doubted, from the very beginning, that I could accomplish this long-time goal of mine despite my own apprehension and lack of faith during this endeavor.

I thank you for your unconditional love and support.

Acknowledgment

I want to thank Jordan and Adam and their team at KDP for making my longtime dream come true. Without their continual support and attention to my project, I would not have been able to finally tell my story with confidence. I feel truly blessed and still hear your kind, uplifting words tweeting happily in my ears.

Author's Bio

Brenda Lynn lives with her husband in Florida, where they both work from their quaint beach home nestled in a gated community close to the Gulf.

Please visit her website at www.brendalynnbooksandbites.com

"You can't go back and change the beginning, but you can start where you are and change the ending."

— C.S. Lewis

Contents

CHAPTER 1

Minnesota: August 2015

There was a county park up ahead, and if I didn't get through the stop sign and take a hard right real fast, I would lose everything in my bubbling stomach on the floor of my pathetically small rental car. I don't know what I was thinking about renting a car this small, but now I could sympathize over the infliction on a claustrophobic. It seemed hard to breathe in such a tight place, especially with my stomach churning as I drove over the numerous imperfections on the road.

I had to keep swallowing, with it rising in my throat faster than the speed I could legally drive on this road. Making it to a decent restroom would have been nice, but I didn't have that luxury. Finally, I pulled into the parking lot and searched for the nearest empty spot furthest from the other cars. I barely got the door open before I hurled what little contents were in my stomach onto the bright yellow dividing line. In my car, I always kept a hand towel in the center console for wiping down the windshield, but unfortunately, I was in a rental car heading to the airport—no such luck in this car. But I found a napkin in my purse as I rummaged around with one arm while I hung my head out the side.

My flight to Tampa was something I'd been looking forward to for three years, and throwing up was just an unplanned item on the itinerary. My best friend, Cassie, awaited me in the Delta Lounge. She'd completely understand why this emotionally driven hiccup happened in the first place; she knew my family all too well. As excited as I was to finally drive away from the mess I left in my parent's driveway, my body would inevitably choose to rebel one more time.

"Ma'am, are you ok? Ma'am?" A security guard approached me and asked.

"I'm fine," I replied, my head still closer to the ground than his face. All I could see were the tips of his black work boots. When I looked up to ask if he had something I could wipe my mouth off with, I recognized him as Chad Jacobs, a guy I graduated with. God, of all people and places to end up. He handed me a small stack of paper towels that looked like he had swiped from the public bathrooms and handed them to me.

"Thank you," I said, embarrassed to make eye contact longer than necessary. The heat mixed with a nauseous stomach made a sweat bath out of my body. Could this get any worse?

Yes, it could. He recognized me. "Raven? Raven McKade? Gosh, I haven't seen you in ages. What can I do to help you right now?" I just wanted him to leave, I was so embarrassed as I wiped my face and my mouth once more before sitting up.

"I'm sorry, I messed up here," I said with the little energy left in me, swirling my finger above the pavement.

"I'll get it cleaned up. Do you need me to take you anywhere?" He offered.

"No, thank you. I'm headed to the airport. Moving to Florida." I cracked a much-needed smile, and a small jolt of elation slipped across my chest, bringing my heart rate back to a regular beat.

Chad wished me luck, and I drove off, heading toward 35W and the Minneapolis/St. Paul airport. The discussion, if you can call it that, between my sister, Rachel, and I weighed heavy on me as I drove north.

"Do you see what this is doing to Mom, Raven? Damn. Your selfishness has raised an ugly head again. Run away and take no responsibility." My egotistical sister, Rachel, fumed yet again about the decision I'd made as an independent adult.

"Run away and take no responsibility? Me?" I said, narrowing my brows.

"Yes, you," she said, pointing an accusing finger my way, her face ugly with anger.

"Oh, do you remember the last time you cleaned up Mom's mess? And where were you when our neighbor had to bring Mom through the window? Who did he call? You or me?"

"So, now, you're keeping count? Great!" Rachel spouted. "So, why don't you stay if you're such the saintly one? This is the way it's always going to be between you and I, Raven."

I chose to stare and not comment. Rachel was well aware of the trauma I'd been through losing my fiancé and enduring the contractor's personal violation against me. But, she insisted that after therapy, those traumatic events hadn't hindered me anymore; that they had washed away with the turning of the lakes somehow.

She was completely wrong.

My silence ended the argument. Rachel flipped her wrist at me before slamming the car door and speeding off, leaving a splat of rubber on the paved road. I thought I saw steam rise from the black tire mark; it was so hot for an August day in Minnesota. It was nearly ninety degrees, and I knew it wasn't even 10 a.m. To see Rachel leave in a huff was typical. Her feelings were the last of my worries. Since our relationship never hit that true sister hood companionship, neither of us felt a love loss.

With my friend, Cassie, it did. We were more like sisters. With my choice to move to Florida, we could easily revive the closeness we once shared before she moved away fifteen years ago.

There were many things I wanted to leave behind me, but it, unfortunately, included my parents. I knew that staying in Minnesota would certainly challenge me mentally in a way that Florida could heal me, which was crucial to my main goal of fixing *me*. Rachel's ulterior motives only proved I was making the right choice.

I hastily shoved the last items into the trunk of my ridiculously small rental car and was almost ready to leave when my mother wobbled toward me. She hugged me from behind with force, her thin hands clasped so close to my esophagus, nearly choking me. The odor of last night's alcohol consumption hung so heavy that I had to hold my breath, and I gingerly pulled her hands away from my throat. That didn't work so well. Now she leaned into me, a waterfall of tears soaking into my shirt. I wore a white blouse and a red skort that was now stuck to me like an extra layer of skin.

My father, dressed in yesterday's suit, now wrinkled with that slept-in look, marched over to encourage my mother to return inside the house. Dad leaned over and whispered, "I'll take care of her. "Don't miss your flight. I'll call you in a few days." And then he kissed me on the top of my head. I handed him a soggy note from my pocket: "Don't forget about the two containers of chicken wild rice soup in your freezer."

She released me from her clasp while her sniffling sobs dissipated and her heeled shoes floundered on the rocky driveway. It was a desperate scene, like watching an Alfred Hitchcock movie. Sadness and guilt were building so much so, my stomach felt squeamish. With their backs to me, I waved and whispered, "Goodbye."

As I entered the Delta lounge, the arctic chill in the air hit me like a wet blanket. It had to be twenty degrees colder in here than outside. Against the drying sweat under my clothes, I felt a goosebump chill. I needed to change and freshen up before I looked for Cassie. She had a seat waiting for me per her text, so I didn't have to worry about that seeing the place was packed. So many were having to stand to sip on their drinks or eat their small plates full of food.

Thankfully, the lounge restrooms provided a few female necessities. Grabbing a couple of their disposable cloths and getting them wet, I wiped down and changed into the clean short-sleeve top I had shoved in my carry-on bag for an emergency. And this was an emergency. I never left home, especially during a hot Minnesota summer, without a change of clothes, and that's why, to me, purchasing large purses or shoulder bags was my style. I was never the girl who'd carry the tiny bag barely big enough to hold my license and lip gloss. With my mother's sobs, perspiration, and, no doubt, residue from throwing up leached into the fibers of this blouse that a change was required. I tossed the shirt in the trash along with the wipes and splashed on some honey lavender-scented body spray from my bag, another necessity for a hot, grueling day. I fluffed my drooping ponytail and applied a light foundation layer, brightening my sunken cheeks and a layer of lavender hand cream. Now I was ready to meet up with Cassie.

"Hey," I said, giving Cassie a shoulder hug from behind. She was engrossed in an article on her laptop: *Atlas Subluxation.* Clearly, a chiropractic topic I'd let her finish while I quickly scanned the double-level Minneapolis lounge. I moved the bag off the chair she was holding for me and sat down. Dressed in dark denim shorts and a mint green top, Cassie's creamy skin looked so fresh, so Florida sun-kissed.

As a chiropractor, Cassie certainly lived the healthy lifestyle she preached about to her patients, and her skin glowed from the fruits of her intentions. A wave of jealousy shimmied through me as I hoped that would be me in six months. Cassie and I were very similar in size and height, but she was an authentic blonde with skin pigment that bronzed from the sun. If I didn't reapply every hour, my pale skin turned the color of an overripe watermelon. We'd actually set a timer when we hung out at her pool as young girls. Her mother reminded me

5

often as she sat outside reading while we jumped off the diving board or raced the length of the pool. Cassie had light green eyes, a yellow fleck on her left, and I had crystal blue eyes, exactly like my dad. My fine textured strawberry-blonde hair matched my mother's when she was my age. At fifty-six, she'd gone mostly gray, the reddish tinge gone.

"Hey," she said without moving her eyes from the screen, raising a single finger in a hold-on-a-moment gesture. A few minutes later, she shut her laptop and slid it back into her carry-on bag. "Sorry about that; I've got some testing I need to study for. Don't you look adorable in that red skort and cute top? And I love your Skechers. You're ready for hot Florida." She flipped me a thumbs up. "Hey," she said, touching my knee. "How'd it go?" I watched her eyes roam my face for answers.

"Horrible as ever." I leaned forward toward Cassie, who sat across from me. I wanted to avoid telling the rest of the travelers seated around me my sad story. "Well, Mom smelled like an after-bar party, and Rachel was her pleasant self." I sighed, pinched my lips together, and nodded my head in a what-did-anyone-expect sort of way.

Cassie nodded; her expression was sad but intent on my words. My family's dynamics weren't a surprise to her in the least. At ten years old, my grandfather disappeared, which left our family in complete unrest and my mother without a motherly presence. That's when she found a bottle to crawl into, and the rest of the family lost faith in what we thought our family unit was. If I hadn't had Cassie's family, who took me in as their own child, I'm certain I would have joined my mother in the pits of self-destruction. Grandma died five years earlier, which was heart-wrenching enough, but then Grandpa up and left one day, leaving my mother crushed and nearly lifeless; the rest of us sank in sadness with her.

Pulling me back into the present, Cassie tapped me and pointed toward the bar with a questioning eyebrow raise. How ironic to be thinking about the horrible drunk my mother had become while I gladly marched up to the bar with Cassie craving a glass of wine. It didn't make sense, but then I never went to the degree my mother did. On the other hand, my sister wasn't below accusing and pointing fingers at my criticism of Mom as I sipped a glass of wine with my dinner. Her voice penetrated my ears like it always did while desiring a glass of relaxation.

"I'm so sorry, Rave. I knew today was going to be tough. 'How's your dad."

The line was long, and I was anxious to just take a moment to breathe, thrilled to be with my best friend.

"Well, he looked like he'd slept on the couch...again. Mom's midnight antics are getting out of hand, and my father looks exhausted most days. My mom's condition is taking a toll on my dad's health. The other night, Mom put dinner in the crockpot early and turned on a burner instead...underneath the crockpot, mind you. Then our neighbor brought her through the front door half-naked at two in the morning. It pisses me off. Rachel lives twenty minutes away but expects me to run from sixty miles away to help Dad with Mom's mess." I shook my head in disbelief. "I think she got the picture this time that it's up to her, now, to help out Dad."

"So dang glad it's going to be behind you now," Cassie said, clutching my face and kissing me on the cheek. She wasn't afraid to show her friendly affection toward me, and it usually didn't embarrass me until now when I noticed the bartender smirk. I rolled my lips between my teeth to keep from chuckling out loud at his observation. Cassie was clueless.

"What would you two lovely ladies like? Champagne? Celebrating something?" His eyes opened wide in question as he nodded, picking up the champagne bottle.

"Yes! But chardonnay, please." Cassie clapped her hands together, glancing back at me. "My best friend, here, is finally taking the plunge and moving to Florida. My husband and I are thrilled to death." She placed her arm around me in another joyous side hug. She scrunched up her nose, smiling like a giddy teenager, and then stuck a five in the jar. The bartender splashed in a heavy pour of the golden liquid into two glasses and then gave an appraising look. His round face, balding head, and squinty eyes led me to believe he was probably one of those guys that liked to hug a woman just to cop a feel. I shouldn't judge, but I couldn't help it.

I followed Cassie with two plates of hummus and chips, the tension in my wrists and fingers nudging me with an annoying ache. Selling my house and my business and packing it all up over the last three months has left me struggling to carry two small paper plates that weighed less than a kitten. I also struggled to keep up my workout routine which hadn't helped, and neither did the many sleepless nights dreaming about breathing in the salty air, watching the palms sway and squishing soft sand between my toes at the nearby beach.

It was good to get *out of dodge,* as they say.

Comfortably seated in first-class, Cassie gave the flight attendant our drink order as I stared out the window at the men shuffling around the plane, preparing for our takeoff. As much as I was hungry to leave, sadness still niggled at my insides. I kept picturing my father holding my mother back as she cried a mixture of emotional tears that weren't about me leaving. It was self-pity. She knew I had enough of her excuses after finding bottles hidden whenever I visited. It wreaked of a weakness I hoped never to encounter, no matter how bad life got. But not now. I was starting a new chapter at thirty-seven and couldn't be happier moving into a new house in a new state. This was also a one-way ticket, which I'd never booked before. I'd be back some time to visit, but my premise for moving was about freeing myself, letting the memories that trapped me stay there. I rubbed away the rumbling that started again in my stomach.

"Are you ok? You're as white as a ghost," Cassie said, her voice soft but full of concern, her hand gently placed on my arm.

"Yeah, I will be…as soon as I get these visuals out of my head," I replied with a snappy tone, regretfully so. "I'm sorry, Cass. My head is spinning with too much…" The flight attendant cordially interrupted, handing us our drinks. *Good, a mood changer.*

"Here you are, Miss Towers and Miss McKade. Enjoy." I looked up to a young woman I guessed to be in her thirties with the perfect Miss America smile. Her bird-like voice switched the snippy button in my head and erased the babbling of Rachel that kept repeating in my ears. I chuckled out loud at how easy it was to do that. Cassie flashed me a whimsical look and started laughing as well.

We raised our glasses in a friendly cheers moment, and then she said, "I'm so flipping excited about you moving." She poked at my hint of a dimple that appeared with an exaggerated side smile. "We're finally going to be close…barely an hour away. Your life is going to be spectacular, Rave. I can't wait to watch how the sunshine lifts your spirits!"

Cassie pulled her laptop out and searched for my most recent cooking video posted on YouTube. It had already been six weeks since I cooked my last walleye dish, thrilled to be switching gears to fresh seafood options like snow crab, grouper, and shrimp. As we watched the video set against the kitchen backdrop I designed with my food vlog in mind, it became unnerving. I kept silent with a tight-lipped grin as Cassie praised my overall appearance and how well I spoke and instructed at the same time. It was hard to listen to all the beautiful things she was saying when all I saw was the face of the contractor who, despite having done such a superb job, assaulted me right there in that very place. A man who came highly recommended by another client of mine. I still felt the punch in my gut. I had to look away.

I let out an audible breath. I hadn't realized I was holding it in for so long, and trying to hide my unease, I gulped a mouthful of wine, letting it simmer between my cheeks before I swallowed.

"Can't wait to see your next video, Rave, in your new kitchen! You're still going to do this, right?" Cassie gave me a side-eye glare as in "no" better not be my answer.

"That's the plan," I said, sitting up in my seat and straightening my skort before crossing my legs.

Just peering into Cassie's eyes, the gold fleck very prominent, and seeing how excited she was for me made me feel small and selfish. Here was the best friend a person could have, one that stood by me through many heartaches and the happiest of times, and all I seem to do is torture myself inside as if, for some reason, I've got to relive those debilitating moments in order to redeem myself. Why? Therapy taught you how not to relive such events. I was to be focusing on my new chapter without the baggage of yesterday's tragedies hindering my forward progress.

"It's the only moneymaker I've got going right now." I sucked in a breath. "I'm surprised I still have money in the bank after all the splurging I've done with this house." I winced, and Cassie made a funny face. A ping of relief settled in my veins while I closed my eyes.

"I'm glad Luke forced me to promise I wouldn't send you any more kitchen pictures. It's so beautiful, and I can't wait to see your reaction, my dearest friend. You deserve every good thing that's coming your way." I lowered my chin and mouthed, *thank you.* She was truly a precious friend to me.

Cassie chatted on while tapping around on her laptop. I had never designed anything as "cheffy", as I preferred to call it, as I did in this new house. I chose all high-end appliances; a six-burner gas stove, a commercial double-wide fridge-freezer combination, and two commercial dishwashers. Unfortunately, it took me months to design and get the appliances in time, which wore on Luke's nerves as it delayed the project at times, but I played on his weakness; food. He's a man with an appetite and loves my cooking. I bribed, showing no mercy to his pertinent deadlines, telling him that when all was said and done, there would be an exquisite dinner made for him. He couldn't argue, instead conceded and wrapped his strapping arms around me in a warm brotherly hug. It was a mutual transfer of sibling love; he was the brother I never had, and I was the sister he never had.

I paged through the newest addition of *Food and Wine* while Cassie typed away on her laptop, both of us sipping our red wine. Flying down the runway, I gazed out the window, watching the oak and maple trees become smaller. As the plane rose higher into the sky through the clouds, my heart filled with an unfamiliar joy. I placed my hand to my heart, letting the oncoming exhaustive fumes of the last three years dissipate into the clouds below us. Pressing my nose to the window, I pinched my eyes closed and felt a rush of hot tears escape while a smile formed. This felt so good, like a pressure-filled tank fully released. I turned a quick glance at Cassie, hoping she hadn't noticed. There wasn't a need for sympathetic or encouraging conversation at this point. It was my time, at thirty thousand feet, to finally forgive myself and accept the start of a new life. It was time to believe in myself once again and realize there was more out there for me.

I finished my drink and closed my magazine; I could no longer keep my eyelids open. Exhaustion poked heavily at my body.

Next thing I felt was the jolt of the tires hitting the runway and my eyes popping open in a delirious daze. "We're home, Raven. Wake up."

Cassie squeezed my hand with an obvious message that said; *we'll never be apart again.*

CHAPTER 2

Wednesday, August 5ᵗʰ

"It's a muggy one here," I said, sounding let down, but that was only because I still felt tired, and the redundant layer of sweat wasn't helping. We walked to Cassie's car parked in the airport parking lot, my feet sluggish and heavy like the air I breathed. I needed to change my Sketchers for flip-flops to at least let my feet breathe. My inside voice kept screaming, *at least it's not ten below or snowing, so shut it down.*

"Still tired, Rave?" Cassie said, amusement slathered in her words. She knew who I was and relished caring for me like the best sister-friend could in this situation. Coaxing me over with a finger swipe in the air, I yawned as I drug three large luggage bags that felt like I was pulling a boulder up the side of a mountain. She popped the back open of her Tahoe and lifted our bags as if filled with feathers. I shook my head in both annoyance and respect. "You can rest your eyes on the way to Tiffany's."

"I don't want to miss the view." I even sounded pathetically exhausted to myself. Though I slept for some time during that three-and-a-half-hour flight, I was still in a trance. After three months of consistent packing, loading, and re-loading, my fight mode had taken flight. I needed coffee or caffeine badly.

"Remember, you live here now. You'll always be able to see it anytime you want." Cassie helped me into my seat like I was crippled and set my bag on my lap. I smiled and poked her cheek this time. "Dig out your flip-flops. It's time for a little sand between your toes."

"Remember when you moved here fifteen years ago?" Cassie started the vehicle and then looked at me, a stupefied expression glaring in her eyes. I chuckled as I watched the memory float to the front of her brain.

"Yes, and I was so pissed at Luke. Seven months pregnant, and he wants to move during August to Florida officially! God, I wanted to kill him."

"I remember like it was yesterday. My heart sank at the same time I jumped for joy. Knowing the twins would be born in Florida, I was so happy for you. But then I hated you for leaving me. I cried all night like a spoiled child. It was exciting that you'd be a first-time mommy without bundling them up in winter to drive them to daycare. What parent wouldn't desire that?" I laid my head back on the headrest and realized that's now me. If I had any children, which was a big *IF*, I wouldn't have to dress them in snowsuits and fur trapper hats like my dad did when Rachel and I wanted to play outside in zero-degree weather. And we thought it was a cool look.

Although mentally drained, my head was filled with the realization I was still emotionally stuck in Minnesota. While Cassie chatted with her office staff on her car phone, I wondered what Dad was doing right this minute and if Rachel was trivializing my decision to move sixteen hundred miles away to her husband, Pete, ranting about my selfishness and how I'd be back in Minnesota sooner than later to reclaim my responsibilities with our parents. Despite our detached relationship, knowing she says things like that still hurts.

The last time I flew to Florida was in January, nine months ago. I didn't remember the air tasting the way it does now on my tongue. The heavy humidity mixed with briny vegetation might not seem pleasing to most, but to me, it confirmed what new senses were in store for me.

"Here we are," Cassie said as we neared Tiffany's.

"Wow! Look at the water and the people. I'm thankful you waited to bring me here," I said, my voice returning to life, my vision clearing from the cloudiness of never-ending fatigue. The swaying palms and Spanish moss dripping off the branches of the live oak trees was a beautiful sight, and had since learned the natives call it *tree hair*.

I like that term better.

Tiffany's Wine Bar & Grill sat beachfront on a small barrier island connected by a half-mile paved road built upon a dam of boulders. Surrounded by intercoastal waters that led out into the Gulf, Tiffany's was *the* popular hangout on Bay Harbor Island. Cassie seemed to be in love with this place. She said, "This is the place to come when you want to feel the sand between your toes, a glass of wine in your hand, and the sea salt air in your nose."

I got the subtle hint she was jealous.

Luke had insisted on building their dream home forty miles inland, in Lakeland, where his business office could be more centrally located. Cassie complained at first, she wanted to be closer to the Gulf waters. I had heard both sides, but when she found the perfect building to house her chiropractic business, Luke jeered her with an, "I told you so."

It was time for Tiffany's initiation. I only wished Jack was holding my hand to enjoy it even more.

The two-story aged building sat perched in the middle of the island. As we drove over the smooth paved road to the parking lot, seagulls darted overhead, pelicans bobbled on top of the wavy waters to either side, and a large clump of tall palms blew in the breeze like a hand waving us in. The time was nearing 5:30, and the parking lot was already packed. I wondered about getting seated or if it would be a long wait for a table. Cassie read my mind and said not to worry as she finally spotted a parking spot.

I was walking toward the main doors when Cassie grabbed my hand and pulled me toward the beach. "You gotta sink your toes into the sand first, Rave. It's a true initiation." She pointed to the picnic table where we set our shoes and then walked closer to the water's edge, where small waves skittered up on the beach.

I stood, hands on my hips, leaning my head back to feel the sun penetrating the skin on my face. Sun-kissed in all the right ways. It felt like a spa moment when you sense the toxins oozing out of you, and the relief it gives is the magical moment. I dug my toes deeper beneath the scorching top layer of sand and felt the cool pleasure like a soothing exfoliation.

"Damn, does this feel good," I said, wiping my hand across my neck and forehead. "I'm ready for some wine and shrimp."

"Let's go then."

A muscular young man dressed in black cargo shorts and a red t-shirt with Tiffany's logo embroidered on the pocket welcomed us as we approached the massive wooden doors. The doors opened to a mob of patrons scattered about, some in small circles, others seated at tables pushed together to accommodate their large grouping. Being short offered me very little advantages, especially in this one. I stood on tiptoe to see an entire wall of windows directly before me. It was like viewing a live-painted picture: a landscape of sand hills dotted with clumps of seagrass and spindly palms swaying in the breeze, the aqua waves pushing foamy ridges along the uneven shoreline. My eyes veered toward the dark wooden U-shaped bar to our left, where three busy bartenders were shaking, mixing, and pouring drinks from behind. I started to feel the electric vibe of celebration.

A young server in Tiffany's attire approached with a waving hand to follow her and seated us at a thick wooden high-top table nestled in the corner surrounded by walls of windows. One of them retracted, fully opened to a large deck with more tables and people. I suspected

Cassie had to have some pull or dibs on this table as I watched a server bee-line toward us, her eyes and mouth in the shape of an "O."

She grabbed Cassie in a one-armed hug as she held a tray of drinks in the other and said in a loud southern drawl, "Hi, sweetie. I got your text but had to shoo the staff off *your* table. Can you believe it? I told them that's why I have a break room, for God's sake." She chuckled and turned to me. "Nice to meet you, Raven. Welcome to Florida, sweetie." She gave me a side hug as well. "I'll be right back and throw in your fave plates, Cass." She threw out a right-eye wink and then weaved in and around the customers holding the tray of drinks that looked glued down.

"No wonder you managed to get us seats at such a crowded hour," I said admiringly. "I take it that was Tiffany, and this is your spot?"

"Oh, yes," Cassie said casually, a satisfied smile on her lips.

Tiffany wore bright red shorts and a black short-sleeved t-shirt with Tiffany's Wine Bar across the front in white letters. Her thick brunette hair matched her nut-brown eyes, and a bun, the size of a cabbage head, hung neatly at the nape of her neck. She had flawless creamy skin and the fit body shape of a yoga instructor.

"A brunette energizer bunny," I said, admiring her spunky first impression.

"She's a doll. You'll love her. Luke always reserves his company Christmas parties here, and that's how we met her the first time. She's got a big room upstairs specifically for events like that, and the view is spectacular. Water view of the Gulf as far as the eye can see. It's wonderful," Cassie said, tossing the menu to the side.

The atmosphere and the vibe seemed to remove the obnoxious heaviness that had lived on my shoulders for the last twenty-four hours.

I took in a deep breath and felt my stomach twisting in an angry growl. I noticed Cassie staring at me instead of the menu.

"You know what you want already? Probably have it memorized," I said, reading the starter list.

"No, Tiffany knows all the good choices and never disappoints," she said. Just as she said, Tiffany arrived with a bottle of chilled chardonnay and a three-tiered platter filled with cold prepared lump crab, shrimps, oysters, lobster with cocktail sauce, and a red wine mignonette. Another server set down a basket of baguette slices and herbed butter. My eyes widened in visual pleasure. Tiffany took notice and winked, which now I see is her trademark.

"Here you go, ladies. Please enjoy," Tiffany said as she poured us each a glass of wine. "I'll be back with more in a little bit." And then she scampered off toward the bar.

Staring at such elegantly displayed food, I wondered how hard it would be to accomplish something like this in my food videos. I snapped a picture.

"I told ya," Cassie boasted.

"This is perfect," I said, wondering what to dive into first. I hated to disturb such perfection.

"Cheers," Cassie said, lifting her glass. "To my best friend, my sister, finally moving to the sunshine state. You're going to wonder why you didn't leave the ridiculous stress of up North sooner."

We clinked, toasting to the new chapter I was about to plunge into, which still brought on an uncanny sense of insecurity even though I felt everything was going to plan. Maybe, it's simply the anticipation of what's next or the fact that my life is changing to the flip side at a hundred and eighty degrees. I didn't have a substantiated answer. I took in a long draw of my wine like a pressured teenager at their first party and slipped into a blasé state of mind, embracing the present right before me.

"Please tell me this is the last step in my forever healing?" I looked at Cassie with my chin down, my eyes nearly touching my raised brows, waiting for an answer that would solidify my being here, which made me laugh inside. If it wasn't for her unconditional love toward me as a friend and her family graciously took me under their wing during those floundering years I experienced with my parents, I wouldn't be here at all.

"Of course," Cassie said after she took a long draw from her wine, and I bit into a shrimp. "You've endured enough heartache for one lifetime, Rave. I know we don't talk much about it, but what your contractor did. God, I'd love to cut off…" She wiped her mouth with her napkin and replaced it on her lap without any eye contact. I sensed her wish to retract that statement, but I let it go despite the sting. She wasn't purposely hurting me by bringing up this particular subject. Finally, she looked up and gazed at me with sadness that bit at my nerves and continued, "I wanted you to move to Florida right then and there. After Jack passed, I knew you were in so much pain; we all were. I'm so sorry, Rave." I felt an affectionate squeeze on my knee, so I patted the top of her hand in a thankful response but then realized my fingers were messy with seafood juice after grabbing crab and lobster with my bare hands. She gave me a confused glare, and I held up both palms and said I was sorry. Laughing it off, we dove back in with our messy fingers and cleared the platters clean.

Cassie was right. We hadn't discussed it much, and I preferred keeping it that way. I think things would have been different if she hadn't been living so far away. Blessed with her presence and support at the trial, being there for me at Jack's funeral was more relevant to me. Jack's memory will always be in my thoughts; he was the love of my life, but what happened to me three years ago was better left buried.

19

I struggled to sell my business because it's who I was and loved, and I became successful squeezing out every penny I could to start it. Raven's Remodeling allowed me life even after the death and tragic loss of the only man I'd ever truly loved. I found it a pleasure to advise homeowners on decorating ideas and updating their homes without emptying their wallets. I never lost sight of my good fortune, and once Jack had entered my life, he became the pot of gold at the end of my rainbow.

One night while talking with Cassie about moving, I said "Yes" before she could finish the sentence.

"Rave, you just said yes to moving to Florida. Are you on a pizza and wine buzz?"

When she called, I was feasting on a homemade veggie pizza with extra mushrooms and had just poured my second glass of wine. I surprised myself answering her so quickly, but it felt right. It seemed as if saying it out loud was like signing a contract that you couldn't back out of for life-and-death reasons. I couldn't retract my answer now.

Cassie pinched her lips together and then continued, "I'm sorry, Rave. The look on your face...I stepped over the line. I'm so sorry."

"No, no. I don't know what to say. I've kept Jack close, and we've chatted about the good memories at times...but that house. To live in it after the fact was horrendous most of the time. But, hey, please, don't feel bad. The last thing I wanted to do was tell you about my sorry life when you were so far away and...." I stared directly into her eyes and watched them fill up with tears. Cassie's strength kept me afloat so many times it was hard to keep count. To see her emotional with tears was rare. It was time for me to show an affectionate gesture. I stepped off my chair and hugged her, my throat cramping from trying to refrain from losing my composure.

We parted, feeling a sense of relief that one more string of unspoken tension between us was now snipped, drawing us closer once again. Tiffany brought two more rounds of savory dishes, she-crab soup and a seared ahi tuna dish with slaw, and asked. "How are we doing, ladies?" Our mouths were full, so we sprung her a thumbs up, and she chuckled. "I'll check in later," she said, her permanent smile never wavering.

I excused myself, and on the way to the restroom, I stopped to check out the infamous wall filled with framed pictures. It was situated on a wall that you had to pass before heading down the hall to the restrooms. You couldn't miss it. Dean Martin, Raquel Welch, and Dan Marino taken years ago. The gold engraved plates pinned to the bottom frame revealed the dates these well-known elites had visited this bar/restaurant. Tiffany's was established in 1952. A framed document holding the first dollar spent on September 6th of that year hung at the top of the collage. I noticed Tiffany Blakesdale, the original owner, gleaming proudly, standing beside the famous stars. I suddenly realized that the first owner's name was Tiffany, the same as the current owner. When I got back to our table, I asked Cassie about it.

According to the original owner's documents, Cassie explained that the U-shaped bar was part of the original design and was never to be removed or replaced. The bar had some famous actors' initials carved in it, and a movie was made here in the sixties titled *Sun & Sand,* starring Frankie Avalon. The bar was to be kept as original as possible.

"When this came up for sale, Blake, Tiffany's husband, pounced on it. He said there was no way they would let it go, not after looking for so long. And then their names…." Cassie took another bite of tuna and looked around at the patrons enjoying themselves while I waited for her to finish.

"And…their names, what?"

"Oh, well, hers is Tiffany, and her husband is Blake. The original owner was Tiffany Blakesdale. Kind of a funny story, right?"

"Guess it was fate," I said, soft moans escaping from my closed mouth. The food was delicious, and I was devouring it like I hadn't eaten in weeks.

If the real meaning of fate is *a predetermined course,* how would fate direct me now? The undesirable fate of my past included the disappearance of my grandfather when I was ten, the loss of my fiancé at thirty-two, and the personal attack on me at thirty-three. Granted, my successful remodeling and design business and my love for cooking and entertaining brought me solace during those doomful events, so what would fate bring me here in the sunshine state? My heart lurched with desire for the unknown while at the same time cringed about the unknown.

The chatter inched toward a higher decibel as the guests talked as fast as the drinks were poured and the food served. Bartenders flung arms overhead, grabbing wine and cocktail glasses while others rattled a shaker between their palms, and servers brought plates to the bar and outside tables surrounding us. I was enamored by the hustle and bustle of women in light printed dresses and skirts, men in business casual linen pants, ties unleashed, and top buttons undone. A clear indication the work day was over.

I daydreamed about my future as a wine and food buzz took hold. Cassie and I rolled our eyes over the amount of food we just inhaled like gluttons. We both noticed Luke walking in with a man that stood a couple of inches taller than Luke, who stood six foot one. The man wore a light gray suit and a loosened red tie against a brilliant white shirt. They both walked with a smile, waving to some as they approached the bar. They hadn't noticed us.

"Did you know Luke was coming here?"

Cassie shook her head; eyebrows knit together like mine. I assumed she didn't know who he was either, but anyone with Luke usually meant a potential client. Cassie kept staring, which made me more curious.

From this distance, especially when he happened to turn our way, he resembled a true twin to Harvey Specter on *Suits*. I'd believe it if that's what he told me.

Cassie's phone beeped with a text from Luke asking where we were. Cassie said he was being stupid and should know. He immediately glanced our way with a look and a shake of his head that he should have known better. He leaned in and said something to the guy in the suit as he pointed our way. Drinks in hand, both headed toward our table. God knows why, but I was stupidly nervous. For a moment, I thought it was Cassie's doing—arranging a date for me, but I shook off the idea as even more stupid. She would never put me in that kind of position especially understanding the hardship of the last three months just getting here. I don't even know why I thought such a thing. Thankfully, I had fluffed my flattened plane hair and freshened my foundation in the restroom, but now I was deliriously relaxed on good wine as the Harvey from *Suits* doppelganger headed my way. I prayed my pounding heart wasn't waving the fabric of my shirt like a flag in the wind.

Luke, in jeans and his navy Towers Construction shirt, attractively stretched at the seams, strutted over to his wife, kissed her, and then stepped around to me. He squeezed me in a sisterly hug and whispered, "About time you bought a one-way ticket," and then kissed my cheek.

"Hi, I'm Cassie, Luke's wife." Cassie introduced herself, as she threw her husband a quick scowl, before returning her attention back to the grey-suited man.

"Oh…uh…this is Drew Hampton, and that is the lovely new homeowner, Raven McKade," Luke said, grabbing his drink from the table, and shoving his free hand in his pocket before he stepped to Cassie's side and whispered something in her ear. He turned to me and said, "He lives in your neighborhood, Raven. Just a few houses down." He rubbed his chin with a shameless smile, as if sending me subliminal dating vibes. I wanted to crawl under the table and twisted my lips in rejection as I glared at him. It only weakened my wine-induced confidence. Not only that, I noticed Drew never wavered his gaze from me. I couldn't remember the last time I had a man's attention, like I undoubtedly sensed this very moment. An image of Jack's face flashed in front of me, summoning the wounds that were not entirely extinguished yet.

It was simply the suited man standing in front of me who innocently reminded me of the estate lawyer I was once engaged to. What came to mind was the closet full of suits that I eventually had to part with after his death.

Gathering what emotional strength I had, I said, "Nice to meet you, Drew." I held out a nervous jittery hand that seemed to calm just by his warm touch.

"Nice to finally meet you, Miss McKade. In the south, we welcome new neighbors with a hug if I'm not too imposing." I questioned this southern precedence, he claimed, but I also found it rude to back off. So, I consented to his welcoming hug, where a light scent of coconut mixed with sea salt rushed through my nose. I closed my eyes and inhaled quietly and deeply as I lifted on tiptoe in a hug with Harvey Specter, or so my dreamy nervousness told me that. When I returned to my heels flat on the ground, he held my fingertips in his hand as I sat back in my chair. I don't know if the wine was kicking in again, but my legs had turned to jello.

"You're the pool guy, right? The famous Hampton Pools? Luke mentioned you stopped by to check on the remodeling progress," Cassie said; her side glances at me were getting annoying. She was making a fool of herself, so I looked at her wide-eyed and pushed a glass of water toward her, diverting her attention from matchmaking to kindly taking a drink instead.

He chuckled. "Yes, I'm the pool guy." He lifted his drink and paused before he swallowed the last of the amber liquid poured neat, just like Harvey Specter. I tried to evade the thought, but his presence kept me in comparison mode. I couldn't help it; the likeness was so real.

"I told Luke I've got to meet the person behind this design. I watched for eighteen months how he took a lifeless piece of property and brought it to life, turning it into a masterwork. He wouldn't take the credit, said it was all you." Drew lifted a poised palm toward me.

I smiled at the compliment and gave Luke a grateful glance. But then I returned my attention back to Drew, who seemed to be drawing the attention of so many others as they walked by, expressing their pleasantries to him. Why was it creating a tiny bit of jealousy in me? I hadn't the desire to feel an attraction to anyone after losing the love of my life, especially after enduring the wicked hands of another, but the sight of him sent a spark traveling near my heartstrings. Cassie noticed my long face and glared at me like a cartoon caricature saying, "P*lease quit thinking about Jack for the moment.*

"Well, Luke is being too kind," I said, shaking my head, my tone dripping in modesty. I needed to quickly pull out of the emotional hole I was headed into. "He's got a good eye for design. I just added a few tweaks that needed his muscles."

Luke put up a flexed arm.

"Yes, my husband with all the brawn," Cassie teased, then glanced at her watch and asked Luke, "Are you going to get the twins from practice?"

Luke nodded and bowed out with a handshake to Drew and hugs for us. "Don't drink too many bottles tonight, ladies." He beamed mockingly as he tilted an imaginary bottle up in the air.

"I've got to go too, ladies," Drew said, and then, facing me, he said, "Miss Raven, would you care to join me for a drink tomorrow at my place? Say...6 p.m.?" His voice was like butter.

I immediately turned to Cassie as if I needed approval, which by the concerned look on Drew's face, I could only wonder what he thought. The heat rose in my cheeks. I wasn't prepared for this invitation. My intention was to spend some valuable time catching up with Cassie and Luke, not be entertained by a meet and greet with the neighbors. I'm not sure why I was having such difficulty, but Drew's velvety voice snapped me out of my reverie. "Would I be interrupting some plans you may already have? If so, I'm sorry…"

"No," Cassie blurted. "Not at all. I'm staying the night but leaving early morning. I have a pregnant office manager close to her due date and not feeling well." She tossed me a simple scowl and knee-knocked me under the table, embarrassing me even more. I felt like it was twenty years earlier in high school during lunch, and I was being asked to prom.

"That would be great, Drew. Thank you for inviting me," I said, trying to keep my composure as a mature thirty-seven-year-old instead of a starstruck teenager. His face softened, and I exhaled, holding a closed-lipped smile.

Drew left, and Cassie excused herself to the restroom. I sat staring at the waves lapping onto the beach and wondered what kind of hot mess I was in just a few moments ago. It went from deeply rooted sorrow on the one hand, then a wave of guilt, then excitement, and then back to guilt. It could be a good rendition of *As the World Turns*.

"Hey, knock knock. Earth to Raven," Cassie said, snapping her fingers, pulling me back from miles away. "What's going on in that pretty little head of yours?"

"Let's go," I said, inhaling deeply as I lifted my shoulders and letting it out audibly. "I'm excited to see my new beach house."

CHAPTER 3

Raven's House - Evening August 5th

For many people, their dream house transcends beyond a mere structure of concrete or some other material; it echoes their persona and epitomizes their achievements. It is a haven of solace where they can withdraw from the world's turmoil and bask in the sense of safety and comfort. The notion of possessing their dream house instills within them a profound sense of pride and accomplishment, enshrouded by an aura of tranquility and jubilation. Whether it is a sprawling, exquisitely crafted palace with breathtaking vistas or a snug and quaint abode nestled amidst an idyllic countryside, their dream house is a place where they can create lasting memories with their loved ones, and it's something they aspire to achieve one day.

And for me, that one day was today. And mine was a dream beach house.

With all that had taken place on my way to Florida and then the surprise elements of Luke and Drew at Tiffany's, these pertinent distractions didn't leave me much time to think about my ultimate destination: my new place of residence. The wait was about to be over.

After saying our goodbyes to Tiffany and a few of the staff that treated us with such piety, we found our way to the gates of Bay Harbor a short fifteen minutes later. I had wondered on numerous occasions what my reaction might be when I took that first step into my new house. Cassie had been filling me in on a few intricate details, accelerating my eagerness to get there. I considered myself somewhat of a savant in the decorating industry, but this project took me outside the box; upscale beach style versus traditional Midwest. I could completely understand, now, from my past client's perspective, how the final reveal affected their first response.

"You're going to love it, Rave. The pictures didn't do it a damn bit of justice," Cassie said, rubbing her palms together, brimming with excitement like a little kid waiting in line to tell Santa what they wanted for Christmas. It warmed me inside to see her youthful expression and excitement for me.

"I don't doubt you." I bopped the end of her scrunched-up nose with my index finger, and she poked at my dimple. Silly antics, but ones I'd missed living so far away. They were a significant part of my memory, full of innocence and spontaneity that I most cherished in our friendship. And memorable moments between friends and siblings. How quickly it was all re-emerging like long-lost sisters. We now have the chance to create a lot more in the coming days.

Unfortunately, with Rachel and I, there were very few. I vaguely remember when my grandfather was in the room before he went missing in 1989, the smiles and sisterly hugs between us as young girls, but that didn't last. Even thinking of her inherent tattle-tale ways saddened me in the realization that I will never have with her what I continually encounter in Cassie. It's probably an empty wish, but I briefly thought of Rachel possibly softening her heart toward me now that I've moved and put distance between us.

Of course, that does need to go both ways.

There it was—my beach house. As we pulled into the driveway, I felt mixed emotions, from excitement and anticipation to nervousness and even disbelief. I was filled with awe regarding the landscape choices I had dreamed of; tall fluffy palms, birds of paradise, and a wide row of Mexican purple petunias. Jack's favorite color was purple, and I insisted on planting something he would have loved if he were moving into this house with me. I needed to somehow dedicate a part of this property to him. To have a tiny note of him, even as trivial as a color, meant that when I'd look at that particular flower blooming in all its glorious purple hue, I'd think of him and believe that if he were here, he'd be bursting with happiness under this wonderful Florida sunshine. I felt a deep sense of gratitude and accomplishment, and I hadn't even seen the inside yet.

The driveway sat to the side of my house. Cassie clicked the garage door opener and then handed it to me. My new blue Escalade sat inside—another spending luxury I took advantage of. I sold my black suburban in Minnesota, hoping to get a luxury car to drive in Florida. And voilà...I did it with the help of Luke once again. Eighteen months from start to finish, and I can now enjoy money well spent on a newly decorated house and new vehicle in a beautiful neighborhood behind the security of a staffed gate. *Dreams do come true.*

I breathed in the salty, briny air with pleasure as I stepped out of the car, the sun sliding into setting mode. My eyes wandered over every color, texture, and vegetation, like gazing at a life-like painting. It was surreal.

"I want you to see how stunning the outside entrance is before stepping inside the front door," Cassie said, grabbing my hand and pulling me toward the sidewalk in front of my house. The full view of my simple Key West-style home, painted in the most beautiful shade of periwinkle, trimmed in creamy white, and the double front doors in salmon, was stunning. Luke and I went back and forth on the steel roof; light gray or a natural dark gray to match one of the three shades in my pavers. I let Luke choose, and the darkest won.

"My dream home," I said, admiring the beautiful house that was now mine. I pushed Cassie toward the front door and told her to get my key out of her purse before I'd rustle through her purse to find it. Jitters brought on pea-sized goosebumps on my arms. I was so excited.

"You've got a code system to get in, but you'll have to change it. It's the one all the contractors used. Here's your backup key." Cassie said, handing it to me.

I slipped the key into my purse as Cassie opened the door. My eyes flew open in complete awe. My intentional design of this house was coastal neutral with pops of ocean and tropical colors. It couldn't have been more perfect. It was more elegant than what I brought together on paper. The minute I walked through the front door, it felt like I was entering a resort, a spa, the most calming environment you could be in, and the Gulf waters were just a few blocks away.

"You're making me cry now," Cassie said, her tone breathy. I covered my face, sopped in tears with my hands. Cassie hugged me.

A blissful cry can relieve a lot of tension. And it doesn't hurt to have wine mixed in with a case of delirious fatigue to bring out the sappiest part of who you are. I have to admit I was not prepared.

Cassie opened the glass doors of my double-wide chef's fridge and pulled out a chilled bottle of champagne. With a touch of a button, the glass doors changed to opaque, which I thought was the most incredible detail in all my appliances. Two champagne flutes and a bright blue bow tied around them sat front and center on my ten by six-foot island—the focal point of the kitchen. Four barstools tucked at one end, perfect for an intimate dinner party. The island was my pride and joy; Cambria quartz in varied neutral tones like layered sand. My heart danced around the image of my counter filled with platters of food for a Sunday brunch gathering with neighbors or my video equipment strategically set up for a live cooking lesson on my vlog Food and Wine Club with Raven.

"Oh, my God, Cass, how have I become so blessed? How..." My voice trembled, and I couldn't form the words to finish.

"You deserve this, Raven. Just remember that."

"I only wish Jack…"

"I know, my sweet friend." Her voice cracked, and I watched her eyes fill with a look of compassion for me. She knew how much Jack meant to me and that my dream was for the both of us to move here, not just his memory. "I'm going to put my stuff in the bedroom, and then let's have our champagne on the back lanai," Cassie said as more of a question than a statement. I had forgotten about the lanai and got instantly excited about the nautical-themed cushions I ordered for the chairs and loungers. In Minnesota, it was pine cones and deer splashed across my outdoor furniture.

Cassie disappeared down the hall on the opposite side of the house from my master bedroom and bath. I took a cool shower to scrub off the film of the day, and I assumed Cassie was doing the same, so I had some time to gather up the rough edges of my emotions and rejuvenate before we met again on the lanai. My contacts were so dry I had to peel them off. Apparently, all the crying I did dried my tear ducts, and there was nothing left to hydrate my eyes with. I slipped on my navy-blue frames--my eyes thanking me--my red lounge shorts and a Minnesota Twins t-shirt and met Cassie on the lanai outside the French doors of my bedroom. Cassie had her arms wrapped around her knees pulled to her chest, wearing a dark gray terry outfit and slippers to match.

"Don't tell me you're chilled," I said, laughing, holding my palm in the air. "It's gotta be eighty degrees still, and you're in long pants." She noticed my confused look and threw back a grimace as I sunk into the lounger across from her. I laughed when she flicked her wrist.

"You just wait. You'll acclimate after a few years, and then you'll know why I'm wearing this, my dear friend," she said, handing me my glass of champagne, and then added, "Besides, the sun is starting to go down. The temps cool fast." I gave her a whatever look, and she threw back a teasing smile.

It felt good to lean back in our loungers, legs stretched out in front of us, crossed at the ankles, listening to the quiet buzzing of nature surrounding us in Bay Harbor. I'd never lived in a gated community before. Minnesota wasn't known for gated communities; outrageously expensive gated private properties; yes. No more mounds of snow to plow. Just green grass and the heavenly sun shining down on me.

I took a long draw of the bubbly champagne and noticed Cassie texting; her face creased in concern. I assumed it was either related to work, Luke, or the kids, but I could've been wrong, so I finished my champagne and let Cassie finish her business while I contemplated what my new daily routine would consist of. My days of owning a storefront and managing employees was behind me now, and although it was a successful career choice, and I loved the design world, it felt like a ball and chain had been cut loose. My job now is cooking and posting videos on Food and Wine Club with Raven and hopefully catering on the side. I'm sure Cassie will have plenty of ideas and resources to set me in motion.

A single car passed, and a couple taking a leisurely walk, their conversation a murmur as they strolled by. Amazing how quiet it was. With darkness approaching, I felt the heat from the day change from a boil to a light simmer, my skin breathing in the cooler air with relief. I looked over at Cassie, who opened her mouth as if to speak but then pressed her lips tight as if changing her mind. And her lips moved again, obviously trying to form words, but nothing came out. After the third time, I knocked my knuckles on the table and gave her an exaggerated questioning look.

"What? Cassie said. Her brows pulled together in a frown as she tilted her head.

"Oh, nothing, I guess...just watching you conversing with yourself. But don't let me interrupt." I used a sarcastic tone and started to chuckle but stopped when her lips tightened. I knew that was not a good sign. I rubbed the back of my neck and swung my legs around to face her.

Placing a throw pillow on my lap, I leaned forward and told her to spill it.

Cassie closed her eyes for a quick moment before looking directly into mine.

"Please don't take this personally." Cassie rubbed her face with both hands, which caused me pause. I wondered what bomb she was about to drop on me.

After a deep breath, Cassie said, "Rave, your sister texted me, and they had to put your mother in a detox unit today. Supposedly after you left, she tried to hurt herself with a kitchen knife. Rachel wanted you to know but not to worry or get upset. They're handling it..."

I immediately stood and threw the pillow on the ground, almost knocking over my empty champagne flute, but I grabbed it just in time. I didn't need to be sweeping up or stepping on tiny shards of glass with my insides burned like fire at this news. "Of course, Rachel, that little...bitch. Somehow, she's gotta throw me under the bus..."

"Whoa, back up, Rave. In her defense, she said after your dad called and you didn't answer, she knew I was with you and..." I raised a flexed palm to stop her.

"You don't need to go on," I said with more of a snap than I intended. Her expression was blank. I went inside to get my phone from my purse and instantly saw that I had missed a call from my dad about the time we had pulled up into my driveway. It was childish to act out this way, but I was so frazzled, especially after a day riding on an emotional rollercoaster. Meeting Mr. Suits, my new neighbor, brought the ride to new heights, throwing me off.

Her empty stare admitted my selfishness.

"I'm sorry I snapped at you, Cass. I didn't mean that. It's just that I know all too well how my sister operates." I sat beside her and put my arms around her. I spoke in a calmed whisper, "Mom should have gone weeks ago, to be honest. Of course, she refused, said it'd never happen again, and my dad let it go," I sighed. I felt terrible for my dad because he had to endure all the hassle. "I don't know why my dad, as wonderful and caring a person he is, let this go so far without forcing her years ago. It makes me angry with him, too. It's like he's enabled her all these years. Pisses me off."

"Hey, stop," Cassie demanded. "Let it go. Rachel took responsibility, and your mother's in a place she needs to be. So, please give it a rest and not let it ruin our time together here. Look at it this way…" She placed both hands on my cheeks, forcing me to look directly into her eyes, and added, "…with you leaving, it prompted a good result. Your mother sunk to a low that required the attention needed long ago. Be happy with this. This could be a blessing in disguise."

I started to speak, but Cassie shushed me and, as she stood, flipped me around so my back was against her thighs. She told me to quit thinking and take deep breaths while she rubbed my shoulders. I'd forgotten the strength she had in her tiny chiropractor hands. She told me to close my eyes and relax, but I couldn't help moaning and twitching from the tiny jolts of pain she was generating. The next thing I knew, I heard a crackle in my ears and felt a surge of heat plunge through my neck after a quick chiropractic adjustment of my head. Even the ringing in my ears stopped. "Tension," she said and bopped me on the top of my head. "Imagine that."

I laid back against the cushion and felt my body pull itself back together, but my heart still thumped at the intentional backstabbing of my sister. At least, that's what I thought it was, but according to Cassie, I wasn't giving credit where credit was due. Was I the inconsiderate, selfish one? Was my anger at Rachel or even my dad, at this point, justified? I'd blow it off like a dandruff spec if I hadn't felt that Rachel was boosting herself up on the "more responsible daughter" pedestal. For the last twenty-four hours, I'd been emotionally rattled and obviously nowhere near balanced enough to choose my battles.

"Clear your mind, Raven Elaine," Cassie said, slapping my knee. I shot her a sardonic look at which she just laughed. Of course, she was right, and I hated myself for being so weak. I wanted to be happy for my mom. I prayed so much as a child that Grandpa would show up, and then my mother's drinking would stop, and everyone would be happy. Such a simple child-like solution, but it didn't come true. Perhaps this was the final straw, and my leaving initiated the dam to ultimately break. I could only hope it might lead to assisting in our sister bond now that I'm, ironically, sixteen hundred miles away.

Magic *can* happen here in Florida. Despite all the food at Tiffany's, we were mindlessly hungry again. I believe it was simple stress for me, but in Cassie's case, she was a person that had to snack while indulging in alcohol. And I get that it's better to drink with food, but we indulged plenty for the day. It made me think about my tiny boned mother who'd fake being full. She'd say, "Oh, I'm already full on this," as she held up a half-empty bottle of vodka but yet drank the rest with a single pretzel if anyone was watching. I'd forget about snacking unless someone mentioned pizza.

"Go scope out your pantry, Rave. Find me something good." Cassie said while also mentioning how a certain "someone" with a list was to fill some cabinets before we got to the house today. I knew who that "someone" was, and if I were correct, I'd find Belgium chocolates in a drawer somewhere. While Cassie scanned through her phone for some background music, I padded barefoot in search of the snacks. I found Belgium chocolates, roasted salty cashews, and almond crackers in the pantry beside the fridge. And if there were almond crackers, there had to be smoked Gouda cheese and roasted red pepper hummus. Cassie knew my favorites all too well.

I arranged everything on a serving tray, and as I walked closer to the door, I heard Cassie's voice, thinking she must be talking to me, but with further inspection, I saw her standing by the screen, chatting with someone. It surprised me, and I wondered what nosy neighbor was making their introductions at this time of night.

I walked over to Cassie after I set the tray on the table to see who she was lurking near the curb.

"Hey, this is Devin, the maintenance guy here," Cassie said, turning to me but quickly back to him.

He waved a raised hand at me, stepped out of the golf cart, and walked over near the bottom step that led up to a small deck attached to my lanai. I thought to invite him up but changed my mind. It was dark. He held a flashlight, and from what I could make of his appearance, he reminded me more of a homeless man than a respectable maintenance man in a neighborhood such as Bay Harbor. His grubby image made me uneasy. I'm sure I was overly critical and mindfully reluctant, but with dirt and sweat stains blotched all over his clothing like he had, gave me the idea he just came from digging a grave rather than carrying-out the duties of a maintenance man.

"Hi," I said through the screen. "Devin, is it?"

"Yes, Ma'am. I'm Devin Hampton." Ma'am? Hampton? I just met a handsome man with the same surname—Drew Hampton and he looked nothing like this guy. It had to be a coincidence.

Devin looked at the ground like a shy schoolboy introducing himself for the first time. Odd. "I didn't mean to barge in, Ma'am, but I know you're the new resident here and wanted to tell you who I was and that if you need anything...well, here's my card." I heard the rip of the velcro flap on his nylon wallet, and he began shuffling through it. He pulled a card out and held it up without moving from where he stood. I walked down the steps to retrieve it.

Leaning toward the light, it was still too dark to read his card. I thanked him and walked back up next to Cassie, who looked like she was trying to remember something, her pointer finger poking the air. "That's right. Luke told me you're the brother of Drew, who owns Hampton Pools, correct?"

I sucked in an audible gasp loud enough for Cassie to jerk her head toward me.

"Ahhh...yes," he said, a bitterness held tight on his words. "He's my brother, but I'm part owner as well."

This piece of information was a shocker. Picturing both men as brothers was difficult to comprehend at first glance. Would he be joining us at Drew's tomorrow night? Did they live together? Granted, darkness was ensuing quickly, and all I saw of him was his basic silhouette under the streetlamp light. But he was giving me a creepy feeling.

Devin continued, his voice slightly raspy and louder, "And he doesn't do any maintenance around here. It's all me. I care for the resident's needs, so please get a hold of me, not Drew. He doesn't know how to do this job." His voice dropped considerably at the end, as if he was lying.

So, this scrappy-looking walking stick was Drew's brother. It was obvious he wasn't a great admirer of his brother like people appeared to be at Tiffany's. It smelled like the male version of Rachel and me.

It seemed that Devin's lack of grooming might have something to do with what hadn't developed beneath his hair follicles. Nothing compared to what I'd had the pleasure of noticing in his dapper-looking brother. He climbed back into his golf cart after he wished us a good night. I kept silent in wonder as I watched him drive away on his squeaky golf cart.

"What an odd duck," I said, opening a box of crackers and shaking my head. Cassie grabbed the champagne from the mini fridge and poured another glass for each of us.

"He was. I'm glad I met Drew today; otherwise, I wouldn't have believed you if you told me this story." Cassie was right. I don't think I'd believed it if I hadn't witnessed it. Complete opposite ends of the spectrum. And then I wondered if daylight might adjust his coarse appearance somehow. I nodded in agreement and shoved a cracker loaded with hummus into my mouth.

Back in 1988, at the end of the school year and right before my tenth birthday, Cassie invited me over to a summer party she was having two weeks later. We hadn't talked or hung out before this, but she was in my reading class during the last half of the school year, and we always talked about books and stories. We loved to read Trixie Belden and Nancy Drew mysteries. After reading every Laura Ingalls Wilder book, we'd playact as Laura and Mary either at school or helping "Ma" cook for "Pa." It never got old.

For Christmas one year, Cassie got the mini kitchen set. The black and gold lightweight metal stove, refrigerator, and sink counter were placed along one wall in her bedroom. I was jealous. It was where we ended up playing the whole time I came to visit. I'm sure this little play kitchen fueled my preoccupation in cooking. I'd go outside to pick clover, the little white flowers it would produce, and some crabgrass and pretend I was "harvesting" healthy herbs and vegetables for our dinner. Cassie and I would take petals from her mother's dying flowers on the table, add maple leaves, dandelion stems, or even acorns from the oak trees, and pretend we were making a salad.

Twenty-seven years later, our sisterhood was more vital than ever. I felt a tug at my heart as I watched her double thumb the keys on her phone, guessing it to be a goodnight text to her twins or Luke about tomorrow's schedule. If it were Rachel, I'd be irritated. But if I were honest, I'd admit I'd feel more jealousy than irritation, as ridiculous as, that sounds, but just knowing Cassie was staying with me was a bonus.

I grabbed Belgium chocolates and stared at the dark morsels. Jack introduced these delicious bites to us. Simultaneously, Cassie and I looked at one another. We both smiled. I motioned for her to open her mouth, and as she obliged, I tossed a piece of chocolate straight in like a bean bag in a cornhole game. She faked choking with her hands to her throat, and then I plopped one in my mouth. We laughed with pinched lips and a mouth lined with melted chocolate, ready to ooze out if we dared to open our mouths. By the time I swallowed, tears pooled in the corners of my eyes from laughing so hard. I immediately recalled the last time we shared in this silly ritual, and that was after Jack's funeral five years ago. In the devastating grips of sorrow, Cassie and Luke insisted I stay with them at their hotel that night to celebrate Jack's life in style with a bottle of Dom Perignon and Belgium chocolates. There was no reason to resist. My head and heart were empty, my legs and arms were numb, and I could barely hold myself up without help.

The lemony violet scent of the hundreds of white roses scattered across his casket sifted through my nose right then. My audible inhale caused Cassie to look up at me, a worried frown creasing on her forehead.

"What made you decide to get these?" My curiosity increased at her hesitation as if she were carefully contemplating her answer.

"Oh, well...Luke brought it up," she said after taking her eyes off me to focus on the ceiling. I thought maybe she had noticed something, so I looked up, too, but saw nothing. I could tell by her silence she might be afraid to bring up the subject of Jack for fear I'd fall to pieces again, and I understood that. Just looking at the box and seeing the same logo and colors identical to the first box he ever gave me made my heart flip with warm memories. I didn't feel sad.

"It's okay, Cass. It was Jack's funeral. I remember. I also remember how the champagne and these chocolates just airlifted me into the sky, and I thought I would wake up in the morning and be with Jack in heaven. Remember that? Instead, I woke up with a headache and a worse heartache." I shook my head while forcing a grin. Sitting out here in the calm, salty air under the stars with Cassie enjoying the first night in my house, I refused to let it end in a disastrous crying session. The whole day felt like I was on the brink of some never-ending madness. "These are happy memories," I added, pointing to the box. "But you forgot to buy Dom. How could you forget, Cass? Instead, we're drinking cheap champagne with expensive chocolates. Shame on you!"

****

Jack's smiling face flashed in my mind's eye, and his scent of cedar and bergamot filled my nostrils as I lay on my pillow in my new house in my new bed. Happy tears fell as I thanked God that I had Jack in my life and how he's comforting me right here and now as my eyes shut.

CHAPTER 4

Thursday, August 6th

Flat on my back, I touch his side of the bed, and it's cold. I sat upright, holding my breath and listening intently for his footsteps. I placed my hand on my cheek, puzzled at my surroundings. The comforter shouldn't be a textured beige pattern. It is supposed to be dark blue with snowflakes on it, and there should be a window in front of me, not a canvas painting of two conch shells. And then I realized it was a dream. A dream so vivid that I expected Jack to be lying right next to me.

It was an awful dream; one I'd never had before. My head was heavy with a distorted static sensation like on a television set that ended its broadcasting for the night. I tried pulling together the images that floated in and out. I gently rubbed a palm over my queasy stomach as I recalled a vision of Jack. It was frightening! He wore a navy-blue Henley sweater, but I couldn't see the bottom part of him. I was in all black, my lips smeared in black lipstick, and the color of my eyes like a brick of charcoal. Jack stared at me, confusion and disappointment painted all over his face. And then his face grew sad as if fighting back the tears, and he walked backward away from me. I held out my hands, reaching for him, screaming that this wasn't me, that I didn't mean to be like this, and that it wasn't my fault. I gasped after holding my breath for so long.

I leaned over, opened my nightstand drawer, and pulled out our framed engagement picture. Jack had on a navy-blue Henley sweater, just like in the dream, but I wore a jade green blouse intensifying the crystal blue of my eyes, an attribute I shared with my father. In the dream, I resembled a phantasm bordering on evil, like an angel coerced into wicked ways and rebelling. I'd never dreamt of anything like this before, and I couldn't shake the bubble of sadness around me.

Anyone could recognize the depth of our love oozing out of this picture. It's the first thing I pack and unpack whenever I travel. Now it's forever placed in this drawer. As I stared at him in this picture, I imagined my fingers running through his wavy brown hair, playing with the tiny curls trimmed close to his ears. His honey-brown eyes had a smile all their own, and knowing I'll never be able to look into them again made my heart sink with the familiar fear I felt the day of his funeral. The fear of being branded with his love is so deep that there isn't room for anyone else.

He wasn't walking around the house like me, in a sleepy daze, though. He was beside me in the drawer, always comforting me. We were engaged on September 6th, 2009, and we posed for this picture a week later-- three months before he was diagnosed with Hodgkin's Lymphoma.

He died on May 30th, 2010.

I swung my legs around to the side of the bed, kissed the tips of my fingers, pressed them on Jack's image, then gently laid it back in the nightstand drawer. With the nightmarish visual, though faint, still haunting me, I was sure the only solution for letting it go would be coffee. Coffee solved many of my issues. Maybe not as much as wine, but this morning, I needed a jump-start to flip my sad morning into a bright day like the billowing sun's rays outside my window.

Cassie left a note by the coffee maker: *Push the button first, then turn this over to read.*

I pushed the start button, and the familiar whirring sound of the coffeemaker ground down hard beans. I closed my eyes, reveling in the sweet floral hints of the peaberry Kona coffee aroma. I had ordered peaberry and chocolate macadamia nut coffee to be delivered to Cassie, who stashed it in my cabinets. Cassie wasn't picky about her coffee like I was, but as far as tea, she was over the top picky, unlike me. In supporting her in her must-have teas as she does with my must-have coffees, I opened the wall cabinet to the right of the coffeemaker and found it filled with her favorite rooibos tea from South Africa, chai tea from India, and her all-time favorite oolong from Taiwan. Her tea fetish warranted a space in my new cheffy kitchen. It's what best friends do.

Raven, my dearest friend, as you sip and enjoy your cup of jo, notice how good it feels to let the emotional baggage slip off your shoulders, and as you go for your morning run, bask in the sunshine and inhale the sea salt scent of your new lifestyle.

Love you,

C xoxo

I loved her poetic air mixed with a sappy note. It made me smile. Once again, I gave thanks to Luke and Cassie as I gazed out the window and watched my new neighbors going about their daily routines while I took pleasure in my cup of coffee. It seemed that with every swallow, I felt the disturbing visions of my dream slip away, hopefully to a place without return. This made me aware of how heavily Jack's memory weighed on my mind. Moving to Florida without him triggered something in my sub-conscience to play such a dirty evil vision.

****

"This is such a beautiful restaurant. I can't believe I've lived here most of my life and have never been here. I'm glad you chose this place," I admired Jack's sense of choice. He said it would be a unique and memorable night that required the essence of an iconic restaurant.

We had reservations set for 5 pm at Murrays, a high-class steakhouse established in 1946 in downtown Minneapolis, a restaurant famous for their "butter knife steaks." Just walking in, a posh sense of the past grand patrons filled the air, as if they could be sitting at your table and enjoying the meal with you.

"I must agree with you; this place is perfect for a romantic dinner," I said after the young hostess had seated us in a private corner booth which I'm sure was Jack's preference. Careful not to upset the perfectly arranged wine and water glasses, I slid into the booth without disturbing the thick white tablecloth, afraid of making an embarrassing scene. Each piece was placed in such conformity it spoke elegance and precision, and no doubt, a depiction in our upcoming service as well. I immediately picked up the knife and felt the weight across my palm. "We need to get tablecloths and silverware like this for our dinner parties, don't you think?"

Jack's face lit up with an amusing smile as he clasped my hand in both of his. "You're telling me you'd prefer this plain white tablecloth and heavy, durable silverware to our cheesy plaid printed tablecloth and Lyons flatware from Target? You don't think our friends would be intimidated?" It was so easy to laugh with him. Problems weren't problems with Jack. They were events that could be changed for the better.

"Good evening, my name is Henry, and I'll be taking care of you tonight," he said, handing us a menu and then folded his hands in front of him. He had hair the color of deep rust; his eyes a minty green. "What can I start you off with to drink, Miss?" As I turned to Jack for a suggestion, another server came with a bottle of chilled Pellegrino and a small plate of perfectly sliced lemons and limes. Another Jack request, I was sure.

Sinatra ballads played in the background. Jack's attention seemed focused on me, and the fact he chose this restaurant for our "special night" intrigued me more than choosing a drink. Although, I was ready for a celebratory drink. I was with the man I knew I wanted to be with for the rest of my life, and if he were asking me to marry him tonight, I'd say *Yes!* Before he could finish the sentence. I was that sure.

"A bottle of your finest red wine, please."

"Excellent choice, sir. I'll return with our freshly made bread platter and sweet butter." We found more time to focus on each other as we sipped out sparkling water and nonchalantly moved to the soft music overhead. I was in "Jack heaven."

It was the summer of 2009, July 13th, to be exact, and the place was packed. I'd only met Jack nine months prior, the best thing that had happened to me. Not a set-up by Cassie or an employee, not a long-lost friend of someone I knew, not a former classmate, but a single lawyer whose office building needed remodeling. A referral from that building sent him in, and when he walked through the door asking for Raven McKade, my jaw dropped, and my stare didn't wander from his beautiful brown eyes. I walked toward him without saying a word, holding my hand out in a welcoming shake as I asked him, "And what may I help you with, sir?"

"I love how you pamper me. It makes me feel so taken care of," I said, snuggling closer into his chest. Henry came with the wine, smiling as he poured us each a glass. Another server brought the platter of homemade dinner rolls and sourdough bread with a heaping ball of honeyed butter.

"I wonder if we'll stay the same way when we're married and move to Florida?" Jack said out of the blue as he lifted his glass, nodding to me to do the same. I nearly choked at his bombshell question. His sly smile told me he knew he knew exactly what he was doing. I recognized the stare and the feel of my open jaw as an exact reproduction of the day he walked through my store's front door and I had laid eyes on him for the first time.

That night will forever be embedded in my memory. We talked about the children we'd have, the area of Florida we preferred, and the fact we had Cassie and Luke already living there to advise us. If we moved close enough to Cassie and Luke, we'd possibly have built-in babysitters. The conversation made the meal seem even more stupendous as I ate every last bit of my steak and imbibed in a third glass of wine. My love for Jack went to a sky-high level that had me floating on clouds right through to our engagement weekend together in September.

I had found the pot of gold at the end of my rainbow that night at Murray's. Jack and I shared our dreams and plans for our future that night. Once we arrived home, we stayed up till 3 am talking and Googling everything we could about Florida and what a move could do for us. Barely thirty years old, we acted like innocent teenagers embarking on our first unsupervised time away; our wishes young at heart.

"I'm so lucky to have you, Jack."

"I feel the same way about you, Rave. And I can't wait to see what the future holds for our family in our dream home."

****

I stood gazing around at the new life before me, a new life without Jack by my side. Could I still live out my dreams without him?

It was time for a run. Yesterday left my muscles aching, and my energy drained, despite the spirited Hawaiian coffee, from a long, emotional day.

I checked out the new clothes Cassie had insisted on choosing for me. She gave out a hearty laugh over the phone when I told her I had plenty of summer clothes for Florida. So, in a foiled disagreement, I handed her a thousand dollars in cash during her last visit to Minnesota and said, "Go for it." It was easy for her to shop for me. We were the same size, although she was a little more robust in the chest department. But she was skilled at choosing the right colors or prints for me; like a personal shopper.

My closet, alone, was bigger than the studio apartment I rented after graduation. I'm five foot three, size four, and the closet cabinets towered above me like the IDS building in downtown Minneapolis. It was fun rummaging through the new clothes, tags still attached. Cassie was the best shopper.

Strangely enough, I hadn't ever looked at the map of my new neighborhood. Unsure of the road names and where they all led to, I pulled the map up on my phone. Bay Harbor was a small development, and according to Luke, there were approximately one hundred seventy-five homes behind the wrought iron gate. The main roads around the perimeter were Pelican Drive and Spoonbill Way. The pool was surrounded by a common sidewalk called Poolpath. Original which made it easy to remember. Osprey Circle was another route I could check out as well, and it looked to be the road you're entering on after the gate.

The coffee helped at least swish out the fuzzy wine fog, but I could tell by my thumping heart it was time to sweat some energy off. It had been weeks since I left my workout routine in the dust in exchange for packing boxes and moving, but now my body was chewing me out. Obviously, the stress of the last few years hadn't caused any weight gain. I'd lost, but I'm sure a lot of that was muscle weight.

As I laced up my sneakers and slipped on my sunglasses, the sun was already high in the sky. I stepped out of my house and watched a young couple ride by on their bikes, a toddler strapped in a seat behind the dad. They waved, and I waved back. And then, an older couple came strolling by with two little dogs but stopped when they noticed me.

"Good morning," the lady said. "Isn't it a beautiful day?

"Yes, it is." I agreed

She had snow-white hair pinned in a bun near the nape of her neck. She wore bright red Bermuda shorts and a white short-sleeve buttoned shirt. Her posture was straight as a ruler, whereas her husband was hunched. He wore jean shorts and an orange faded University of Florida t-shirt. Both of them sporting identical pitch- black sunglasses. He smiled and waved at me, which urged the dogs to bark as they looked up at me from the edge of my raised patio. "Bunny...Willy...shush." The man stood quietly as his wife barked back at them in her raspy voice. The leashed pets immediately obeyed, sitting their butts down and staring at her as if waiting for a treat.

"You did a nice number on this house," the lady said.

I was happily amused. "Thank you. I appreciate you saying that. My best friend's husband gets all the credit," I said. "Are those Westies?" It was comical how the dogs turned their attention to me but didn't bark.

"Yes, the white one is Bunny, and the black one is Willy," she said, pointing, holding the leash just taught like a trained dog owner. "They can be naughty once in a while. And by the way, we know Luke Towers very well. He worked on our place when we bought it. Very good contractor. Very pleased with his work." Her husband nodded his head in agreement and then looked at me.

"Do you live alone?" The man's voice was surprisingly soft and monotone, opposite his wife's. I assumed they were married.

I wasn't sure if I had heard him correctly, but she said, "Roger, speak louder. How can anyone hear you at this distance?" He repeated the question louder, raising his bushy eyebrows above his sunglasses in a questioning gesture. I nodded.

"Yes, I do. I'm a transplant from Minnesota." I saw her shiver at the word Minnesota like every other person does when you tell them where you're from.

"Oh, sweetie, my body wouldn't be able to handle that blizzard-cold state. Born and raised here in Florida. Wouldn't want it any other way." She gave me a tight-lipped grin.

"We've lived here all our lives," Roger said, "It takes some getting used to, but you'll learn to love it." Both nodded in understanding.

"What brings you down here from Minnesota?" The lady asked.

I took a deep breath and said, "Oh...I just...I wanted a change of pace. I've always lived in the Midwest, and I just needed something different." The simple answer was best.

Roger spoke up, his voice still barely above a whisper. "I know what you mean. Sometimes, you just have to take a chance and try something new—"

The lady interrupted him and said to me in an exemplary manner, "By the way, if you haven't been warned already, it's an unwritten policy here in Bay Harbor to leave Harry Fishmen alone. No contact with him, don't try to befriend him. He lives at the end of Spoonbill Way; there are woods behind him. Don't ask why, but he prefers to be alone, and we're happy to let the ole geezer be that way." She shook her head. "I'm just being the friendly neighbor so you don't get chewed out by Devin or Frankie."

How strange. I didn't know what road Spoonbill Way was, but this wasn't a large community, so it wouldn't be hard to figure out. She was urging her leashed pets to get moving.

"Why doesn't he want to interact with anyone?" I heard what she said, but my mouth still blurted out the stupid question.

"If we knew, sweetie, we'd tell you, but that's what he wants, so it's how it is. Nice chatting with you. Welcome to the neighborhood."

"Yes, nice to meet...you too," I said, completely baffled by that last bit of information. And then I realized I hadn't gotten her name when they were already a distance away. Next time, hopefully.

I checked my phone before I took off and saw a text from an unknown number:

Hi, Raven. Luke gave me your phone number. Hope that's ok. Still on for drinks at my house tonight? Come any time after 4 pm. Looking forward to it."

I had forgotten entirely about meeting at his house. How could I lose site of an invite to Harvey Specter's house, I joked to myself. And then I realized I didn't know which house was his. I looked down the street both ways. To my left stood three mammoth houses, the middle a replica like that you'd see on *Miami Vice*. I pegged that one to be Drew's but to make sure; I texted him back:

Which house?

He immediately responded:

The one between the Spanish and Hemingway house.

I was right, the gray contemporary skyscraper house with two large balconies spread across the second and third floors belonged to him. It looked befitted for a well-manicured man. The clean lines and angles of the stucco exterior, the manicured lawn thick as a rug, comparably, not to mention the symmetry of the jacaranda trees and the pygmy palms beside the small pond underneath the fountain. I imagined the Harvey Specter look-a-like expected nothing less than precision.

My house sits on Pelican Drive near the fork of Pelican Drive and Spoonbill Way. Regarding what the lady had said earlier, I took the fork to the right—Spoonbill Way--laser-focused on finding the house tucked up against a wooded area. I could meander some other time and take in more of the sights and sounds of my new neighborhood, but my curiosity for this Harry guy stuck like glue in my mind ever since that nice lady warned me.

I had run maybe a quarter mile, and there it was, a celery green vinyl-sided three-story house nestled up against a thick tree line that towered over part of the roof line on one side. I could barely make out the metal peaks of a pool cage without squinting or moving closer to his house, which I was afraid to do. Afraid he'd see me approaching and then possibly yell at me or something worse. I hid behind a clump of trees in the open lot across from his property. It seemed lonely at the end of this part of the development. I noticed one house had a car in the driveway and a few kids' toys out front. A baseball bat and mitt lay on the top of the wrap-around porch, and a couple of big toy trucks sat on the concrete path leading to the porch steps. The lots were vacant to either side of Harry's, and the only other houses built near this dead end seemed void of human occupancy. The one had a for sale sign in the front yard.

I had to admit that it was hard to catch my breath in this heat. Sweat ran down my forehead and soaked the back of my thin running shirt. Without a breeze, the heat and humidity felt like I was stuck in a sweatbox. I had to seriously rethink my jogging times in Florida, especially in the dead of summer.

I knelt by a tree trunk wide enough to hide most of me; one of the few virtues of being small. I pretended to re-tie my shoelaces while I kept an eagle eye on Harry's house. It felt eerily quiet as I took steady, slow breaths, listening for voices. Instead, the trill and warbles of the osprey and blackbirds filled the air. There wasn't a sign of the old man anywhere. I pictured him feeble and bent over like a crotchety old man; characters you read about in stories or you see as the mean man across the street on a TV show. I laughed at the thought that I might be living in a neighborhood that housed such a fictional character. Or, maybe he was a nice-looking old man that would wag his finger and tell you to beat it if you came too close.

Amusing was the operative word.

And then I heard a high-pitched motor sound in the distance. I scampered to the road facing the direction I came since a big, bold sign in front of me read: DEAD END. I had to turn around. When I did, Devin came trolling around on his golf cart, the odd noise I heard in the distance.

"Hey, Miss Raven, what are you doing here?" Devin said with a harsh note of disapproval as he brought his golf cart to an abrupt stop, the smooth tires sliding some. He stared without moving his head. Odd-looking black sunglasses that nearly covered the top part of his scrawny face, reminded me of enlarged fly eyes, the way they fit on his face.

"I was just out for a run. Checking out my new neighborhood," I said in a rebellious tone. I've been here one night, and the maintenance guy is acting like he's the neighborhood police. "I don't know the neighborhood yet. I was just checking it out." I started jogging away from him, and he followed, which forced me to stop and turn around.

"You have another question for me?" The sweat dripped into my eyes and started to sting. I cursed at myself for not bringing a towel, but I respectfully waited for his response.

He stood, and I watched him give me an obvious "once-over" look before he spoke, which infuriated me even more. "I'm just letting you know that the gentleman that lives in that house likes to be left alone, and the unwritten rule is never to approach him per his request," he said. Pointing toward Harry's house, he immediately returned his gaze to me. I stepped back, demanding more distance between us. A thick sweat line had formed across his light blue baseball cap bill with Hampton Pools embroidered in dark red. He pulled it down further on his forehead, pushing his stringy hair back around his ears that hung down to his shoulders.

His disposition curdled my insides.

"Ok, thanks for telling me, Devin. I'll remember next time." My heart started to pound unnecessarily faster, and I was extremely thirsty. My feet felt like they were swimming in a hot tub. I wasn't in the mood to waste my time with Devin. I desperately wanted to get home.

"Well, I just don't want our newbie in the neighborhood to get reprimanded so soon after moving in. Frankie doesn't mind giving out fines if you decide to disrespect the privacy of others," he spouted in an I-told-you-so tone as a smirk formed on his lips. I wasn't oblivious to how men ogled at women, and looking at him wearing those god-awful sunglasses, that he probably stole from a blind resident in the neighborhood, made me instantly leery of his motives at this very moment. This person, whom I regarded as our community maintenance man, rubbed me the wrong way.

"I get it, Devin. I need to get back home, so thanks for the warning." I took off in a run rather than a jog, but before I rounded the corner and out of sight of Harry's house, I quickly turned to see Devin drive his golf cart onto Harry's driveway, get out and walk around to the back.

What the heck? Who is this Harry person, and why can Devin enter his property?

And who is Frankie?

CHAPTER 5

Evening, August 6th

It took over an hour, but I finally decided on the printed short-sleeved romper in jean blue and rusty red. I assumed this invitation to be more of a casual than a formal affair, so I slipped on a pair of simple brown sandals and pinned my air-dried hair behind my ears; medium hoop earrings for the final touch. I had gotten so lazy about my appearance with all the packing and moving over the last year that I'd forgotten what it was like to dress up, to choose something more than a t-shirt and running shorts. I never imagined I'd be picking out a suitable outfit for a drink and sunset date with my fantasy Harvey Specter look-a-like neighbor on my second day of Florida living.

If God himself told me that this would happen on August 6th, 2015, I'd have to respectfully laugh and tell him you've got the wrong person.

But it was true, and I was excited and beyond nervous at the same time. For all intents and purposes, it was merely a *welcome to the neighborhood* introductory sunset occasion, not a proposal in marriage.

I still couldn't get past the idea that Drew and Devin were brothers. Granted, I'd barely met either one, but it didn't take a genius to recognize a distinct difference. I had a strong opinion of both; one bordered on the edge of creepy and tactless, whereas the other reigned in the charming and debonair department. It didn't make sense to me. If it wasn't for their similar features--narrow faces, deep-set eyes, and the exact shape of their mouths--I'd say one of them has a different set of parents. Devin was definitely the older one, from what I could tell. How could they be so different yet related?

And why was I obsessing over this fact?

I thought about my sister and me and concluded it could be true. Our relationship pulled us in opposite directions depending on the situation in front of us, but I never felt, from the outside looking in, that we could ever be as diametric as I noticed in the Hampton brothers. Maybe I was being too critical. Maybe Devin didn't cut it in the professional world of luxury pools, and the two brothers had some amicable agreement between them and their set positions, which was really none of my business. Who was I to judge?

With a lightweight sweater hooked on my forearm and the house alarm set, I exited down my front steps on my way to Drew's. I'd noticed Cassie always having a sweater with her for that "just in case moment," so I simply followed without question. You always wore layers in Minnesota. The weather was that unpredictable.

"Hello! Miss McKade?" My thoughts were pulled away by someone yelling my name from behind me. I saw a woman approaching me in a small compact car embellished with security guard logos and the windows down.

"Hi," I said, bending slightly to face the driver through the open passenger window. I recognized her smooth chocolate skin and white-toothy smile as Cassie, and I came through the gate yesterday. I just couldn't remember her name. "What can I help you with?"

"I'm Carly, the security guard at the gate. I saw you come through last night with your friend...Cassie, is it?" I nodded. "Remember the paperwork I gave you to fill out?" Carly reminded me.

It slipped my mind, just like Drew's invitation.

Oh, Carly, sorry. I'll get that to you tomorrow. I haven't had a chance."

"No, no... Miss McKade, I wasn't trying to harass you about it. I just wanted to make sure you remembered is all. How are you coming along? Cute outfit, by the way." Her voice was smooth and cheery. It was hard to imagine her taking an authoritative stance with someone at the gate with a sweet timbre such as hers. Her polite gesture made me feel welcomed and appreciated. And then she added, "I just love rompers, but my thighs don't."

She let out a self-deprecating laugh.

I let out a soft snort of disagreement and said, "Don't be so hard on yourself, Carly. If we went shopping with my friend, Cassie, she'd find you a romper that would look great on you. I promise you that." I don't know what I was trying to prove, but Carly gave me the impression that she was happy, fun-loving person and would enjoy a girls' shopping day. "And thank you, but please call me Raven."

"Okay, Miss Raven..."

Carly stopped mid-sentence when we were interrupted by Devin pulling up in his golf cart. My stomach twisted into a knot.

He was a hot mess of sweat and dirt up to his elbows, and by the egotistical smirk on his face, which I would have preferred to slap right off of him, seemed to enjoy his narcissist intrusive need for attention that very moment.

Carly, in her welcoming sweet voice, said, "Hello, how are you doing, Devin? Looks like you're working hard?" I wasn't about to infuse my questionable angst with this guy in front of her, so I also cordially acknowledged Devin.

"Hello, Devin." The hood of the car blocked his view of me, so he pulled his cart forward. He folded his arms, leaned back in his seat, and pulled his mouth to one side as he intentionally stared without saying a word. I had to laugh at his cavalier insolent behavior. He clearly missed the mark of looking seductive or even the least bit provocative. Unlike his brother, who naturally, without effort, personified such likeness.

Men like this infuriated me. I recalled one such contractor that used this type of haughtiness in order to control me and won. To compare Devin to the likes of that despicable contractor put me in a bad place. I don't know why it was happening right now. I closed my eyes and prayed for the Drew gods to sweep me away.

"Well, hello, Miss Raven. Nice to meet up again." Devin stood propping his arm on the hood of the cart. "You look really nice. Meeting someone?" His tone drooled with spite and disdain as if this was any of his damn business. Did he treat the other women in the neighborhood like this? What did Carly think about him? My hand made a fist, and I smiled through gritted teeth. He was disgusting, and I wish I could say as much.

"I know, she looks ready for some fun in the sun," Carly said in an overly excited manner, clearly not feeling the intrusive vibe I was getting from Devin. Turning to me, she said, "Well, you have fun, Miss Raven. I got to keep going on my neighborhood check. Bye, y'all." A wave of her hand out the window as she drove away, leaving Devin staring at me.

I waved back to Carly and proceeded toward Drew's house, my heart racing, my steps wobbly, hating myself for letting him get to me. I clutched my purse in front of me like a protective shield as I listened to the sound of Devin's golf cart behind me, wondering where he was, but I was afraid to make eye contact with him. Looking up ahead, I saw Drew by his mailbox, and my face lit up like a neon sign. So much so, it gave me the courage to look behind me and see Devin turn his golf cart around and head in the opposite direction. A much-needed relief surged through my veins.

Dressed in khaki shorts and an untucked dark purple striped shirt, Drew looked like the star of a Hallmark movie, displaying a brilliant, confident smile at me. I was relieved to see how comfortable and casual he looked with sleeves rolled onto his forearms and leather flip-flops.

"Hi, welcome to Bay Harbor, my new neighbor. I'm so glad you could make it." Drew greeted me with a warm smile, and I held out a hand that I quickly drew back as he pulled me into a friendly hug. I momentarily forgot he was a hugger and that my formality of shaking a man's hand wasn't necessarily the proper approach in Florida. He released and held me by my shoulders, taking in the sight of me for a moment. I smiled and playfully wondered, was this a fantasy Harvey moment on TV?

"Wow...Miss Raven, don't you look like an angel sent from heaven," Drew slathered me with a compliment I didn't know how to respond to. I'm sure my skin turned the color of an overripe strawberry, but too hard to tell with the sun blaring its rays directly at us.

"Well, that maybe pushing it." My voice flitted away out of embarrassment.

He gently touched my back and pointed toward the back of his house. A large, curved pool shaped like a pear with a waterfall streaming down a mountain of rocks at the smaller end sat in the center of his backyard. Bluish-gray soapstone tile and crushed shell carpeted the rest of the area. High-top tables and chairs, chaise lounges, and a small seating area decked out this area like a private resort. The Gulf waters sprayed against a wall of boulders connected to a thick row of mangroves. The perpetual bounce of the sparkle on the calm waters from the sun's rays was stunning and mesmerizing.

"By the way, thanks for inviting me. Your outdoor area is absolutely breathtaking!" I took a moment to look around, admiring the details of the house. "Is this your design, or did you have a special designer?"

Drew took an audible breath, nodding his head. "You got me between a rock and a hard place...you being a designer and all. If I said *I* did it, and you thought it was short on proper design trends, I'd look like a dummy, but if I said I hired someone to do it, I'd look like I didn't know what I was doing!" He took me by surprise. I was shocked this charming, confident man was afraid of a possible failed attempt at design when, in fact, it was stunning beyond anything, I was sure, I would have come up with.

He handed me a chilled chardonnay and poured himself a glass of bourbon on a cube of ice after we chose a seat at his outdoor bar.

"I've been looking forward to your visit since I saw you at Tiffany's last night. I'm so happy you're here. I know you just moved in and maybe would have rather stayed home tonight….I didn't want to interfere in your personal life." I heard the sincerity in his voice and appreciated his thoughtfulness. It touched my heart. And for instance, a millisecond, I thought about Jack and how he wished for me to be happy again and hoped I'd find another I could trust and love as much as I did him. I never thought it would happen, as tortured as I've been with the loss of Jack, but now I wondered; could this be the man?

Or was I being starstruck foolish?

While sipping our drinks, our conversation mainly consisted of him asking me questions about my decorating store in Prior Lake. He seemed to be impressed that, as a single young woman, I was able to achieve such success. I didn't take it personally. He didn't seem to be chauvinistic in any way, just surprised at my ambition. That's why he had asked Luke so many questions about me while he worked on my house, and when he mentioned he'd seen a few of my cooking videos, I was, again, shocked.

"So, I suppose you're aware of my next big wish or venture, whatever you want to call catering?"

"No, I didn't," He responded, eyebrows raised. I could see the cogs in his brain turning as he lifted his glass to his lips. I wondered what he was thinking.

Drew had the perfect spot for an outdoor party. It could easily handle a hundred guests. I imagined servers dressed in smart black and white perusing the crowd carrying large silver trays over their heads filled with champagne flutes and savory delicacies. I dreamed of catering parties in outdoor tropical settings where the guests were dressed in light linens and flowery prints. I loved planning dinner parties for my friends, but that was usually outside on our deck next to the grill or inside during the winter next to the fireplace. An outdoor party with a view such as this would be an exciting challenge. The vision was inspiring. And then it dawned on me; maybe a new reveal for "Food and Wine Club with Raven" could be just that—finger party bites and cocktail sippers.

"Looks to me you're thinking pretty deep about something." Drew set out a small bowl of pistachios and tiny square crackers and then came around from the bar to sit next to me.

"Tell me about it. Why do you want to cater?" He took a sip from his cocktail, grabbed a cracker, and popped it into his mouth. I did the same.

"I've always loved to cook and throw dinner parties. Well, that's what I did in Minnesota, and when Jack..." I stopped and looked down. I then took a deep breath and slowly let it out through my nose, hoping he hadn't heard, and I could continue with my catering story. Drew tilted his right ear toward me as if waiting for me to finish. "In the back of my mind, I always wondered about catering a party, but I never got that far."

"Jack?"

"My fiancé. Jack was my fiancé," I said, gazing out to the large body of water in front of us, wishing I hadn't slipped. It felt like I was crossing a fragile line of something that just belonged to Jack and me. I'd never opened up to another man about my relationship with Jack nor anyone other than my family or Cassie and Luke. It seemed sacred, and now I felt like I was breaking a promise or a special kind of confidence.

"I wasn't aware you were engaged. I'd..."

"I'm not. He died five years ago." I said with a hint of apology and wondered why. The words just fell out of my mouth. I re-crossed my legs and finished the last of my wine before Drew said his condolences, which always follows after someone hears devastating news. I didn't want to hear that from Drew, and I didn't think I'd be talking about Jack and me, but I couldn't stop now that it had started. "Jack was the love of my life, and yes, it has been the most devastating thing to ever happen to me." I flinched as the image of Farren hit me like a bat slammed on my fingers. Of course, Jack's death wasn't the most devastating compared to the cruel hands of my attacker, but he was never going to be a part of this conversation. I looked down to gather my thoughts before I continued, "But I'm fine now and realize it was better to know and have him for the short time I did. I experienced true love, and I couldn't have been more blessed when I was with him."

Drew nodded as if agreeing with me and took my one hand between the both of his and said, "Luke mentioned you hadn't been interested in a relationship for some time, but he didn't tell me why, and I didn't ask. I just knew I wanted to meet the person Luke told me he treasured as the sister he never had, so I left it at that." His voice was laced with emotion. The melancholy sound of the lapping waves against the rocks and the unending trills of the osprey in the background felt as if we were filming a romance movie; a light breeze sifting through our hair, touching the parts of our open skin. He inadvertently released the tight squeeze wrapped around my heart with his words.

I excused myself to the bathroom and could tell by the concerned look on his face that he knew I needed time to readjust. The vulnerability in my heart stuck out like a sore thumb, and I was overwhelmed by the subject of Jack. And not only that, but what Drew mentioned about Luke and what he had said about me nearly choked me to tears. I hadn't known Luke felt that way. Sure, we joked and playfully acted like siblings, but his words "treasured as the sister" struck a sensitive chord. I had to swallow and bite my lip to stave off the water boiling behind my eyes. I needed to refresh in private and pull myself together. Between the subject of Jack and the words of Luke, I was a hot mess.

"You can cater my parties," Drew said softly but with intention as I hoisted myself back onto the bar stool. He lifted his glass to his lips as creases lined his forehead. I could tell he was closely observing my reaction, possibly tiptoeing around certain subjects to avoid more emotional disruptions, which I understood. It pained me to think he might see me as weak and vulnerable. Finding so many faults with myself seemed easy, but I couldn't find one in this man.

"Really? You don't even know if I'm a good cook."

"I don't need to know. I trust Luke. He promoted your cooking as much as your design capabilities. He could have been wearing a big sign that said 'I work for Raven McKade'. Another reason I had to meet this talented person."

"Luke? He loves my cooking, but he's a contractor with a meat and potatoes appetite, and that's not hard to cook for.

Now, catering a highfalutin party is something of a different caliber, and I'm not sure..." The hint of catering seemed to revive my semblance all of a sudden.

"I know you could."

He patted my knee, but I sensed he would have rather left his hand there as he gave a tiny squeeze before wrapping his fingers back around his glass.

Thoughts buzzed around in my head like a swarm of bees fighting for nectar in the middle of a sunflower. I mentally scoured the stack of food magazines I had piled in a box somewhere.

He poured me another glass of wine, took my hand in a secure, gentle hold in his, and led me to a high-top table at the far corner of the pool area. We stood like gawking first-timers at the view of the sun closing in on the horizon. Definitely, a breathtaking view as I sipped my wine. I started to pull my hand from his as the sweat building in our grip felt a little uncomfortable, but he grasped tighter. He looked down at me and said, "Is it okay if I hold your hand a moment longer?"

I nodded, watched his smile spread wider, and then tilted my head back to let the salty-scented air fuse through my hair and nose. I felt my insides awaken as if my hands ran lightly up and down my body in a sensual massage. I squeezed his hand in appreciation for this moment.

Moments later, Drew pulled out two small plates from the under-counter fridge and then pointed to the chairs at the end of the bar where he set the two plates. He told me the arugula salad was dressed with his mom's version of lemon vinaigrette, which consisted of a "splattering of limoncello," per her words on his recipe card.

I hopped on the end bar stool and watched this charismatic man grill me up tequila-glazed shrimp and champagne-salted buttery scallops while I inhaled the divine salad chilled to perfection.

I was in a happy place.

"I might have to steal this for my food vlogs," I said, teasing, but Drew just shrugged his shoulders as if that wouldn't be a problem. "So, this party. Does Devin take part in anything since he's part owner?" I stopped chewing when I saw the sober look on Drew's face. I obviously said something that struck a nerve and nervously pushed my hair behind my ears as Drew tapped his teeth together.

He flipped the shrimp and turned the scallops to make a cross-hatch char mark before he spoke.

"Ahh... that's a story too. Devin thinks he's more of an owner than he really is. He's still part of the company, but the jerk-off, excuse my language, decided to assault one of our best clients' daughters. His wrongdoing got him, me, and the company into serious legal trouble. He made a mistake, and we all ended up getting into trouble. I had to pay them to avoid pressing charges. It wasn't a good situation, but thankfully it's all in the past now." He shook his head, focusing on the seafood on the grill. I noticed his jaw clench as he poked at the shrimp.

I was shocked, but only for a moment. Devin manifested narcissism, although subtle to most, it wasn't to me, and this proved it. I sensed a temper.

My sympathy poured out for the poor girl.

"Hey, I'm not interested in ruining our inaugural introduction by having to bring up my brother's faults," Drew continued. "He's my twin and, unfortunately, started out at a slower pace, if you know what I mean. It makes me feel I still need to protect him, although he pisses me off sometimes, and he knows it."

My God, they were twins, and I thought Devin to be older than Drew. He continued, "And there I saw a twitch."

"I'm sorry. You said 'twin,' and that threw me. I... assumed Devin was older. It's..."

"Everyone says that. I get it." He placed an ocean blue platter stockpiled with scallops and shrimp on the bar between our salad plates and then moved around to his seat.

The blazing red-orange of the sunset would forever be implanted in my mind's eye; it was such a stunningly beautiful frame-worthy sight. Drew and I sat in silence as the sun hit the horizon for what seemed like just seconds before it disappeared into a hazy atmosphere. The subject of Devin stayed a moot point, which was okay with me, but I still had concerns. And I didn't push the issue about Harry when I asked Drew about this odd man. He just said, "Yeah, Harry's an odd man, but we should leave him alone like he's asked. He owns this development, you know?" He paused and continued as if he had just remembered an important detail, "And, if I'm not mistaken, your house is the first he built." My antennae raised high in the sky.

By the time I was ready to leave, the annoying no-see-ums were biting through the fabric of my sweater, and I was tired. The information I had learned from Drew was both interesting and disturbing. Although, on a lighter note, it was an interesting night spent with a doppelganger from Suits. I don't know why I never brought it up to Drew. I'm sure he'd heard it before. Besides, it was my little fantasy.

"Damn it, Devin. You startled me," I shouted.

It was extremely quiet in the neighborhood except for the cicadas and grasshoppers in their nightly chorus but I still never heard the ping of Devin's cart approaching. I noticed he was using a flashlight rather than the headlights on his gold cart. I'm not sure what the purpose of that was but I didn't care to ask. I checked the time on my phone: 9:45. "What are you doing out this late?" Driving around in the dark for what? What could he possibly be doing at this time of the night?

"You shouldn't be walking by yourself in the dark," Devin said quietly as if someone could hear him. And his presence agitated me even more after what I'd just learned from Drew. I wanted to shout in his ear, *You know it's wrong to assault a defenseless woman, you pervert.*

"Don't change the subject, Devin. Why are you out at this time of night?" I didn't wait for his answer. I started to step away when Devin grabbed my arm but quickly released his hand. I don't know if the fear he saw explode in my eyes made him let go, but I raised my palms in protest. I faced the street lamp's glow, and I knew he could see the terror on my face.

"I'm sorry. I didn't mean to scare you, Miss Raven. I noticed you walking out of Drew's driveway and wanted to ensure you would be alright."

I didn't care what his excuse was. I punched the code in from my phone, ran to the front door and slammed the door shut as fast as I could, and locked it.

This man scared me.

CHAPTER 6

Friday, August 7th

While the coffee brewed, I snuggled into the corner of my couch, tucking my feet under me, and checked my phone for messages and my last video reviews on the walleye dish I prepared weeks ago. At a glance, many of my avid followers anxiously awaited my first vlog set in Florida, something I'd need to decide on sooner than later. I was more than excited to perform it in my new kitchen. And I'm sure my viewers would give me "Rave Reviews" on just the setting.

I was actually ecstatic to be done recording my videos from my kitchen in Prior Lake, Minnesota. Farren James Humboldt, the highly recommended contractor who took five months to renovate my kitchen, had decided to make one last visit on that chilly night on October 16, 2012.

As I stood watching from my new garden window, the familiar stray tabby cat made its nightly appearance and jumped onto the arm of my wooden chair. And that's when I felt a warm heavy hand slap across my mouth. Of course, I screamed, but it was a hopeless case for anyone to hear since the closest neighbor to either side of me was a full block away.

I lived on a little over two acres close to Mystic Lake Casino, and now the distance would hinder any screams for help. I tried recalling where I'd left my cell phone. Not that that would have helped me anyway.

The slap was just the beginning of the worst inflicted on me. His monstrous hands covered most of my face crippling my breathing efforts through his fingers. His biceps parodied those of Sylvester Stallone's in *Rambo,* which now made me wonder why he was built like a mini Schwarzenegger; to be in control of his victims without much effort. He seized my hands and dragged me to the living room, where he tore at my plaid flannel lounge capris, throwing the buttons he tore from my shirt across the room. I kept fit and was vital for my height, but I was nothing compared to his beastly strength and consumed anger. He had at least fifty pounds of muscle on me. As much as I twisted and fought back in his grips, he resorted to pinching my inner thighs and skin at the base of my neck in order to gain control. The more I struggled, the more vicious he became.

His weight on my body suffocated me and exhausted my energy to scream. I eventually collapsed into submission.

I was defiled from behind, where he scratched and prodded me so hard it was painful to sit or use my legs without cramping or stumbling from extreme muscle fatigue. The garage door slammed. He left me lying there, barely able to move in a mess of my blood and tears. My mind went numb. I was so messed up; I couldn't recall the day or time it was. I felt like a small animal hit by a car, left to wither and rot away on the side of the road.

All I thought about was why this happened to me, and did he, during those five months, plan this all along? Was this vicious act something he did to his other clients? Was this a typical last act after getting paid in full?

He was a referral by a long-time client of mine. How could I not trust him?

I was ashamed to tell anyone, including Cassie, my best friend. The one person I should have run to immediately. That was shame all by itself. But I finally did weeks later and filed a restraining order. Cassie insisted I tell my parents and sister. It was a night of pity and hugs, my dad sitting in silence with tears wetting his cheeks, my mother sobbing as she sipped on vodka, and my sister, so full of anger and rage I thought she was going to get in her car and hunt him down to put a bullet in his head the way she talked. Cassie flew up from Florida to be with me for as long as I needed, and during that time, Cassie begged me to start making plans to move to Florida.

"Hey, I know it's been tough and scary for you after what happened. But I want you to know that you don't have to go through it alone. Luke and I think you should consider moving to Florida and start over in a sense. Live closer to me and take advantage of what Florida offers besides no snow!" I could tell she was trying to lighten the mood and I appreciated her for it. It seemed as if the attack was replaying on a TV screen above my head, so the mood in the room was continually somber and depressing.

It was hard to shake.

Moving had never crossed my mind, and staying in that house felt like being buried alive with fear most nights.

"I don't know, Cass. I've always thought I'd need to stay here in Minnesota. My mom? My business? What about that?" I hesitated and struggled with the realistic measures I'd have to take to make it happen, but in the same sense, it sounded appealing, a fresh start far away from the agonizing memories.

"You're strong, and you can overcome this. Just think about it."

"Moving to a new state and starting over just seems daunting, having to sell my business, and I just started my food vlogs."

"Sometimes we have to take a leap of faith and trust that everything will work out for the best. Sometimes it's greener on the other side, Rave. And remember that you're not alone in this. You have Luke and me here to support you. I will be here for you every step of the way. Florida is a beautiful and vibrant state with so much potential for your career. Keep your food vlogging. It just has a different background and food flair, is all."

Cassie tried her best to convince me, and I could feel the intrigue of living in a beach-style home. "I know, but what if I'm too scared to live on my own again? Maybe I'll need to find a roommate."

"Rave, I won't pretend that bad things can't happen anywhere, but I promise we'll take every precaution to ensure your safety and security in Florida. And as for starting over, sometimes a fresh start can be just what you need to move on from the past and create a better future for yourself." After a brief pause, Cassie continued while I sat as still as a mouse. How I could possibly get my act together and do what it took to leave my home state and start over somewhere else? "I understand, and I'm here for you no matter what you decide. Just remember that you don't have to face this alone, and we can work together to overcome this fear," Cassie said, her motherly nurturing voice pleasant to my ears. We were at her parents' house, sitting on the couch having this conversation, and when we finished, she coaxed my head down on her lap, rubbing my shoulders and back till I fell asleep.

Days later, I started to think about moving to Florida. I also thought about my parents. Mom needed a constant watch, and my dad was not in the best shape of his life to care for himself and my mother. And Rachel, well, I knew she would flip out at my decision and cause an unneeded ruckus within our family unit.

But…Cassie's offer was already influencing my decision.

I got a text from Rachel:

I'm sure you're very busy and not too concerned about Mom knowing she's safe behind doors without alcohol, but she asked about you and has wondered why you haven't called her yet. She doesn't understand you just can't willy-nilly call and expect to talk to her. If you want to learn more, you'll have to call me or Dad.

As I expected, there was no **Love, Rachel. How are you doing** or **Hope everything is going well.** But what was I really expecting? This was Rachel purporting her importance in our family now that I was hundreds of miles away.

Not to be cold about it, but Mom needed to be in a place like this long ago. And Rachel was the one to bring it up with Dad and me years ago.

****

"You know, I think we need to push her into therapy," Rachel said to Dad and me at the table the night Mom passed out in bed after the neighbors found her lying in their backyard.

It was 2 a.m. Dad called Rachel and me after he got Mom back to the house and felt devastated about what to do next. Rachel made the fifteen-mile trek, and I made the fifty-mile trek with a small packed bag. I knew this would be the start of a bumpy road that would need the full benefit and cooperation of the three of us.

"I'm...I'm...not sure that's going to work," my father said, his hands constantly rubbing his forehead, switching to his chin every so often. Rachel and I looked at each other and knew it had to work. Mom was hiding vodka and gin bottles in obvious places as if she wanted us to find them, like calling out for help. But when we'd approach her with that opinion, she'd accuse us of lying, trying to make her look like an awful mother, slamming the door to her bedroom, where she'd hide out for the rest of the day.

Fifteen years later, Rachel and I are still in fight mode. I personally blamed it on Mom. We all grew tired of her antics, which was something different every week. She could never realize that it wasn't just her that was hurting; it was all of us.

When Grandpa disappeared, she carried on as if it only affected her. It tore my father apart, but he still had to go to work, so he lifted his chin and took the badgering my mother imposed on him for acting "aloof," as she called it.

"It isn't your father, so what do you care" she'd say, which hurt him. According to my father, my grandpa Ben treated him like his own son, so my mother's words penetrated deep into his heart, but he had to refrain from arguing with her about it. She never understood, no matter what you said to try and make her realize she was in the wrong.

****

"Dad, hi. How are you?" I asked, feeling positive, hoping my dad was in a better place.

"Raven, so good to hear from you. How's Florida?" I was surprised at how calm he sounded.

"It's great, Dad. The sunsets are stunning. And the neighborhood is perfect for running. I just need to realize that midday is not the best time to run in the Florida humidity this time of year." I chuckled and walked over to the window, coffee cup in one hand, the phone in the other, and stared at the blue skies above.

"You've gotta be careful about that humidity, Rave. It could be treacherous on your little bird-like figure if you don't hydrate enough." His tone more scolding, which warmed my insides. "God knows you eat like a bird. I'm not sure how you have the energy you do at times." He wouldn't say that now after what I ate at Tiffany's.

It was nine in the morning in Minnesota, and I could hear the news channel in the background. Dad loved a pot of coffee and his news channel Friday mornings. Close to retirement now, he only worked Monday through Thursday.

"Dad."

"Hmm?"

"I know it's only been two days, but how's Mom?" I heard him inhale while I held my breath. I assumed he knew I found out from Rachel via Cassie from the other night. I was sorry I missed his call.

"It's only been two days, and she's still detoxing. They're giving her benzodiazepines to help her, but she's at least resting more instead of fighting them." It was a relief to hear. It was also a relief to notice the strength back in my dad's voice. The last few years wore us all so thin that when he did speak, it sounded more like he had a chronic case of laryngitis.

"Will you let Rachel know we talked?"

"Sure. But it would be nice…." I could tell he preferred me to contact my sister, but not today. I didn't need her fault-finding finger-pointing at me on top of everything else that's flipped my mind upside down since I woke up.

"I know, Dad. I will. Just not today." I know it hurt my dad to hear that Rachel and I are still poking at each other from different sides of an emotional track. I had hopes that if Mom could be healed, then all of us could as a whole.

I poured another cup of coffee after I changed into my running outfit. Cassie had left a text saying Luke forgot to tell me he had a box of "trinkets" he found in the walls of my house. They planned on coming by to drop them off, but I was to call her later to set up our "dinner date," which meant I was cooking for them, and I was more than thrilled.

"Trinkets"? I liked Luke's choice of words. This should turn out to be a fun night. And if this was Harry's first house, then why would there be trinkets hidden in the walls? Intriguing is all I could say.

After this interesting news, I wanted to get another look at Harry's house. I'm not sure if you'd call this an obsession with Harry Fishmen, but he was luring me in like a walleye latching onto a spinner bait; hook, line and sinker.

CHAPTER 7

Devin, Friday, August 7th

Feisty. I like feisty girls. They are attractive and intriguing; they are bold and confident in their skin. I greatly admire their unapologetic attitude toward life, which fascinates me. To me, a feisty girl symbolizes strength and passion, and I can't help but feel drawn to them. Now that I know Miss Raven is feisty, I'd have to handle her differently.

But, boy, is she a looker, with a small petite figure and skin as smooth and flawless as a model. I just want to touch her soft blondish-red hair. It seems it would be silky soft wrapped around my fingers. And the one-piece thing she had on. I don't know what you call it, but it worked, showing off everything that mattered to a man, everything that sent a man's groin aching to touch. She's a perfect size, including her breasts, a perfect handful.

Just picturing her naked made me hard. And what kind of deranged parent would name her Raven? It doesn't fit her petite presence. Her perfect petite body. It's like her name is too big for her body. Besides, a raven's a big ugly bird, and she's a gorgeous dainty thing, well, feisty, but dainty in size. What parent would name a gorgeous little girl after a nasty blackbird?

Another thing is she has red-blondish hair. Wait, it's strawberry blond. That's the color. Not black like the Raven. Doesn't make sense to me. It doesn't matter, though; I still want her.

She's living in this area for a reason.

She seems disinterested in my concern for her, and that's a problem. I will have to make her change that perception once she realizes I'm here for her safety and not just as the maintenance guy.

This job sometimes sucks because all the snooty people think I waste their time if I'm not doing what they tell me to do. They don't have time to chit-chat or say a nice "hello" to me. Well, Frankie is a great friend, and, of course, Carly is at the gate. They're always lovely to me.

Time will change Miss Raven's mind once she sees that lots of others like me and appreciate me, especially Harry, who I noticed, she is kind of snoopy about. She just moved in and wants to know why there's this unwritten rule about leaving him alone. Well, duh. It's what he wants, and he owns this place. She doesn't get it, but I'll gently guide her when I see her get too close. Harry pays me to keep him protected. Miss Raven will want to be closer to me when she realizes Harry prefers me as his right-hand man or his sidekick, just like Watson and Sherlock. I make a great Doctor Watson watching out for Harry's welfare.

What really pisses me off is how Drew swoops in and invites her to *our dad's house*. I have rights to living there also, but greedy Drew thinks it's all his, and he thinks he's such a lady's man that he's in Miss Raven's face before she can barely spend a night in her new house. At least I introduced myself the first night when she was with her friend out back. I didn't need to invite her for drinks and a sappy sunset so soon. For crap's sake, she just moved in. I would wait and let her enjoy her new house, get to know some neighbors, and let Frankie do her thing first, then I'd ask her for some personal time.

I can see she's not only feisty but shy as well. I saw her eyes roaming over me like mine were all over her. Again, just thinking about her naked, with a flat hard stomach and a beautiful tight ass, sends twitches through my groin. I've got to keep my desires at bay, though. I don't want to scare her with the thought she's got twin brothers going after her. It makes her have to choose. That's unpleasant for anyone. I'll win in the end, so it's easy to let Drew slather on his charm dressed in custom-designed Don Johnson look-alike suits from Miami Vice just like our dad does or custom-ordered linen and silk from Rio de Janeiro in a tropical Tommy Bahama model look. Makes me sick. Doesn't offer to buy me anything like that. Says, "There's no reason for you to have a suit custom-made. You don't wear anything but cargo shorts and a T-shirt. If you need a suit, you can borrow one of mine." Asshole.

The stinking prick thinks he's the top dog. But I still own a portion of Hampton Pools, so he better be careful with his egocentric mind. It will hurt him soon enough.

I stopped by Frankie's to pick some fresh flowers she had planted. I had a smiley face vase that I wanted to put in front of Raven's door before she went out anywhere today.

"Devin, what the hell are you doing picking my flowers?"

Frankie caught me digging around in her garden. "Hey, be careful. I just planted some seeds where you're standing." She started down the back steps toward me, wearing a funky disco-designed spandex outfit that molded around her fleshy curves. She looked plumper than usual.

"For god's sake, you could have asked for a flower arrangement. I would have done it for you." Her scolding tone was like that of my kindergarten teacher.

"No," I said, clipping the last of what I assumed were yellow daisies. "I want to do this myself. They're for Miss Raven. You know the newbie?" I shoved them in the vase and walked over to Frankie, who tried to wrap her hair into a bun or whatever you call it when a girl winds her hair through some binder at the top of her head. But it didn't look good.

"Oh, gosh, I need to make up a package and bring it to her for signing," Frankie said.

"I could do it for you."

"Really, Devin? I don't think so. That's my job. But now I've got to get to the spa. We're starting a new yoga class today, and I need to watch my new hire to see if she's as good as she says she is. Toodle doo, Devin." No wonder she was in that god-awful outfit. Frankie isn't much older than me and usually wears those fifties dresses with wide flared skirt bottoms. It covers her rear well, especially after what I just saw.

"Thanks, Frankie, I owe ya one."

"Damn right you do," she said, walking up the back steps and disappearing inside.

I used the hose to fill the vase with a little water before I placed the vase outside Raven's door to ensure the flowers wouldn't wilt before she could see this colorful arrangement. I was proud of what I developed at a moment's notice. I could be thoughtful and romantic. Maybe this will make up for last night, her thinking I was spying on or trying to scare her. I wasn't. I just wanted to see her again in her hot shorts outfit. Plus, Drew hugged her. It wasn't fair.

Drew's already snatched enough from me: my stake in the company from forty percent down to ten, living with him in my dad's mini-mansion where I know I'm shoved to the outside of the gate in a twelve hundred square foot bungalow and the right to find another job. He forced me to sign a contract for the position of maintenance man for the next five years. All because I made a mistake with a young girl. Granted, I used the wrong head that day, but I'm sorry and have paid for it.

And now, he thinks he can get his hands on the one person that could change me and my life forever. I can't understand why he attracts all the good-looking women. We're twins and look almost identical. I'm a good-looking, charming person with a good heart, and more hardworking than Drew.

I'm also sociable. And I'm even friends with Harry, who doesn't see anyone else in the neighborhood. Drew always gets what he wants while I clean the dirt. I know Miss Raven will eventually like me for who I am, but I also know that might take a little convincing or romantic swagger on my part.

And these flowers are just the beginning.

I pulled up in my cart with the vase in one hand and a small note in the other. As quietly as I could, I walked up the front steps and set the vase down toward the one wall, and situated the note that said *Have a great day* gently on top of the thick bulb-like flower colored in bright red. I didn't know what these flowers were called, but this was a beauty, and the white note was prominent. I ensured I wrote in all capital letters neatly so she could easily read it. Otherwise, my handwriting wasn't the best, but I didn't want it to look like a kindergartner spelled it.

As I put down the flowers, I wondered if she would find it cheesy or possibly be creeped out by my gesture. What if she were indifferent and didn't care at all? I quickly dismissed those thoughts. I know she'll appreciate my gesture, especially since there's no reason not to like me. We exchanged pleasantries. I'm a genuinely nice guy; she'll recognize this and be grateful for the flowers.

I rode by numerous times this morning, and the vase was exactly where I had put it. I thought maybe I'd see her drinking her coffee, or whatever she has in the morning, out front in those comfy cushioned chairs that look too expensive for my pocketbook. She must have money after seeing all the remodeling she's done to this place over the last year. If a woman I like has money, all the better. We'd share everything, especially every night in bed, spooned tightly together, touching every part of each other's bodies. I couldn't help but moan; my carnal desire supervised my thoughts as I stared at her house from a distance.

I wondered if she hadn't noticed the vase yet or if she simply didn't like the flowers. I started to feel a bit edgy, wondering if I had made the right decision to leave the flowers. I also considered calling her to confirm if she received the vase, but I didn't want to appear too pushy. I decided to wait a little longer and hoped she would eventually see the flowers and appreciate the gesture.

As I roamed around the area of Raven's house, picking up the dead branches and fallen palm fronds, I remembered that Harry needed me before lunch, so I'd better switch my thoughts from the ravaging Miss Raven --a perfect pet name for her--to my required duties. But first, I needed to stop at Drew's before he left for the day.

"Hey, can I have some extra dough to buy new shirts and shorts? I need new shoes, too," I said, lifting my leg for Drew to see I was telling the truth. One side of my sneaker was blowing out.

"Do you always just show up in my house without knocking? Damn, I could have been walking naked out of the shower. And don't give me the crap about this is your house too. No. It's not. I live here and bought you a house close by, so quit with the alarm bit and knock or text that you want to see me. Is that so hard?" He finished tying his tie and headed back toward the bedroom. My patronizing pompous ass of a brother flinging his rules at me once again.

"Hey, grab me some cash while you're back there," *Asshole,* I said under my breath. God, he's such a greedy prick. Another thing he likes having control over is the money I get on the side. Like he's my personal stingy banker.

Instead of acting like he was my father and handing me my allowance, he actually, to my surprise, handed me five one-hundred-dollar bills and said, "Go buy some nice things and get outta here." It was hard to get a single C note from him most of the time.

I don't know what I did to get this, but I said a quick "thanks" and a "goodbye" and split. As I left, I wondered why Drew had easily given up that much money. He's always been reluctant to part with his cash; he often gives me just enough to make do.

This sudden change made me suspicious.

And then I thought a bit harder. It was probably some connection to Miss Raven. Perhaps he was hurrying to see her, or maybe he needed to impress her by spouting how generous he was with me. Have they talked about me when they've been together? If so, great.

I'll buy some new stuff and show her I can clean up, too, like my fancy prick of a brother. I'm not arrogant and have to show off the material things to impress her. Since it was Friday, I had to decide whether to go shopping at the mall and check out all the date hookups by the movie theater, which were so obvious it was hilarious, or dabble in a little online shopping with a few brewskis. That way, I can have a little fantasy session with myself, and the images of the sexy ravaging Miss Raven I can't seem to get out of my mind.

And there she was. My heart leaped as I drove my golf cart out of Drew's driveway, catching the back-side of her walking the other way. She wore tight, bright red biker shorts that molded around her perfect ass cheeks and a black bra-like top, walking fast, arms pumping back and forth. I couldn't stop staring. I decided to drive by her house again once she rounded the corner on Spoonbill Way to see if she picked up her vase. And there it still sat, as if she hadn't opened her front door yet. I didn't see what door she came out of but assumed she'd come outside that way. And then it dawned on me. If she was rounding on Spoonbill, she would walk past Harry's.

Harry needed me to move some things from his shed anyway, so I headed that way via the pathway by the pond. Harry and I were talking by his pool, my one eye on the street watching for Miss Raven, and there she was, walking by slowly, scoping out Harry's house. I didn't want to upset Harry, so I told him to go inside and make me some fresh tea, and I'd return in a jiffy. He gave me a funny look, and I waved a hand at him like it was nothing, but I had to take care of it.

I watched her walk over to the open grassy lot, her back to me as she put her phone to her ear. I bet it was Drew. That would piss me off. But a mile-wide smile formed on her face as she half turned to look back at Harry's house, and I wondered if it was him she was talking to. I marched over to confront her, struggling to hold my frustration in without looking pissed; I opted to smile as if I was coming to wish her a nice day. As I approached, she had deer in headlights look, but she quickly slid her sunglasses back on and her phone in the pocket of her spandex shorts. I knew I needed to be nice and sound nice, otherwise, she might get mad and feisty again. I wanted her close to me as much as possible. I wanted to smell her sweet womanly scent.

While looking at Miss Raven, I felt nervous and excited as I approached her. I forced a friendly smile despite my disappointment in catching her in this part of the neighborhood again. "Hi, Miss Raven," I said as congenially as possible. I want her to smile back, but all I see are pierced lips in a half grin. There's no way I can ask her to remove her glasses so I can see her sparkling eyes. She'd definitely run from me then. I see her tilt her head to the side just enough to see past my arm, which makes me turn to look. And Harry is standing at the front door, partially shielded by the scrolling ironwork covering the screen door watching us. I wave him away and then hear a slam of his heavy wooden front door, which brings Raven's attention back to me.

"What do you help him with, Devin? Is it something I could help with too? Like cooking meals or something like that? Maybe a cake?" She's noticeably jittery. She fiddled with her fingers, pretending to crack each one. Her voice is soft but not a high girly voice. It sounds authoritative but in a sexy way. I didn't notice it while she was yelling at me last night. Or maybe I was just too buzzed up to notice.

83

"Miss Raven, I've told you. Harry doesn't want any contact with visitors or the neighbors around here. I help because I'm the maintenance guy, and he trusts me. That's all." She nods her head like she understands, but I see her still staring in the direction of Harry's house. "You better get back home, Miss Raven. Please."

As we began talking, I couldn't help but wonder if she had found my flowers yet. I didn't want to sound presumptuous by asking, but at the same time, I was curious to know if she appreciated this small, warm gesture of mine. I hoped that the flowers would convey my admiration for her and make her smile as she was smiling on the phone while, I assume, talking to Drew. I couldn't hold back any longer, "Hey, did you get my flowers?"

CHAPTER 8

Saturday, August 8ᵗʰ

A wave of nostalgia slithered through me as I fine-tuned the placement of my dishes and the lighting screens for my cooking video this morning. A significant but pleasant surprise was the image of my grandfather's face straight out of the depths of my memory bank. I heard the phrases he used to say: "I'm in my happy place" or "I'm cooking up a storm." It's precisely how I felt as I prepared the ingredients for my first Florida post on Food and Wine Club with Raven. I remembered my grandfather as sort of a burly man, always full of love and affection toward Rachel and me. The memory has stuck with me because, during that period, Rachel and I were sisterly close. The distance grew between us after my grandpa disappeared, and my family slowly fell to pieces and left without answers. I still miss him terribly, and I have a small hole in my heart that still aches for his return. I especially miss his warm hugs and the twinkle in his eyes.

Unfortunately, we never got to say goodbye to him.

Nevertheless, a smile emerged as I readied myself in the mirror for my camera appearance. I was, once again, going to be cooking up a storm, relieved to be in my happy place. *Thank you, Grandpa.*

I chose a soft pale peach V-neck short-sleeve shirt and tucked my hair behind my ears with a small clip for this video. The dish for today was shrimp fra diavolo with jasmine rice. I've had it before, but I had never cooked it. I paired it with a pinot grigio from Veneto, Italy, but I also suggested a prosecco in case the other was not to a viewer's liking. Today, I wore my black apron with my logo in ombre colors of reds, oranges, and yellows stitched across the bib part, which was easy to see on camera. It was sometimes tricky to stir gently enough not to splatter, but with an apron, I wouldn't have to worry when I chose to wear a light-colored shirt. I also liked to dress in a shade close to my primary course color, so the colors of the veggies or other condiments popped while presenting them to the camera. Some vloggers liked using different colored and textured dishes, but for some reason, I always thought that detracted from the food itself in a video. Every chef or home cook has their opinion, but I preferred to use all white or cream-colored dishes and platters, so the reds, greens, and yellows burst on the camera.

It felt good to fall into the rhythm so quickly as I heated up the olive oil in a large sauté pan, added the shrimp and red pepper flakes, lightly stirred, and salted as the sizzling sounds permeated in my ears and the slight ocean scent wafted through my nose.

Barely leaning over the hot pan and closing my eyes, I inhaled slowly and deeply, letting the viewers experience through me, via the camera, the smells, and tastes as I described them. I remember watching Rachel Ray's first cooking shows, and she always said, "I wish we had smell- a-vision; it smells so good in here."

Before I finished the dish and was ready to plate, I took off my apron and lightly reiterated what I did to bring this dish together while spooning the rice, that I had premade earlier, onto a plate and then scooping two heaping spoonful's of the tomato shrimp sauce on top. Tiny black flecks of char and fresh ground black pepper were easily seen in the deep red roasted tomato sauce, the shrimp a soft pink, and the green dots of fresh parsley scattered evenly about. The steam rose from the plate in front of my mouth, swirling up to my nose as I took a bite and then recaptured, for the viewers, how the garlicky tomato flavors with a hint of red pepper spice in the sauce sucked in the juices from the shrimp and how the herby oregano was left lingering on your tongue even after you swallowed.

I clicked the stop button and devoured what was on the plate with the last bit of white wine I had in the fridge. It was so scrumptious I plated another serving and ate that as well. I slipped the recipe into my **KEEPER** folder.

I focused on editing with a different eye this time…something I read in a magazine about food vlogging that surprised me. It mentioned that showing a tiny blooper here and there makes one, as the teacher, more real and more human to the viewers. It couldn't hurt, so I slipped in the part where I had lost count and added too much salt. The tug at the side of my mouth and raised eyebrows explained how that was a mistake. And the part where I said to use a wooden spoon but caught myself stirring with a spatula became the other slip-up. Usually, I'd delete those clips, but not today. Weird how it felt a little more empowering and personalized.

Yesterday, Drew reminded me through a text that his party was a little over a month from now. A nervous excitement hit my chest thinking about his party, and my mind circled around plates of small bites like ricotta and roasted grape crostini with fresh rosemary or smoked salmon and dill flatbread, or even an apricot with goat cheese and walnuts. And then, of course, the pairings. Possibly a crisp rose or pinot grigio, but the cocktail must be something with gin and cucumber. The question was, what should I decide on first; food or drink? What's more important?

I had texted him back that I'd be working on it and looked forward to meeting up soon on the details. I also asked where I should go for fresh fish. He said nowhere but Bill's Fresh Catch, a mile away from our neighborhood as you zigzagged through town around Golden Pond. I laughed at the name and made sure he spelled it right. *It's Golden Pond, just like the movie* he texted back. I made a mental note to check out that movie again on Amazon or Netflix. You can't go wrong with Kathryn Hepburn and Henry Fonda, especially with homemade pizza and wine.

It was easy to find the seafood shop, and Bill, the owner, was as friendly and helpful as possible.

"Good morning, ma'am. What can I help you with?" A bulky medium, height man with thick fingers and balding white spiky hair approached from the back, wiping his hands on a rag matching the color of his bluish-gray eyes. He reminded me of what Guy Fieri might look like in twenty years and had that comical lilt to his voice. I still had to get used to this "ma'am" thing. Wasn't it specifically addressed to old ladies or a woman of stature? Neither was me.

"Drew Hampton sent me and said this was the only place I needed to go to buy my seafood." I watched his eyes light up and his eyebrows raise at the mention of Drew. I took it as a positive sign. I then wondered if I would have said "Devin" if his reaction would have been the same.

He chuckled and said, "Now I owe the little pool punk another twenty. My name is Bill, as you probably already know." I nodded, and he reached a hand over the glass cases to which I gave him a friendly handshake. "What are you looking for today?"

I was enamored. Mounds of shrimp and scallops filled the case adjacent to the one I was peering at with glazed eyes. It was filled with tuna, grouper, mahi-mahi, and the most significant piece of salmon I had ever seen. And then my eyes locked onto what looked like a thick piece of pinkish-white steak, but I knew it wasn't, and then I said, "Is this swordfish?"

Bill chuckled and said, "That's what the sign says, ma'am."

I rolled my eyes as I lifted my head. In my defense, the sign was smudged and looked like it read *Susfish*. "I guess I better pay more attention."

"New in town?"

"Yes, I am. I live in Bay Harbor." I pointed to the shrimp and held up a peace sign for two pounds. He grabbed a clear bag and tongs and started filling it up.

He let out a whistle like one does after hearing the price difference between a Ford and a Tesla.

"Pretty nice area you chose. Good for you, young lady," he said, nodding his head with a glimpse of a wink as he asked if I wanted something else.

"How do you prepare swordfish? I mean, is there a favorite among the Floridians? I've never seen this fish but in pictures. Walleye was the choice in Minnesota." As a food vlogger living in Florida, I'd better up my ante now in the seafood category.

"Minnesota, eh?" He chortled, confusing me with the people from northern Minnesota, close to the Canadian border. Oh, well. I grew up twenty minutes from the Iowa border, where you'd commonly hear; *ya, ya betcha*. "Well, let's see...it's a meaty fish. Most folks marinate and then grill it. Others might pan-sear in a bit of butter and wine sauce. More recently, I'm seeing people cutting back on red meat choose this as an option to steak because of the texture and the omega 3's. I may work here alongside fish all day, but I'm a meat eater." He patted his belly and laughed.

My culinary decision-making mind told me this was the perfect choice for Cassie and Luke's dinner at my house; grilled swordfish and vegetables with couscous dinner paired with the perfect wine. I couldn't believe how fifteen years had gone by so fast. They moved to Florida right before their twins were born. I'd missed cooking for them, but here was my chance to make up for lost time.

I wanted to make this a special dinner and thought about inviting Drew. I wondered if it would be too forward. On the other hand, he obviously was acquainted with Luke and now Cassie. A little guilt niggled at my gut. I knew I needed to put Jack's image in the proper spot in my heart and keep it there. No one was trying to replace him. I needed to keep reminding myself of that. I'd sleep on it.

"I'll be back to pick up some fresh swordfish when I make a date with my friends," I said, grabbing my bag of shrimp and a big piece of tuna. I waved goodbye and skipped joyfully out the front door to my car.

As I drove into my driveway, I noticed a short, plump woman standing at my front door, a large leather bag hanging from her arm that nearly touched the ground. I continued into the garage and parked, hurriedly grabbing my bags and purse to get out and see who this was. And then I remembered Drew said Frankie would be by soon to greet me with paperwork to sign as the newbie in the neighborhood.

"Hello," I said, walking around to the front of my house. She stood staring at the door, ringing the bell again. She obviously didn't see or hear me drive up. I own a Cadillac Escalade, more like a mini bus, and I wasn't sure how she missed me pulling up in the driveway. "Hello," I said again, but nothing. I needed to get the fish in my fridge, so I walked back through the garage and into my house to put the fish away and then answer the front door.

I opened the door, and there she stood, graying brown hair clipped short around her ears, blue tooth earbuds in. No wonder she didn't hear me. Without a greeting or nod, she walked straight in and dropped her leather case down on my foyer rug with a thud. I thought I was short. She could have been a shoo-in for a munchkin on *The Wizard of Oz*. Her skirt flared around a robust bottom like those knitted dolls used to cover toilet paper rolls back in the day. I couldn't help but chuckle to myself. My great-grandma had them in her bathrooms and changed colors per the seasons. I preferred the red and orange hues of the Fall; Rachel loved the purples and pinks in Spring.

She pulled out her earbuds and shoved them into her skirt pocket. "Hi, I'm Frankie, the HOA president. I've got some papers for you to sign. Is this a good time?" she asked, looking over the top of her glasses, her voice nasally. Her beady, scrutinizing eyes looked me up and down.

"Well, I wasn't aware you were coming today, otherwise, I would have made us tea or sangria or something," I said, a true nip in my voice, immediately taming it back. I didn't want to sound unneighborly, but people who just showed up at your door unannounced was an irritant to me. Clicking the button on my refrigerator door, it changed from opaque to transparent. I eyed up the bottle of white wine and noticed enough left for my shrimp dish. "Oh, I see I have a bottle of ginger ale."

"Oh, nothing for me, thank you," Frankie said. "I've got a date later on...with my own bottle of wine." Her shoulders moved as she laughed, amused with her own joke. But when she glanced at me, looking for approval, I could only muster a weak smile. I sat down at the table where she was unloading a file cabinet full of papers and brought my knees to my chest, watching her mouth move but no sound. I drank from a bottle of water and waited.

Finally, she pushed two thick piles closer to me. "I've got to sign all these?" I was in shock.

"Oh, no, sweetie," she said, patting my hand with her chubby little bear claw. "I'm just sorting. I didn't do this before I rushed over." I sighed heavily and noticed her spotting the smiley vase on the corner of my console table. The vase Devin placed by my front door yesterday.

A bright yellow smiley vase filled with red, pink, yellow, orange, and white flowers with a card propped in the center of the arrangement. It must have been there for a while; some flower heads drooped, and I wondered how I could have missed it. It was bothersome knowing this lovely collection came from Devin. I thought of tossing it, but that seemed extremely rude. So, I displayed the ray of flowery sunshine inside on my corner console table by the window, where it was more of a decoration rather than a focal point. Devin was nowhere a focal point.

"Oh, Devin brought you these, didn't he? They shouldn't be stuck in a corner. Why don't you put them in the middle of this table? You know he cut them from my garden out back. I'm good at growing flowers. If you ever need a little sprucing up for your counters, just let me know, and I'll provide you with the best arrangement possible," she said with a self-assured grin as she moved more papers around.

I could not imagine this woman, with the way she dressed, had an eye for arranging flowers in a vase.

Without thinking twice, Frankie picked up the bright yellow smiley vase and placed it in the center of my table. The fact she seemed to closely cohort with the likes of Devin proved that it was best to keep my discrepancies about him to myself. And my passing thought, since she mentioned how good she was with flowers, of using her to help with the fresh flower arrangements at Drew's party, was just that, a passing thought.

With a polite smile, I explained that I needed to return to my project, agitated with her company and nasal-sounding voice.

"I bet you didn't know I own a spa down on 4th Street." She dug through her leather bag and pulled out a card, and said as she handed it to me, "Adam is a great masseuse. You'd love him. Take this in when you make an appointment. I'll give the first one free."

I took the card and nodded politely. Once the door was closed, I let out a deep sigh of relief and threw the card in the trash.

I couldn't believe the audacity she had moving the vase. I couldn't imagine her and I becoming friends anytime soon.

CHAPTER 9

Saturday Night of the 8th

Months after our engagement, our life changed drastically. His symptoms worsened by April of the following year, and he could no longer dream about leaving Minnesota. The fatigue, the swelling, and the weight loss left him no choice but to rest in a hospital bed permanently. We had it in the middle of his bedroom, facing a large bay window overlooking Lower Prior Lake. We'd get him into a wheelchair when he wanted to look out onto the rippling waters that edged his property.

****

Jack had asked me to flip the plantation shutters open all the way. As I folded back each shutter carefully onto itself, the sun rays spilled onto the floor, illuminating the otherwise dark room and bringing a sweet smile to his face. The view was beautiful, and thankfully, during this time, it was a view we cherished together. The sky was a perfect shade of blue, the clouds fluffy and white. The leaves of the trees rustled in the wind.

Due to Jack's declining health, it was nearly impossible for him to go outside. I turned back to Jack, who had a peaceful expression. "It's beautiful," I whispered, looking back at him, who lay in bed, weak and frail, the color of his skin growing paler as the weeks went by.

"Yeah, it really is."

Tears began to well up in my eyes, but I blinked them away, determined to be strong for him. "I'll always be here for you," I said, taking his hand in mine and placing it to my cheek.

Jack looked at me with a mixture of gratitude and sadness in his eyes; the glossy golden brown color fading to dry wheat. "Thank you for everything," he said, his voice barely above a whisper.

I leaned in and kissed him softly on the forehead. "Of course," I whispered back, kissing the tip of his ear. "Anything for you."

****

I chose to relax in the sitting part of my bedroom. Luke insisted on knocking out the half wall in the master that divided the bedroom from a small office area to incorporate a sitting area with a love seat, an ottoman, a side table, and a lamp. A small quaint place for my own privacy.

"Damn," I said when I caught sight of the shrink-wrapped box. I knew exactly what it was, and it's exactly where I told Cassie to put it when she unpacked the box labeled **PRIVATE.** I only came into the closet to change into something more comfortable. I wasn't expecting this. The box was barely noticeable beneath the crazy amount of shrink-wrap layers. Every personal item Jack and I wished to never part with lay inside. It was sacred to us, and we vowed to show our kids someday.

A sharp pain poked me between my shoulder blade, and my heart beat sped up like a hummingbird's wings just looking at the clearly wrapped bundle. Inside were items special to Jack and me. These were items, we had joked, would be buried with us unless we had children, and it was decided we'd share with them the importance of what we put in this box.

I needed him. My heart was breaking open again. I wanted him to touch me, just one more time. I know I'd feel better if he could just hold me one more time. I closed my eyes and felt his breath on my neck, his strong arms wrapped around me. But it faded away. His hugs were always gentle, and I could feel the love in his heart pour into mine as we embraced. It was a feeling I'd never experienced before or since.

Torn and splitting apart like unwinding a woven rope, one part of me said to leave it be and put it back on the shelf, while the other begged for it to be opened, to relive and recapture some of the beautiful memories stuffed inside. I closed my eyes and tilted my head back, letting the tears stream over my ears into my hair. I let out a strangled cry of heartache. My emotions flooded to the surface so fast I felt like they would burst through the skin of my temples.

I cut through the layers of shrink-wrap. I held my breath briefly before removing the lid. On the top was our CD, which we made specifically for us; songs that meant something special between Jack and me. The first song, our favorite, was "Time in A Bottle" by Jim Croce. The words *"If I had a box just for wishes"* was the reason for doing this. This was our box of wishes. I hummed a few bars of the song as I stared at the items Jack had once touched and why they belonged in this box. My throat quivered, and my eyes prickled with tears while the rest of my body weakened from the sight of these things that I hadn't looked at since his death.

Wiping my face dry with the back of my hand, I dug some more, pulling out notes and cards we had given each other, and then I found his personal towel, the one he'd only use on the boat. Our initials were inscribed near the bottom hem in deep purple, with two gold wedding rings linking the letters. He was a true Vikings fan and joked about wearing purple socks and a gold tie at our wedding. The funny thing was, I knew he wasn't joking and would somehow convince me it would be a necessary shenanigan that highlighted our wedding day. I gently chuckled in my throat and felt my cheeks lift with calm happiness in remembering that moment. Initially, I hesitated, but now, I only wished I could have married Jack Finnegan; it would have been my greatest joy, and I'm positive that I would have gladly welcomed purple and gold at my wedding just for him. I stared through watery eyes, circling the gold rings with my finger as teardrops fell.

I slumped to the floor and crossed my legs, which had turned jelly-like. As I unraveled the boat towel, a blue velveteen jewelry box fell into my lap, and I opened it. Inside, shimmering like the day he proposed, was my pear-shaped diamond engagement ring, even more stunning than I had remembered. I linked my finger through it. The day he proposed was Wednesday, September 9th, 2009. It was a gorgeous Fall Minnesota day on Prior Lake, where the sun's reflection sparkled on the water like the diamond he had put on my finger. He purposely waited till after the Labor Day holiday to make the maiden voyage of his new boat — *Rave Reviews* — because there would be fewer boaters and distractions. The colors on the trees started to change, and he wanted to open a bottle of champagne without the DNR or water police hanging too close.

****

The weekend came, and Jack took me on the boat ride as promised. The trees were ablaze with vibrant red, orange, and yellow hues, a sign of the season. He'd had the boat for a month, the summer nearly ending. "Excuse me, Miss, but are you enjoying yourself?" Jack said, a sarcastic grin spread across his perfect lips. I never got sick of kissing them.

"You know how I love the Fall." I sat up and pulled my sweater tighter around me as the cool breeze chilled me. I didn't mind because the sun was full and the sky was clear. We only hoped we had another six weeks before the white stuff would appear. "Look at how the trees are changing colors so quickly. I hope a heavy southern wind doesn't come and blow them all down so early like last year. I like to see them on their branches a little longer," I whined.

"I know, it's a beautiful time of the year. I wanted to bring you here for another reason," Jack said, raising my curiosity. I thought it might just be the maiden voyage of his new Aviara and lunch at Charlie's.

"What is it?" I got up and sat next to him.

He slowed the boat to a stop. We floated in the center of the lake, other boats off in the distance. He stood up and pulled something out of his pocket. It was a small box with a ribbon. I lightly gasped but waited for him to continue on. "Well, I just wanted to tell you how much I love you and how much you mean to me. You make me a better person, and I can't imagine my life without you." Jack said with an emotion that made me cover my heart with my palm, my lips quivering with heartfelt excitement.

"I feel the same way about you," I said, touching his cheek.

He waved me over to the bench seat, where we sat with one leg lifted onto the seat, looking at each other. He opened the box to reveal a pear-shaped diamond ring. "Will you marry me, Raven Elaine McKade?"

Tears welled in my eyes as I had been anticipating this moment and couldn't believe it was here. I gasped, covering my mouth with both my hands. "Oh, my God, yes! Of course, I will marry you! It's so beautiful! I can't believe it. Oh, Jack. I love you, and I love this ring," I said as Jack slipped the ring on my finger.

He stood up and engulfed me in his embrace. Holding me tight to his chest, he added, "I want to spend the rest of my life with you."

He poured us each a glass of champagne, and then we toasted our future together. But that future never happened.

That day has been engraved in my memory forever.

My whole body wrenched as I sobbed in despair. I kissed the top of the ring and set it back in the slot where it now belonged. My head was heavy with so many precious memories; memories I never want to forget. My heart was so drained of emotion that I just slumped on my side.

I woke up hours later in a fetal position in the dark on the closet floor.

CHAPTER 10

Friday, August 14th

"Hello, Chica. Miss Raven!"

I turned from grabbing more grocery bags out of the back end of my car to see a woman half-running to me from across the street. She was waving frantically as if I might run, but I was too intrigued by this smiling, well-dressed woman with long black curly hair pulled in a ponytail at the top of her head and painted bright red lips coming my way.

"Hi, Chica, my new neighbor. So glad to finally meet you. I'm Deidra from over there," she said, her voice high-pitched but still sweet sounding. She pointed a finger to the very light terra cotta-colored mansion with two gigantic Queen Anne palms in the front to either side of a half-moon balcony. And then I noticed she lived right next door to Drew.

"Hi, Deidra. Nice to meet you. I'm Raven," I said, holding out a hand, which she quickly grasped with both of hers.

"I know, I know you *nombre,* Miss Raven McKade. Luke told me. What a nice *hombre,*" she said, elongating the word nice, dipping her chin, and lifting one shoulder. She was very bubbly, and I liked how she flipped between Spanish and English. At least I understood so far. "How do you know him? Oh, is he your *marido?* Husband?" She covered her mouth, and her eyes opened wide as if she had crossed a line.

"Oh, no. Luke's my best friend's husband. They live in Lakeland. Basically, he's the brother I never had, and I'm the sister he never had. And he's a good contractor," I said, waving my hand like Vanna White at the outside of my house. Deidra nodded, and the smile on her full red lips lit up her whole face.

She had large round eyes, black as coal, and soft brown skin with a coppery glow. When I glanced at her feet, I wondered how she could run in four-inch laced-up espadrilles. And not only that, she was quite top-heavy. I would have fallen flat on my face. She wore a solid black blouse over a pleated skirt in every color under the sun. It looked like she was ready for a party, but it was barely noon.

"Yes, Luke was *muy amable conmigo*. I'm sorry, very nice to me. I told him I had to meet the person who would be moving into this beautiful house. And then he told me your name and when you might be here. And here you are!" I wished I had a giggle as cute as hers.

"Deidra, I'm so glad to meet you. You're a warm, sunny hug on a rainy, cold day," I said, trying to sound as serious and meaningful as possible to this stranger. Something about her drew you in, like a long-lost trusted friend; as if I'd known her for ages. I wanted to talk to her more, so I invited her into my home.

"Oh, Chica, *eres tan dulce*." And then she pulled me into a full bosom hug, which was slightly embarrassing as sweat had defiled the back of my shirt. Oddly, I hadn't seen a sign of perspiration on Deidra. Had to be that acclimation thing Cassie kept telling me about.

I asked her to come in while I put away the groceries before they'd spoil in this heat.

"Hey, Deidra. Miss Raven. You two ladies look lovely as always."

I had just pushed the button to close my trunk while Deidra was helping me with a box of dried goods when Devin pulled up in my driveway with those god-awful, bug-eyed sunglasses and a calculating grin. No matter what, this man seemed to appear out of nowhere. His

101

presence immediately sent shivers down my spine. With Deidra in the mix, I tried to keep a composed and polite demeanor, but my repulsion toward Devin was palpable. The strong urge to tell him to leave would have suited me just fine.

As we were standing there, I noticed that Deidra didn't mind the arrival of Devin. I felt my body tensing up, but Deidra seemed oblivious to the situation and greeted him with a smile. I sensed her innocence and ability to see the good in people, which I admired, but in this case, with Devin, something was off about him, and I seemed to be the only one that perceived that. However, I know deep down that my own experiences have skewered my trust in certain people. I couldn't help but feel wary of this man.

"*Gracias,* Devin," Deidra said in a genial tone.

Devin replied, "You are welcome, Deidra." Then he turned to me and started saying,

"Miss Raven, how a—" I cut him off mid-sentence. Forcing a smile, I said, "Thank you, Devin, but I'm kind of busy to chit-chat right now." I wasn't interested in talking to him and started walking toward the door through my garage into the house.

Devin yelled loud enough for the next block to hear. "Miss Raven, how are the flowers holding up? Would you like some more?"

I cowered in embarrassment, wondering why he was making such a big deal out of a vase of flowers? And why loud enough to draw attention. And then I realized it was narcissism poking its ugly head out. We all have a little narcissism in us, but Devin proved to be drowning in it. I was beginning to understand what Drew meant by "slower," but I'd love to correct that and say "obnoxiously slower."

I didn't want to come off as rude or ungrateful for the flowers, but I didn't want to encourage further advances from him either. I wondered why some men just couldn't leave women alone and respect their boundaries. I said, "I'm good. They're still good. Thank you." I lied to him. I tossed the flowers two days ago and set the vase in a cabinet in the garage. Deidra opened the door for me and waved to Devin, saying something in Spanish to him. I was surprised to hear him respond in Spanish.

"He tries to be nice. He's actually harmless," Deidra said, setting the box on the island. I could tell she was trying to smooth over whatever she sensed from me the minute he showed up. I couldn't help but hide my disregard for this person. She obviously didn't see him in the negative way I did. I'd been here just over a week and already had a list of outcasts: Devin and Frankie.

"I know, but he's hunted me down daily since I moved in. And I've only been here a week." My angry tone caught me off guard, and for the first time since Deidra approached me, her smile disappeared. "Sorry, I don't mean to sound so hostile."

"Raven, my sweet neighbor. He just likes you. Look at you," she said, her smile rising on her full cheeks, her arms stretched out as she addressed a crowd. "*Chica, eres hermosa personita...y*ou're a gorgeous little person." I laughed so hard my eyes watered. Then I heard Deidra's childlike giggle, and I laughed even harder. My cheeks were on fire when we finally stopped. Arms wide open, she came around the corner of the island and pulled me tightly into her large chest in a sincere hug.

Deidra walked around the house as I put the groceries away. She commented on my decorating features while explaining that being born in Ecuador with lots of siblings and a large extended family, their house, though large, was simple and filled with colorful murals and paintings by local artists such as Manuel Rendon and Eduardo Kingman. I had no idea who they were, but I enjoyed listening to her. The more she talked, the more excited she became, and the more her English turned to Spanish, making it harder for me to understand what she was talking about. But I wasn't going to interrupt; I enjoyed watching how animated she was as she spoke of her family. Her hands, arms, and feet moved the whole time she spoke.

"Let's get together for a sunset. Oh, but a happy hour first. What do you say, my new friend, Miss Raven?" Deidra's voice was soft, her palms in a Namaste position.

"Of course," I said with enthusiasm. "You don't need to beg me." I laughed and touched her pleading hands, and she sighed as if she was holding her breath, waiting for my answer. "I'm dying to see your house. I bet the view is to die for!" I put my hand to my chest and watched her glossy red lips form a smile as wide as the Gulf.

Deidra clapped her hands together, "How about tomorrow night? Trey is coming back from a business trip, and it would be lovely for you to meet him. My *marina* is so *guapa!* He's so handsome, I mean." Her eyes became misty with tears and that touched my heart.

"Regrettably, I can't. I'm having my friends over for a long-awaited dinner. Maybe next week?"

"Oh, Drew is coming? *Si?* I talk with him all the time. Oh, *Chica.* He's an *atrapar....* catch, my dear friend." She winked, and I was taken aback. I flashed her a raised eyebrow.

"Well, he invited me over for drinks and seafood the other night, which was very nice of him." I laughed and told her he was a true doppelganger for a guy on TV that I lusted over like a soap opera junkie, and she gave me a confused look. "Oh, never mind. I'll tell you later over drinks at your house."

"*Si, Si.* I will call you." Deidra said, her hand up to her ear, imitating a phone, "I got to cook for my man who comes home tomorrow." And out the door she went, quickly turning around before closing the door, her skirt twisting about her legs as she blew me a kiss from an open palm.

I pretended to snatch it from the air. The only other person I've ever done that with was Cassie.

It was a hit in the reviews after I posted my swordfish dish with vegetable couscous and tomato vinaigrette. I was sure it would be a hit with Cassie and Luke and now Drew.

In my Vitamix, I lightly blended the fresh plum tomatoes, red wine vinegar, and seasonings, including a dash of oregano, and let that marry overnight in the fridge. I'm exceptionally excited about the Dom Perignon champagne. I had chills. It behooved me to make this gathering special since Cassie and Luke were the most precious people I had in my life. They've been there for me more than anyone, and I feel I will die still owing them my sincere gratification.

After a quick ride on the Peloton and a shower, I made a lemon chamomile tea and started writing more notes in my food blog journal when Deidra's words about Drew flashed at me like the lights on an ambulance, the ones you just can't miss. 'He's a catch,' she said. Yes, I was easily enamored and taken in by his immaculate good looks and polished presence. His congenial hospitality as my new neighbor also checked the box in the gentleman category.

But my mind was still stuck in repel mode. I hadn't reached the courage to allow another man in my life. I couldn't do it; Jack seemed forever emblazoned in my heart. Granted, the feel of Drew's hand holding mine as we watched the sunset was amazingly romantic and tugged at my heartstrings. There's definitely a chemistry, a connection that can be talked about. After opening the box that held my engagement ring, I felt as if I'd fallen a few steps backward and still felt that Jack was the love of my life, that there was never going to be another man that could give me the amount of love and joy I had with him.

"I always thought that finding someone who could truly understand me was a distant dream. But meeting you, Jack, has changed everything. The way we connect is so natural, like two missing pieces finally coming together. Honestly speaking, I still can't believe we're engaged! It all feels like a dream to me." I watched his eyes glitter as they filled with watery tears.

I could only hope that the torn part of my heart could be stitched back up in complete repair as each day passed. It's the only way I will be able to move on and embrace this reason for moving to the wonderful sunshine state in the first place.

CHAPTER 11

Devin-Saturday, August 15th

"Dammit, Devin. Get out of my way." Drew slapped a hand on my shoulder and shoved me, which pissed me off. I don't know why he thinks it's okay to manhandle me like this when I only asked why I wasn't invited to Raven's dinner.

He got all obnoxious and in my face. "She's not interested in socializing with the maintenance guy." I simply asked why, and he shoved me.

"Fuck you, Drew. You act like it's all about you. Even though you got me this job and, God forbid, I made a mistake that I'm no good to be seen with anymore. That we're not really brothers anymore..."

"Shut your trap, Devin." He grabbed me by the neck of my t-shirt, the ribbed edging clearly stretching as he wrapped his fist in the material. "You know damn well why you belong where you are. Don't ever call what you did a mistake. It was called attempted rape, you son-of-a-bitch."

Yes, I made a mistake in the past, but everyone deserves a second chance, no matter how big or small their mistake was. I was sorry I scared that girl. I didn't mean to hurt her; people shouldn't be defined by their mistakes. Drew's the only one that keeps harping about it. And I know, in doing so, he has ulterior motives. For him, it's one great excuse to relinquish my involvement in the business.

He owes me another. This was a brand-new shirt. I was hoping Raven would see me wearing something nice and new. "You owe me. I just bought this." I said, trying to reshape it after he let go of me.

Damn, everyone thinks I'm the one with the temper. He's the asshole with one too. He tossed a C note behind him as he slammed the bathroom door and yelled, "Get outta my house. Now."

I watched the C note flutter before landing on the floor. On the one hand, yeah, I like the cash, but on the other hand, it sucks that he throws the money at me like I'm some skank beggar. Per our dad's agreement, he's supposed to pay me monthly, but the jerk acts like he's doing me a favor. I scooped up the C note and shoved it into my pocket. One day, I'll make him realize my value and the respect I deserve. Total prick. I didn't do anything wrong.

I just stopped by to show him I was wearing my new black dress shorts and a yellow Guy Harvey shirt with a big blue sailfin on the back. I thought it was really cool and that Raven would like it. I bought it with her in mind. I know she likes yellow and black. I saw her running in those exact colors the other day—black shorts and a yellow bra top that formed over her perfect curves, the hint of her cleavage mesmerizing. I couldn't take my eyes off her.

My attraction to her has gotten obsessive, but it's not a bad obsession. I always think about her and wonder what she's doing when I can't see her. Harry brought it up yesterday. I thought it weird how he noticed me watching her, told me to quit it, and said it's rude to treat women like sexual objects. Why shouldn't I? I'm a man with needs that need to be met, and Miss Raven's a perfect choice. I can look and want, so let me dream, Harry.

Besides, I can care for her better than Drew; he's just a damn womanizer. I have a cool house and car. Drew bought it and all, but he's supposed to share the money our grandpa left us, so it's purchased with money I was supposed to get anyway, I guess. And I can cook. I'd make her my excellent burgers on the grill, like my grandpa taught me, with grated onion instead of chopped, making the burger juicier. Something I do that Drew doesn't. Too lazy. It definitely makes a difference, though. And with Miss Raven being a chef with a cooking video show, or whatever you call it, she'd understand precisely what I mean. She'd love it if I cooked a good burger for her.

Plus, I sent her that vase with beautiful flowers. I'm sure she appreciated my nice gesture. It was hard for her to say that in front of Deidra. I could tell. But either way, I'm doing nice things to welcome her to the neighborhood just like Drew; only mine is more heartfelt. Anyone can put on a show, grill up fish, drink wine, and watch a sunset. And then he was so careless, letting her walk home alone in the dark. Thank God I was there to accompany Miss Raven for her safety. I could see on her face how scared she was to be alone in the street. She got scared to death when I called her. But it seemed all good once she realized I was there to protect her.

The other thing I like is Miss Raven seems pretty educated and quite sophisticated. I'm confident in myself too, and if she'd just spend some time with me, she'd see I'm just as smart, if not smarter, than Drew. For instance, I'm good with computers and the Internet. Last week, I did all my shopping online, and I know how to look up many things online, like her cooking videos. Harry told me she cooks and shares it online for others to learn. I watched one she made in Minnesota. It was wild rice soup or stew, maybe with chicken. Supposedly, it's a big deal up there. I tried to make it and told Harry about it, but he said I probably did it wrong and didn't pay attention to her directions well enough. It wasn't my favorite, so maybe I made it correctly; it didn't taste good because I didn't like wild rice. Harry's wrong about a lot of things. His age is showing, and he seems distracted, so I let it go.

It was fun shopping online. I sucked down a couple of beers while I shopped at J.C. Penney and Kohl's. They have good brands for lower prices. I don't need to be a show-off like Drew and order custom-made clothes. God, he's so into himself and so damn egotistical. His haircut costs ten times more than my shirt, but I got it on clearance. Supposed to have a manufacturing flaw, but I didn't see any.

No wonder Harry picked me to be his right-hand man; Drew barely gives Harry the time of day. And the good news is Harry said he'd will me his house if I kept people away, especially Miss Raven. I'm not sure why he specifically pointed her out. Maybe because she's the newbie in the hood, and he's seen her, like me, come around too often these past few days, but it doesn't matter. I'm going to get his house and pool and, more than likely, his old blue Dodge truck, maybe even his Tesla. He never talks about kids or family or anything. Even if I ask, he shuts me down with a raised palm.

That's right. Harry wanted me to stop by and pick up his favorite meal in town at the Irish pub, Katie O'Leary's. He loves the corned beef platter with mashed potatoes and extra pickles. Says he's got something to tell me, and he's got a cold Guinness waiting for me.

Tonight, I'm going to stop by Miss Raven's anyway, even though she has a dinner deal and Drew will get so pissed, but Frankie gave me some discount cards at her spa to give away to the neighbors, so I'm going to give one to Miss Raven. And I'll wear nice new clothes, and my hair will be washed and combed instead of dirty and sweaty underneath a cap. I dream about Miss Raven. She's the best-looking lady in this whole place. There's no one like her. Even her friend is gorgeous. I forgot her name. Maybe I don't know it, but perhaps it's her sister or cousin or something. I only saw her once when there was a large group of guys unloading a semi, and she was the only lady carrying in a few boxes, but that was it. Never saw her again. In more ways than one, I'm getting excited just thinking about seeing Miss Raven later.

I didn't do much in the neighborhood today other than check out Miss Raven's house and pick up a few missed pet droppings. I hate these neighbors who are lazy and don't pick up after their dogs. What do they think? That it's the maintenance guy's job? Hell no. It sucks that I have to do it, but if I don't, it's called into Frankie, and she just yells at me and tells me to do it and then shoves in my face that I'm getting paid more than they usually pay this position. If I didn't have this job, I'm sure Drew would find something way worse than driving around in a golf cart checking out the residents in their bikinis by the pool or getting paid extra money to help the residents who don't want to hire someone else for menial tasks that they prefer not to do like weed their gardens or clean their pools or even wash their cars. It's excellent easy work sometimes, and the money is good.

But, now that Miss Raven has moved in, I don't want to work elsewhere. I want to get to know her better, take her out, and keep her safe. I'm sure she'll appreciate me sooner than later.

I dumped the debris bucket in the garbage and looked at my watch. It was time to pick up Harry's food already. He likes to eat early. And I couldn't wait to hear what he needed to tell me. Plus, I drain a few Guinness dark beers while he eats and talks to me. I don't eat. I just like the beer.

CHAPTER 12

Saturday, August 18th

For tonight's occasion, I wore the outfit Cassie had slipped into my closet and hung a small yellow ribbon with a note over the hanger; For **a special night for a special friend – Love Cass.** And tonight was that special night. It was a knee-length rayon wrap dress in royal blue. Below the shelf (she had an arrow on the note pointing down), white slip-on wedges sat in an open box with another box nestled between the shoes. I pulled out the most beautiful ruby pendant necklace with a gold chain and tiny ruby earrings. Tears stung my eyes, and the last thing I wanted was mascara dribbling down my cheeks. I had guests coming in less than an hour, and I still had some minor things to do before they arrived.

I heard the rumble of 'Luke's Titan pull up in the driveway.

"Damn, look at this gorgeous woman," Luke said as I opened the door. I could have been offended, but, in his defense, the last time I'd slipped into a dress of this caliber in his presence was at a classmate's wedding when Jack was alive. He stepped in first and kissed my cheek, quickly setting a large department store bag on the floor before wrapping me in a bear hug. Cassie stood patiently behind him with her hands full and winked when I flashed her a funny face as Luke lifted me up.

"You wouldn't say that if I was your real sister," I said before kissing his cheek, and he lightly pinched me near my ribs.

"Hey, let's move the party inside the house before all the bugs want to join," Cassie said in her worst sergeant commanding voice. We all laughed while she set a bottle of Caymus Merlot and a wrapped box large enough to put a small caged animal in on the counter.

"What's this?" I lifted the box, surprised at the weight. I looked at her and then back at the box as I furrowed my brows in confusion. She had held that box with one arm before setting it down.

"That's for later. No touchy." She lightly tapped my hand, which I grabbed and pulled her in for a tight squeeze. As long as I could remember, she'd made me gifts, bought me gifts, and just simply had given me gifts for no reason; "Because I love you" was always the response." Twenty-seven years of friendship, and Cassie hadn't let up on the gift-giving. "Beautiful outfit, by the way," she said, twirling me, touching my ear lobe. I gave her a pouty look of appreciation, staving off a bout of tears stinging to be released. I lightly ran my fingers over the costly pendant necklace.

After I poured Cassie and me a glass of pinot grigio and offered Luke a beer, I walked over to the bag Luke dropped by the front door. "Is this the box of 'trinkets' you mentioned?" I pulled out a man's size thirteen shoe box and set it on the breakfast nook table. It was taped shut. Antsy and wanting to dig in to see what goodies Luke and his workers found, I was interrupted by the doorbell. And then I sucked in a low-level gasp.

"Oh…the mystery guest?" Cassie asked, her tone slathered in pleasurable amusement. She tilted her head with one eyebrow raised. I didn't have a chance to respond before Luke opened the door.

"Drew, my man. Good to see you," Luke said, both men joining in a strong manly handshake and a friendly pat on the back.

I had to blink away the sudden pounding in my heart and the fire rising in my cheeks. Drew's smooth tanned skin and perfectly manicured hair looked like he just walked off the set of *Suits*. He had on wheat-colored linen pants and a black polo, ironically matching the tan pants and black shirt Luke wore. I glanced back toward the kitchen, hoping it would reset my composure before approaching him. But it didn't. I pressed my hand to my neck as if that would stop the throbbing in my carotid.

"What? Did you two message each other?" Cassie said, laughing, poking fun at how Drew and Luke had dressed alike.

"Hey, if I'm going to be twinning with anyone, I'm glad it's Drew," Luke said, tapping Drew's shoulder. A boyish grin appeared. My thoughts went to-*there surely wasn't any "twinning" going on between the Hampton brothers. Not in the dress category anyway.*

We all smiled and laughed at the light-hearted camaraderie between the four of us, and then I looked at Drew, smiling and chatting with Luke and Cassie, wondering what it could be like if I just opened the door to my heart; just let the beautiful memories of Jack be a guidance, be a way for me to allow someone else to cherish me the way he did. It's a longing rising out of the depths of my broken heart of hearts.

As Drew walked toward me, the heat rose to an uncomfortable level. My head spun with mixed emotions as my heart ached for Jack, but, at the same time, I had this gorgeous man right in front of me, and not so ignorant that I didn't detect his alluring signals; the chemistry was felt. Out of the corner of my eye, I saw Cassie posed with a twisted smile and a green-eyed sensual look. She knew me too well and could instantly tell I had questions flying around like a kite lost to the wind.

Drew approached me, kissing me on my cheek, my balance wavering just from the sense of his touch. I felt like a star-struck teenager without fortitude as my cheeks flared pink Cassie's matchmaking eyes, roaming back and forth between Drew and me, didn't help. As she's hinted numerous times, I could hear her tell me *it's time to move on, Rave.*

Why was it so much easier to say than do?

While the three of them chatted, I brought the bottle Drew handed me to the bar and pulled it out of the fancy rope-handled bag that read: Sullivan's Liquor. Looking at the bottle, I realized I had completely forgotten to buy a bourbon for him. I stocked up on wine and beer but missed this important item. How did I do that?

I turned to ask Drew if he preferred ice or neat and was met with a penetrating stare. Luke was talking, but I'm unsure if Drew was listening to him. His intense focus on me made me think of the scene from *Suits* where Harvey and Donna were locked in a passionate stare before their lips touched for the first time. And then my peripheral vision slowly disappeared as I locked my eyes onto his. I finally mouthed "ice"? He signed me a chopping signal near his throat. No ice. Perfect. At least I had a nice snifter to pour it in. I'd be embarrassed to pour it into a rocks glass. And then a giddy snicker slipped out as I poured.

I waved everyone over toward the other side of the kitchen near my living room, where I had a platter of crab Rangoon wonton cups, asparagus and strawberry crostini, and goat cheese drizzled with a sweet balsamic reduction sitting on the bar top. Cassie's eyes lit up as I hoped they would. Her favorite was the asparagus and strawberry crostini, and I knew Luke loved anything with crab. All three took a plate full, Luke and Drew continuing a conversation as they sat in the living room. Cassie waited for me to fill my plate and replenish our wine.

"Cute sundresses," I said. She wore a small flower-printed smocked halter dress with a white background; the white against her skin emitted the perfect tanned glow.

We chatted briefly about the twins, saying that they were getting their driver's licenses soon. "They're my babies, my babies are growing too fast, and Pheebs is developing…" Cassie cupped under her own breasts. "She's going to fit into my clothes soon she's growing into such a young woman, it makes me sad." She pouted but then resumed a smile and said, "So, we need to change subjects. Love my kids, but I'm more interested in you and Drew. Dating?" Her glossy green eyes probed mine for an answer as I stared back over the rim of my glass.

"Are you kidding? I just moved in, Cass. Come on. I've been working on my videos. Posted two so far." I bit into the crostini smothered with the most strawberries and waited for her reaction.

"And I watched both!" Cassie said loud enough for the men to turn their heads. I shook my head, and they went back to conversing about boats. I caught the part where Drew said we'd all need to spend a day together on his sport fishing boat, and Luke about leaped off the couch to hug him. I could see these two were hitting it off real well. And then I saw a light bulb go off in Cassie's head, "You're making that swordfish dinner, aren't you?" I nodded. She emptied her glass and stepped toward the bar for a refill. "I can't wait to taste it."

The wine was finally taking effect, and my nerves felt less frazzled. This was the perfect dinner party to kick off my new adventures in Florida. I thought about how safe I was right here with these three people. I fluffed my bangs and pulled the wrap of my dress a little tighter, gearing up for the next course.

When I invited him a few days ago, I asked Drew if he'd help grill the swordfish. By his momentary hesitation, I felt positive that he'd already had plans for tonight. But he said yes and would gladly help me with anything I needed.

"You had plans for tonight, didn't you?" I asked without making eye contact. Drew and I were on the deck getting the grill ready. On one burner, I had a small saucepan with the fennel and summer squash reheating.

"What makes you say that?" Drew brushed and oiled the grill next to me.

"I just sensed there might have been something, and I'm only bringing it up because I didn't want to—"

"Raven, it's okay," he said, touching my shoulder and looking at me with a side cheek grin. His chiseled features let the butterflies in my stomach loose. "I was to take my daughter out, but her mother made other plans, and Violet was happy about it, so it worked out just fine."

My lips curled around the words 'daughter.' "Oh, I had no idea you had a daughter…Violet. That is a very pretty name. You never mentioned her the other night." I was surprised at this information, yet, not to a heightened degree. I imagined hundreds of women throwing themselves at him wanting to be his baby mama.

A few minutes later, I looked up, and Drew took my chin in his fingers and planted the softest, gentlest kiss on my lips. Our eyes locked briefly after we parted, but like a shy schoolgirl, I immediately dropped my eyes to the couscous pot and nervously stirred. My body tingled all the way down to my feet. I couldn't feel my toes beneath the cotton fabric of my sandal.

"I've wanted to do that since I first saw you in Tiffany's." He flipped the swordfish steaks with an impressive crosshatch mark precision. All I know is that asking for his help ensured a Michelin star-looking dish. "I hope I didn't cross a line," Drew said, his voice softer, with a hint of noticeable regret. It must have been his voice.

"No, no. I'm sorry. I don't know what to say, let alone…think." I shut the burner off. The couscous was slightly al dente, and I was so nervous that if I didn't stay in control, I'd be burning our dinner.

"Luke told me about Jack, but very little. Just enough to let me know what you've been through. I won't push. I understand about healing. Just know that I'm here for you." He side-hugged me before we shut everything down and set the food on a large tray to bring inside.

I couldn't help feeling a bit disturbed by this admission. I wasn't aware that Luke had told him anything about me or Jack, for that matter. I almost felt a possessive hold on my life with Jack—as if it wasn't a subject for anyone else to talk about behind my back. It angered me enough that I couldn't look at him, but I also knew it wasn't Luke or Drew's fault that it was mentioned. It was foolish of me to think that Luke would need my permission, silly at best. But this wasn't the time nor that place to display my disappointment either. There was too much joy in having Luke and Cassie beside me to get flustered over something trivial about my past.

Everyone has secrets. I just thought this one would be a longer-kept secret. *Stop being selfish and get back to hosting a gracious dinner party.*

Lifting my chin, I raised my eyebrows and placed a wide-open smile on my face. Arms fully loaded up with our freshly grilled dinner, I purposely grabbed Drew's attention with a nudge before we went inside and said, "I appreciate what you said." He smiled and leaned in to kiss my forehead.

"Wow, everything smells amazing," Luke said, opening the French doors for Drew and me. "Did I ever tell you you're my favorite person, Rave?" He winked, and I threw him an exaggerated eye roll. He kissed the top of my head and nodded at Drew.

Luke was unusually quiet, and Cassie kept talking between bites, "Oh my God, Rave, everything is perfectly seasoned and so yummy. I've never had swordfish this good." Drew nodded and agreed, adding words like "divine" and "tender" on top of Cassie's "yummy" and "delish." I soaked in the compliments while a healing calm passed through me. The last dinner party I hosted was in July of 2014 after officially signing the papers for the sale of Raven's Remodeling. My sad but supportive staff begged me to cook for them one more time, which broke my heart but inspired the future chef in me. Cooking puts me in a happy place. And as I cherished this group gathered around my formal dining table tonight, sharing the results of what I most enjoy, I'm truly grateful for this pure gift of friendship. One I will undeniably never take for granted.

I couldn't wait to serve my champagne and dessert.

And I couldn't wait to find out what was in the box.

CHAPTER 13

Cont'd -Saturday, August 15th

I chose a nautical-themed tablescape using Anchors, which are "stake-like" in comparison to the swordfish I served that Bill mentioned was "steak-like". They all got my fun play on words and laughed. They loved the little gold and navy-blue anchor confetti scattered on top of the white textured tablecloth and the striped navy chargers underneath the light ocean blue plates that brought the swordfish to life right before you. I had see-through glossy blue water glasses and tiny dark blue votive candles surrounding a small pirate's chest overflowing with keychain anchors and gold coin-wrapped chocolates as my centerpiece. I thought it looked amazing and had a ball designing it. A far cry from pine cones and blue spruce twigs that I used to use.

The warmth of having my friends right next to me and the budding connection with Drew breathed new life into me. The delicious dinner, enjoyed by all, had been a resounding success, leaving us all satisfied and my spirits uplifted. I was grateful for the beautiful evening that had unfolded.

"I'm stuffed, but I can't wait to dive into this!" Cassie said as she helped me carry out the dessert bowls printed with black anchors and gold accents.

It was such a beautiful night that I suggested we eat our chocolate crème brûlée and enjoy our Dom Perignon on the lanai. The forecast called for a heavy storm, thankfully, not a hurricane, brewing out in the Gulf heading our way tomorrow or the next. I embraced a good thunderstorm, and this would be my first in my new house. The temps had dropped just enough, and a light breeze slipped through the screen.

My heart was whole as we all engaged in fun conversation and one of the best desserts I'd made to date. I carefully admired Drew from a distance, my eyes darting between the three of them with each spoonful of crème brûlée. A phantom brush of Drew's lips on mine made me touch my own. I still felt a flutter, but I cheaply blamed that on his looks. Even Cassie whispered earlier that she had almost slipped and called him *Harvey* instead of Drew. It was that uncanny of a resemblance. At times, at just the right moment, you'd think Gabriel Macht himself was sitting here drinking champagne with us. But, instead, it was my neighbor Drew Hampton, with dark, deep-set eyes like the *Suits* character, who was effectively sending signals that he was interested in me.

"Even Luke had the champagne with your dessert!" Cassie said, her tone filled with surprise and amusement. We scooped up the empty dishes and brought them inside. Luke and Drew were immersed in boat talk, which gave Cassie and me a few minutes to chat alone. "He usually snubs his nose and grabs a beer. Good choice, girlfriend."

"I hope you and Luke have enjoyed getting away for a bit I said. Cassie nodded as she rinsed the dishes handing them to me to put in the dishwasher. "Since the twins are with their friends, you could let loose some more and stay. There's plenty of bedrooms to choose from," I said, hoping she'd seriously consider. I didn't want the night to end. With the wine, champagne, and an exceedingly blissful ambiance with them all here, I hesitated to think what might become of Drew and me if left alone. My world was quickly spinning in directions too fast for me to relinquish.

"Oh, Rave, I would love to take you up on that, but both kids are in a high school event tomorrow. High school. I can't believe I'm a mother of teenagers. They're in high school, Rave." I laughed at her dramatics as she feigned a silent movie actress in distress, except she covered her forehead in dish soap bubbles, which made me wonder why she was even using dish soap. Champagne induced for sure, and I wasn't too far behind.

It was a complete joy to be laughing, the two of us finally together in the same state in my new house cooking for her again. "Remember, Cass, you're the one with a great husband, excellent kids, and I have—"

"Drew...you have Drew now!" She said it so loud that I instantly looked to the lanai to see if Luke or Drew heard, but thankfully, their heads never turned. I looked back to Cassie with my fingers at my lips, shushing her. She cowered some but continued on as if I needed to hear more. "He's such a great guy. So was Jack, Rave, but Drew...is...is a perfect runner-up." I saw her struggle to find the right word.

Jack will always be number one.

With Cassie mentioning Drew's name and the prospect of embarking on a new romantic adventure was both exciting and daunting, especially when my purpose for moving was not only to be closer to Cassie but to start over and begin a new life at thirty-seven; preferably in a safe community behind a secure iron gate. It still left me grappling with a slight fear of the unknown. Considering the potential of a new relationship was the last thing I thought about while packing to move to Florida. I know for Cassie, it wasn't. It was brought up numerous times in the previous three years, but while in Minnesota, I just couldn't think about letting Jack's memory fade into the background.

I met her playful eyes without blinking, my finger over my lips to shush her politely again. "Cassie, stop that. He's not here because we're dating. I invited him because he's been a wonderful, hospitable neighbor." As the words spilled out, I realized who was I kidding?

"I saw the kiss," she said with a smirk, wiggling a finger at me. "You tell yourself what you need to."

I was caught. I lowered my chin, wrapped my arms around my waist, and stared at her as I chewed my lip. Now I was stuck. Damn. "Did Luke see too?"

"So, what if he did? He's lovin' this guy. And we both think he's a good catch, right here by the water." She laughed at her pun, and while I thought it silly but funny, I tossed her a semi-scolding side glance. I peeked toward the lanai, and both men still seemed engaged in deep conversation, obviously not concerned about where the two of us were.

"Come on, Rave." Cassie turned me to face her. "Listen, I'm trying to have a little fun with you. Look at this man. Harvey in actual color. Right? And single? He adores you, and it's obvious. If the man didn't want us to know how he felt about you, he'd never take the chance of kissing you in front of a window directly in front of Luke and me." I gave her a blank stare. Did he do that on purpose? Did he mean for Cassie and Luke to notice? My heart picked up unevenly because it was precisely what Deidra said.

My nerves started to spark, and a little fire burned beneath my skin. I felt trapped, so I held up my arms and said, "Enough. I get it, Cass. Please." I saw her wince and mouthed *sorry*. "I'm dying to know what's in this package," I said, quickly changing the subject, sporting an *I Love Lucy* smile like she did when hiding the truth from those around her.

"A lefse maker!" I was shocked when I pulled the wrapping off. Dishes loaded, Cassie and I had filled our wine glasses and joined the men on the lanai. I wasn't expecting this. It was a Bethany Housewares model, nothing like my mother's vintage one but definitely a keeper. "So, we're starting our own Florida tradition?"

"Yes," Cassie said, touching my hand, "I thought this would be a great time spent with Phoebe now that you live so much closer, and she's been asking about us and how we first met and how I learned to make these delicious buttery wraps." I could tell my attitude moments ago sobered her a bit, and a wave of guilt flushed through my gut as I peered into her glossy green eyes. I suddenly felt shameful for the way I treated such a wonderful friend. She meant no harm.

Luke chimed in after downing the last of his champagne and setting the glass away from him, "Always remember; a double batch just for me. I'll ensure Phoebe knows, as you ladies will selectively make what you want." He lowered his chin and turned his eyes sharp to the left at Drew, sending him a hint that he should be aware of. He smiled and nodded at Luke, but with a momentary look of confusion spread across his face.

As I pulled the pieces out of the box, I caught Drew's tilted head and pierced lips. "You don't know what lefse is, do you?"

This amused me for some reason. I saw a boyish grin play across his face in agreement. I flipped through the instruction booklet, found a full-color page of a perfectly cooked piece of lefse, and handed it to him. He studied it briefly and then said in a questioning tone, "Looks like a tortilla. Isn't it?" Cassie and I instantly rolled out a full belly laugh and high-fived.

The men looked at each other, mumbling, clearly unaware of our inside joke.

When he popped out the word "tortilla," I knew Cassie, and I had envisioned the exact moment when we were eleven. It was the first time Cassie had come over to make lefse with my mom and family around Thanksgiving time, a yearly tradition. After she saw the finished product, round with dark brown marks, she blurted out the identical word Drew had. It's hilarious because not once did that cross my mind, and I'm sure it's because we didn't grow up eating tortillas. Taco night was hard shell only. I had never heard of a soft-shell taco until standing in line at a Taco Bell across the street from my high school during lunch one day.

I disliked hard shells ever since.

"But it's potato-based with cream. Tortillas are mostly flour and butter," I said, giving Drew an impish smile. I neatly put everything back in the box and set it aside, grabbed the shoe box of found items, and set it in the middle of the table. I couldn't wait any longer. I was dying to know what was inside.

"You'll love it," Luke said. "Slather it with butter and brown sugar, even a piece of baloney." Luke pretended to be rolling up a prepared lefse piece like a burrito while Cassie and I made gagging sounds, faking a finger down the throat. We thought Luke was absolutely crazy for adding baloney. That's not the Norwegian way, but then again, he's not Norwegian, so Cassie and I marked him off the list for giving suggestions on the right way to eat lefse.

"And by the way, you *must* say 'Uff Da' after you take a bite!" I said, remembering what my grandmother Elaine insisted on teaching Rachel and me. We had to say it before she'd handed us the rolled-up goodie, but not before lightly pinching our cheeks as she smiled at us. As they chatted about lefse, memories of my grandmother, faint as they were, came to me. I remember thinking she had a tiny mouth and a tiny smile, her eyes large and bright blue behind her round glasses. She smelled like baked bread or cake.

"I definitely got to try this lefse thing now," Drew said with a slight reluctance yet a playful note.

As we continued talking, my attention went back to the box. I was now living in the house Harry first built in this development. It almost felt deliberate how I came to buy this place as if somehow calculating or premeditated. Is this the reason I've become so obsessed with this man? Or, maybe it was simply that I've become overly sappy about an old man living alone, which I can't fathom such a desire, especially in a neighborhood such as this. I guess I just need to find out more about this Harry Fishman.

Everyone's eyes were glued to the box as I spread the contents onto the table. Crushed plastic Zephyrhills water bottles, two skeleton keys that interested us all, a ripped piece of material stained with grease or tar or possibly, with closer inspection, dried blood, according to Luke, which raised our eyebrows. Cassie picked up a chain with a locket dangling from it, but the clasp was missing, and the ends were tied in a loose knot. I immediately went to fetch a flashlight. Luke had a Swiss army knife in his pocket; he gingerly pried it open as I held the light, inspecting every detail. His large fingers dwarfed the locket; it seemed so small, as if for a young girl. Inside was a tiny picture of an older lady with short blunt-cut hair, wearing round wire-rimmed glasses; we couldn't make out the face. My first thought; Harry's mom? Was this lady related to Harry? His wife? The chain was tarnished, and some links were severely bent, but the locket seemed to be in fair shape, just discolored. I put the necklace to the side to avoid more damage.

Drew noticed something else stuck to the bottom of the box. He pulled out an envelope, dingy with dirty fingerprints, and handed it to me. By this time, the three of them had sat back down, quiet and intent on the items. I stayed standing, my legs too restless to sit. As I retrieved the envelope from Drew, my finger felt the spot where it had stuck to the bottom of the box. It smeared like lipstick and felt somewhat greasy. I wiped my hand on a napkin before opening the envelope flap. A newspaper cutting was neatly folded numerous times into a tiny rectangle. As I gently opened it up, careful not to tear the delicate paper, Cassie held the flashlight on a faded newspaper article. Parts of the report were smudged, and so was the picture. But not bad enough for us all to understand it was a picture of an accident. The car in the wreck looked to be from the 1950s. Drew and Luke pointed to the round headlights and specific grill detail, wondering if it was a Chrysler New Yorker or a Cadillac. Luke took a pic on the phone, mentioning that one of his workers is a vintage car fanatic and that he could find some answers for us.

"Why would Harry hide these things in the walls and then sheetrock over them?" I asked, examining the keys again. "And what could these possibly open?"

Drew said, "Those belong to an old lock box from a bank. That style went out thirty years ago, at least."

"Just a thought, but it seems like Harry may have purposely built this home to "bury" these things." Cassie used her fingers as quotes for the word bury. "But why?" I couldn't begin to understand and thought it creepy myself.

It seemed mysteriously odd that he or whoever wanted this stuff forever buried, never to see the light of day again. We sat silently a little longer, each person checking the other items closer. I felt like I was stuck in a *Nancy Drew* mystery, and it made me smile. I loved those stories. Her determination to solve was how I felt at this very moment—determined to figure out the mystery of Harry Fishmen.

"It looks like in Lake City?" I was squinting so hard my vision was getting worse. "I can't read the state, but it ends with an 'O'? Or is it an 'A'?" I could barely decipher it since it was so faded. Something seemed oddly familiar with this picture, though. I laid it back down, pondering that idea. Luke and Drew took the flashlight to give it a try.

"I hope I'm not bringing up a forbidden subject," Cassie said, inhaling audibly before going on, "but wasn't your grandmother in an accident in a car like this? I remember seeing a picture you had shown me." She looked up at me, eyes wide with question.

"You're right. That's what's pecking at my brain and why this seems kind of familiar or whatever," I said, waving my hand in disbelief and shaking my head. There couldn't be a connection; it was absurd. But she was right. My mother had a photo album of stuff, for lack of a better term, in regard to my grandparents, including items related to the accident. As her drinking escalated, she'd take out that photo album and cry like a wounded child with every page-turn. Finally, my father and I decided it was best to hide it where she'd never look; my dad's office at Hormel.

"I can't tell if this is Montana or Oklahoma or..."

"Or Minnesota?" Drew added. "That's where you're from, right?"

It caught me off guard, especially now that Cassie mentioned my grandma dying in an old car. We're talking about Harry, not my family in Minnesota or my grandmother's car. These things came out of the walls of Harry's old house, which has nothing to do with my family. It can't. Obviously, they had to be put there before he sheetrocked. But why and where did Harry come from? Lake City, Florida? Where's his family now? Are they aware that he lives like a hermit? Or did he write them off, threatening them never to come around like he does here in Bay Harbor?

The only other item in the box with significance was a pair of stone cufflinks that looked similar to a mood ring from the 1970s. It instantly brought to mind the mood ring my parents bought Rachel and me at an antique store in northern Minnesota. We thought they were so cool, and I remember giving mine to my grandpa to wear, hoping it would change his sad face to a happy face. At least, that's what I thought it would do. After my grandmother's passing, the once vibrant man I knew as my grandpa seemed to carry the weight of the world on his shoulders, his eyes reflecting deep, unspoken grief. I understand now that pang of sorrow he had felt for the love he had lost.

It was a poignant reminder of the fragility of life and the enduring power of love.

"Come on, Grandpa. Just try it. We don't want you to be sad all the time," I said one night after dinner. It had been two years since my grandma had died, and it seemed to me, at the age of nine, that my grandpa was dying too. He was so sad and didn't want to play checkers or *Sorry* with Rachel and me very much; he said he was just too tired to play. He always went for walks with us, explaining how exercise was necessary to stay healthy and live a long life. I never forgot that when I handed him the ring, he just looked at it as if asking it to bring Grandma back, like you did with the plastic billiard 8-ball toy, hoping for a positive answer.

"Raven, nothing will take my sadness away. I love your grandma too much to be happy with her gone." I cried with my grandpa that night, sitting beside him while Rachel sat on the floor at his feet, looking up at him with tears staining her red chubby cheeks.

That Christmas, Rachel and I gave him a set of cufflinks with a mood stone, ironically similar to the ones I held in my hand. We hoped he'd wear them whenever he dressed in a suit. He wore them to church and our house on Sundays for dinner every so often, but then he disappeared two and a half years later.

"I understand... you never found him?" Drew's voice was slightly husky, tired sounding. It seemed telling the sad story of my grandparents had lulled our happy occasion some. And how did it switch from Harry to my grandparents?

I let out a sigh and said, "Yes. My father had hired a P.I., but the trail ended at my grandfather's cousin's house in Tennessee. Supposedly, they said he left to return to Minnesota and didn't think twice until we said he never showed up. Honestly, I've forgotten some of the details and why my dad stopped the search." I finally felt the need to sit. I asked Drew, "Do you know anything about Harry? It seems silly I haven't asked that question tonight."

He shifted forward in his seat and said, "Actually, I don't. I was told the same as you, 'Stay away; he doesn't want to be bothered.' Didn't concern me. I'm busy running a business, but when my brother said Harry was paying him to do particular errands and whatnot for him, I wondered why. Devin's good at lying, so his reasons are erratic. He's never straight up when it comes to Harry; I haven't cared till now. I've let it slide, but after seeing this, I think there's a legitimate reason." Just then, we all heard my doorbell ring.

Cassie got up to go with me. To my surprise and dismay, standing on my doorstep was the last person I wanted to see. Disturbing that we were just talking about him, and here he was, again, in the dark at nearly 10 pm. I was rendered speechless and struggled to maintain my composure.

"Devin...what are you doing here?" I said sternly, my arms tightly folded across my chest.

"You're the maintenance guy I met last week," Cassie said, never taking her eyes off him. I wanted to catch her reaction to him showing up at my house. I wondered if she realized how ironic it was that his man, standing at my front door, was Drew's twin. I could only wonder what possible excuse he had, knowing a truck parked in my driveway clearly spelled out that I had company.

I never welcomed Devin in, but I did notice how cleaned up he looked, even under the dim light of the outside fixtures. He wore a clean, bright yellow t-shirt, and his hair was noticeably washed, combed back in a feathery look that barely touched the top of his shoulders. It still didn't change my opinion of him.

"Yes, that's me, but I wanted to talk privately with Miss Raven if that's okay. You're...?"

"Never mind. She's my friend, Devin, so you can speak openly. What is it?" It was hard to keep my tone neutral.

Just then, Drew and Luke came through the French doors of the lanai heading straight toward us. Devin lifted his chin in a nod, and when I turned to Drew, his expression was grim. I could tell Luke was contemplating the situation, sucking in his bottom lip.

Looking straight at Drew, Devin said, his black eyes unblinking, "I saw Miss Raven's lights on, so I thought it would be okay to bring by the gift cards Frankie wanted her to have and forgot to give her the other day." I heard a quiver in his voice.

"Devin, you need to leave now," Drew said with an authority I wouldn't debate. Devin handed me a stack of plastic cards that I grabbed without looking at him. I didn't care what he was bringing me from Frankie. I abhorred that he showed up this late on a Saturday night, knowing I had company. And now that Drew was here to witness this, I felt my angst toward his brother was justified.

"Excuse me, all. I'll be right back." Drew walked out the front door, wrapping a strong brotherly arm onto Devin's shoulders before I shut the door.

"Why the hell is he showing up this late? He's still the maintenance guy, right?" Luke said with a scowl, shaking his head. "He's rubbed me the wrong way since day one."

"Yes, he is," Cassie said, "but I think he's a little taken by Raven. He showed up and introduced himself when I stayed here the first night. I have to say he doesn't look as creepy as he did that night." I nodded, surprised as well, but he still rattled my nerves.

It was out of the question to mention what I had learned about Devin from Drew the other night. At the slightest mention of the word *assault*, Luke would put two and two together and immediately bring Farren Humboldt into the vision. And I'd never sleep again if I heard him say that name in this house.

131

Luke stared at me, his eyes burning with a seriousness I'd not seen in some time. "Is this guy Drew's brother?" I nodded.

"You've got to be fucking kidding me. That little son-of-a-bitch. You know he cocked off to some other resident about me not having a permit, which was false, but it cost me three days of work." He ran a hand through his hair.

Cassie looked at me, and I shrugged. I added, "He's got some issues, that's for sure."

I stood, arms folded, while Cassie found her purse and Luke's keys and put them on the counter. I didn't want them to leave. I could see the wheels grinding in Luke's head, his jaw muscles moving. He looked at Cassie and said with apprehension, "Are they twins? Is this the guy you mentioned the other day, Cass?" We both nodded, and Luke shook his head in protest.

Cassie looped her arm in mine as Luke approached, wrapping his arms around us like old times. He kissed my cheek and said, "Despite his asshole brother, Drew's a solid guy." His eyes lit up, and I smiled, knowing I'd take to heart everything he just said, although, with the two of them pointing out such apparent sentiments about Drew Hampton, I was more mixed up in my heart than ever before. I trusted him like a brother who would do anything for a sister. Undoubtedly, his protective nature was unflappable, and Luke Towers was a person you wanted on your side.

Drew flung the door open. "Sorry about that," he said, a little breathless. "He's not supposed to be in the neighborhood after 8 pm. It won't happen again, Raven. I'm sorry." He touched my shoulder. "Sometimes, Frankie can manipulate him like the little child he can be. Again, sorry. He doesn't always use common sense." He held out a handshake to Luke. "Hey, we're boating as soon as you can get away, my friend. You too, Cassie." After he hugged her, he walked them out to their truck as I hung back in the doorway and watched how cordial and respectful he was to my long-time friends. I rubbed my hands over my face, trying to brighten up my sullen demeanor before Drew returned, reflecting on how wonderful the four of us got along. It's like it was meant to be. Another blessing in disguise.

"Sorry," Drew said, closing the door behind as the headlights bounced through my window.

I now found myself alone with Drew. My heart raced with excitement and nervousness, and my mind was filled with anticipation about the unfolding conversation between us. I was already feeling a sense of vulnerability, being he kissed me earlier. He expressed precisely why he did it, and it hadn't left my mind. Drew joined me at the breakfast nook where I had brought in the box of miscellaneous items we had looked at earlier.

"Luke didn't know you two were brothers, let alone twins, till tonight." Drew's eyes noticeably weary around the edges, exactly how mine felt.

"Luke explained outside what my prick of a brother did while he was working on your house. I had no idea," His voice whisper-like as he rubbed his forehead, his thumb on his temple. I could sense humiliation in his words. With his other hand, he reached for mine and squeezed.

Drew stood. "Please, let me know if he comes around ever again after eight. Okay?"

"Why eight?"

"It's a rule with the maintenance position when they live outside the premises. It's not allowed per the covenants."

"I see. Who do I call if I see him after that time?"

"Me."

And then he kissed me exactly the way he did earlier, only this lasted much longer.

CHAPTER 14

I heard a sheet of rain hit my steel roof with such forcefulness that I jumped out of bed, slid the drapes open, and watched the heavy downpour. My first Florida rainstorm. It was beautiful in a cozy way. The way droplets created a soothing rhythm as they pattered against the windows, and the earth seemed to come alive with the nourishment provided by the showers. I couldn't remember being this attentive during a rainstorm in Minnesota. I jumped back at the flash of lightning and the crack of a thunderboomer. It was so loud that it scared me into laughing at how jittery I was. I'd never heard a thunderbolt that sharp. It had to have hit close by.

I had done a little research on the area of Tampa and found out it was the lightning capital of the world, that the Calusa Indian tribe called them "sticks of fire." I recalled a conversation with Luke last summer as we stood inside this house, completely gutted, making decisions on wall placement and a million other things when the loudest lightning strike I had ever heard to date, caused me to jump into Luke's arms. It sounded as if it had landed directly behind me. I couldn't stop shaking, and we both couldn't stop laughing.

Checking the weather on my phone app, it looked like a thunderous storm would hang over Bay Harbor Island all day; an excellent day for relaxing and catching up on my video recipes. With a semi-dark view outside the naked panes of glass, I sipped my coffee as I thumbed through a mound of magazines, searching for the perfect party bites for Drew's party. There was plenty of time to organize this event, but since I'd moved here just a short time ago, it seemed the days were rushing by. I tore the pages out and placed them in a folder labeled **Drew,** making it easy to show him a picture rather than trying to describe it. And then a funny thought crossed my mind; how to incorporate tiny filled lefse rollups?

I'd have to pick Cassie's brain on that one.

Ironically, I received a text from Drew.

Drew: Good morning...lightning crashes scaring you? Do you want me to come over?

Of course, I'd love him to come over and hold me and kiss me like he did last night. I can still feel the tingling, but I can't admit that to him yet.

Me: (Emoji laughing face) It did shake me a bit, but I'm good. Hawaiian coffee does wonders for anxiety.

Drew: The offer still stands.

Me: I am going over thousands of recipes for your party. I'll text when I narrow it down to six.

Drew: (Emoji with party hat) You sound serious. Sorry about last night.

Me: Please, don't worry!! I'm fine. With the rain and all, I enjoy getting some personal things done. If you're still available later, maybe I'll have the choices figured out, and we can go over them here.

Drew: I'll be there. Time?

Me: 5?

Drew: Done. See you then!! (Smiling emoji & blowing kiss emoji)

I don't know what forced my fingers to type those words, but inviting Drew over later cramped the pleasure of a worry-free personal day. I wanted to forget about fixing my hair or face, but something persuaded my fingers into typing the message. Drew had been nothing but a gentleman to me from the moment we met, and then I remembered the kiss: both times. It made me stop what I was doing. I felt the sensation of his warm lips gently touching mine. I carefully set my coffee cup down, the image producing a fluttering in my stomach and a shaky grip.

I admitted I liked this feeling, and the challenge was realizing that the last time I'd experienced such a passion was the day Jack asked me to marry him. I closed my eyes, the vision of Drew slipping into the more rugged features of Jack. I held my hand to my neck, inhaling his deep scent. A clean woodsy scent as I kissed his temples near his hairline, the musky smell of the changing leaves, and the vision of his bright smile after I said "Yes!" so loud it seemed to echo against the waters of the lake we were floating over. It startled me how prominent the scene reappeared in my mind's eye. I rubbed my face as I let it slowly fade away. It tore at my heart too much to let it linger and relive the details of that day.

I got up to refill my cup before my eyes filled with tears. Deidra called me just as I thought about roaming the fridge for something to eat.

"*Chica,* how are you doing? Nice rain, huh?"

I loved hearing her accent, her lively girlish voice. "Morning, Deidra. I love this rain. I'm getting a lot done sitting on my couch, drinking coffee, paging through a magazine." Her bubbly personality was like a drug; she could bring an instant smile to Darth Vader if he met her.

"Oh, you are such a funny one, Miss Raven." She paused, and I heard a smack like a kiss, and then she said, "Bye." "Okay, I'm back. Trey leaves for business. Back on Wednesday. How about Thursday for drinks and sunset? *Por favor venga?*"

"You've got to teach me Spanish. I just love listening to you…you're like a verbal party," I said, trying to figure out what *"venga"* meant. Her laugh was contagious.

"I will! *Lo Hare!* Thursday at *cuatro*?"

"*Si…cuatro.*" It sounded awful. Rolling the R's takes practice, lots of practice for me. Listening to Deidra's girlish giggle, I was genuinely elated for having such a delightful person living just a few feet away. Her infectious laughter and sunny disposition seemed to have a magical quality, effortlessly brightening even the gloomiest of days. All it took was a simple giggle to brighten your day with Deidra Palermo nearby.

I immediately plopped that date into my phone calendar. I didn't want to miss this, especially now that I'll be meeting her husband. I forgot to ask if I should bring something. I quickly texted her back and then wondered how she got my number. I never gave it to her the other day at my house. Maybe Frankie? No, because it had to be Drew. She mentioned they talked often, and my gut told me it was him.

By mid-afternoon, I had the perfect stack of what I considered elegant bites to serve at Drew's party, a couple of dessert options, and wine and cocktail pairings. I slipped into a pair of jean capris and a dark peach Henley. I let my hair dry naturally, spritzing in a coconut curl enhancer to let the soft waves come to life, and felt it a good time to call my dad.

"Dad, hello. How are you?"

"I'm fine, Rave. More importantly, how are you? You've been gone now for a few weeks. How do you like it so far?" I sensed a genuine light-hearted tone in his voice. My shoulders relaxed with relief.

"I'm thrilled, Dad. Met a few neighbors now and had my first dinner party with the Towers last night. Grilled my first swordfish." I wouldn't admit that I hadn't actually done it myself, that I just watched Drew work his magic, but he didn't need to know that. Plus, Dad didn't really concern himself with cooking or a grill. It wasn't his thing, but a microwave was. With Mom gone, I knew the cabinet over the microwave was full of popcorn, a favorite of his that my mother constantly scolded him on, saying, "Tom, it's not a meal. Eating microwave popcorn does not replace your dinner." It's the one thing my father refused to give in on.

While my dad talked, I walked over to see what was happening outside. I pulled the blind away just enough to peer out and see that the rain had begun to pick up again. Quiet under the darkened sky, every house had a light or two on, all hunkered down in the safety of their homes, thunder boomers overhead creating the only sounds other than the sheets of rain hitting the roof.

It was nearing three in the afternoon, and I told Drew to come at five. Would he expect dinner? I didn't say as much. All I had was gouda cheese, apples, cream cheese, and some grapes—that looked like they were at the end of their life, or close to it anyway—in the fridge and almond crackers in the pantry for something quick. I peeked while Dad updated me on Mom and her therapy sessions.

I was listening but distracted by Drew coming over, something I wouldn't mention to my father. And then I remembered all the wild rice I had sent down. I had to remember what cabinet Cassie put that in when she kindly helped unload my boxes sent via UPS. I opened every cabinet door, finally locating the big bag of Minnesota wild rice. I'm sure Drew will be fine with whatever I whip up. He might dress and carry on with a degree of vanity, but I also believe he's not beneath a beer and a pizza if that were the only choice.

"Are you making plans to maybe visit when Mom's out?" My father was very talkative, and I didn't catch any strain or worry in his voice. I actually believed he was happier and felt a sense of relief. Unfortunately, it seemed it took me to move sixteen hundred miles away for the shit to hit the fan, as they say, but Mom should have been admitted long ago when we first tried. But I guess three times was the exhaustive number, so we never attempted again. I wondered why it was working this time. Dad didn't have an answer when I asked him, but he added, "Let's just count our blessings and not ask questions why." I agreed, noting his adamant tone and no need to argue.

I hesitated to ask but felt it necessary, "Dad, has Rachel been helping you? Meals? Visiting with Pete and the girls?"

Before I could finish my question, he eagerly divulged that he'd hardly been alone and that Rachel set up a meal delivery plan for me. "I guess one of her co-workers created this business with her husband. She does the cooking, and he delivers. Three nights a week, I get a fully prepared meal that's easy to reheat in the microwave. It's like a modern tv dinner." He chuckled.

"You would love it here. Both you and Mom." Just then, my eye locked onto the box on my breakfast nook table. I picked out the article from the envelope and tried to lay it flat with one hand, careful not to tear it. I couldn't shake the urge to come straight out and ask my dad about Grandma's accident, but my mind raced around the potential infraction of raising the delicate subject. He certainly wasn't as sensitive with this subject as my mother was, but I hadn't conversed with him personally in a long time.

Finally, I decided to only ask about the car involved. "Dad, what kind of car was it that Grandma had the accident in?"

Without hesitation, he said, "A 1959 New Yorker. Why?"

My heart jumped. Drew and Luke thought it might be a fifties New Yorker but weren't sure. Was this a coincidence, or was I making too much of a simple car make and model? The photo was black and white and, of course, very faded, the front of the car visible, the backend crushed.

"No reason, really. I saw an old car from the back. I thought it might have been like the one in Grandma's accident. This one was white and turquoise." I had to lie.

"Your Grandma's was red."

When I had hung up from Dad, I immediately turned my phone flashlight on to look closer. And then I Googled 1959 New Yorker. The front of the cars online looked similar to the one in the article, but I couldn't see the back of the vehicle; the photographer took the photo at an angle from the front, not the side. Online it showed the backend of the 1959 car with fins. It was perplexing to me as to why Harry hid this in the wall and who was it? What tragic loss did he endure? Had he suffered in the same way my own mother has? I was itching to know and wondered if he was a person that just simply needed to talk with someone; someone that could relate and one who cared enough to help.

That person was me.

I don't remember what the picture from the paper looked like anymore; it's been too long since my dad took the album to his work office, so I texted him:

Me: Dad, can you text me a picture of the article about Grandma's accident?

Dad: What for? Is there something you're not telling me?

I thought he might say that. Now what do I do? I didn't want to raise any alarms and rehash this subject, especially knowing what it did to my mother and what my dad's gone through because of it. But I needed to see that picture again. Just to ensure I wasn't going crazy connecting two matters that may or may not be connected or even existed simultaneously.

Me: Oh, never mind. It's nothing. Just something Luke asked about, but it's no big deal. It was great chatting with you. Let's talk soon. Love you!

Dad: Love you too.

Again, I lied. I hated doing it, but *why can't I look this up on the computer? And while I'm doing that, why not also search for Harry Fishmen?* I had time before Drew was to show up. I brewed an herbal tea and sat at my computer, searching for anything I could find on Harry and my grandma's accident.

CHAPTER 15

Cont'd...Sunday, August 16th

The only single item I found on Harry Fishmen was an article stating he was the original developer of Bay Harbor Properties in 1990. However, the report didn't mention a single detail of his background or where he came from, if he was a native Floridian or even married. Nothing! The article read boring and uncaring about this individual; just a number to call if interested in a plot to build on. All the other Harrys were spelled Fishman with an "a," not an "e." I thought that odd as well.

I decided to switch to searching the *Austin Daily Herald* for anything on my grandmother's accident from 1985, but with that option, you had to pay for access to the microfiche. I wanted to rethink that option. I was beginning to doubt my intentions, teeter-tottering on the feeling that seeking out this information was all for naught. Searching for over an hour and coming up with zilch was enough for the day.

Since my search found no noteworthy results, that potentially meant I needed to talk with Devin, which created a sense of frustration and uncertainty. I questioned how I could extract any serious information from him about Harry. Just peering into those salacious eyes of his sent the creepy feeling of a bug crawling up my spine. Plus, his responses were often vague or dismissive, which proved to me his narcissistic tendencies made it hard to find common ground with him, just like I remember Drew stating.

Drew gave me the impression he's bothered, maybe somewhat fearful of his brother. I can't blame him, especially after learning his capabilities. I shuddered inside, thinking about that poor teenage girl. I didn't want to engross myself in how well I understood her situation. My heart ached just thinking about her tragically falling victim to this

143

perverted man. The unspeakable suffering, she must have endured haunted my thoughts, and a sourness developed in my gut since I knew all too well, having gone through it myself. I can't fathom how someone could be capable of inflicting such cruelty on another person, especially a vulnerable young girl.

I had to shake it off.

I got up to change and pull something together for a light dinner or at least a worthwhile snack for when Drew arrived, but, unfortunately, he texted, having to cancel because of some work issue that required his immediate attention. I felt sad, I was geared up to enjoy a few casual hours with him, talking over the menu for his party. He left three crying emojis at the end of his text which made me laugh but also palm my heart, knowing his desire to want to be with me. I was looking forward to seeing him again, especially after he had successfully broken through one of my barrier walls by planting a gentle kiss, without fear, on my lips, unknowingly to me, in front of my friends. A repeat of that moment would be very welcoming right now.

I slipped on a heather gray capri lounge outfit with a matching elbow-length t-shirt and poured a hefty glass of Merlot. As I walked around the island to flip on the under-cabinet lights, I heard a small banging sound like a door slamming off in the distance. I took a large gulp of my wine before setting it down on the counter and then went to check the door to my garage on the other side of my corner pantry. It was slightly ajar, so I closed it thinking that couldn't have been the sound, so I checked the doors out on the lanai, and they were all shut and locked too.

Had to be a car door.

I returned to the counter to pick up my wine glass and walked past my pantry again to shut off the dining room lights. As I headed toward my living room, a hand came around from behind and covered my mouth while the other pressed hard against my throat. The wine glass flew out of my hand, landing with a splash, the sound of glass bursting into shattered pieces. My blood-curdling screams were muffled by a large gloved hand covering my mouth and nose, nearly suffocating me. I grasped the gloved hand with both of mine, trying to pull it off my face. Then I felt a pinch at the base of my neck that forced me to release my grip on the hands pressed against my mouth and throat, and I fell back into this person's chest.

My thoughts whirled around like fireflies in the night, wondering where this person came from and how they walked into my locked-up house. I swore I had locked all the outside doors, the only one unlocked was the door I just checked, and there wasn't a need if the outside service door was bolted. I tried to talk, my words stifled beneath the gloves that pressed tighter against my lips, causing a pinching pain. This obviously was a man, the height and strength a challenge for me despite my own built-up physical strength. His chin dug into the top of my head as he pushed me from behind toward my living room. He forced me to shut the lamps off except one as he grasped me tighter around my shoulders, his arm across my chest. After he released two fingers, I smelled beer and sweat. I needed him to speak. I wanted to hear his voice. I knew so few people in this neighborhood. It could only be one person. And then I curled up with rage as I connected the dots. I began to cry so hard my body shook with tremors.

"You smell so delicious, Miss Raven." The moment I heard his raspy whisper, I knew it was Devin and realized my horrific situation. I pushed the sobs out as hard and loud as possible through my throat. He clamped harder on my mouth as I furiously wriggled myself out of his grasp. His strength was still too overpowering.

"You need to settle down now. I need your cooperation; otherwise, you get nothing from me about Harry," he said, still whispering, his lips touching my ear. I could feel his lips move as he talked, and then he started kissing my ear, down my neck, ripping my shirt off my shoulder, leaving it partially hanging, and exposing my left breast. He removed his one glove with his teeth, placing his bare hand on my chest and pushing his lower body against my back. I felt sick at the sounds he made.

With fear rising and my heart thumping through my skin, I thought of something I learned in high school during a self-defense class; if attacked, try to urinate or vomit to persuade the attacker from further violating your person. I was desperate to try anything, to get this beast off me. Could I do it? While he groped me with his left hand, I tried to concentrate on releasing my bladder, but I was too tense, so I tried forcing bile into my throat, but that wasn't working either. It took solid mental willpower, and mine was failing me right this crucial moment with him rubbing his grubby hands all over me.

I was sure he would restrain my hands with something sooner than later. I undid my fingers from his grip on my mouth and started jabbing my elbows into his ribs. Since he was so thin, it wasn't hard to hit them directly. As he lifted me, I started choking, and my hands had no choice but to release the pressure off my neck. The next instant, I was slammed to the ground, knee in my back, his hands finally off my mouth but now holding my head down. He tied my hands behind my back with a rope of some kind, but it was soft on my wrists. He kept swearing, breathing heavily, mumbling but still in a whisper as if he had laryngitis.

I focused on staying quiet for two reasons; if not to release my bladder, I hoped to hear him say something else about Harry. I didn't know what he meant by "...you get nothing from me about Harry." That statement surprised me. But it led me to believe he wanted to tell me something, and then I flinched, wondering what he'd make me do to get that information.

"Miss Raven, so lovely but yet so stupid. You think I don't know what you're up to? Lingering around Harry's house so that he notices you in hopes he'll change his mind. You want to take my place with Harry and get all the benefits, don't you? You want what is rightfully mine, don't you? You're just like my brother. You want it all for yourself. *What benefits?* "You want Harry to accept you, so he'll give you all his belongings after he dies, right?" He sat over my rear, one knee to either side, squeezing tight. He leaned forward, kissing my ear, my cheek, and the side of my mouth, at which I lifted my head and turned my face the other way. He attempted to kiss me again, making me sink my chin into the thick rug he slammed me onto. Shoving the coffee table across the rug, it hit the fireplace, and then I heard wood splintering, the slap of books and magazines sliding, and the vase of shells tumbling across the tiled floor.

I cringed from the harsh-sounding bang, and my muscles felt so tight that I couldn't feel them. Tears seeped out from my tightly pinched eyes, the pain of my hair being pulled as he lifted my head up, forcibly turning my face onto one cheek. "I want to kiss you, damn it, Raven." This wasn't a whisper; his voice was deep and scratchy. His lips were wet, his breath filled with the stench of lingering beer on his tongue, his nerves increasing the heat emitting from his body as he leaned in close, licking and kissing my body in every direction.

"What do you want from me, Devin?" My voice weak, cracking as I tried to spit out the words. My throat was so dry I could hardly swallow.

"I want you to want me, not my brother. Do you understand? He's an asshole. Total prick. Womanizer. Did you know that, Miss Raven? Did you know you're hanging out with a womanizer who's got a daughter? He was having an affair with his other girlfriend and knocked this one up. What a fucking loser! Do you like hanging out with a loser like that? Huh?" He slapped my rear so hard I screamed loud, and then he slapped my face. I felt the warm blood drain from my nose.

I could feel the tension in his body as his knees dug tighter into my ribs, frustration emanating in his voice, a palpable tension that seemed to hang in the air. I understood that his emotions were running high, seemingly to put the blame on Drew and then me for wanting to know more about Harry. I could only hypothesize that Drew was unaware that his brother felt this way nor had intentions with Harry and his property. I bet Drew was clueless about the deep disturbances crawling around in the crevices of Devin's brain, and I am now witnessing his devious actions because of it.

Holding my arms, tied at the wrist, so high up behind me, my muscles screamed in pain. I bit my lip to keep quiet, avoiding another slap to my face again. He sat on my legs now, making sure I couldn't kick him as he ripped my pants down and tore the rest of my shirt off my back. I felt his nails scrape my skin. He sat quietly and didn't move. I breathed as quietly as I could, listening for a possible clue as to what he was going to do next while, at the same time, I kept trying to figure out how I could get out of his stronghold. My clothes were now mere shreds of material—a painful reminder of the brutality I endured at the hands of Farren. Warm blood mixed with tears and sweat trickled across my lips. It felt like the air was being sucked out of the room. Tracing my spine with a sharp fingernail, I could feel my skin open up and then a stinging sensation, probably caused by his dirty sweat. I could tell he was enthralled and pleasured by this. He'd mumble under his breath and then rudely laugh.

A quiet determination grew with intensity, a resolve to overcome this situation.

Since the option of vomiting or urinating on him didn't work, I elected to be brave and ask, "What about Harry, Devin? Is there something I should know?" I said it slowly and softly in hopes he'd converse gently and not become irate, punishing me again for asking this question. Still no movement.

He brushed my hair with his palm and replied, "Miss Raven, you're a lucky lady, you know that? Huh?" He tugged at my hair as if he was braiding it. "This was Harry's first house, and I know you know that. He just told me he was thrilled you were moving in now."

He paused, but I waited for more. I could hear him inhale as if he was about to continue. His fingers moved all over my body, touching everywhere he could without moving off of me, but he wasn't physically hurting me. I lay as still as I could, trying to blank out how revolting his touch was while listening intently to what he was saying. Finally, he continued, "And do you know why, Miss Raven from Minnesota?" He took a deep breath and started poking his finger in my back hard enough to make me wince, but I kept my full attention on his voice, seemingly hoarse. "Because he knew your grandpa. Remember the one that just took off and deserted your whole family? Yep, that grandpa."

My eyes shot open in shock. I should say one eye, the other was crushed to the rug. I tried twisting my body so I could look into his eyes, as hideous and black as they were, to see if he was telling the truth and how he found out about my grandfather's disappearance.

He was bribing me. I hated even him more.

"Now, little Miss Raven." He leaned close again, his tongue swiped across my shoulders and neck. When he reached the side of my mouth, I pinched my lips together, refusing to taste his saliva. He continued, "…you need to keep your mouth shut about our time together in your beautiful little beach house. If you had just invited me to dinner last night, we could have had a nice time together, but instead, you invited my brother, who had to throw me out after I so nicely brought you a gift from our acting president. I didn't like that one bit." He roughly ran his fingers through my hair, and I cringed as he twisted. "You should know that I'm nice, and people in this neighborhood trust me, Miss Raven. You should too. So, you keep your fucking mouth shut on this, and I'll tell you more about Harry since you're so obsessed with him. I still don't get your concern with some ole' man but whatever. It's on my terms. Not yours. So, stay away from his house, and I'll tell you what you think you need to know. Only if you meet with me when I ask you to."

I saw him pick up my phone but couldn't tell what he was doing with it.

After, what seemed like several minutes, he lifted his upper torso off my legs, which were now numb from his weight on them for so long. Upright on his knees, I heard him fiddle with his belt. I turned my head ever so slightly, stretching my eye to the side as best I could to see what he intended to do to me next. And then I heard him unzip. I put my face into the rug, my mind racing with options, once again, on how to escape his grip on me. The quiet unnerved me, and suddenly, I felt jerky moves against my legs. I pinch my eyes closed in disgust. And then he gasped. I quickly decided to take advantage of his distracted, weak state of self-induced pleasure and immediately flipped my body around with every bit of adrenaline and strength I had and pulled my knees up into his groin, shoving him back into the coffee table with my feet. His temple hit the corner where curse words, unfit for a sailor, flew off his tongue.

With both of his hands, he covered his naked groin. As he lay there groaning, I found the opportunity to slide my tied hands underneath me and run for my bedroom. I locked my door and then wriggled my wrists free using my teeth. Not too many minutes later, I heard a door slam. Afraid to go out and see if he actually left or decided to play an evil trick by pretending to have left, only to be hiding and ready to pounce again, made me shudder with disbelief that I didn't have my phone to call for help. It was in the living room. I couldn't risk leaving the bedroom. I checked the locks on the doors to my lanai, ensuring they were also locked at the top.

My heart pounded with a vengeance now that I was out of his grasp. My nerves were so frazzled, and with no phone, I felt like a lost sheep without a shepherd. Grabbing an old long-sleeved shirt and yoga pants from my closet, I covered my primarily naked body as I shivered from the chills and fear. The only item lacking was my phone. My throat was parched, and my hearing seemed slightly impaired by the rushing of my blood into my ears. One ear to the door, I held my breath and listened for anything suggesting he was lurking around in the house still. I heard nothing.

If I were to call anyone, it would sever the link to Devin in the only way I'd want to be linked to that low-life, and that was Harry Fishmen. No one else seems to know anything about him but Devin. I had to find out what he knew about my missing grandfather. And if I didn't connect with Devin in his way, I know he'd find a way to hurt me again, paralyze me with his twisted narcissistic demands.

As I sat on the shower floor, my arms wrapped around my knees pulled tight to my chest, I let the hot water wash the blood from my nose and cut lip. Desperately needing to remove every last trace of the traumatic encounter, I let the warm water cascade over my body as I dropped my forehead to my knees. Minutes later, I scrubbed my skin with fervor, hoping to erase every fingerprint he had left on me, every unwanted lip mark, the lingering stench of his breath, and all traces of the body fluids that had come into contact with me. The overwhelming desire to cleanse my body of these physical and emotional reminders consumed me.

What did I do to deserve this?

CHAPTER 16

Wednesday, August 19th

I had lost track of time on how long I sat on the shower floor, shedding his obnoxious traces from my body. As I traipsed into my bedroom, trembling and utterly shocked, I processed the reality of being attacked in my home for a second time. I tried to fathom how this could happen to me again. The walls that symbolized my new sense of safety now felt like a prison, trapping me within a nightmare that refused to end. I struggled to hold back my tears. I was sick of crying and feeling a sense of helplessness and vulnerability.

I know now, after very little sleep and watching the sun rise and fall, that a few days had passed, and with every roar of a passing car or the chatter outside my window of people walking by, my nerve endings sparked like a firecracker, ready to go off. My anxiety grew exponentially. I wondered what I had done to deserve this; I questioned my worth and the life I dreamed I'd have moving to Florida. Was this a wrong choice? I longed for peace and the ability to live without the constant shadow of fear hanging over my head. However, at that moment, my world seemed to be closing in, and I debated whether praying could offer an olive branch of hope for my recovery.

For two days, I hid. Faith in myself and the world around me wavered as I tried to face my nightmarish reality. I cowered at the thought of anyone knocking on my door or calling me. I looked like a squatter; my hair and face frazzled from neglect. Cassie had texted me a simple question about a quiche recipe I'd posted a few years back. I texted her back with a simple answer. Even though the last thing I wanted was for her to suspect anything odd, I held a ball of anger directed at her and Luke. They promised me this was a safe neighborhood.

Supposedly no one, who lives in this neighborhood, has a record, and that's why they were accepted, and the staffed gate was adamant about who they let through. I guess Devin was the exception. We were all convinced that this was the answer to my prayers. And that's why this anger toward them is uncalled for and humiliates me further while the rage pokes at my heart.

After two days, my top lip was still swollen, a small cut visible where he thwacked the side of my face with nails needing a trim. The scrape on the side of my nose was nearly gone, but not the bluish-yellow tone growing under my left eye. What excuse do I use when I show up at Deidra's tomorrow night for a happy hour and sunset occasion? I can't cancel on her. She was one of the calls yesterday that I purposely ignored, but I texted her and told her I was in the middle of something. I had left my bedroom earlier to run out like a scared rabbit and grab my phone and lock the front door. Noticing the front door slightly ajar, I realized that's where Devin ran out. And then it made me wonder how he entered in the first place, when I knew damn well, I had the front door locked. My only choice was to check the service door to the garage, and when I saw it open, I cringed with self-deprecation as I lunged onto my bed in a sobbing mess of tears. It was all my fault. I left the outside service door to the garage open after I took the garbage out. I pounded my fists into my pillow, drowning myself with self-pity. I'd been behind my locked bedroom door ever since, wondering how I could have done such a stupid thing, averting my blame, also, on the iron gate at the entry. It wasn't another resident that walked into my garage and then into my kitchen, it was Devin who took advantage of the gate and my door allowing him to waltz in and violate an innocent person.

"We completely understand your fears and apprehensions, but please trust us when we say that it is an entirely different environment in Bay Harbor," they both told me after I chose this house. Luke and Cassie promised I'd be safe and happy here. How do I tell them they lied? That it's a completely hideous lie?

I believed Luke, but I guess he forgot to mention the maintenance guy with a record and one who hides behind the façade of someone you should trust. It seems Drew hasn't realized his brother, despite anger management class and sitting in jail for a time, didn't fix him. He's still a pervert walking around the neighborhood, ready to pounce. And he chose me, why? Because I have an interest in Harry? If I didn't, would he still have pursued me? I'm hard-pressed to believe that the towering black iron gate Carly opens with a push of a button is anywhere near a symbol of security for the neighborhood I now reside. It's fake. It's bogus. I'm angry, pissed off, and so hurt at my best friends for suggesting this was the place for me. If it allows a letch like Devin to come through and terrorize whom he pleases, the safety feature has failed. Has he done this to other women in this neighborhood? Is that how he attacked that young girl? Through a private gate on private property?

I turned to slam my fists into the pillows and the pile of blankets in front of me. I wailed and screamed with such force, it made me dizzy. Sweat accumulated under my arms, around my waist, and forehead to the point I had to grab a towel from the floor and vomit; I could not run fast enough to the toilet. The hot, acrid vomit had splattered onto the cold floor, leaving me trembling and weak. And then, the darkness enveloped me, my consciousness slipping away as I crumpled to the ground and fainted.

None of this would have happened if Jack were still by my side. He had always been my shield, my unwavering protector, even while bedridden in the depths of his sickness. His presence was like a sense of security and strength to me, repelling any danger approaching me. I remember feeling so lost and weak while he lay in his hospital bed, slipping away from us little by little each day, but he had the ability and mental capability to build me up, encouraging me to carry on and reminding me how precious life was. My eyes were non-stop pools of tears. I missed him so much, more than words could describe, especially now. I felt even more vulnerable and exposed. I brought the boat towel to my lips, inhaling deeply, wishing Jack were here to shield me from the pain and fear that now haunted me in my new home; a home I had hoped to be my healing retreat.

How was I going to go on living in a neighborhood that failed to protect me?

CHAPTER 17

Devin, Monday, August 17th

Mindlessly flipping channels, I finally landed on the game show channel airing Hollywood Squares from the seventies. God, these people looked like morons. Listening to the stupid jokes of Paul Lynde or that weird lady Rose Marie was the worst entertainment, but I didn't care. All I wanted to do was dream about Miss Raven. I couldn't shake the events of last night. I know I shouldn't have treated her that badly, but she was a bundle of resistance the minute I touched her. I had to use some force. Even so, I got to press her body into mine, and that's what a man likes; a gorgeous woman's body sucked into his. And that's what I did.

I've been told I have a twisted psyche, primarily by my brother when he's pissed at me. "You know you're a twisted fuck-up, right, Devin?" All I asked him to do was set me up with the chick he uses to help with his *lavish* events. He's gotta look so important and throw these god-awful expensive parties that he hates when I attend, but I don't give a shit what he thinks about that. This Samantha chick he hires to organize these social gatherings is hot. Well, not now. Miss Raven is hotter, so I don't care about Samantha anymore, but I just asked him if he'd set me up with her, that I'd love to get inside her someday soon, and he damn near punched me in the gut. It's what all men think about a sexy woman, right? I don't know what the hell his problem was but fuck him. I've got Raven now, anyway.

The image of how terrified Raven looked replayed in my head like a twisted highlight reel. It was a source of satisfaction, leaving me feeling powerful and in control. Something I strive for when I really want it bad enough. I needed to see her, first and foremost, and I needed to touch her and feel the smooth skin on that petite body of hers and the lean muscles she has. She's fit and strong, but not too strong for me. I get riled up just thinking about her, but I know she wasn't pleased with me. That's why I had to restrain her a little more. It excites me to feel the adrenaline rush through my body and to hear her heavy breathing while I roamed my hands where they pleased, over the soft curves of her delicious body.

I couldn't help but fantasize about my next move. The rush I felt during it all was intoxicating, and I craved more. My insides pounded with anticipation. I was ready to plot my subsequent encounter, which to most sounds twisted, but the rush of creating a scene like that again was compelling.

I got off the couch, slower than usual, to grab a beer while I sat here dreaming about Miss Raven. It wasn't even noon yet, but I said fuck it, I don't care. I called in sick to Frankie, not my asshole brother, who thinks I'm supposed to check in with him first. I told her I had the flu. Of course, she freaked, insisting I stay home and not spread it around even though I'm outside and never work in anyone's house, so how the hell is that spreading it everywhere? I'm not stupid, but that sounded stupid. Last night was a wild ride, leaving me with little energy to go to work. If it wasn't for Miss Raven, I'd at least be able to walk some, but she's got a strong knee jab. Despite the hard knock to my groin, which I'm sure will be back to its ole stout self soon enough, my mind wandered back to her luscious naked body and what I did to it.

I remembered all the good things; her perfect naked back, turning her to the side to clamp my eyes on her breasts, how she smelled like fresh citrus, my lips grazing across her smooth skin on her cheeks and ears, and my hands moving over every curve scoping out all the sensitive places. I got what I wanted--mostly. I would have preferred to sink right in between her legs, but I want to save something for next time. I could only imagine how wonderful that would feel now that I've got this extreme tightness blowing up in my pants that won't go away unless I do something about it. I know Miss Raven will enjoy making love to me.

I slammed my beer and got up to get another one. Drew thinks he can keep me from being out after eight, like a kid with a curfew.

Right.

Ha…jokes on him. The night guard is some young punk now who just watches TV. As long as I park my golf cart nowhere near a street light, I can jump over the massive row of thick brush on the other side of the gate, where it's completely dark. The guard doesn't notice. There's no camera by those thick bushes. This HOA is stupid. They don't even realize that anyone can get in if they're not afraid to jump over some bushes in the dark. It can get muddy on the other side, especially after a good rain. But thankfully, last night, the rain let up some, so I wasn't completely soaked, and thank God she had her garage door open. Otherwise, this wouldn't have worked.

I never call in sick, so it's hard to sit here and do nothing, pretending I am sick. I love thinking about Miss Raven and wish I could see how she's doing today, but Harry entered my mind. I forgot. He's going to be mad today. I promised him I'd help clean out his shed. Plus, I wanted to get paid. Harry owes me about a hundred, and I need more clothes and beer. I aim to look even nicer the next time I visit Miss Raven's house. I'll try not to be so physical. I'll let her wait on me, cook me something, and maybe make me a drink. I noticed her nice bar. Not many bottles, but I did see the bottle of Remy XO. She bought it just for Drew, I'm sure.

He's such a prick. Has to drink this expensive shit and show off about it. Like the jerk can't drink a beer like a regular guy. I felt a twinge of jealousy seeing how Miss Raven interacted with Drew. Her interest in him disgusts me. I bet he tried to suck her in the other night by bragging about his cooking or his car, something that would impress her. But, for some reason, I could see her rejecting him, not liking the affluent dick he can be with his nose in the air, all puffed up about owning a pool company now run by the third generation in our family.

This does include me, but Drew insists I'm in the background for now, still getting compensated, just not a face in the forefront. Fine. As long as I'm still associated, Miss Raven will still be more interested in my connection with this company being the one with some humility. She'll respect my position more than she'll respect Drew's as head honcho. More like a master prick, in my opinion. I deserve the same level of care and attention that Miss Raven showers upon Drew, that's for sure.

Harry being an old guy, he's good with technology. I texted him and told him I had to be gone today and I'd be there tomorrow. He texted back that I better be there tomorrow. He has a lot of things for me to do. I'll just hurry up, get the debris picked up, the dog garbage dumped, and then go right to his house. Harry better keep his promise of giving me his house and cars because Miss Raven would like to live in that house. He has a massive room with a pool table, a custom-built bar with a huge TV in front of a black leather couch shaped like a U. Miss Raven, and I could have parties there. She'd love it. I know she loves to cook and wants to do more catering, from what I heard her say to Drew at his house. They didn't see me dropping some tiles off, but I heard her say that. She can cater for my parties anytime, that's for sure. I watch her food videos all the time. I'm glad Harry told me about them. I asked him how he found out about them, and he just told me it was none of my business.

Again, I'm not that dumb. I know how to use a computer, so I found them myself. It was easy to find her name from Luke, the contractor, that sort of arrogant jerk like my brother, but he gave up her name the instant I asked who was moving in. I posted a review. I wonder if she'll know it's from me. I loved watching her cook up that shrimp davi something or another. I went to the fridge and grabbed a couple of brews. It was time to watch Food and Wine Club with Raven. I love getting off watching Miss Raven from Minnesota.

When I turned on my computer and clicked on her YouTube channel, my eyes were glued to the screen as I watched Miss Raven, the most beautiful person I know, move gracefully around her kitchen, her hands skillfully prepping and chopping. I didn't catch what this meal was, but it looked delicious. I love how she smiles and laughs for the camera. Seeing her ignites an undeniable urge within me, a feeling that grows stronger as the video progresses. My body tenses, and I can feel the unmistakable sensation in my shorts about to explode. She's the woman who's captured my heart and fueled my fantasies. It's true love, I feel as I fidget in my chair, watching her chop red peppers, tossing them in the pan with onions she's already started sautéing. It's erotica to me just watching her.

My heart's racing like I ran a five-mile race, but I didn't. It's just watching her and wishing I could see her right now. I wonder if she's thinking about me in any way. I'd love to know. Oh, that's right, I put her number in my phone last night. Now, I can text her. Damn, I almost forgot. Just the thought of being able to text her and talk thrills me. I know my messages to her will be welcomed by her. She'll hopefully see me as charming. So, I'll be patient and not bombard her with any notes. I'll send her a text tomorrow or maybe Wednesday. If I see her out running, I'll try to snap a picture of her without her noticing.

After watching five of her videos, I clicked off my computer and grabbed a bag of chips and another beer. I started feeling a little bad. Seeing her gorgeous face on the screen, I didn't like that I had to slap her face. Pretty hard too. I didn't want to. She's so pretty, but she pissed me off, squirming and shit when I was in control. I was there to make love, but her behavior ignited a fiery anger I couldn't control. Miss Raven must understand that it was her own actions that triggered me. The situation would have been different if she didn't resist. I know our relationship will work out and soon. As soon as Drew realizes it's me she will choose.

If she wants complete control in the bedroom, that's a different story. I'm up for that. But I want that time to be special. She's got to warm up to me a little more. And to find out Harry's ticket is something of interest. She perked up when I told her Harry said he knew her grandpa. How does a guy just leave his family like that? Must have been an asshole in the first place to leave behind an absolutely stunning granddaughter. Well, I picture her stunning as a little girl. Don't cute little girls grow up to be gorgeous? And I guess she has a sister. It's what Harry thought. I wonder what she looks like and if she shares any physical traits with Miss Raven or possesses her own unique beauty. Probably as gorgeous as Miss Raven. Wait, no.

No one is as gorgeous as Miss Raven. In my eyes, no one could compare to her, not even her sister. Miss Raven is incomparable—a unique gem I will cherish forever.

CHAPTER 18

Thursday, August 20th

It felt as if I'd gotten some much-needed sleep, but I was still reeling from the egregious attack, the lingering effects pulsating through my muscles with every move I made. It made for a complex progression of moving forward. Life had to go on, and if Deidra hadn't invited me to her home today, I'm not sure what kind of debilitating mindset I'd be wallowing in.

It's amazing what twenty-four hours can do. The greenish-yellow bruising had mellowed into a minor stain just under my eye. And my lip had lost its fat look, but the cut was slightly visible. I would need to apply extra foundation and blush for disguising purposes. By the time I'd make myself up for Deidra's sunset and cocktail gathering, my appearance shouldn't be the center of attention. If I wore sunglasses, that would be a bonus.

As I sipped my coffee and iced my lip, I reflected on Deidra's unique qualities and couldn't help but think of her as a living embodiment of therapy right this moment. Little did she know I was genuinely grateful to have someone like her as my neighbor. The fact remains, wonderful neighbor or not, I'm not willing to open up about this anytime soon, not until I understand more about Devin's relationship with Harry.

I chose nautical blue and white striped Bermuda shorts with a white flowy top and navy-blue flats. With mascara applied a little heavier than usual, I hoped it wouldn't draw unnecessary attention from the extra layer of foundation directly under my eye. Either way, it is what it is, and my expectations of meeting Deidra's husband, Trey, and having cocktails while watching a sunset will be my only chance of feeling like I have a normal life again. In desperate need of a new view, I had high hopes that getting out of the house could eradicate the poison that hung on my nerves.

All dressed, I stood in front of the mirror, glancing at my outfit and makeup; it was time to leave and meet my new neighbors. I pinned my hair up in a messy bun and wore the ruby earrings Cassie had gotten me. I looked presentable. Honestly, anything passed compared to the disgruntled homeless look I stumbled out of earlier. I took a deep breath, letting the nerves settle, and whispered a little pep talk. I spun around on my feet and headed for the door, the beginnings of excitement trickling through my body as a welcomed sense of butterflies fluttered around in my stomach.

Before leaving the house, I checked every window and door to ensure they were all locked and then set the alarm. I made a mental note to talk with Luke about getting an alarm strictly for the garage and service door and wondered why I hadn't thought of it from the beginning. I also thought about tossing out the question as to what made him believe this neighborhood was safe in the first place? But that would be unreasonable. No, it was completely unfair. My utter disgust was talking.

Big pillowy clouds dotted the sky, blotting the sun from its rays as they slowly swept by, heading East. I brought a shawl along just in case the temperature chilled, or the noseeums started biting. My eyes like a hawk's, I gazed at my surroundings before I proceeded down my steps toward Deidra's. No sign of Devin or the low hissing hum of his golf cart brought relief. Just as I turned the corner off Deidra's driveway to ascend the stairs, Drew popped his head over the railing two floors above me and waved. I did a double take, a palm to my chest in complete surprise, my heart leaping out at the sight of him. My infatuated senses climbed upward, starting at my toes, my heart racing at seeing him dressed in brick-red shorts and a white linen button-up, sleeves rolled to his elbows. I wished I could have taken a picture right then, his poise and striking presence like that in a movie starring Rock Hudson. It was inviting.

"Hey, I didn't know you were going to be here," I said, delighted yet taken back by a dash of fear. My concern revolved around the frenzy building in my gut with these two brothers. The blame I threw at him and Luke after what Devin did, was still ruminating, but the rational side of me put shame on myself for even beginning to blame them. Don't twins have some kind of spiritual connection?

It's obvious Drew has no clue how evil his brother is. Devin had attacked me, and it was a harsh truth that he would eventually have to face. He held out his hand at the top of the steps like the true gentleman he was, just like I imagined Rock Hudson, even Harvey Specter would do. Either way, I wasn't going to flinch at a man treating me with respect despite the tiny nudge in my gut wanting to repel the essence of any male touching me.

"Deidra motioned me over a little while ago. I was out back in a meeting," he pointed over to his pool area, "and asked if I'd join you all for a happy hour, that our newest neighbor would be here." His smile filled his face, and it was evident he wouldn't miss this occasion.

"Well, it's a pleasant surprise to see you here," I said, my tone icy. All I could see was his twin lurking behind the identical nose and brown eyes that peered directly at me. Drew leaned in to kiss me on the cheek, and with a guided hand on my lower back, he walked me over to the seating area where a spread of finger foods and a salad sat on an ice bath. A large, colorfully painted ceramic pitcher sat on a flat red platter ringed by four margarita glasses.

"*Chica! Me allegro de verte!*" Deidra pulled me into a full bosom hug, squishing me like a tiny ant at one point. "I can feel your bones, my friend. *Necesitas comer.* Eat!" I exhaled as she let go. *If she only knew why I didn't eat for three days.* Dressed in a multi-colored sundress, her wildly curly hair, pulled up in a high ponytail with a red ribbon, Deidra was the spark in the middle of a dull party which I'm sure this wasn't going to be.

"Deidra, you are such a delight. Your smile is contagious." I sincerely meant that and could already feel my cheeks cramping from smiling so much since I'd arrived. My muscles had grown weak from crying and frowning for three days straight.

"You're too sweet, Miss Raven." I gave her a funny look. "Oops, Raven, my sweet Raven." My eyes instantly darted toward a tall thin man with hair as black as Deidra's dressed in dark gray linen trousers and a white golf shirt walking toward us. Drew immediately got up and shook his hand, both men shoulder-slapping one another in a man hug, and then their eyes turned to me.

"You must be Raven. A true Minnesota girl, I understand." He said, his voice deep but smooth, his accent smoother. He took my hand between both of his in a small handshake, then kissed the top of my hand before letting go. And, surprisingly, I didn't feel the need to pull away from his touch. I couldn't believe how hospitable and welcoming these people were. The "Minnesota nice" thing didn't compare to this.

"And you must be Trey, a true Italian?" We all chuckled. "Nice to meet you," I said, my voice wavering slightly. For some reason, a nervousness encompassed me standing between two men. I quickly turned to the sparkling inner coastal waters below us, the Gulf out past the small island that seemed a short boat ride away. "You have a stunning view, and your house is a… South American dream mansion with a European flair?" I intended it as a question. I'd never designed a house in this theme; not a Minnesota style at all, but its beauty favored a Florida attribute.

I didn't want to remove my sunglasses for fear my makeup job failed me, but I did, so I could take in all the colorful decorating features right before me. A tall statue of two parrot-type birds stood in the corner as if safeguarding the lanai next to a giant wall of glass doors now fully opened. Dark woods, sunset gold on the walls, ceramic pieces set about, and large canvas paintings decorated the walls to either angle. It felt like I'd be walking into a personal museum. I slipped my sunglasses back on, returning my attention to my hosts.

I pointed, and Deidra explained, "Those are Lilacine Amazon birds. My favorite. They're a critically endangered species now. *Es Triste.*" I wasn't sure what that meant, but I was more enamored by the bright green of the feathers and their red and white heads with the yellow cheeks.

I felt Drew's gaze on my cheeks.

Deidra added, pouring four glasses from the pitcher, "My cousin made that statue for me. Trey likes it but doesn't love it like I do." She elongated the 'o' in the word love, and Trey looked up at her with an amused smile that told me it was a story she told often.

I noticed how stunningly beautiful this couple was and thought about how gorgeous their children must be. We all had donned sunglasses with the sun's full brilliance on top of us as we made small talk. Deidra's laughter filled the air as she giggled while Trey related stories about her entertaining specialties. Deidra handed us each a glass as Trey warned us that his "lovely wife loves tequila, so beware." I took a sip and completely understood; goosebumps ran down my arm like a rolling avalanche. I instantly laughed, giving a thumbs up to Trey's alert. I definitely entered a state of relaxation. My tightened stomach muscles and the tension etched in my back seemed to ease up, and so did my breathing. One too many of these, though, and I'd be making a fool of myself or, worse, unconsciously blabbing how the maintenance guy attempted rape, that he's fooling everyone into thinking he's a trusted human being.

I would be a complete idiot to let that happen.

In fact, the little bastard texted me before I walked out the door. I refused to read what he said. Even though reading it might send me into a worrisome frenzy, I wondered if he may have revealed more about Harry, which pestered me. I still wondered at his audacity to text me after what he did to me. I'd prefer to block him, but I second-guessed that action because I rationalized that maybe acquiescing and texting with him would allow me to learn more about Harry. That's the only reason why I'm not going to block him.

Deidra explained our food choices. Over a separate bucket of ice, there were four small dishes of ceviche with shrimp and halibut sprinkled with bits of green onion and cilantro. A small frisée salad and cherry tomatoes on the side, and on another platter, three rows of bite-size mini cheesy potatoes called llapingachos lay on a bed of curly kale, all worthy of pairing with a strong margarita. We ate and sipped, and I listened to their stories about how they all ended up here in Bay Harbor. But I hoped someone would mention Harry and his involvement in Bay Harbor. I shifted around ideas in my head on how to bring him up.

And then I heard Trey complain about Devin; I couldn't understand what it was. My eyes darted at both of them.

"Yeah, I'll talk with him about getting that back to you," Drew said, taking a long draw of his drink.

"I don't know why the board can't allot some funds for him to buy his own tools. I don't know what the hell Frankie thinks sometimes. Her time's almost up, isn't it?" Trey hissed, setting down his empty dish of ceviche. He looked to Deidra, pointing at his empty dish. She shook her head, so he grabbed another cheesy potato.

"Frankie's reign is done next March," Drew said matter-of-factly. Motioning for Deidra to refill his glass, she glanced at me with a questioning smile since I couldn't see her eyes, but I waved her off. I'd barely finished half of mine and felt quite light, near floating. I popped another shrimp in my mouth.

I got up the courage to participate. "Sounds like you're not a fan of Devin as the maintenance guy? He uses *your* tools, Trey?"

"Yes, and the idiot conveniently forgets to put them back in my garage." He quoted with his fingers on the word conveniently. He sounded pissed off, and Drew didn't try to justify Devin's actions, which surprised me and led me to believe he wasn't happy with it either.

As I observed them discussing the topic of Devin, I recognized an innocence and an embarrassment resonating from Drew's posture. The muscles in his jaw twitched as Trey talked.

"He doesn't mean to *roba tus herramientas*, Trey." Deidra forked two more cheesy potatoes on her plate. "*Comer mas.* Eat up. Come on, Drew. I know you love these." She smiled and took a bite while we all grabbed another plate.

I noticed Trey didn't respond to Deidra. Again, I was oblivious to what she said in Spanish, but I knew Drew understood. He tilted his head toward Trey and said, "It'll be fine."

Both men got up to get a drink from the bar, and Deidra asked if they'd bring us both water. She explained that Trey set up companies, advised clients on business-related options, and prepared tax returns. He was Drew's tax preparer, and they often talked of business and future options. It was all over my head, and Deidra made it known that it wasn't an interest to her. I moved next to her on the couch. I wanted to face the water and watch the boats and jet skiers cruise by. I noticed a few fishing boats trolling close by. They waved at us. The sounds of osprey trills and, of course, the blackbirds flying above us. We laughed at a pelican diving into the water with a splash.

As we took in the lively scene on the water, I felt an overwhelming sadness. The extent of work I had put into the design of my new beach house with the sole intent of it being my "safe haven" was now scarred and blemished. I'd barely spent fifteen days in my new house and wondered if I'd ever be able to recover from this devastating dream destroyer.

Deidra and I talked about food and my online presence with my food vlog, at which she went bubbly nuts over suggesting I could make some Ecuadorian dishes and volunteered to be my special guest; which I thought was a fabulous idea. I told her we needed to make a date to discuss all of this, but it would need to be after I cater Drew's party. "Oh, you're catering his big shindig, huh?" Deidra said, reapplying the glossy red lipstick she pulled out of her skirt pocket. "That's wonderful, *Chica!*" She got up and waved her hand for me to follow.

As I walked through the massive wall of open air into a space filled with furniture, built-ins, and a black grand piano in the corner, I fell in awe at the décor. I slipped my sunglasses off, thought about how I should have moved here years ago, and opened a decorating store. To decorate and furnish a house like this would be an honor for me; definitely more fun than work, in my opinion.

There were so many textures; marble floors, colorful ceramic pieces, ceramic tile on the backsplash of the built-in bar, etched mirrors surrounding a buffet cabinet, a thick white plush rug under the piano, and furniture in a mixture of scrolling wood and black iron. The focus was the larger-than-life canvas paintings on the deep golden walls.

Trey and Drew entered from down a hall past the biggest bay window I had ever seen, with a small built-in seat and a mound of throw pillows in colorful satin brocades, all fringed in different textures of colorful yarns. Both men stopped at the window facing Drew's house, Drew pointing at something and Trey nodding. I walked over with my glass of white wine Deidra had handed me, the four of us gazing at

Drew's property. There was Devin pulling up in his golf cart beside Drew's pool. My body felt like it jumped out of its skin. When I stepped back, Drew turned to me with a smile at first but then quickly turned to a confused scowl. He leaned in close, which made me wonder what he was doing, and then I remembered my eye. I sucked in a breath behind my pinched lips. I'd forgotten entirely.

"What happened here?" he said, softly touching the edge of my eye.

I touched it, pretending not to remember, and then said, crinkling my nose, using my hand to rub out a fake itch, "Well, I was at Cassie and Luke's house the other day, and a board fell on me when I was helping Luke unload his trailer." I hoped they couldn't see the rush of blood rising in my ears.

"Oh… that's why you didn't answer my call? You were busy?" Deidra said, lightly touching the top of my cheek. "Do you want ice? Are you okay?"

"Oh, gosh, yes. It's no big deal," I said with over-exaggeration in my voice. Even to me, it sounded phony.

Later on, after Drew had to excuse himself, Deidra leaned toward me, and half whispered, "He really likes you, you know." She pointed to the spot he was sitting in.

"Are you being a matchmaker, my lovely wife?" Trey interjected; his smile as handsome as he was. He lifted his glass in an air toast to me and nodded.

Apparently, Trey agreed, which made me smile and toast him back. What was I going to do? Tell them I'm not interested in a man with a brother who likes raping women in the neighborhood? That Drew's good looks and charming behavior tainted by the likes of this twin who represents a flaw in the Hampton name? So, why would I want anything to do with that? I took in a long draw, the smooth chill down my throat pressing my trepidation further away.

The sun's position was now directly in front of us, nearing the horizon with a glow that shimmered across the water. The four of us stood near the white-painted iron fencing that ran the perimeter of their open lanai and gazed out in awe. Drew brought it up, and we all agreed that a person could never get sick of a sunset, no matter how many times you've seen one. They're amazing each and every time.

Moments later, after we decided to sit back down to watch the remaining sunset glow filter into a myriad of pink and orange hues, Drew asked, placing a hand on my knee, "Find out any more things about the stuff in the box?" This cued the curiosity of Trey and Deidra, and both turned my way. Drew went on to tell them what the box was all about and listed some of the contents we'd seen. Deidra's expression told me she knew nothing about Harry or the house I now live in, but Trey's body language told me something different. He emptied his glass and set it on the table before him.

Drew finished, and I asked Trey, "What do you know about Harry and this house I live in? You look intrigued." I was hoping for a million-dollar answer to this million-dollar question.

"Well…I know he built the house he's in now, like in '93 or '94." He leaned back, placing his laced fingers behind his head. "What some of the other neighbors were saying, and this is hearsay since I never talked with the guy even before he became this lunatic warding everyone off his property. No problem by me, but I guess he fell apart after someone in his family died or something to that effect. Not sure what that has to do with moving out of one house and building another, but that was the rumor."

That's exactly what I thought when I saw the newspaper article about the accident. He lost someone; now, he is hurting so deeply that he doesn't know how to handle it. I suddenly felt so bad for him, and my heart ached because I understood the heartache myself with the loss of my grandma and Jack and then my grandpa disappearing. I could help him. I know I could.

And then Devin's words fluttered in my ear: *Harry knew your grandpa, you know, the one that up and deserted your family?*

"What qualifies Devin to be the only one helping Harry?" I said, irritation biting at me. I couldn't hold back as I darted my eyes at each of them, hoping for another million-dollar question to be answered.

"I haven't a clue. It's what Harry wants, I guess," Drew said, shrugging his shoulders. I was disappointed in that answer.

"It's possible it's just a simple fact that Harry knows Devin could use the money. He's fully aware of what Devin did ten years ago," Trey said, turning his view from the water toward Drew. "At least that's what Frankie told me." And then, as if he got a notion that I needed to know this particular fact, Trey added, "It happened right here in this neighborhood. The people moved out right away for obvious reasons. Harry and Devin connected somehow after he came back from rehab three years later." Drew nodded.

I shifted so my back was at an angle on the loveseat, my eyes directed at the three of them, especially Drew. It was clear he was uncomfortable. I watched him rub his chin, turn his view to the water as he ran a finger comb through his hair. He'd be even more uncomfortable if he knew what his slimy twin did just four days ago.

Deidra didn't comment, but I watched how she scrunched her nose when Trey relayed the details about the girl. She shifted around, picked at her skirt, and reapplied her lipstick, giving me the impression that this conversation irritated her funny bone because there wasn't anything funny about it. She seemed all about fun and pleasurable conversations, not ugly outcomes with that conclusion.

Appalled at what I was hearing as Trey spoke about the tragic incident, I watched Drew sit in silence, neither defending nor accusing Devin, as if his lips were zipped shut on this subject. What set my stomach on fire was that it happened in this very neighborhood. I assumed it was elsewhere the way Drew talked last week. But then they allowed him back in this neighborhood? To actually troll around, scoping out the residents and their routines, watching family and friends come and go while he derives a plan of attack? That's exactly what I imagined he would do.

Thank God it was dark enough to hide the flare-up on my neck. I wrapped my shawl around me, bit my tongue, and wished my heart to stop pumping out of my chest. Drew pulled me closer with his arm around me, warming me from a chill I wasn't getting from the outside air. Part of me wanted to remove his arm. The infatuation with his Harvey Specter good looks was taking a hiatus.

CHAPTER 19

Friday, August 21st

If regret was a positive characteristic, I'd be very happy this morning, but instead, I'm sulking beneath a cloud of I should haves". I should have spoken up about Devin and let Drew accompany me back to my house last night.

"Hey, Rave, I'll walk you back." Drew offered when we decided to call it a night. Deidra had made her and I an herbal tea while the men sipped on a cognac Trey had shipped from France as our last drink of the night.

"No," I said so bluntly it made everyone's head turn. "I mean, I'm fine. I'm just across the street." I touched his arm to let him know I appreciated it, but it wasn't necessary. And then I wondered why he offered. Was he trying to convey something? Did Drew know about Devin, and would Devin have the guts to show up again? He did threaten me if I said anything to anyone.

"Ok, as long as you're safe," he murmured, unconvinced. He lowered his chin and raised his eyebrows, almost in a begging manner. And then I wondered why he used the word "safe"? The judge and jury part of me was simmering on a high level. From what I had been through living in Minnesota and now in Florida, the word "safe" sounded like a far-fetched dream. A cruel blend of nostalgia and sadness washed over me. For me, the term "safe" had become an elusive concept, a mirage that seemed to vanish as I tried to grasp it. It was a dream once within my reach, but now it felt distant and detached from my reality.

All because of his twin brother.

I believe Drew, optimally, wanted to come over to be alone with me. It's what I read from the questioning look on his face; implied without actually asking. My immediate response would have been, "I'm sorry, but I'm really tired when in fact, I was really scared. Scared of him noticing my missing coffee table and rug, leading to questions I was not ready to answer. It was hard enough to restrain myself from spilling my guts about Devin when I observed Trey's loathing for the guy. Seeing how this small community has made Devin out to be a good guy, the good maintenance guy that helps Harry, has my insides bundled up into a knot. Who lets this convict into this neighborhood anyway?

And I had to remember Harry was the imminent factor in keeping my mouth shut for the time being.

When I hugged Deidra and Trey goodbye, Deidra made me promise I would help her remodel the two bathrooms that she thought needed updating. Trey rolled his eyes and agreed that they were impeccable, but if Deidra wanted a change, so be it. Trey praised me for the extensive improvements and renovations on my house, which, according to him, looked like an abandoned fort before I bought it. Trey also mentioned that if I needed any help with a business startup for my food vlogging, I should talk to him before some other lawyer or tax consultant steers me the wrong way. I gave him a thumbs-up and pecked his cheek. It was definitely something I'd need to seriously consider, especially if I wanted to branch out into the catering business.

At the end of the driveway, before Drew went one way and I went the other, he said, "I hope I'm not being too forward, being I've just met you, but I can tell something is eating away at you." He paced and kicked around a few loose stones while I held my purse tight to my chest as if I needed protection from his implications. It felt like a probe drawing out my inner fears too far in advance. He can't know the truth yet.

"Why…why would you say that?" I tensed and had to pinch my lips shut, afraid of bursting out the truth that was holding me prisoner right here in the middle of the street.

"Because you seem a bit distant and guarded." I immediately let my purse fall to my side and looked at the ground. Trying to relax and smother the pain and fear of him finding out didn't seem to get by him. I guess my acting failed. We were standing underneath a street lamp, his eyes glossy, his facial features sharp, and he took my hand and added with a note of hesitation, "I saw you flinch a couple of times at the mention of my brother."

My God, was he that fixated on my reactions? And why? What does he know? I thought I kept my composure during that conversation, but clearly not. I looked down to the ground, gathering my thoughts, wondering exactly how I should end this conversation before I said something I'd really regret. This was not the time to talk about Devin. "I'm really tired, Drew. Right now, finding out more about Harry and those items in the box is what I'm really interested in. The idea of your brother working with Harry and that no one knows why Harry is the way he is seems ridiculous to me." My voice rose a couple of notches in volume. I didn't want to come off angry, but that's what was happening. I reeled my emotions back and continued, "It may sound silly to the rest of you, but for some reason, it's got my full attention, and if your brother doesn't tell me more about Harry, I'm going to—"

"Tell you more? What's he told you so far?" Drew interrupted me.

"Ahhh…" I scratched my neck and adjusted my purse before I remembered something else in place of what I was initially thinking, "He said Harry told him he was happy I was the one that bought this house. I only assumed he said that because the last owners didn't take care of it, and I'm clearly taking care of it now." I turned to look at my house, feeling a deep stab of violation within those walls. It was a true statement, but telling him Devin told me Harry knew my grandfather wasn't anyone's business but mine right now. The subject of my grandpa wasn't a concern to anyone else. This had to be something between Harry and me.

"Yes, you have. This place looks fantastic; there's no comparison." He slid his hands into his front pockets, his lips forming a thin line as he gazed at me.

I clenched my teeth together as I roamed the quiet streets, half expecting Devin to charge at us in his cart. "I just wish I could actually talk with Harry. But the minute I get close, I've got security patrol Devin in my face with a barricade."

"I don't have an answer. I wished I'd paid more attention to how they connected." His body language changed. A smile appeared, and he opened his arms to me, which I reciprocated in a mutual hug. He kissed me and said, "Let's meet soon about my catering job. Let's talk food and drinks."

"I believe I have a full list to go over now," I said and. Then thought it *was ready on Sunday, but unfortunately, your brother interfered, and I couldn't invite you over.*

I curled up in my wicker chair, coffee cup held between my palms, watching the busy Friday traffic of parents running their kids to school and pet owners walking their fur babies. It was close to 8:30 in the morning, the perfect time to sit out front. The sun had a few hours before it doused my head with its heated rays. As I settled into the shaded corner of my front patio, I cradled my hot coffee, feeling the warmth permeate through my fingers. Despite the day's heat, the steaming beverage didn't feel out of place. Instead, it offered a strange comfort, the bitter notes of the coffee juxtaposed perfectly against the bright, sunny day.

Drew pulled up in my driveway, and at the same time, Rachel texted me. I quickly read her text:

Hi...hope you're doing well. Just an FYI, Mom is doing great in a few short weeks. She says hi and sends her love. Can I call you later today after I drop off the girls at a birthday party? It would be around 6 pm. Is that ok?

I was shocked at the cordial tone of her text. Something big must be going on, or she's had a coming-to-Jesus moment. Either way, I responded with a big **YES** and a sunny smiling emoji, and she returned with a thumbs up. That was satisfyingly easy.

"Morning, Raven. Wow! Your smile's as bright as the sun," Drew said, pointing upward as he walked up my patio steps and sat next to me. He placed his elbows on his knees and clasped his hands together, giving me the impression he had something important to say. Dressed in cargo shorts, a Tommy Bahama shirt with a parrot on the pocket, and a Tampa Bay Bucs hat, he slid his glasses off and looked directly at me as I took another sip of my coffee. And then I thought, *oh shit, no makeup and flat uncombed hair.* An uncomfortable warmth plastered my face.

"Would you like some?"

"That would be great if you have more." I sprung out of my chair like a firecracker had gone off underneath me.

"I'll be right back." I didn't want him to enter my house, so I quickly grabbed a cup and poured, warming mine up and returning to him seconds later.

"Thank you, I'm going to need this," he said, taking the cup from me. His eyes looked a little droopy and bloodshot. "You look refreshed today." He smiled and then sipped his coffee. Perhaps I didn't look as bad as I thought.

"I am, actually. With all the fresh air last night, I slept very well." I crossed my legs, leaning more toward him. The blackbirds squawked back and forth, and an egret chased another away, making a deep angry clucking sound. It grabbed both of our attention. "It's so interesting to live here and see all this. You're lucky to have been raised here."

"Yes, I'd say that. I couldn't imagine suffering through Minnesota winters. I have no inkling as to how you could possibly manage the roads and still keep a business running."

I laughed, and he gave me a goofy eye roll. "To be able to live in shorts every day is a true blessing." I pointed at his shorts.

"Well, I'm in grub shorts today. I'm going to help a team of my guys with this elaborate pool we're building, and the owner said if I wasn't there some of the time to oversee his project, he would reconsider who he refers. So, I'm a grunt man today." He gave a throaty chuckle and finished his coffee, setting the cup on the small table between us. It was amazing how attractive he was in his so-called "grubs. I had to avert my eyes away from him. Somehow, the sibling connection kept my heart at a distance, but I had to admit that watching how the muscles twitched in his forearm as he raised his coffee cup and the bulge of his calf in the length of his lower leg was arousing. I chewed on my lower lip and turned my view to the other side of the street.

"So, clients use threats for good business' sake, huh?"

"This one does. He's spending two million dollars on this outside pool and entertainment area, so I better put my tail between my legs and get to work with my boys." He sounded proud to do just that. "But, I stopped because I wanted to ask you out on an official date. You might think I've been clowning around, but I'm not." He got up and stood in front of me, removed my coffee cup from my hand, placed it on the table next to his empty one, and prompted me to stand up, which I did. He placed both hands on my cheeks, his dark chocolate eyes penetrating mine, and said, "I don't care what you think, but I'm madly in love with you. Will you join me for dinner tonight to discuss this catering job? You know, the one you'll have fun planning and cooking for?"

His Adam's apple bobbed as he held a chuckle in his throat. I gave an indulgent laugh and repeated his words, "…fun planning and cooking, huh? I suppose I will." And with that response, I saw his eyes light up as if that was the answer to his question. I really meant "yes" to discussing his catering job.

My response was a shocked double-take after the realization of him officially asking me out on a date for tonight. He was picking me up at 4 pm sharp.

Did he just say the words: "madly in love with you"? It's every woman's dream to hear those words. It was my dream, and Jack made that dream come true; in a very similar way. Instead of standing outside facing a somewhat busy street in front of neighbors and their pets, construction workers, and garbage trucks passing by, we were snuggled on the couch on our third date. After the song "I Want to Make It with You" by Bread ended, Jack placed my face in his hands and said, "I'm madly in love with you."

Feeling a surge of enthusiasm, it was time for a run. After quickly changing into a light-colored running outfit and luxuriating in the cushioned bottom of my new shoes, I filled my water bottle with electrolytes. Before I left, I carefully placed the necklace and the article from the box in an envelope and then placed the envelope into my fanny bag. After two times around the neighborhood, avoiding the back part of the development where Harry lived, and five miles carved into my new running shoes, I stopped half a street over and pulled my usual stunt, hiding by a thick trunk of a live oak. I pulled out the tiny binoculars I just found in my box of gardening tools in the garage. It dawned on me that these could be useful for this spy-like surveillance.

Hiding most of my body by the tree trunk, I peeked around, looking through the binoculars, and my first image was Harry's tall, slightly slumped body coming out the front door. Immediately, he grabbed the wood railing for support, stealthily climbing down the stairs and rounding the corner to the side of the house, where he bent down to pick up something. And then I saw Devin's face peek around the back of the house where he said something to Harry, and Harry pointed out toward the woods. I watched Devin get into his golf cart parked on the open lot. A surge of hatred spilled through my veins, and wished I could have mind-numbingly gone over and choked him without repercussions. The mere sight of him flipped my stomach. I realized I needed to use more caution, though, having missed seeing his cart parked there.

Once Devin left, I ran over to Harry, working to get the envelope out of my fanny pack. I called out his name, "Harry. Harry Fishmen." I waved to get his attention.

He turned and stared without moving a muscle for what seemed like minutes: statue-like, barely seeing his chest move as he breathed. And then anger crossed his face. He pointed a long arm toward the road and demanded, almost savagely, "Leave. Get off my property. Now!"

I didn't. I was determined to get some answers. As he took a few steps back, I walked closer and stopped. "Harry, I have something for you. I know it belongs to you." I held out the envelope. His eyes forced slits from the glowing sun above us. I stood in the shade of his large palm tree, sunglasses propped on my head to get a clear view of this man. I watched him inspect the envelope, his jaw moving as he ground his teeth, and then he looked back at me. "Here, I found it in my house. Your house."

Devin came right up to me in his golf cart, hitting the brakes hard enough to make a squeal, startling me out of my hypnotic state. I escaped his grasp and ran closer to Harry, who ran around the back of the house, where we heard a door slam with a loud snap. Devin caught up and grabbed my arm, squeezing so tight it hurt. I slapped his face hard with my other hand. He pulled me into a tight body hold, lifting me up, his chest to my back, my legs kicking at him, trying to wriggle out of his arms.

"You little bitch. I told you to stay away from this man. He doesn't want to see you or anyone. Don't you get it?" He screamed at me.

I could smell beer on his breath, and his shirt was filthy with sweat and grass stains mixed with dirt. A car pulled up, honking, and Devin threw me hard out of his arms to the ground. As I got up and brushed myself off, Devin walked over to the car, where I witnessed Frankie peeking her head out of the car window, shoving Devin to the side. Evidently, Frankie wasn't interested in hearing what I had to say. She wagged a stiff finger, yelling like a scolding teacher at an unruly student. Looked like the two of them were a team effort.

Pressing the binoculars back in my fanny pack, I took off in a dead run. I didn't need to listen to her; all respect was lost now that I saw her position loud and clear. I'll be back. I saw Harry's scared but interested look before he fled the scene. I held onto that tiny bit of hope.

While I showered, I thought about the visual of Harry. It was the first time I saw him in detail. He had a long face with a wide-set jaw, and he still had a good amount of snowy white hair, somewhat shaggy, though thinning, and he looked sad. I felt sorry for him. I know this accident had to be his wife, mother, or someone very close. I could feel it in my bones, especially after he just stared at me and then briefly glanced down at the envelope. He couldn't have known the contents, but I felt he had a sense of what it could be.

Four years after Grandma passed, Grandpa went out to run errands and never returned to his home. It was the year 1989. After days of calling the hospitals, neighbors, and friends and driving for hours looking for my grandpa's truck, my parents demanded the authorities search his house again to look for anything they may have missed. It didn't matter. My dad had hired a private investigator, and the trail ended in Tennessee nine months later. Grandpa's cousins lived near Nashville and told the P.I. he had stayed for a few weeks, helped them with landscaping projects, and then said he was heading back home to Minnesota. However, that trail was never found. It was as if he had disappeared between Nashville and Minnesota into thin air.

One night, my father gathered us all and said, more directed at my mother than Rachel and me, "We need to face the facts. We've spent thousands on private investigators, searches, and every lead we could find, but we've got nothing. We're no closer to finding your father than when he first disappeared."

"So, what are you saying? That we should just give up on him? That we should stop looking?" My mother's lips quivered, her voice coming out in a staccato pattern, emphasizing every word.

"I'm saying that we've done everything we could within our means and have already exhausted our resources. We need to come to terms with the fact that we might never find him," my father said, trying to console my mother as he reached for her hand.

"No!" she said, whipping her hands out of my father's reach. "We can't just stop trying to find him. I can't accept that!" Suddenly, my mother's demeanor changed, and she sounded very aggressive.

In anger and frustration, she picked up a lamp from the side table and hurled it across the room, which crashed against the wall, shattering it into pieces. She then kicked over a dining room chair, sending it crashing into the curio cabinet.

I'll never forget that night. Rachel and I actually hugged, and when my father ordered us to go to our rooms, we cried ourselves to sleep after we had prayed, folding our hands in a steeple position, our heads bowed as we sat cross-legged on the floor. I don't know what Rachel prayed for, but I prayed Grandpa would return so we could play games again, eat lots of lefse, and watch old Mickey Mouse cartoons. Rachel cried as much as our mother did while I tried to be strong like Dad.

I was almost eleven when the search began and had just turned thirteen when it ended. I clearly remember it, Wednesday, July 13th, when my father told us. That night, I watched my mother drink herself to sleep. At thirteen, it was difficult to understand how a parent could stop being a parent because I was still a young kid and needed a mom. But that's not how it was. Dad was there to oversee certain household chores, keeping the normal functions of a family together. If Mom, in a tipsy stupor, burned something on the stove or in the oven because she passed out on the couch, we'd clean it up, and Dad would take us to McDonald's or order George's pizza; our favorite. Mom became notorious for boiling everything to mush or forgetting to season anything. Nothing tasted good anymore. I remember thinking that I would never cook like that.

Drew said we were going to Tiffany's, which excited me. The place had a good vibe. It's where I first laid eyes on Drew, but being together will be different this time. There's a plight stuck between us that he's completely unaware of. My acceptance of his invite, puts me in the position of being thanklessly two-faced. On one hand, my heart screams for a second chance at love, and Drew would be an over-the-top candidate, but on the same note, my gut points a blaming pistol at the brother who's guilty by association.

How do I reconcile my broken heart?

CHAPTER 20

Cont'd...Friday, August 21st

Just a few short days ago, I was crushed into a ball of despair at the hands of the twin brother of the man taking me out on an official date. A man that has confessed his love to me, like you might see in a Turner Classic movie from the 1940s.

How ironic.

I put on a jade green button-up blouse and skinny white jeans. I pulled my hair up in a twisty bun and slipped on a pair of black canvas wedges. The height would definitely improve the balance standing next to Drew. I applied a final swipe of my sparkling rose lipstick when I heard the doorbell.

Drew greeted me with a warm hug, the aroma of a manly ocean scent mixed with a hint of coconut and vanilla lingered between us as I stepped back from him. Tiny goosebumps speckled my arms. A simple gratification that my hormones had not died at the hands of a deviant. I was still sensitive to a man's proper touch.

During the short drive to Tiffany's, Drew asked, "How do you feel about what I said this morning? I didn't put you in a bad place, did I?" His voice calm but loaded with anticipation as his eyes switched back and forth between me and the road. His thumb beat like a drum against the leather steering wheel. I wondered if that was a nervous twitch or just his driving habit.

I hesitated because I wasn't sure what my answer was or should be. I turned to him, unsure of what I felt because I was still punch drunk with his confession of being in love with me. I had never imagined I'd hear those words again. "Honestly, Drew...I'm...I'm not sure," I said in a strangled voice but then blurted out, "I think we need to have a conversation." He nodded, but I saw the worried look on his face despite the hopeful smile beginning to form.

"Tiffany," Drew said, wrapping his arms around her for a quick hug. She happened to be by the front door as we entered and scooted right over to us. The place was fairly packed, but she found us a table near a window opposite the side where Cassie and I sat last time. I was happy to have the distracting view of the beach and rushing waves of the waters if my inner turmoil got aggressive.

"Hi, sweetie. You look stunning, my friend," Tiffany said, flashing me that signature wink. A radiant whirlwind of energy and a vibrant aura buzzed around her as she took care of her customers.

"Thank you, Tiffany." I had on colored lipstick and didn't want to mark her face up, so I leaned in for a quick hug.

"The usual?" Drew looked at me, and I nodded, impressed if she remembered white wine for me. I knew she knew what Drew would like. Drew nodded and added crab cakes for starters but held up a peace sign to her.

"Two orders of crab cakes, a chardonnay, and a bourbon neat. Be right back."

"She's something else," I said, envious. "I wish I was that spunky."

Drew did a full head tilt back with a big laugh. "Believe me, I already know you can be just as spunky." I didn't know how to take that. It sounded like he was throwing a dagger.

"Is that a... bad thing?" My hands clutched my elbows as I asked the question.

"Oh, my God, Raven, no. I love it." His eyes changed from a surprised look of abhorrence to now roaming over my face as he rubbed the back of his neck. My eyes didn't veer away from his lips, anxiously awaiting his response. "Why do you think I told you what I did this morning? I love a woman who can hold her own, and you've clearly proven that." I wanted to add *if you only knew how much I've had to hold my own on*--but kept my lips zipped tight. "That's spunk. It's the first thing I noticed about you."

"Oh, please. Not the first time you met me. I was here with Cassie and a hot mess." I was craving a gulp of wine about now and hoped someone would be bringing it sooner than later. For some reason, this conversation was raising the anxiety scale that had started in the car.

"No, I knew you had just flown in and the mess you were leaving, so no, not then. When you came to my house, remember, we talked business, your goals, the things you're planning on doing now that you're here." He flashed that beautiful Drew smile, the one that puts a blip in your heartbeat.

I leaned toward him with complete curiosity, "What mess did you hear about me?"

"Well, Luke mentioned what was going on and why you were making the move from Minnesota. And I completely understood." He rubbed his palms, keeping his gaze on me.

I felt my guard rise and turned to the window for a moment to realign my thoughts and then turned back to Drew. "Luke? Luke told you about me? What all did he say?" I strained to keep the angst out of my voice.

"Yeah, he did. Are you okay with him telling me about your mother?" His eyebrows came together in a concerned look.

"I just didn't realize Luke was trying to set you up with me before we even met." Tiffany brought our drinks and two orders of crab cakes and then quickly scooted away to deliver the rest of what was on her large tray. My eyes gladly took in the essence of what she displayed in front of us.

"Well, that's pretty presumptuous of you," Amusement splashed across his face. I allowed myself to stare into his eyes, not caring one iota how he'd take that. We both took a swallow of our drinks, but I let my lips linger a little longer on the rim before I had to respond.

"No, that's not what I mean," I sighed and waved my hand, negating his impression of my comment. "He's telling you things about me, but he never once mentioned *you* the whole eighteen months it took to do my project. How am I supposed to feel?" I slid a bite of crab cake in my mouth and made a melting face; it was so good.

"These are the best," Drew said, imitating me, and then added after he swallowed, "I asked him who he was working for on that house and what person could possibly design something like this without being here, and he said, 'The one and only Raven McKade.' And I said I needed to meet her. Then he forwarded a video of you on your cooking show. And again, I said I need to meet her." He picked up his glass and, with the same hand, pointed a finger at me as he nodded with a sardonic grin. I sensed his playfulness in trying to loosen my tight grip on my defense, and it was working.

I felt foolish jumping to conclusions. But it's what I seem to be good at as of lately. "You watch my vlogs?"

"I did catch the one with wild rice. Something I don't know anything about. Not a popular item around here, obviously, so I was interested."

"So, did you post a review? Recently?"

"Ahhh….no, should I have?"

"I saw the initials D.H. and thought that was you. It said something about wanting me to be your private chef anytime. The tone was suggestive."

"No, I didn't post a review. And I'm pretty sure I wouldn't say anything online that would be inappropriate or 'suggestive.' Had to be someone else with the same initials." Tiffany came by to pick up our plates and ask about our order. I gave Drew a raised eyebrow. We hadn't checked anything else out on the menu, our conversation more pertinent than choosing our next course, it seemed. Drew lifted the menu for Tiffany's eyes only, pointing to a few items, and said, "How about this or this or this? You choose."

She took the menu, smiled, and said she'd be right back with another round.

"It's weird because most of my followers never use initials; it's always a first name or a nickname. Weird. Oh well, it doesn't really matter."

"Unless it's Devin. Does he watch your videos?"

I gasped; my hands balled into a tight fist in my lap. Grabbing my phone out of my purse, I instantly deleted his post. Why would I know if he watches my videos?

"You okay, Rave? Your face went pale for a minute." He reached across to touch my cheek.

"Bad cramp." I lied rubbing my stomach and watched him turn away, rolling his eyes before a deep red lit his cheeks. I shouldn't have done that to him, but it was the only subject a man didn't inquire about any further. "Sorry." I haven't had to use that excuse for any reason for quite some time and just remembered how relevant it can be in a time of crisis.

189

"So, what's on the menu for my party food options?" I could see the relief on his face changing the subject, which made me laugh inside.

I pulled three folded sheets of paper out of my purse and opened them up for Drew to see. I had pictures of ten food options and three drink options. It was fun to watch him inspect every picture and then pointed out the three choices I had thought the best for this outside party. We agreed on roasted grape crostini, salmon tartare on cucumbers, and prosciutto-wrapped pears with brie and arugula. We fist-bumped like high schoolers in complete agreement.

I had one small problem; servers. I know Cassie would do it in a heartbeat, but who else? "I'm going to have to find some more servers."

"If you need help with serving, my daughter, Violet, would be very helpful. She's a food lover and very smart." I had forgotten about him mentioning a daughter. I don't think he mentioned her age, but I assumed no more than college age.

I cleared my throat. "I supposed I should meet her. At least see if she'd even like me first to want to work with me."

"There's no doubt she'd like you, Raven Mckade. She likes your videos too." Oh, I have a young fan!

We made plans for a pool party on Labor Day weekend with Violet, Cassie, and Luke with their twins, Deidra, and Trey, if they were around. I texted Cassie on the way home. I was concerned because Luke usually hosts a big cul-de-sac party over that weekend, but when she responded with a quick YES! I was elated.

My sub-conscience kept spitting at me. It was as if I had the devil/angel situation posted on my shoulders. One side poked me to tell Drew the truth about Devin, while the other whispered *it was not the right time.* My agreement with the latter stemmed from the fact that I needed and wanted to find out more about Harry, and Devin was, unfortunately, a critical component in that regard. I let the incident earlier today with Frankie, Devin, and Harry sit on the back burner, although it still flared up in my mind. So, I fixated on pushing it away during this time with Drew. It wasn't an important subject.

I definitely felt a strong assurance of Drew's feelings toward me and only wished I could reciprocate them. Putting all anxieties aside, just being able to gaze at a man of Drew's quality, knowing he has a heart-professed interest in me, reminds me of the scene where Harvey finally spilled his romantic feelings to his secretary, Donna. And here he was, mine for the taking, but that rigid wall of twin association kept him at a distance. It wasn't fair to me, especially to him, after professing his heartfelt feelings the way he did this morning.

And there was still Jack.

As we arrived at my place, the stars glimmering subtly overhead through the open moon roof in his Bentley. Drew turned toward me, his face gently lit by the dashboard lights. His gaze was soft as he leaned over and placed an affectionate kiss on my lips, as light as a feather yet laden with a million unsaid emotions.

In that instant, I felt as if I was floating in a dream, my heart fluttering like a bird released from a cage. And I wanted more of him. I wanted to feel the hardness of his body and the gentleness of his lips and hands as they freely caressed me.

And that's when I sensed, with my eyes tightly closed, Drew's lips on my ear whispering—*only if you let it.*

CHAPTER 21

Saturday, August 22nd

I've always felt that a relationship can't be a fully engaged circle if there are secrets and hidden truths. During our dinner, I could feel my heart reaching toward Drew when I successfully lynched the image of Devin in mid-air. I only hoped that with each glance we shared, he experienced the same electric vibe I had. Those moments let me know I was safe. (There's that word again) But, there were also moments when I felt I had to lift my protective wall, and he'd tilt his head in question.

The dinner at Tiffany's with Drew was not just a meal; it was a platform performance of push and pull with an underlying current of palpable chemistry between us. Drew tried pulling me into his romantic grasp while I, at times, couldn't help but push him away when I failed to remove the visions of Devin that seared beneath my eyelids. It wasn't fair to him not to understand my grief and the pain I was hanging onto. The food, the ambiance, his company—everything had been too perfect for my selfish insecurities to ruin it. We had bridged the gap seamlessly in the driveway.

And then Rachel flashed in my mind.

I finally dialed Rachel's number after downing half a cup of strong coffee. There was no avoiding the inevitable reprimand, but at least the caffeine would help sharpen my wits. "Hi, Rachel. I'm so sorry. I was out on a…I was out preparing for my next food video and left my phone on mute. I completely forgot." I lied, but how would she know what I was up to anyway? And why was I feeling so intimidated? I certainly wasn't going to tell her I was on a date. She'd give me all her analytical opinions about letting Jack go and how I shouldn't let my past get in the way, blah, blah, blah. I guess my guilt derived from how nice she was in the text. I doubt she was going to use nice words in this conversation.

"What's your new recipe?" While she responded so quickly, it was a bit shocking that she didn't retort at all; she didn't even acknowledge my apology.

"Ahhh…cucumber gazpacho or…" The intimidation had me reaching into my food-brain of recipes to pull out another as if it was such an undertaking. "…or my green pizza with artichokes and pesto."

"Oh, jeez. Not the green pizza *again*. You did that one up here all the time. Pick something that relates to Florida. Something fresh from the ocean. You just made a wild rice chicken salad with grapes. You're still in the Minnesota state of mind, Rave. Get with it." She let out a sigh while I rolled my eyes. "You live in Florida now. We'd like to see what people down there eat."

Did I hear that right? "'We'? What do you mean by 'we'? Are you watching my videos?" I knew she had watched a few in the past, but she rarely took an interest in my personal life with her being married and raising two daughters; she was always complaining about being so busy as if no one else had children or was married. Rachel was all about Rachel, and if the time suited her, she'd engage in a discussion in whatever hobby or subject you might be involved in, but it was rare. Despite this, the notion that Rachel was investing her time in viewing the content I created stirred a strange warmth in my heart, and I appreciated it. Maybe it was the distance between us that triggered her small transformation toward me.

"Well, why wouldn't we? Dad and I watched a couple the other night while the girls had a sleepover and Pete was out fishing with his brothers. Dad said he missed you and wanted to watch you on YouTube. So, we did."

As Rachel uttered the words, "he missed you," I heard her sneer. This was the typical Rachel I was accustomed to, masking her true emotions with snide remarks and condescending smiles. Her hidden message, clear as the chirp of a robin at the first sign of Spring, she believed I had abandoned them, just like our mother had done so emotionally years ago. "What's so bad about that?" I asked Rachel with a bit of agitation.

"Bad about what?'

"That Dad misses me."

"Nothing. Anyway...I wanted to talk to you about us all coming down for Thanksgiving and you're cooking. We'd help, of course, but Mom thought it was such a good idea. She wants to book tickets now, but I told her to wait till I talk with you. So, it is alright if we come to stay with you for a few days?"

"Sure," I said, my tone even, void of emotion. If it had been my father saying these exact words, I'd still be excited, but it was Rachel and her dismissal of passion in planning a family get-together. It was a chore for her. I smiled into the phone and injected a lilt into my voice, "That would be great. I've got plenty of room. Book it."

"Okey dokey. Thanks, Rave." Rachel said quickly.

"If you would like..."

Rachel hung up the phone before I could complete my sentence. I just stared at a blank screen and shook my head.

Ever since Luke brought me the box, Harry has been like a ball and chain on my mind, weighing me down with questions I can't seem to get the answers for. I wish I knew if Devin was gone for the day or if he always worked Saturdays. I feel he's always around, even when you don't want him to be. I guess I could go for a run and check it out.

By the time I reached the doorbell of Harry's house, the anticipation of what I was about to encounter sent my determination up a notch. I pushed the button to his doorbell till I heard a yell from the back of the house. "Go away. I don't talk with anyone here, now go. I mean it."

I waited to see if he'd come to the front door or if he'd peek around the side of the house at me. I waited another ten minutes and then rang the bell again, holding it in longer than any respectable person regarding the sound of an annoying doorbell should. But I was determined to get his attention. From behind the door, I heard him finally say in a firm tone, "Listen, Raven, you need to leave right now." I was surprised to hear a deep calm voice from the other side of the door.

And then I realized he said my name. I was in shock. I stood on my tiptoes, stretching to look through the two rectangle-shaped windows in his front door. There truly wasn't an advantage, in my opinion, to being short. I hated that I couldn't come eye-to-eye with him. I even jumped up twice to see if he'd maybe reconsider and open the door, but he didn't after I waited a couple of minutes. "Harry, you know who I am. I have something that belongs to you." I held the envelope up to the windows. "Please, let me help. Please, Harry, open the door."

"Put it in my mailbox and then leave. I'm not opening the door till I see that you are gone. Now, git!" He was back to shouting, so I changed my mind and decided to be happy to do just that.

At least there was some type of communication between us.

I put the envelope in the mailbox, shut it with a bang so he'd hear the clank, and then I ran across the small wooded area to a large tree trunk and hid behind it till I imagined he sensed I was long gone. Looking through my binoculars and keeping myself hidden as best I could, I saw him open the door, his bare arm reaching into the mailbox, snatching the envelope out, and then slammed the front door shut with a bang.

CHAPTER 22

Saturday, September 5th

Today was the day of Drew's pool party. The thought of relaxing by the pool under the glorious sun, indulging in delicious food, and just spending quality time with friends had been a source of my mental switch. After all the challenges and turmoil of the recent past, it felt like a breath of fresh air to be able to look forward to something so simple yet, so fulfilling.

"Oh, my God! Phoebe, you are the spitting image of your mother in high school," I said, opening the door to let the Towers family in. "The blonde waves, the perfect smile. And look at your brown eyes. Just like your daddy's." I hugged her, kissed her cheek, and touched her silky hair. "I can't believe you're taller than me now." I guess it had been a year and a half since I'd seen the twins, according to Phoebe.

"And I have a boyfriend too, Aunt Raven." Her smile all braces. Cassie protested with an exaggerated eye roll. "Mom, really? Stop." It sounded more like "stahhhhhp."

They set their food and beach bags on the island, and then Phoenix and Luke came through the door with a large cooler and pool noodles. I walked over to hug both of them, immediately noticing I had to get on my tiptoes to wrap my arm around Phoenix and look up, not straight ahead anymore.

"What...did you grow five inches since the last time I saw you?" He's reached the age where his hugs are much looser than Phoebe's. I felt proud, though, as an honorary aunt to see how he's grown up into such a good-looking young man. Obviously shy about showing affection now that he's older, whereas as a little boy, he was all about the hugs.

"I guess so." He stood just a smidge shorter than Luke, and his voice had definitely changed. Both kids wore braces, their smiles a million bucks already. Phoenix had sandy-brown hair like Luke's, while Phoebe's matched her mother's golden locks.

"So, everyone ready for a pool party?" I asked, both kids waiting at the door with big smiles and beach towels around their necks, pool noodles in their hands.

I had learned days ago, when Drew and I had the sunset dinner at his house, that Violet was also fifteen, like Phoebe and Phoenix. This made Cassie nervous as we walked the half block to Drew's house. "Nix is girl crazy, and you see, Pheebs is happy to tell everyone she's got a boyfriend. This will be the death of me," Cassie said, putting her hand to her throat, shoulder-bumping me.

Walking through the gate to the pool, Trey and Drew were relaxing on loungers closest to the bar, their legs crossed at the ankles looking suspiciously in vacation mode. I waved, and instantly Drew popped out of his chair, sprinting over to give me a welcoming hug and kiss. Trey stayed lounging, lifting a hand in a wave, and smiled as he saw our crew gather around the pool area. After the introductions of Phoebe and Phoenix to Drew, he pointed out a large table with several open munchie bags and a couple of bowls of rich, creamy dip, their tantalizing aroma mingling in the fresh outdoor air. It made my stomach growl. The dips were placed on a bed of ice, so I grabbed a chip and dipped it into the first bowl; onion and garlic with fresh herbs. I wondered if Drew made this or bought it. Adjacent to the table sat a large cooler filled to the brim with chilled beverages. A big sign in playful letters was taped to the lid: Soda-Water-Lemonade. The kids were thrilled, and each grabbed their choice, cold water dripping on their feet as they opened the bottles.

The sound of the sliding door echoed, and I turned to see Deidra emerge onto the sun-drenched patio, her entrance stunning. Her solid coral swimsuit hugged her form perfectly. As she sauntered toward us, her white lacy cover-up fluttered in rhythm behind her with each step while her lips shined in fire-engine red. *"Chica!* You look so *hermosa mi amiga.* So beautiful!"* She hugged me tight and kissed my cheek, leaving a bright red lip mark that she rubbed away lightly with her thumb.

I was so happy she and Trey could join us and meet Cassie and the kids. Deidra is becoming a special person to me and is very important to have in my life. She's definitely becoming a true trusted friend. Just last week, we had so much fun spending a day together. She taught me how to make homemade empanadas stuffed with cheese and vegetables, and we drank a sangria that went down like a fruity Kool-Aid drink from our past. To date, that sangria is definitely on my list of favorites, and I was so thankful she offered to share the recipe. And then told me her secret ingredient was tequila. I was shocked because I couldn't taste the tequila, but after two heavy glasses full, I could feel it.

I introduced Deidra to Cassie, Phoenix, and Phoebe. And then, when she noticed Luke, she kissed the tips of his fingers and placed them on his lips. She said, "My dear Luke, *gracias, gracias* for bringing this wonderful *esplendida amiga* to this neighborhood. La amamos!" She turned to kiss me again and brought my hand to her cheek. Deidra charmed all of us as we stood in awe of her genuine gratitude. I definitely needed to brush up on my Spanish.

Drew approached with a young girl as Deidra went over to sit by her husband. "Hi, I'm Violet. Nice to meet you," she said with an impressive young adult confidence. She held her hand out to me first, which I shook, and then introduced her to the rest.

Violet, in all her modesty, was dressed in a bright pink bikini that complemented her fair but perfectly tanned skin beautifully. Her long, dark hair was elegantly woven into a single braid that fell gracefully over her one shoulder. Her smile was as striking as the length of her legs. As I introduced each person to Violet, she attentively listened and repeated each of their names in turn. Her demeanor was marked by a maturity well beyond her years, her manners impeccable, and her approach to each introduction sincere and respectful. I couldn't help but admire her refined behavior. It was unmistakable evidence of Drew's influence.

Deidra, Cassie, and I sat on the edge of the pool, close to the rock ledged waterfall, feet in the water, chatting and sipping on mojitos Deidra had mixed up. The pool area was a riot of laughter as the kids engaged in an energetic game of water volleyball. Phoenix, being the only boy, played against the girls, demonstrating admirable good-natured competitiveness.

The three men lounged nearby, their chiseled figures on display. They sat side by side in cushioned loungers, bare feet propped up, faces shielded from the sun by baseball caps. I checked out Drew with a sly eye as he kept one eye on his daughter, the other talking business and construction with Trey and Luke. I could tell they were all having a great time, telling stories, throwing jabs at each other, rolling in laughter, and pointing at one another. It was hard to turn my attention away from them. Or rather—him.

Luke and Cassie brought burgers and hotdogs for Drew to grill, and I made a watermelon and feta salad to go along with Deidra's Italian pasta salad. Drew said he made popsicles for dessert, and Violet slapped at her dad and said to the group, "And the freezers at the grocery store helped him." He teased her about telling on him, and we all chuckled.

I asked Violet as we were cleaning up the paper plates and silverware to put in the trash, "Would you want to help me serve at your father's party, Violet?"

Her eyes lit up, pausing her dirty plate stacking duty to look at me.

"Are you serious?"

"Of course."

"Yes, I'd be delighted!"

I don't ever remember hearing a young person use that word.

"Well, then that's a deal. Do you need to talk with your mom about it first?" I don't know why I asked such a stupid question when her father was the one that offered her assistance to me in the first place.

"No, Mom won't care. Besides, I think she's gone to Australia or the Bahamas for the next three weeks. I can never keep track, but that's why I'm staying with Dad." She laughed and then added, "He hates driving me to school because of the traffic. Says it's ridiculous the way they make you zigzag just to get into the school to drop me off by the front door. I told him I'd walk a few blocks, but he insists on driving me all the way to the door."

I sensed Drew's pride in caring for his daughter by the way she spoke of his insistence of driving her to the door as if he was concerned for her safety. "What does your mother do?"

"Oh, she designs arts and crafts kind of things and sells them on Etsy. She travels to different trade shows all over the world." I noticed that while the twins started playing card games with Cassie and Drew, she opted to stay helping me.

"Do you want to get in on the card game over there? Looks like they just started." She glanced over to where they were sitting but kept wiping down the table as if this were more important.

"I'll finish helping you first. It's no problem." And then, out of the blue, she said as she continued wiping down the table, "You know my

201

dad really likes you." She stood upright, dirty dishtowel in her hand, staring in my direction, obviously waiting for my response. Needless to say, I was taken aback. "Did you hear what I said, Raven?"

"Ah…yes, I absolutely did. I'm sorry. I'm a little shocked your father would tell you that."

"We're very close. And he trusts my opinion." She leaned in to hug me and whispered near my ear, "I can see why he does." She scampered off to take the trash into the garage, and as I watched her, Drew was staring straight at me. His smile told me he enjoyed what he had just witnessed.

We were all lining up the outside chairs to view the sunset before the Towers needed to leave. The three teens grabbed their chairs and placed them where they wanted, grabbing another drink from the cooler. I stood by the bar with a glass of Merlot and watched the kids interact. Violet was a hospitable host to both, but I could tell Phoebe and Violet were going to be close friends. They'd already exchanged phone numbers and email addresses. It reminded me of Cassie and me when we met at the age of ten and couldn't wait to call each other. Only we wrote out numbers on a piece of paper, hoping never to lose it before we got home after school. Phoebe already asked Cassie if sometime she could stay the whole weekend with Violet.

Trey was standing by the pool gate talking on his phone when Frankie and Devin came barreling through, spouting about something the rest of us couldn't make out as we were standing on the other side of the pool area. Trey shoved his phone into his pocket and yelled, "What the hell is going on?"

Pointing at me, Frankie shouted out, "You…you caused this, Raven McKade." She marched over, still pointing, Devin following behind her; her face twisted in anger. "Harry is in the hospital because of you!" She emphasized the word *you* which made the rest of the group look directly at me.

I stood frozen, my palm to my chest, appalled at her accusations but also in dismay with the news of Harry. What happened that he had to go to the hospital? The envelope I left in his mailbox…did it somehow cause him pain?

My knees felt like they were going to buckle.

Next to me, Violet grabbed Phoebe and said, "Let's go up to my room. I hate Devin." Phoenix followed with Luke's arm pointing toward the girls scurrying away.

Frankie hustled over to me, invading my space, so I pushed her back with a frantic wave of my hand. A waft of onions mixed with a strong spice of some kind puffed out of her mouth as she gasped. Devin approached closer, but I held up a flat palm to stop him, staring at him with such an evil glare that it seemed to stop him in his tracks. My heart pounded so hard, and the blood rose in my ears so fast it echoed.

"What…what in the hell… do I have to do… with Harry being in the hospital?" I choked on my words. The others had gathered around me like I was in a high school fight, and they were going to pounce in my defense if I gave them the right signal.

"You gave him an envelope…of stuff. We found it on the floor." It was Devin shouting and pointing now. Trey grabbed him by the arm to shove him away from us, and then Drew pinched his scrawny neck between his thumb and fingers, strong enough that it forced Devin to walk back even further. *He used that method on my neck the night he assaulted me.*

Deidra and Cassie stood next to me in silence, both periodically touching my arm in support. I watched Drew eagle-eye Devin, raising a poking a finger in Devin's chest as he told him he had no right to come in here and accuse me of such a thing. Devin's arms flailed in the air as he tried to stop Drew from pushing him.

"You've been warned, Raven," Frankie said, her voice like ice. "You were to leave poor Harry alone like the rest of us have. Have you no respect for anyone?"

"Oh, for God's sake, Frankie. Get off your high horse," Trey said, his arms talking as much as his mouth. "The old geezer made this 'so-called' demand a couple of years ago. So, what…he didn't associate with anyone anyhow. He walks into the annual board meeting with a written letter he's had signed and dated stating no one comes near his house except for Devin Hampton. It's all bullshit. What do we care anyway?"

Devin pulled away from Drew's grasp just enough to say in an oddly strained voice, "Because he's Miss Raven's grandpa."

"You liar, Devin. You lie like the rug you assaulted me on." As these words slipped past my lips, a profound silence fell over the gathering. The gravity of my accusation hung heavily in the air, a volatile charge that seemed to electrify the space. I hadn't planned on confronting him publicly. But my emotions surged ahead of my rationality, and the confession had exploded out of me like lava spewing out of an active volcano; raw information so hot it lit the air with fire. It felt as if the time had stopped for a brief moment; everyone's attention was now riveted on me and Devin. Acutely aware of the eyes boring into me, their shock and confusion only amplified by the prior revelation about Harry.

I heard gasps as I covered my mouth. Cassie and Deidra turned to me, their eyes probing me for answers without asking me questions. Drew held Devin back while Trey walked over to me, begging me to repeat what I had just said. But I couldn't. I was tongue-tied by the words that came out of Devin's mouth. It was as if my body floated above everyone else while I tried to make sense of it all.

In the aftermath of my outburst, I felt a wave of exhaustion come over me, leaving me feeling brittle and raw. The atmosphere seemed to thicken with their silent questions. I could sense the concern and confusion radiating from everyone present, but I was in no state to deal with it.

I didn't want anyone to touch me or talk to me.

I held up my arms to keep the others at a distance and then walked over to Devin, looking him straight in his bloodshot, droopy eyes while Drew, as if cued by my body language, held Devin's arms behind his back. Trey walked at a distance beside me and then stopped right before I took in a deep breath and said, "You fucking liar…you rapist."

Before I knew what I was doing, my open palm connected with Devin's cheek in a swift, resounding slap. The sharp crack echoed as Devin's face whipped to the side from the force of it. I watched as a red imprint of my hand quickly developed on his skin. I had no regrets, just a strange sense of satisfaction and relief as if I'd finally released the pressure valve on my deep dark secret.

CHAPTER 23

Cont'd...Saturday, September 5th

Fury coursed through me like a speeding train. I was livid, and the slap I landed on Devin's face was a poor representation of the storm raging inside me. I wanted to hurt him more, make him feel with every inch of his body the torture he inflicted on me, but, unfortunately, I stopped with only a slap and my piercing words, forcing everyone to momentary silence.

The three of us headed directly inside while the men dealt with Frankie and Devin. I needed to get away from Devin's malicious semblance and Drew's problematic intentions about me. I just knew that the spark that had started between Drew and I, would now be in question with my formidable accusation. And I felt a strong stinging bite with that thought.

Deidra sat next to me on an oversized cinnamon leather couch, gently rubbing my back. She grabbed a throw from the backside of the couch and laid it on my shoulders while Cassie brought us all a bottle of water from the refrigerator in the kitchenette. I didn't know if I was chilled from the air conditioning inside or from the alarming information I had just heard, or even the blatant truth I ejected at the end. The last thing I remember was Devin yelling about me being a liar and then Trey gut-punching him till Drew pushed him off. I struggled to grapple with the words he'd said about Harry.

It had to be a lie.

"Where's the kids?" I asked, my voice barely audible, my arms wrapped tightly to my stomach in hopes of stopping the urge to puke.

"Don't worry about them. Luke's handling it." Cassie dismissed my concern taking my face in her hands, and asked, "Did he really assault you, Rave? Did he hurt you?" Her brilliant green eyes had turned to watery pools of tiny red roadmaps. The gold fleck in her eye was missing. I could only imagine what mine looked like. I felt like I had been dragged through a field of dust and dirt. I rubbed my eyes with the heels of my hands, contemplating how to respond to Cassie.

I looked at Deidra, her thick mascara lashes now clumped together by her tears; her lips pale, void of her normal bright red lipstick. She nodded her head. "That's why you had a bruised eye, right, *Chica*?" She delicately touched my cheekbone while her other hand steadily rubbed my back.

"Bruised eye?" Cassie exclaimed, anger spewing through her vowels. She grabbed two more blankets out of a closet and handed one to Deidra. We were all dressed for a night outside in the August heat of Florida, not inside in a cold air-conditioned house.

I finally admitted that I had lied to Deidra and Trey the night they had me over when I said I was at Cassie and Luke's house and had a fight with a board unloading Luke's trailer. Cassie waved it off as if this tiny white lie was nothing in comparison to the real truth I had unintentionally disclosed. She started pacing, and that unmistakably told me what was going on in her head, making me even more nervous. With every step she took, my fear rose with the possibility of her exposing what happened to me three years ago in Minnesota. I could almost sense the questions swirling in her mind about why I hadn't confided in her about this attack. I had endured the torment alone out of fear of dredging up the buried anguish from the past, but now I saw how it'd created an unseen barrier between us. Her eyes, normally filled with a sisterly warmth, now held a flicker of pain and confusion, sending a flurry of guilt grumbling through my veins.

"But, instead, that son-of-a-bitch attacked you?" Cassie stood directly in front of me, eyes loaded with an ire that scared me enough to believe the next thing out of her mouth might be Farren Humboldt.

And that's not what I needed right now. Especially when Deidra, although a very trusted friend, wasn't aware that this had happened to me before, making it excruciating to answer any questions she might have. I could only imagine Deidra's round, shiny eyes suddenly drooping like a basset hound's if she heard this bit of news about my past. It didn't take me long to understand how empathic Deidra was.

Deidra started rattling off a written page of Spanish words, none of it making any sense to Cassie or me except one single word *Bastardo*. Deidra's sweet girlish voice took on a sharp, angry tone, and we ended up in a giggling session. And how good it felt to laugh with these wonderful ladies next to me. Cassie and I gaped at one another with surprised wide eye look, slapping a hand to our mouths to hold back from bursting behind our closed lips at Deidra. Just the sound of all that Spanish jargon spoken so fast with an emphasis on every other word was comical in the silliest of ways.

Deidra couldn't help but laugh at herself as we tried to imitate her actions. It grew into more laughter. Something that tamed our inner angst, especially after the scene we'd just experienced outside. All three of us wrapped our arms around each other in a purely satisfying much-needed hug. Despite the gravity of the situation, I felt a surge of happiness and relief. I was not alone in this battle; I had these two great women, my companions in this turbulent journey, standing right beside me to help me navigate through a series of unknowns with Harry and, hopefully, the removal of Devin forever.

It made me sad for Drew. How could I forgive him for what he's allowed? And if there's the truth that twins have this unbreakable bond of sorts, then it might be me that Drew can't forgive. Time will tell.

After I drank the rest of my water, Cassie grabbed three more bottles from the fridge. As she walked them over, I shook my head and said, "A glass of very chilled wine, please." As soon as I said it, my mother's face appeared before my eyes, and I grimaced, thinking *was this how she started*? My God, I was heading down the same path. The shameful part of me justified how the water satisfied my thirst but not the nerves twitching around my heart like a million pins poking at me. I raised my chin and narrowed my eyes in a *don't argue with me* look. Her eyes shot open, and she immediately looked to Deidra for approval, which made me laugh only on the inside. I hit Deidra with a friendly tap on her leg, and Cassie whipped around in a pretend huff.

A minute later, we all held a glass of chilled wine, and I said, "Here's to finding out the truth about Harry and if Devin needs to be castrated." We clinked, and I downed a large mouthful, the cool liquid releasing the tension in my throat.

"Castration's too good for him," Cassie said, her face still twisted in disgust as she shook her head.

"*Si, Si.* I agree." Deidra raised her glass, took a sip, and then placed her tiny hand under my chin. "Grandpa?" I raised an offering hand to Cassie to be my spokesperson, which she kindly stepped into.

She gave a short version without the detail of how my mother's response to the traumatic event ended with her now in rehab. Then Deidra asked, "If he is, would that be a happy moment for you, my *amiga especial*?"

I'm not sure why, but I had to take a moment to think about it. "Of course! Never in a hundred years did I think I'd hear those words. It's almost as if I blacked out when Devin said them. I was sure he was just saying it to get to me. Although, in my house that night that he had said Harry told him he knew my grandpa. *Knew him,* not *was* he. Then Devin threatened me to silence about what he had done to me, so I kept quiet because I wanted to know more about Harry and thought the only way was through Devin. I'm so stupid." I dropped my forehead in my open palm but looked up when I heard a sniffle. Cassie dabbed continually at her tears. Again, afraid of what she was thinking and what might slip out, I put a finger over my lips, and with a quick tilt and side glance at Deidra, I could tell she understood.

I needed desperately to talk with Harry.

"Honey, you should have told Drew right away what his brother did to you." Deidra kissed her fingers and then put them on my cheek. Her eyes melted with pity for me, which I appreciated, but it also made me feel defeated—as if all the therapeutical healing I had worked hard at over the last three years had sunk into a black hole, and starting over was the only way out.

Cassie's eyes were glazed in a mixture of vengeance and the effects of the wine. I could see the cogs spinning in her head. It looked like me a few weeks ago, but my cogs were spinning in a different direction. "After what Trey said the first night I met him...about the young girl he assaulted and it being right here in the neighborhood—"

"What? Are you flipping kidding me, Rave? This asshole assaulted someone else in this area?" Cassie cut me off; her voice had risen to almost a scream.

Deidra and I nodded.

"And he was allowed to come back and work here in this neighborhood? What idiot allowed that?" She finished her wine and walked to the bar to set it down, but instead, picked it back up and grabbed the bottle out of the fridge. I watched as Cassie divided the remaining wine between our glasses. The weight of the day had worn me down, and I accepted the glass, staring at the buttery liquid that swirled within it, my mind a whirlpool of thoughts.

"It was...Drew." Deidra's voice dropped at his name. Cassie put her hands on her hips and gave a sideways glance. "But he put trust in his brother. Not to justify, but Devin had been in therapy and was given a clean record and a high recommendation for a job. I'm sure Drew only wanted his brother to be better. Maybe to hurry and get past it all." Deidra seemed a little flustered, a nervous energy manifesting in her hands as her fingers twisted and turned.

"Where are they now?" I asked, realizing we'd been sitting here for quite some time. I looked at the clock above the fridge, and it was almost ten-thirty.

Cassie said, "Drew and Trey drove Devin to his house to shower and pack a bag. They are taking him to the St. Petersburg/Clearwater Airport, where his uncle from Miami is coming to get him on his charter plane. That's all we know, according to Luke's text" Cassie knew what my next question was going to be, so she added, "Luke and the kids are up on the third-floor shooting pool, listening to music. According to Violet, she refuses to be around Devin; that's why she ran into the house as soon as she saw him."

Deidra also added, "The girl Devin assaulted was a few grades older than Violet, and the kids at school gossiped about the incident. Because Devin was her uncle, Violet was harassed, so her mom homeschooled her for the rest of the year."

Seeing Violet so vibrant and positive pained me to imagine the hardship she might have faced due to Devin's disgraceful actions. No child deserves to carry the weight of an adult's shameful conduct, yet Violet was thrust into that unfortunate position. And, now that she knows how I've been added to his list of victims, I wondered if it would diminish the respect she has for her dad and also, how is Drew going to justify all of this to his daughter?

Unfortunately, my respect for Drew has plummeted a few notches.

"He should be castrated," Cassie said. "And tell me, what kind of therapy did this deranged piece of…did he have that he supposedly was released on 'good behavior'?" She used finger quotes.

"Trey was really upset, too, that Drew made the deal for him to work in the neighborhood. I didn't want to talk about it much because it would send Trey into a rampage sometimes. He and Drew had it out one day, and since then, it seems they've been able to deal with one another." Deidra walked over to her beach bag to retrieve her phone. No message from Trey.

I questioned Drew's motives for wanting to protect his daughter while still allowing a known pervert to roam around in the very same neighborhood he was convicted in. He's charismatic, he's classy, he's intelligent, he's sexy. However, he faulted on the one thing near unforgivable—trusting where it didn't belong. And now it's hurt more than just him. His daughter had been affected and possibly even more on a different level. I felt an immense sense of pride for the incredible young woman she was despite it all. I was torn, caught in the crossfire of my thoughts as I pondered over the culpability of Drew. Could I, or should I, hold him accountable for allowing Devin back into the neighborhood?

"Hey," Luke said, peeking around the doorframe. "You all good here?" He sat down on the other side of me; Cassie still paced while Deidra hung close to me on the couch with her phone held tightly in her hand. She kept checking her messages. "Sorry to hear about this, Rave. God, it pains me to think I didn't check into this neighborhood a little more. Small neighborhood, staffed gate, excellent reviews…meeting Drew who's lived here a long time and…." He rubbed a heavy hand across his face, sighing heavily after each point he was trying to make.

"Luke, stop. It's not your fault. Like you knew the maintenance guy was a narcissist." I said, turning to hug him. "Although I did swear at you for half a day. I sort of hated you and wished I'd never laid eyes on this property." I was half joking but didn't want him to feel it was his fault in any way…because it wasn't. If blame was to be pointed at anyone, it was me for leaving my doors unlocked and Drew's renewed faith in his twin brother.

I excused myself to the restroom. I needed to freshen up and remove the salty sweat and the stench of this so-called confessional of earlier. I splashed my face with warm water and used the corner of the hand towel to wet it and wipe down my neck and arms. It gave me the sense of wiping away the grime Devin left on me while he went on ranting lies to all of us.

And then I recalled the conversation that had taken place outside.

I believed they all thought Devin had raped me. Not that what he did to me was less invasive or hurt any less, but it's just not the whole truth. For some reason, though, I didn't want them to know any different. If I could get away with it and not press charges, I'd prefer that. To enter into a court setting again would put me in the same tormented bubble I was in with Farren's trial. The accusations, the scant evidence, and the daily emotional terrors suffered all for a few years behind bars were not worth it. The crucial element in all this is that Devin never touches a woman again.

I want him permanently removed from this neighborhood.

It was decided that the Tower's family was opting to forego the hour-long trip home and stay with me, which I happily embraced. The twins were excited and couldn't wait to have an "Aunt Raven breakfast". It gave me something to look forward to in the morning. Thankfully, I stocked the fridge and pantry. I always hated having to run to the grocery store first thing in the morning, especially over a holiday weekend. I was set for a houseful of company.

Cassie gave me an innocent pouty look when she disclosed a couple of extra overnight bags stashed in the back seat of their truck. "It was a just in case, but so glad I packed these." I smiled and realized how wonderful it would be to wake up to a house full of people I love and trust. I couldn't remember the last time it happened.

We all said goodbye with long, warm hugs to Deidra while the rest of us, including Violet, went back to my house.

Violet said quickly, near a whisper, while I prepared us all a chamomile tea, "I won't be calling you Aunt Raven as they do. I'm hoping you will be my step-mom someday." A large lump emerged in my throat as she pulled me into a tight hug, her cheek against mine. I felt the rapid beat of her heart and couldn't help but wonder what she would think if she knew how I detested her father right now. I was stupefied by her reaction.

I just smiled as if the negative thoughts ruminating in my head had no effect on the wonderful sentiment she just declared.

CHAPTER 24

Sunday, September 6th

After a family breakfast feast of scrambled eggs, bacon, a fresh fruit bowl of cantaloupe and berries, a pitcher of fresh orange juice, a mound of toast, plus my ultimate blueberry muffins made with rice flour, Cassie and I cleaned up while Violet took the twins over to her pool to hang out for a while before they drove back to Lakeland.

I looked at Cassie bussing the table, bringing the dishes to the sink to rinse them before loading them into the dishwasher. With the teens gone, I decided to tell Cassie what was niggling at my gut. After wiping the table, I said with slight hesitation, "Hey, ahh…last night Violet mentioned how she'd love to be able to call me her step-mom someday."

"Well, she knows her dad's crazy about you. I heard the girls talking about it when I met them coming out of the bathroom at Drew's last night." Her eyes were focused on the plate in front of her, and I could see she didn't understand my problem.

"But…I'm not interested in Drew. After all, that's happened? Especially after finding out he's the reason why that scoundrel was able to work in this neighborhood again," I said, holding my hand out so Cassie could hand me the next dish to load into the dishwasher, but she just stared at me with a look of disbelief.

Now my heart quivered.

"You're pushing Drew away? And Violet? Doesn't seem fair." She handed me the dish and returned to rinsing the others. *What was I missing?*

It's as if she expected me to forgive and forget what just happened. And then she shut off the running water, and while drying her hands on a towel, she continued, "Hey, I'm not happy that Drew and this HOA allowed that scum to work in here and then raped you, for God's sake, but, dammit, Raven, Drew didn't mean any harm by it. How was he to know that his brother was going to hurt the woman he'd fall madly in love with? Or any woman, for that matter. In fact, he was convinced he was doing the right thing. You can't blame him for this, Rave." My eyes started to water, and I clenched my teeth to stop the tears from dripping. This was such an ugly mess. I inhaled deeply through my nose and continued to load the dishes. "Rave, listen. Luke told me that Drew's so messed up inside right now that Trey's trying to keep him composed. He hurts as much as you...."

I waved a hand at her to stop. I backed up a few steps. I felt I needed more air space between us. I drank the rest of my bloody Mary and chewed on the olives without looking at her. My stomach churned with anger.

After I took in a large breath and turned to face Cassie, I let it out like a rush of wind and said in a calm but decisive tone with one finger pointed in the air, "I cannot and will not forgive Drew for what he's caused. He needed to help his brother, and he thought this was how to do it. Unbeknownst to him, he let his perv brother work as the maintenance guy under the supervision of him and Frankie. Then he provided him with a house outside the gate where he wouldn't be privy to socializing with the neighborhood residents and had a so-called curfew which obviously didn't work. That's what he thought would be a good idea. And that's where he made a huge mistake." Cassie didn't move. Her eyes probed mine, her chin to her chest in sole concentration on me. It seemed minutes before she even blinked. I carried on, "And besides, I'm confused about Violet. She's fully aware this is her dad's doing. That he's the one that's allowed Devin to work inside Bay Harbor. How can she possibly think that after finding out what her nasty uncle did...plus, she's admitted she can't stand to be in the same room as him! How does she think I could possibly...?" I couldn't finish. I brought my hands back down from flailing in the air.

I started walking toward my bedroom, my hands rubbing the disgust from my face, but Luke came in through the garage, grabbing my attention. "Rave, I got a question for you." He waved a finger to follow him but then noticed the grim look on his wife's face and turned back to me, his forehead wrinkled with confusion. "What's going on with you two?"

"Nothing," Cassie said sharply, towel-drying the glasses she knew I never allowed in the dishwasher.

"What do you need, Luke?" I didn't want this conversation to go on.

"Are you two fighting?" Luke stood in the middle of the doorway, both hands flat against the frame like it was holding him up.

"No," I said and then darted my eyes at Cassie; her mouth was open, but nothing came out.

"I just told her I want nothing to do with Drew. He's caused this mess."

"Rave, listen..." Luke's voice was quiet but tense. He looked to the ground and kicked lightly at the tiled floor. "Drew is suffering...."

"Oh really! As he should. Now what the hell were you going to ask me?" I couldn't remember the last time I'd used fighting words with Luke, if ever. It hurt.

But neither of them talked back to me.

They were fully aware of the tragedy I endured under the hands of that deviant brother of Drew's, although, at this very moment, I was going to let them think I had endured an actual rape; my anger ran so deep.

While fixing my faulty circuit breaker, Luke noticed my rug with a coffee can-sized blood stain on it, covering a pile of broken furniture. As we stepped out to the garage, he just pointed and peered at me with suspicious but discerning eyes.

"Yeah, they're ruined. I've ordered new replacements sitting in the boxes right here," I said matter-of-factly, my expression stone cold. I hated feeling like this and treating Luke with such disregard, but I felt as if their promises when choosing this neighborhood for me--deeming it safe and secure--hindered more of a joke than a conscience choice for me. To have a demented maintenance guy was just part of the deal, but you have a staffed gate that won't let the "crazies" in. I know that's not what Cassie and Luke meant to happen at all. They would never wish this upon anyone, but my unabashed anger spilled over into believing such a distortion. And if I ever had Devin in my presence again, I could only imagine what I would do to land me in prison for life.

When Luke approached me with reluctant steps, it sent a surge of guilt up my spine. Tears sprung instantly and poured out of me as if a dam had broken. My anger hovered at the surface so long that I couldn't hold back anymore. He put a gentle hand on the back of my head and pressed it to his chest. I wrapped my arms around his waist like I was hanging onto a life-saving device. My body was racked with sobs. And then I heard Cassie open the partially closed door where she stepped down and pressed her chest to my back and squeezed.

I suddenly could see a new sense of hope perched on the horizon, waiting to rise up and shine on me again if I only let it. "I'm so sorry. I love you both so much."

Luke put my new coffee table together. I didn't have to explain why they ended up like this and out in the garage. Cassie rolled my new rug out, flattening the creases, and commented on how the horizon scene was a beautiful sign of happiness and that my new, though much cheaper, coffee table in creamy white brightened my living room like a Florida house should be. I nodded in agreement with Cassie's assessment and flashed her a cheerful smile that said *I love you for saying it that way.*

I didn't get to say goodbye to Violet. When the twins arrived back at my house, Phoebe said one of Violet's friends' mom picked her up for the day, but she was still excited about helping serve at her dad's party. And that made me stop in my tracks. I'd forgotten about it and now would need to somehow find a way to deal with letting Drew down. Right now, my brain was consumed with finding Harry once the Towers family had driven away, and I was on my own again. My first step was stopping by Frankie's and demanding to know what hospital he was in.

I waved one last time before I shut the door to my empty house.

A significant sense of relief passed through me as I wrapped my arms around myself in thankfulness for these true friends. Living alone has its perks, but I know all too well the changes after being violated. The quiet alone afterward can seem like a violation. Just hearing the kids early this morning as I made coffee put a cheer in my walls that I know would last forever. Watching my friends wallow in a pang of sadness for me since last night's disaster, and after my clashing of heads with Cassie and Luke this morning, actually gave me a new-found strength to carry on. We may not agree on how I'm to move forward, but with Devin out of the picture, that puts me in the ultimate power seat, and all I have to do is take control of Harry and how he's associated with me and my family.

I know Frankie is next on my list of what to control.

I walked with rigid steady steps up to the front door of Frankie's house. Resolute determination coursed through my veins as I approached the facade of her house. My flip-flops snapped rhythmically against the pavement. The morning sun cast long shadows behind me, stretching and skewing with each deliberate step I took. It reminded me of when I first saw my shadow and tried to run from it as a small kid. I remember my dad laughing while he tried to hold me still and explain how a shadow comes to be, but I screamed, wrestling to get away from him. I chuckled, watching my shadow project sheer determination with each step I took. It seemed like a therapy session of sorts.

With my posture straight and my chin held high, I fought to exude an air of controlled calm, yet within me, a flurry of emotions threatened to break free. As I reached the front door, I paused momentarily, taking in a healthy breath before raising my hand to ring the bell. I could feel my emotions seeping to the top like a bottled-up genie in a jar begging to be released. And then I wished I could have three wishes.

I rang the doorbell and banged on the door the way a mean neighbor would. My calm control was slipping away like the air hissing out of the pinhole of a popped balloon. I was raised to show respect to all and prided myself on being a pleasant person, greeting most with a wave and a *hello*, and helping when someone needed it without passing judgment. But this particular person rubbed all of that away when she showed her support for Devin last night. Finally, I heard footsteps and a huff before the door opened. "Oh, it's you. Hello, Raven. What can I do for you?" Frankie opened the door leaving one hand on the handle as if ready to shut it in my face and the other hand on her hip, her mouth twisted. Standing before me, dressed in maroon spandex leggings, her torso engulfed by an oversized white t-shirt that could pass as a small tent that nearly hung to her knees.

"What hospital is Harry at?" I glared at her, not caring a single minute if she told me she despised me and hadn't an ounce of respect for me. In fact, I'd encourage it. It was despicable how quickly she disappeared when I shouted that Devin was a rapist. Cowardly in my book, especially for an HOA representative whose job it is to oversee community situations. I watched her face bloom in shock and then push past Drew like she was just told her house was on fire.

"I'm not at liberty to tell." As the words rolled off her tongue, a level of snark and sarcasm grated across my already twitchy nerves. I wished I could have slapped it off her face.

I leaned in close enough to smell eggs and onions on her breath and poked my finger close to her face. Her chin melted into her neck as she backed away without moving her feet. "Well, that's too bad. Because you're going to tell me; otherwise, I will write a letter to all the other residents and tell them you support Devin in his devious behavior of assaulting and raping women in this neighborhood." The color drained from her face, leaving her looking pallid and shocked as if I had just informed her that her mother was a woman of the night and the man she'd known as her father had no blood ties to her. Her reaction was as dramatic as if I'd revealed a deep, dark secret from her family history.

"I'm shocked at you, Raven McKade. I took you for a nice young lady. And really hoped you to be a cordial resident in this neighborhood."

Her whiny voice was an irritation to my ears, especially how she said my name like it was peanut butter stuck to the roof of her mouth. "One that could be raped by your perverted maintenance man, right?" I screamed in her face and watched the color rise in her cheeks. I turned to see a couple and their dog walking by, staring up at us, and a group of kids on bikes laughing and pointing our way.

I wasn't the least concerned because by the time they'd learn who I was and why I just said what I did, they'd congratulate me and probably join me in protest as I stood outside the house of the HOA president.

"Hey, Raven." I turned to see Drew pulling up in his Bentley with Trey in the passenger seat. It was Trey who yelled out my name, waving me over. Frankie shut the door as soon I turned toward them. *Such a coward.*

"Do you want to go see Harry at the hospital?" Drew asked the question. By the look on my face, Trey gave me a thumb gesture to hop in the back seat, but I told them I needed to stop at home first to get my purse. I was desperate to see Harry.

How was I going to get in Drew's car without strangling him with an emotional lecture? How could I possibly sit in the same air space? Sweat built up so fast on my scalp I could feel it starting to stream down my forehead. I was caught between a razor and the blade; it was such a thin line I was teetering on with this decision. Trey lifted his sunglasses, looking directly at me as he poked his thumb in the air toward the backseat, and Drew stared straight ahead. He had one wrist bent over the steering wheel while his other hand cupped around his mouth, his elbow perched against the window. It was all awkward, and I was screaming inside for an answer.

Harry was my answer. "I'll be right back. Pull into my driveway."

I needed to bring a couple of more items that were found in the walls, but I wasn't going to tell Trey or Drew that. They were not involved in this battle; it belonged only to me.

Harry was at Mease Hospital off McMullen Booth. I didn't ask how they found out, just assumed it was Devin, and the last name I wanted to hear was his. It was a twenty-minute drive, and for most of that time, there was silence except for Trey talking to Deidra, who he said sends her *amar,* and then called a few tax clients, which surprised me being a holiday weekend, plus a Sunday. I guessed the life of a tax preparer never ends in April. When I didn't respond to Deidra's message, he translated and said, "It means love. She sends her love." I touched his shoulder, and my mouth formed a big smile to let him know I thought that was very sweet of her, even though he couldn't see my face.

Drew didn't offer up any information about Devin, and I was surprised by his silence. Maybe it's because Trey was in the car, but I had to assume Deidra told Trey about my assault. Maybe something was said between the two of them before they saw me, and they agreed this wasn't the time to bring up Devin and what happened to me. They were smart men, and I'm sure they realized bringing up his nasty twin brother had no room within the confines of his car.

Trey and Drew were going to the cafeteria to get something to eat and asked if I needed anything before finding out what room Harry was in. I shook my head and watched them walk away.

He lay still and quiet, his eyes closed with oxygen tubes in his nose. He seemed bigger than what I remembered just a few feet away from him at his house before he had run from me. I stood in the doorway of his room, observing everything about him; how his feet nearly touched the end of the bed, how his shoulders filled out the width of the bed, barely leaving room for his arms to rest beside his hips, and how his breathing was shallow but steady. If this was my real grandfather, how come I don't remember him being this large of a man or his face having such a strong square jaw?

After so many years, I stopped looking at pictures of him. I was so young, too, so maybe I didn't remember as much detail as I thought I had. At thirteen, when the private investigator had lost the trail of my grandfather after he'd left his cousin's residence in Nashville, the pictures were put away. I hadn't remembered him to be such a large framed man and couldn't remember examining the pictures in a way to remember him after that. My mother would pull them out often in her drunken state, but my father and I didn't want her to ruin them, so we'd take them away and quickly place them back in the box that eventually ended up in my dad's office so none of us looked at them.

I was happy to be left alone with Harry. I had to lie to the nurse that I was his long-lost granddaughter in order to be considered a visitor. I told her he hadn't seen me in over twenty-five years as he didn't want anything to do with me or my family. I couldn't tell her that my grandpa's real name was Benjamin Pierce III, not Harry Fishmen. So, maybe this man didn't lie to Devin, and he really did know my grandfather. Or, maybe my grandfather legally changed his name somehow, and that's why the trail ended. They were looking for Benjamin Pierce when instead, he was now Harry Fishmen after 1990.

I'm sure I was wrong. Why would my grandpa do something like that? It sounded absurd in my head, and besides, why would he tell Devin that he knew my grandfather but really was my grandfather? Didn't make sense.

I sat in the chair next to his bed and stared at his face, taking note of how this man had aged, the lines and crevices telling a story I'd like to learn about. I lifted my jittery hand and placed it on his hand, his skin thin and slightly cold. I'm not sure what I would do if he opened his eyes and saw me here this close to him, but I had to touch him. If this was my grandpa, I wanted to feel him. Or at least I thought I would feel something out of the ordinary, something that would tell me it was true, but there wasn't anything of this sort.

Just as I was about to get up to find a bottle of water, I heard my name spoken, the voice a rough whisper. I was standing and slowly turned back to the man lying in the bed. His eyes were watery and bloodshot, the color grayish blue. He spoke again, "My granddaughter." I fell into my chair so hard the metal legs squealed as they shifted over the composite flooring. My jaw locked open, and in my mind, a million questions escaped like butterflies released from a cage into the open air, but there was nothing. Nothing but silent air-space that hung the few short feet of distance between us, our eyes never wandering from the other.

"You're my Grandpa Ben?" My stomach somersaulted, and a large lump formed in my throat as he nodded ever so slightly, as if afraid admitting it would send in a SWAT team to arrest him. I could see how scared he was. I panicked, not knowing what to say or do other than take my phone out of my purse. What was I going to do with that? Call my mother? Of course, I couldn't do that. I wasn't thinking straight. I wanted to show him the cuff links and the two skeleton keys. I wanted more proof that he was who he said he was, and if he showed me some type of recognition of these items, I would have my answer. I pulled the bag out and laid them on the side table next to his bed, where a pitcher of water and a notepad with a pencil sat. I looked at him, staring at me, trying to raise a hand, but I didn't understand if he was trying to say something or wanted me to do something with his hand. So, I touched him. Immediately his eyes closed, which made me question whether he actually saw the cuff links and the skeleton keys in the bag.

The nurse explained he had fainted at home from dehydration and a weakened heart. She pleaded against stressing him with anything serious, to just keep him quiet. Was it what he saw in the envelope I put in his mailbox that day? I wanted to ask him if that picture in the locket was his mother or sister or even…his wife, my grandmother. Was the accident in the clipping the one that killed my grandmother?

Was this why the pictures were hidden in the walls? Because he couldn't deal with the tragedy of losing his wife? Is this why he ran away? I wanted to ask him all these questions without the chance of causing him pain or the possibility of having a heart attack, like the nurse alluded to. But I believe he's too weak to handle all of this. Was this why he refused the company of everyone, especially me, because he knows what I had found?

The turmoil spinning around in my head felt like a tornado that had latched onto pages of possibilities but first ripped them to shreds before I could piece them together to see the answers. It's why I wanted to call Dad and Rachel. I wanted to share this possible good news with someone that would understand the realm of what I was dealing with. For twenty-five years, he'd been gone from our lives, and now we deserve answers. We simply want to know why. We couldn't even speculate as to why but if he could prove he's our missing father/grandfather, the missing Benjamin Pierce III, I want to be able to tell my family. They need to know.

I had been yearning for the day when my mother's burden would be lifted and when the shadows cast by our grandfather's disappearance would dissipate. I hoped for a time when our family could remember Grandpa with fondness instead of questioning murmurs and an ever-present sense of loss. It was my deepest wish to see my mother unburdened, relieved of the worry and suspicion that had hung over her since that fateful day when our beloved grandfather vanished without a trace.

With his eyes still closed, I picked up one cuff link and inspected every inch of it, remembering the Christmas Rachel and I were so proud to give him this present.

We had giggled with a sneaky impression that by giving him something he could wear, despite his disbelief in the mood stone, we felt he'd see a difference and somehow be happier. Every time he wore them, we watched in eager anticipation for a change. It was a silly gesture.

While Harry—I couldn't bring myself to call him Grandpa just yet--rested, I decided to go down to the cafeteria to tell Drew and Trey they could go and that I'd take an Uber back home because I didn't know when I would be ready to leave. I spotted them at a blue Formica table next to a window. I'm not sure how he managed it, but I watched

Trey type double thumbed on his phone while carrying on a conversation with Drew, who seemed miles away as he held a Styrofoam cup of coffee between both hands.

His lips moved, but the dewy glaze in his eyes told me he was feeling the wrath of his brother's actions as much as I was. They insisted on staying with me till I wanted to leave and asked about Harry. I noticed by the intent looks on their faces how curious they were to find out the truth about this particular man that lived just yards away from the three of us; their eyes lifted in question at me, but I didn't offer anything other than he was resting. With a shrug of their shoulders and a courtesy nod, they continued on with what they were doing before I had approached their table.

They were being gentlemanly and patient with me while I felt a need to protect Harry. I really had wished they'd leave because I wanted to keep this secret about Harry, my newfound grandfather—if that was the truth. My future is going to change if what he's telling me is complete truth, but in order for my mother to heal fully, I'll need to know why and I don't want the opinions or needs of others to get in my way. Coffee sounded like a good idea, but I assumed it to taste like burnt beans compared to the preferred choice of Hawaiian Kona coffee.

I stirred in three extra creams, took a sip, and then walked over to a thick concrete pillar where I could covertly keep my distance without them knowing. It was perplexing to me to be in the same building as Drew. To feel him this close and to observe his morose mannerisms put me in a quandary. There were so many words unsaid. A dense fog gapped between us. I don't know how, as close neighbors, this will all play out, but I sensed that once one of us starts the monologue, it will be pages and pages of sordid rhetoric before it comes to an end. And how will that end? Will his love for me fade into a mere friendship at the expense of my safety and sense of security? Or will I succumb to the pool owners' pleas for a passionate affair of the heart? A simple Harvey Specter fantasy?

I laughed the image away and finished my coffee. I felt the caffeine starting to sift through my veins as I tossed my cup in the trash can. I started to text Rachel, then Dad, but erased it, then started again, but it didn't make sense to alarm them if, for some unbelievable story, he was lying to me about being my real Grandpa Ben. I was still in a speculative state of mind as I rode the elevator to the fifth floor. But that didn't last. When I came back to his room, a nurse was taking his vitals and giving him something to drink with his medication. When she left, he seemed more alert and motioned for me to sit in the chair I was in earlier. He pointed to the cuff links, which I grabbed and held in an open palm. He lifted his head and touched one and said, "Rachel," touched the other and said, "Raven." As he laid his head back, tears slid down from the corners of his closed eyes onto his pillow. Sobs rose in my throat with the realization that this really was my grandpa. This man, lying in this bed, was my Grandpa Ben. I covered my mouth to smother the wails that were about to burst out of me, and then I placed my forehead on his hand. With his other hand, he tapped the top of my head.

Within minutes, two nurses walked in with glaring eyes and their lips pressed into a straight line. In an authoritative tone, the older nurse told me, "He should not be allowed in this kind of emotional state. It could cause pressure on his weakened heart." The other stated I would need to leave him to rest. I understood their position, but unfortunately, I didn't want to leave just yet. I needed more answers. I wanted them to leave so I could be with my grandpa, my newfound grandfather, but that didn't matter to them, and I had no choice.

I also needed him to get stronger.

I leaned into his ear and whispered, "I love you, Grandpa Ben. So does Rachel, Mom, and Dad. I'll see you tomorrow." I kissed his forehead and noticed his hair smelled like chlorine. His eyes fluttered open, but I mouthed *close your eyes* and touched his lids.

I took the cuff links and keys and put them back in my purse. Tomorrow, maybe, I could go a little further, ask more questions, and let him tell me why he left us.

I finally found my missing grandpa.

CHAPTER 25

Thursday, September 10th

A mixture of exhilaration, relief, and fear hung in my gut like a bowl of sour, but sweetly macerated berries. After spending the last few days with my new-found grandfather, I knew it was time to relay the stunning news to Dad and Rachel. My hesitation hinged purely on just that fact; it was stunning. In my heart, I felt like screaming it to the world, while at the same time, I wanted to keep it to myself, to savor the essence of what I had stumbled upon merely by chance in the neighborhood and the specific house I chose to move into. Granted, in the short period of time I've actually lived in this house, I hadn't realized there would be an unforeseeable attack on me that would lead me to this end result.

So, was I thankful or angry or somewhere in between?

For the heartache my family has endured over the last twenty-five years, the happenstance of finding my grandfather outweighs the torment and physical pain I had to go through. As long as my family never finds out, I can easily bury that incident as if I had watched Devin himself fall to his grave six feet under.

The keys found hidden in the wall jingled as I twisted them in my palm. I stopped by the day before to visit my grandpa, who had seemed brighter and cheerier as I walked through the door. Someone had opened the blinds a little more than usual, allowing the sun to shine at an angle, fixating its rays upon the mottled grays and blues of the VCT tile on the floor. I settled into the small fabric chair next to his bed. Since I'd been coming and staying so long, the staff thoughtfully switched out the hard metal chair for a softer, more comfortable chair during my visits. Many times, I'd end up closing my eyes and getting in a little cat-nap while Grandpa Ben dozed off. He's the one that whispered the word *cat-nap* to me which made me smile as I vaguely remembered, as a little girl, that my mother would call it that when she begged Rachel and I to lay down for a short time. "It's just a little cat-nap, girls. And then when you get up, I'll get you a root-beer popsicle," my mother would say during the summertime when we were out of school. As I got older, I realized that the bouncy energy Rachel and I had during the summertime had caused anxiousness in my mother. It also inhibited her day drinking which made her edgier toward us, tossing out activities for my sister and me to entertain ourselves with instead of hanging around her and interrupting her daily routine. Cat-naps next to my grandpa in his hospital bed were welcomed.

Without a true sense of urgency, I couldn't muster the nerve to ask Grandpa Ben what these keys were for. I know he noticed I held them in my hand. His gaze swept from my hand to my eyes, but he never said anything and I didn't ask. I imagined, though, a locked box possibly hidden in his house that held even more secrets from his past. Maybe he was waiting and would tell me later. He had acknowledged the cuff-links, but not the keys which increased my curiosity. A little part of me embraced the belief of waiting awhile longer, my questions would be answered. It surprised me how patient I already had been sitting next to him in his hospital bed for hours without bombarding him with questions that were bursting at my seams. Where did you go in 1989 and why did you go? Why would you leave your family? If you missed Grandma that much, why didn't you come to us for comfort? Didn't you love us enough? Why such lies?

Instead, I pulled up a few of my cooking videos on my cell phone and watched him with wide-eyed interest as he pointed at certain recipes. He'd then turn to me with a satisfied smile as he nodded. He wouldn't talk but a few words; "Yes" or "Really good." He pointed more than spoke, but I couldn't tell if that was because he was afraid to speak or if he had an impediment of some sort. It would behoove me to hastily rock the boat of my good fortune by being overanxious.

Grandpa Ben kept pointing to the wild rice dishes and used the thumbs-up gesture on the blueberry muffins and the parmesan-crusted walleye, which made me laugh. I said, "Then, you have to get better so we can fly back to Minnesota and go walleye fishing!" He wrinkled his nose, the corners of his mouth turning upward in a smile much wider than I'd seen so far. I noticed the color of his skin had taken on a rosier tone, not so ashy and dehydrated. It had only been a few short days on an IV, and they believed his heart had shown such an improvement that he'd be back home soon, but with stipulations on diet and rest.

That bit of news brought me a great sense of hope; hope that our relationship would soon evolve into a genuine grandfather/granddaughter bond. We could go back to playing games and going for walks like we used to. I couldn't wait to cook up a stack of lefse just for him to spread on rich butter and sprinkle with brown sugar. A pure Norwegian treat that just envisioning my family sitting around my dining room table and sharing anything I cooked, had me skipping to my car in the parking lot as I left the hospital.

I had texted Rachel earlier and asked her to either go to Dad's or ask him to drive to her house, that I had something important to tell the two of them, but they had to be together. She chose to drive the twenty minutes from Owatonna to Austin, and she was to text when they were ready.

Rachel: This better be good because you got me all riled up.

Me: Do you think I'd tease you?

Rachel: Really???

Rachel put me on speakerphone. I struggled on how to begin and half expected them to respond by asking me what I was smoking, it was such a mind- boggling revelation. Tears started warming the corners of my eyes as the excitement of revealing such news flooded my veins. I smeared whatever mascara I had left on my lashes as I wiped my eyes dry.

"Hey," I said, my voice trembling as I prepared to deliver the long-awaited news.

"What's going on, Rave? I can hear your heart racing through the phone," Rachel said, a touch of impatient annoyance in her tone. I could see her sitting on the edge of the couch perpendicular to Dad's chair, with her knees bouncing like a little girl dying to open a Christmas present.

"I found Grandpa." The words just flew out of my mouth. I drew in a breath and then took a long quiet draw from my wine glass.

"Where?" It was Rachel again, her tone demanding and hinting at disbelief. I could hear my dad clearing his throat but wasn't sure which one was fidgeting in their chair to make such a rustling noise in the background.

In a flat, precise tone, my father said, "You found Benjamin Pierce III? Your mother's father?"

"Yes, I did, Dad. Right here in Florida…"

"Raven Elaine, if this is a joke," Rachel cut in. I figured she'd say something like that.

For her to insinuate I'd play such a trick pissed me off, but this wasn't a battle worth fighting about with her. She would soon understand and change her tune.

"My God, Rachel, of course not." I swallowed another gulp of my wine and eye-rolled toward the ceiling before I started to explain to them about the sad old man named Harry, and how he refused to associate with anyone in the neighborhood, that as soon as I had moved in, I was essentially told about his request not to bother him. And then I said, "He intrigued me even more after I learned my house was the first he had built in this development. Luke found a bunch of items hidden in the walls after the sheetrock was torn away, and we wondered why and who put them there in the first place. It was such a mystery to me that I had to know why someone would do that.

"What proof do you have that it's him?" Dad asked.

"Yeah, what proof? Spit it out, for God's sake," Rachel practically yelled in frustration. I heard Dad whisper in the background telling Rachel to settle down, to let me talk.

"Sorry…I'm just overwhelmed telling you this. When I found out what hospital he was in, I brought the mood stone cufflinks that were found in the empty walls and had them in my open palm when he pointed to one and said 'Rachel' then pointed to the other and said, 'Raven.' I was shocked. He remembered Rachel. He remembered we had given them to him."

"Wait…he's in the hospital?" Rachel said.

"You found the cuff links in the wall?" My dad's voice faded at the end.

"Yes, and yes," I said. "He was taken by ambulance last Saturday. And Luke also found a locket in the wall with a woman's picture in it, and I think it's Grandma when she was much younger. And, Dad, I think I found a newspaper clipping of the accident that was also hidden. That's why I asked you what kind of car she was in during the accident." My excitement started scrambling my sentences together, so I stopped to take a breath and let them process what I'd said so far. "He also said 'granddaughter' when our eyes met for the first time. When I said, 'Grandpa Ben,' he nodded. Dad, Rachel, we found Grandpa Ben." I heard sniffling and my dad clearing his throat. I heard the familiar squeak of the recliner my dad usually sits in.

He mumbled something to Rachel, and then I heard her say, "Okay. Dad's going to get something to drink. Are you sipping on something, Rave?" I hesitated before responding because I sensed a hint of chastisement from her. Rachel was so good at criticizing at the wrong moments.

"Listen, Rachel…"

"Hey…I'm not pointing a finger. I just wanted to ask because I think that's what Dad's doing, and I was going to find something too. This is a celebration moment…for real! Plus our nerves are on fire."

Dad resumed his seat in the recliner and said as much as Rachel fetched a drink of some kind. I heard a heavy sigh from him, and then Rachel said, "Okay, I'm back. Dad's got his Coors Light, and I've got a…a tasty margarita in a can. Let's cheers to the best news this family has been waiting to hear!" A soft clink on the other end of the line had me raising my glass in the air, and then finishing what I had in my glass, I reached for the bottle and refilled it.

The only sounds were the sniffling on the other end and my own shaky breaths mingling with the tears streaming over my cheeks. I was so overjoyed to be telling them this great news. I hadn't even told Cassie and Luke the news yet, but at this very moment, I was too thrilled and happy to be sitting alone, my dad and sister at the other end of the phone line, enjoying a celebration drink together. The three of us share in a hallelujah moment. It made me think of my mother, and I grew sad. She's the one that has been the most emotionally damaged by the disappearance of my grandfather, and guilt crept through my veins not being able to have her here during this reveal. My heart ached for her to finally learn the good news.

My father cleared his throat again, a clear indication of his struggle to regain composure. "Oh, sweetheart…," he began, his voice thick with emotion, but then the words seemed to get stuck. Rachel had gone strangely quiet. She was usually the outspoken one, always quick to respond. But this time, her silence spoke volumes. It was filled with the shock and disbelief that mirrored my own when I first stumbled upon Grandpa Ben.

"I... we need a moment," Rachel finally managed to croak out, her voice barely a whisper. The line went quiet again, but the silence was no longer awkward or anxious. It was heavy with unsaid words and sniffles that sounds muffled by a tissue, our hearts brimming with the possibility of a reunion long overdue.

"Rave, do we know why he left?"

"I didn't want to ask yet. I couldn't ask. The nurses are watching him closely because of his condition. They already chewed me out once for causing an emotional upset in him. And besides, I had to lie to be able to visit him."

Dad asked, "Why?" I heard the crinkle of his beer can as he took a drink.

"Well, the man in the hospital is named Harry Fishmen, not Benjamin Pierce."

"Then how do you know it's really him, Raven." Rachel was getting a little frantic. "Are you sure? How do you know you're not being played?"

"I've already explained the proof. And besides, why would this man pretend to be our grandfather? What would he have to gain from that? It doesn't make sense."

"That all makes sense, but do you think the recognition of the cufflinks is proof enough?" Dad asked. Then I heard him say under his breath, "That makes him seventy-seven this December."

In my mind, it would be a silly question. "Why would this person call out me and Rachel's name when he saw the cufflinks? You're not suggesting this is a common occurrence and that…"

Rachel chimed in, "Raven, jeez, that's not what Dad's saying."

"We're all under happy stress right now. Let's not overdo this. Please." I let out a huff of breath, trying to rethink my next step. "I'm hoping we can stay positive with all this until I get more information from him?" It was more a question than a statement directed at Rachel. "Are you okay, Dad?"

"Raven, in over twenty-five years, I haven't felt this much relief. Getting your mother the help she needed for years comes close, but not like this," he said, his voice much more stable.

It had occurred to me, while I watched Grandpa Ben doze off into a deep sleep, that he might not tell me everything my family wished to learn about his disappearance, that he won't open up to me once he was home. We had started off so strangely, him peering at me through his windows, a scowl pressed deep into his face as he yelled at Devin to get rid of me. Those memories still vivid and hurtful. But now that he's accepting me and sees who I really am, and can trust me now. But will that allow or hinder him from telling me the whole truth?

"I guess I'm still in shock and can't quite believe it," Rachel's tone airier and distant as if she still needed convincing that this was the truth. I understood all too well. It took hours of sitting next to him in his hospital room, staring at him while he napped, observing the way he grabbed his spoon to bring a bite of food to his mouth and watching the way he winked and smiled at me instead of using his words before I realized that he cares, that he wanted me close by. I could feel in his heart that he enjoyed my company and was relieved that I had found him.

."Will you two book flights here, and can we get Mom out of treatment early, or do we have to wait till October before she'd be able to come?"

."We'll figure that out," my dad said using a cautious tone. "I'll call or email the details once Rachel and I talk with her counselor. I'm sure there can be an exception to the rules in this case."

."Raven, thank you for this. If this is real, and I know you believe it as well, life is going to change drastically for all of us," Rachel said. "I can't believe we'll be seeing our grandpa again. We all thought he was dead. I can only imagine what Mom…" It had been a long time, but I definitely heard the sincerity in her voice toward me.

Maybe inadvertently, my obsession with Harry was the catalyst to stitching the gap in our relationship. It may bring us closer. Stranger things have been happening lately.

."Hold off," Dad said, responding to Rachel's over-excited enthusiasm. "One thing at a time. We need to look out for your mother's welfare first. I mean, this is purely the reason she went down this road in the first place." We all sighed, and then I heard him take in a breath before he went on. "Raven…has he asked about your mom?"

."No, Dad. Not yet."

"That's understandable. I don't know what I was thinking. I'm sure he's in as much shock as you are and now the two of us sitting here miles away." I think the beer might have eased his tension some. I sipped more wine and ate a few bites of cheese while I listened to them reminisce about past memories and ponder the future. Minutes later, we said our goodbyes.

The two of them were going to go out for dinner and talk over a plan, which made this all seem even more real. So much had happened since that disturbing last day just over a month ago when

Rachel cursed me for abandoning the family, and my father stood holding my drunken mother back from falling all over me. Now, I'm the one bringing us all together, and it filled my heart with a new sense of purpose and a confirmation that I hadn't made a mistake in moving away. Unfortunately, I've had to withstand the demons of Devin Hampton behind the iron gate of Bay Harbor. But my outlook can change as this dream comes true.

I made notes of the dishes I wanted to prepare for Grandpa Ben once he arrived home. I would have to wait for the green light first. *Grandpa Ben-* To roll those words, that name, around in my head and out loud on my tongue still felt strange no matter how many times I'd tell myself it was the truth. It created a panicked excitement inside of me that lingered, never fully going away. It was like a permanent Post-it note reminder stuck to your heart.

I pondered with how the man known to most as Harry had placed his trust in people who were far from deserving of it. Devin, with his deceitful charm, and Frankie, with her cunning guise, had manipulated him and played on his vulnerabilities and expected to inherit his belongings when he died. It pained me to imagine my grandpa, isolated and misguided, having faith in such unsavory characters. The trust he had for them was supposed to be a safe haven, but instead, it was exploited. The thought left a bitter taste in my mouth, yet it also hardened my resolve. I would make sure my grandfather would never fall prey to such people again.

Today, as I left to hug him goodbye, I said, "See you later, Grandpa Ben," and then the nurse walked in. Not nurse Susan, who was in charge the last two days, someone different.

"Ben?" I couldn't believe how careless I was. I'm sure she saw the color rise in my cheeks.

Stammering to make up some excuse, I lied and said, partly chuckling, holding my hand on my chest, "Oh, well, my sister and I liked his middle name better; Benjamin. So, we always called him Grandpa Ben instead of Grandpa Harry. He didn't mind." I glanced back at the man lying in a hospital bed, and saw him squint his eyes.

"I see," said the nurse who I hadn't met before. Her name tag read: Brita. She was dressed in flamingo-pink scrubs and had the creamy brown skin of Whitney Houston. She had her hair pulled into a tight bun at the top of her head. "Are you the contact on this gentleman's paperwork? Miss…." Her hands flipped through papers on a clipboard.

"Yes, I am. Raven McKade." I held out my hand.

"Oh, I see now, Miss McKade." She walked over to me, limply shook my hand with her left and then pointed to a cell number to verify. I nodded and signed where she told me. "I, or my supervisor, will contact you when we will be driving Mr. Fishmen back to his residence. It's already stated he will be arriving by ambulance and will have a staffed nurse with him 24/7. They will introduce themselves and give you the parameters and particulars of his healthcare while they are attending to him."

"I could drive him home."

"No, ma'am. It has to be by non-emergency ambulance. He'll be in a hospital bed, and a medical assistant needs to handle the medical equipment and whatnot associated with his proper care." She smiled and asked, "Is there anything else, Miss McKade?" I shook my head. She turned and walked out, leaving me with a man they knew as Harry Fishmen.

My phone rang, shaking me out of the hazy stupor I was in. "Hello, this is Raven."

"Miss McKade, this is Brita. How are you doing?" I was going to answer, but she carried on like there wasn't time for small talk. "I'm calling you to let you know that your grandpa will be arriving at his home on Saturday the twelfth. It will be after twelve noon, and please be aware that you may not spend a lot of time with him that day as he'll need to rest and recuperate in his own surroundings first before he can be entertained by friends and family." I understood and told her so, but unfortunately, the nurse didn't realize I'd be the only one "entertaining" him till my family arrived.

I had two days to grocery shop for all the ingredients on my list for the dishes I was looking forward to cooking and baking for Grandpa Ben. After I hung up from the hospital, I had a boost of energy, so I set up my video equipment and box lighting on the island in preparation for my food vlog postings tomorrow. I wanted to start first thing in the morning as soon as my coffee buzz kicked me into gear. The plan was to post two featured videos. The first recipe was a gochujang glazed salmon with garlic spinach, and the second--a complement to the first--a mango yogurt tart. My mouth watered, just writing them down in my notebook. I was so excited for my grandpa to try them.

I took the copper-tarnished keys held together by a knotted rubber band out of my pocket and held them. A memory came to me of my grandmother. I faintly remember making lefse with my mom, my aunts, and cousins and envisioning my grandma sitting in a tall wooden ladder-backed chair at the dining room table, stacking lefse in cling wrap packages. She had a permanent smile on her face like she was a statue in a department store window. And then the memory disappeared; I couldn't remember anymore. Did these keys belong to Grandma? Why did I think of her while I held them? I rubbed some more and thought about Grandpa, my eyes pinched shut. Nothing.

Grandpa Ben will tell what these keys open.

CHAPTER 26

Friday, September 11ᵗʰ

Unfortunately, I had procrastinated to the nth degree. Violet was coming at 4 o'clock today to go over the details for her father's vendor party. I never canceled with Drew and never justifiably mentioned anything to Violet. I stared out the window and wondered why I so decidedly neglected or refrained from having this important conversation with Drew. We haven't spoken in days. And now I've got Violet coming over, thinking I'm still head over heels with delight in catering Drew's party.

And how do I explain it to a fifteen-year-old girl in a way that she'd understand? That the potential of being her stepmother was next to nil? To explain to her that her father faltered to the point of dismissing her concerns for her uncle and allowed the despicable man to associate with everyone? No matter how chocolate-covered the words, they're going to come out spicy and hurt with a hot chili pepper zing.

While the coffee brewed, I responded to Violet's text confirming our time of 4 p.m., and then I wondered what her father had been telling her. Has he admitted his mistake of allowing Devin to work in this neighborhood? Or, did he pretend that our lack of communication was due to something else going on in my life, that I was distracted at the moment? Wrapping my fingers around my second cup of coffee—the first didn't make it ten minutes--I settled into the corner of my couch and pulled my legs to the side of me. I had a nagging push-pull motion going on inside like a taffy-pulling machine. If I was to be honest, I believe one of the reasons I hadn't declined my services for his vendor party was simply because of the feelings I have puttering around my heart like a craving that needed to be satisfied. One minute I'm swearing at him and hating what I've had to go through because of his brother, and in the next minute, I'm swearing at myself for not forgiving him and allowing the man who already confessed his love for me to be in my life. It's as if I'm needing something from him and can't seem to let go despite the anger and resentment that's built up. You'd think I was starring in some soap opera with the way my emotions feel so dramatized.

I got up to pour another cup of coffee.

After changing into my yellow silk top and navy-blue capris, I gathered all the dishes I was going to use in my cooking video. For this video, I decided to clip my hair behind my ears for that uncomplicated look. The recipe was gochujang-glazed salmon with garlic spinach which sounds like it could be complicated, but in reality, very simple and quick.

After grating the ginger and garlic into separate small sauce dishes, I cut the salmon into four filets. By the time I made the glaze and generously brushed it over the salmon, the spinach was just starting to wilt, so I put the salmon under the broiler and set the timer for the required amount of time. In ten minutes, the dish would come together. I explained to the viewers that the prep was the catalyst for bringing it all together in a jiffy. I served it on an oval white platter, the dark green spinach lightly scattered beneath the blush tone of the salmon filets, and added a sprinkling of chopped green onion over the top. The kitchen smelled of fresh ginger, and sautéed garlic in toasted sesame oil. The earthy spiciness of the gochujang hung on my tongue.

For my next video, I slipped into the blue and white striped boat neck top and slid on a wide navy-blue headband for a different look. I was preparing a mango yogurt tart. It took an hour to prepare the tart crust. Once that had cooled, I set out the dishes I'd be using and the ingredients for the mango tart recipe. It was nearly 2 o'clock, and Violet was coming at four, so this would work out just fine. It wasn't my intention to hurt her in any way, but telling her it would be a mistake to cater this event could put her in an ugly situation in regard to me. I couldn't disregard the fact her father lived just three houses down.

After I blended the filling ingredients, notes of vanilla and cardamom filled the space between me and the camera. I smiled, and with a wave of my hand, I took a whiff and described the scent to the viewers; "it smells just like splitting open a vanilla bean and crushing a cardamom pod." Peeling the mangos, a sweet fruit aroma permeated the air and smelled so delicious I slipped a juicy piece into my mouth while I sliced the rest. I had to shut the camera off one more time to let the tart cool down in the freezer for twenty minutes, a shortcut to get it chilled enough to cut and take a bite for the viewers. I couldn't believe how luscious this dessert was. I'd never had the chance to make it, but the recipe hung out with many others I'd been holding onto for some time.

Violet rang the doorbell at 4 p.m. sharp. I still felt on the edge of decline and somehow needed to explain to this pretty little daughter of Drew's that I couldn't cater his party, that it didn't feel right, and I simply wouldn't enjoy it. I poured a small glass of wine and grabbed the recipes and notes I had taken, anyway, and set them on the island in hopes this would all blow over, ending with a friendly hug. When I opened the door, an exquisite example of a young model dressed in a printed, smocked sundress tied at her tanned shoulders stood before me. Her radiant smile, perfect in its symmetry, was as genuine as it was captivating. She was the epitome of youthful beauty and poise and made me proud even if I wasn't her mother. Drew had to be proud of his daughter. With a hand on one hip and a bouquet of flowers in the other, she walked through to the kitchen as if she'd been through runway training.

She handed me the bouquet, a mixture of yellow and orange daisies and baby's breath and said, "Here's the note that goes with it, but you're not to read it yet. Not till I leave." She nodded her head once and grinned, proud that she carried out her mission with precision. And then she quickly added, "And, oh, by the way, hello, Raven." She leaned in and gave me a warm hug and a kiss on my cheek, which I wasn't prepared for. In fact, the heat rose in my cheeks from what possible devastation lay ahead.

"Hello, Violet. Don't you look adorable?" I said, my eyes quickly giving her a once over before taking the bouquet and lifting my chin in curiosity. I centered my nose over an orange daisy and slowly inhaled the slight fruity aroma.

"Remember, don't read till I leave," she demanded, holding up a finger; a side smile dimple appeared on her left cheek.

"Is that so?" I replied with a playful tone as I placed the vase on the table. "These are beautiful, and they're my absolute favorite." And then I remember telling Drew that same thing the night he had me over for my first sunset. I swallowed hard and turned to see Violet staring at me. I gestured for Violet to take a seat at the end of the bar and asked her if she wanted something to drink.

"I'll have sparkling water. I know you have that because it's one of your favorites, too," she said in a matter-of-fact tone. "And, oh, here's a list we need for our planning." She took a folded piece of paper out of her tiny pink leather purse hanging from a thin strap across her body and handed it to me.

As I opened it, a credit card fell out. I picked it up and noticed it had my name on it. I shrugged my shoulders in defeat as I tilted my head at Violet, my forehead twisted in confusion.

"He said you might do that." She moved closer to me, her voice more like a whisper, and put a hand on my shoulder, then added, "Dad wanted you to use this at your leisure for his party. He completely trusts you, Raven, so there's no worries. Isn't that great?" There was an excited catch in her voice. Her smile braced by tiny dimples at each end. It made my guilt run deeper. This may be a fifteen-year-old girl, but at the moment, it was more like a fifteen-year-old matchmaker.

I gave her a gratifying smile and realized Drew was trying hard to connect the dots between us through his daughter. Surprisingly, I wasn't as disappointed as I thought I would be. In fact, my insides softened a bit by her words, but I still felt the need to be cautious. If it wasn't for her father's twin brother, who nearly raped me, I'd see things differently. And if I spoke my concerns with Violet, would she have the answers or at least a legitimate response to the security breach in my own home? It would be a tragedy to tell her what her uncle did to me.

With our drinks at the island, we spread out the lists she had brought and the recipes I had chosen. Drew had picked the same three choices I had secretly hoped he'd choose when he took me on a date to Tiffany's, but I was curious as to what Violet might choose.

"Oh wow! Prosciutto wrapped pear and arugula? Never had that before. Yum. I think my dad will love it!" My eyes didn't move from watching the enthusiasm light up her face as she flipped through the choices, her eyes widened with excitement.

I suddenly realized I couldn't go through this. A vice clamped around my stomach. Who was the adult here? Me. And that meant it was up to me to say something. "Violet." I rubbed my forehead so hard I felt heat generating and my skin starting to peel. I lifted my eyes directly at hers and said in a broken voice, "I… can't…do this. I'm sorry. Your father will have to find someone else." I formed an "O" with my lips and let out a breath as if I'd been holding it for hours. Violet's eyes darted between the ceiling and me. She pulled in both lips making a tiny chomping motion. In the silence, my heart picked up an unhealthy rhythm, and I suddenly felt dizzy.

I got up and grabbed a bottle of water. When I finished, I turned back to Violet, who seemed to read and understand my abrupt movements. "Raven, can I ask you something?" I nodded. "Are you in love with my father?"

I nearly choked and, instead, coughed into my closed palm to cover it up. That was the last thing I thought would come out of Violet's mouth. I didn't respond because I didn't know what to say.

"I know I'm young, and you don't really know me, but I know my dad, and he's in love with you," Violet said in a tone so sweet cake icing had to be melting close by. My breath quickened, making it an arduous task to look at her. I had to admit, I was a little intimidated with her forwardness, although not aggressive.

"How do you know this?" My voice held a bitter note, but I didn't correct it. The push-pull reaction started again.

"Because he told me. He's going to ground me for telling you this, but he can't stop talking about you. See, we're close, and he trusts me. He's been miserable all week, Raven. All he does is sit around or sleep…or lay by the pool staring into the sky like he's begging for you to show up. I swear he's started praying." She took a drink of her water, and I could see how nervous she was becoming. Her hands noticeably shook as she set the glass back down. As she bent her head, I saw a tear drip onto the counter. She quickly wiped it away and lifted her head to look at me. "Uncle Devin is a cruel man, and my dad knows what a horrible thing he…."

"You know what he did to me?"

"Yes, my dad told me. When you called him a rapist at the…" Violet stood and approached me, but for some reason, I held my hand up for her to stop. I was livid inside. The fact that Drew told her Devin had attacked me pushed me over the edge. I didn't need this fifteen-year-old young girl to know this about her uncle, whether she claimed him as a family member or not. It was my business and my business only. I hadn't realized that she'd heard me say that. I didn't want her feeling bad for telling me.

I lowered my head in an apology to her, and she sat back down on the barstool with a mature poise of understanding. "I'm not trying to hurt you, Violet," I said, touching her hand. "You're a wonderful sweet girl, but for you to know what he did to me…"

"He tried to do that to me," she blurted out in a solid angry tone, her eyes filled with shock. She withdrew her hand from under mine.

"And your dad knows this?"

"No. He just thinks I hate Uncle Devin because of what he did to a classmate of mine. He doesn't know he tried to do that to me. I think my dad would kill him." Her head fell to her chest, and she fiddled with her nails. And that's when her body jerked with sobs. I immediately went to her and wrapped my arms around her.

We cried, holding each other for a long time without speaking. Finally, after tear-stained cheeks and my tear-soaked shirt, we released each other. I stood close enough to hear her labored breathing and saw a depth of sorrow in her golden-flecked hazel eyes that gave me solace. She has been fighting the demon of Devin while shouldering her dad's pain of losing me. This young girl had taken on an adult matter with such courage. Protecting her father at the cost of her own safety and security humbled me to my core.

"Violet, you are a beautiful child," I said, taking her face in my hands. I had no idea what it was like to be a mother, let alone a mother to a near-adult, but now, I could sympathize with Cassie. "I can't disappoint you anymore." I placed her cheek to my chest and closed my eyes as new tears fell onto her silky mahogany-colored hair. I felt her shoulders tremble ever so lightly, and then I heard a soft giggle. I let go of her and watched her pat the top of her head.

"You're soaking my hair now." Both of us laughed and wiped our faces clean with tea towels I had hanging nearby. "Does this mean you will cater my dad's party?"

Of course, I hesitated, but only for a moment, and then I drew in a deep breath. "Yes, I will, Violet. Just for you." I winked and pecked the end of her nose. While we continued with the party planning, a permanent smile replaced the frown from earlier.

By the time we were done, we had three different lists in front of us: Food, Drinks, and Decorations. We had fun picking out most of the decorations online. Violet said she would get what we didn't order online at Party City with her friend, Felicia, who was also going to help us serve at the party. We decided to wear black shorts and white short-sleeve cotton tops with small black and white striped aprons. Violet's idea to wear something red in our hair or even a bright red baseball cap was the perfect addition to this occasion.

It was a joy to have her help me plan this, especially after spilling our hearts to one another. I will treasure this day and never forget how she taught me that forgiveness is the only way to heal and that I don't need to bury myself in seclusion. It was a relief to have it all out in the open, knowing Devin is far away from the both of us and that we have each other to depend on when it comes to safety and security of our secrets.

With the commitment to catering her father's party, I had a million more questions filling my head as I made copies of the itinerary for Violet and her friend before she left to go back home to her dad's house. I wondered what she was going to say to him? Should I tell her I'd prefer she not say anything or let her be the trusted daughter and just let it go? That I had enough to worry about when it came to addressing Drew myself and how I was going to initially react to him? I really thought Drew and I were on the backburner, that we'd soon learn to be friends again but that was where it would end. We'd courteously say or wave a "hello" as we drove or walked by one another since we lived so close to each other. After all that's happened and now that I have a very important task on my hand—reuniting my family with a long-lost family member—my personal life has to take second place. I feel too weak to have to endure both at the moment.

Granted, Violet has shed a new light on the subject of Drew and me, but it will have to be at my pace. I slipped the credit card into my purse and then opened the note inside the tiny white envelope tucked into the flowers that Violet happily reminded me to do on her way out the door.

It read:

Dear Raven,

Please, forgive me, for my heart has never known a woman like you.

Please, forgive me, for my heart can't be without you.

Please, forgive me, for my heart is in love with yours.

Drew

Texting Drew felt like the right thing to do. I picked up my phone, my trembling fingers barely able to tap on the correct letters, and sent him a message. Within, what seemed like minutes, I heard a knock at my front door. I opened it to find Drew standing there, his eyes filled with a mix of surprise, relief, and concern. The lines and puffiness around his eyes confirmed what Violet had said earlier. *So, this was Harvey Specter on a bad day.*

"Drew," was all I could manage before I leaped at him. He wrapped his arms around me, his sturdy presence a comforting anchor in the emotional storm I had pent up inside me for so long. I thought I had more control, but just seeing the distressed look in his glossed-over eyes and the bristly shadow on his face, I melted like a whipped teenager. Thankfully, my embarrassment was hidden against his shirt as I inhaled his beauty and manly scent.

"Shh... it's okay," he murmured, holding me tighter, his own emotions spilling over. His shoulders shook slightly as he, too, allowed his tears to fall. This wasn't just a moment of shared sorrow; it was an intimate weaving of our spirits, an acknowledgment of the deep-seated empathy that linked our hearts together.

Right then, I realized the origin and gave credit to the only one responsible for this; Jack. On his deathbed, Jack wished for me a good life and prayed for me that I'd find another despite the massive protesting I did as he spoke. He laughed at my resistance and told me he loved me more for even suggesting I was never going to find a love like we had ever again. I didn't want to hear such things from him. It hurt my very soul to hear him say such things while he was slipping away from me.

But now, my heart has been opened to such an opportunity.

CHAPTER 27

Saturday, September 12th

Over a breakfast of smoked salmon toast and a fresh avocado dotted with cherry tomatoes, I began to unfold the story of Benjamin Pierce, aka Harry, to Drew. I could see the surprise register on his face as I recounted the details.

"So, you mean to tell me that our Harry, the Harry who lives at the end of Spoonbill is actually your long-lost grandfather? And you didn't mention this last night?" Drew asked, pausing mid-bite on his toast.

I nodded. "Yes, Drew. It's hard to believe, isn't it? It's an incredible fact to swallow for me and my family, but it's true." I took a sip of coffee before I continued. "I wanted to get our differences out in the open first before I felt comfortable talking about Harry."

His eyes bore into mine, searching for some sign that I might have been mistaken, but he saw nothing but sincerity. He combed his fingers through his hair and sighed, setting down his toast. We had looming signs of a late night; puffy eyes, and strained expressions of why and how we ended up in each other's arms last night. We'd barely had four hours of sleep. On top of that, for me, waiting till this morning to reveal the astonishing truth about Harry Fishmen had me waking every so often with anticipation.

It was hard to fathom that I woke next to Drew, who seemed to have slept like a baby while I tossed and turned with an insatiable need to tell him this good news.

"But... how? When? How is this even possible?" He sputtered, still in shock.

I detailed the entire happenings, explaining the search my family conducted, the keys and cufflinks he had witnessed us pulling out of the box, and finally, the revelation. His surprise turned into fascination as he listened to me, and his eyes held a newfound respect.

"According to the medical assistant that would be riding with Harry—Grandpa Ben--back to his house, we wouldn't be able to see him till closer to dinner time. So, I've made arrangements to bring him dinner tonight. They advised a light meal, something gentle and easily digestible. I thought about a simple chicken soup," I added, breaking the flow of the story.

Drew nodded, processing the information. "No wild rice, though."

"Ah…you're right, Drew," I confirmed that the medical assistant had put a nix on wild rice. "I guess it's going to be just the soup and some bread then."

Drew's gaze softened, and he took my hand, giving it a reassuring squeeze. "I can't believe it. Your grandpa...our Harry. This is insane, but...it's also kind of wonderful, isn't it?"

Despite the complexity of the situation, I found myself smiling at his words. Yes, it was indeed wonderful, a mix of miraculous coincidence and fate. "Yes, Drew," I finally responded. "It truly is." Simultaneously, we leaned in for a kiss.

Last night, under the glow of the moon, we exchanged stories, laughter, and silence in equal measure. The lanai had been my sanctuary, but now it was becoming our shared retreat, a testament to our growing bond that both of us had discussed in depth.

"You know I never in a million years thought that son-of-a-bitch would ever hurt anyone, especially you," Drew professed as he straightened himself on the lounger. The night was so beautiful we decided to carry on our conversation outside with another bottle of

Merlot. It definitely helped in talking out what we needed on the subject of his devious brother. It had to be resolved in order for Drew and I to move on.

I could feel the sorrow and how repulsed he was as we discussed his brother's actions. I poured another glass for each of us and kept my gaze to myself for the moment. Inside, I had opened up to him with caution and still needed some type of solidification that this was the right man for me, that resuming what we had started weeks ago was the right direction for me since my security and safety were the only reasons for moving to this location.

"Drew," I said, turning to face him, placing my elbows on the tops of my knees as I held my glass of wine, I inhaled and leaned my head back to gaze at the ceiling before I looked at him. I continued, pushing all resentment aside, "I know you were just trying to help your brother after that shameful thing he did, but I can't fathom allowing him back in here…."

"I know, Raven. That's where I could just…I know that was the biggest mistake." He took in a large gulp of his wine and held it in his puffed-out cheeks for a few seconds before swallowing. His body language made me uneasy. I'd hit a nerve, and he seemed as if he was going to explode. I intended this to be as relaxing as possible despite the subject matter, but I'm seeing that's more naivete on my part.

"Okay, let's back off this subject. Let's change it to us." I said, shifting back in my lounger and crossing my ankles. I'd slipped on a sweater and the fuzzy black flip-flops Cassie had purchased for me. I heard him sigh as he turned his attention to me. "Why do you feel it needs to be me?"

"Why it needs to be you that I want to marry?" He said, his tone slow and deliberate. I nodded and placed my lips on the edge of my glass, waiting very still for his answer. "For every reason, Jack fell in love with you."

I gasped.

"You can't compare…"

"Yes. I. can." My heart lurched at his words, and I started nibbling the edge of my glass. I couldn't tell if I should have been insulted by him bringing up Jack or honored by his recognition of who Jack really was.

Minutes later, after staring into each other's eyes like lovers in a classical movie, I finally responded, "Oh…kay." My voice broke, a lump caught in the middle of my throat that swigging my wine and swallowing hard didn't remove it. And then Drew snickered, which embarrassed me.

"Okay? That's what you say to a man who wants to marry you in the worst way?" He chuckled lightly as he rubbed his chin, a baffled look on his face.

"Could it be the…best way?" I asked much later, my voice timid.

The lanai was now becoming the haven where our love story was unfolding. Just like in a fairy-tale.

The temperatures had dropped overnight, and my weather app said it was only sixty-six outside compared to the normal eighty-degree range. It was 9 a.m. I slid on a sweater and yoga leggings, and we took another cup of coffee out to my lanai. Thankfully, Drew had gone home last night to grab his toothbrush and some other clothes, including a white Hampton Pools sweatshirt, which he put on over a t-shirt and tan cargo shorts. The morning sun nearly blinded us, so I ran in to get our sunglasses. It was a comical scene, bundled up in layers of clothing like a crisp Autumn day in Minnesota and drinking coffee with sunglasses on. Only in Florida? We clinked our coffee cups, toasting to a mutual coming together of our hearts, letting the forgiveness thrive and the past linger with or without answers.

"When does Violet come home?" I asked.

"Well, being it's a Saturday, and she's at Felicia's, they usually come up with something that she'll ask permission about. I doubt I'd see her before dinner time." He took a drink of his coffee and turned to me, "What were you thinking?"

"Oh, nothing in particular." I looped my messy hair around my ears and drank from my cup, looking at him. Shock wasn't the right word for what my body was sensing, but it was close. I giggled, remembering I called him Harvey last night. I believe it started with the opening of the second bottle of Merlot around 10 p.m.

"You're laughing at me again, aren't you? Something I did?" He raised his eyebrows, nodding as if claiming he was right in his accusation.

"No, no, Harvey."

"Oh, God. Please, not the Harvey thing." He let out a hearty chuckle. I couldn't help but laugh along with him. It felt so simple to be enjoying coffee and the sunshine with a man that radiated like a protective shield around me—a protective aura that was palpable and soothing. I found myself basking in this comforting radiance. It felt good to have the control of letting it seep into my skin and chase away any lingering shadows. A simple pleasure, yet so profound.

It was time to bring Grandpa Ben his dinner. My heart raced as we pulled up into his driveway. I had no idea what to expect as we walked through the door or how we were going to react to each other. Would he change his mind and refuse our visit? Would he wish he'd never admitted who he was? Is he going to refuse my questions and tell me to leave him alone? The anxiety building up inside me those few short blocks nearly sent my blood pressure into the universe. I also had to remember his name was Harry to everyone else, so that made it sketchy as to how I should address him. Drew warned me the medical person staying with him knows him only as Harry. That made me wonder if we'd be able to have a private meeting with him or would they, by protocol, have to be in the room with us.

I knocked, and it didn't take long for a tall curvy woman around the age of forty to answer the door. She had creamy white skin with freckles and long, bright red hair braided in the back. "You must be Miss McKade. Please, come in. Harry said he would be expecting you."

"Please, call me Raven, and this is Drew. He lives in the neighborhood as well." I said, looking for a name tag.

"Sorry, I'm Terri. Pleased to meet you, Raven. Drew." She only nodded. Her hands were covered with medical gloves, and her scrubs dotted in Disney characters. Only in Florida.

Terri walked us to the back of the house in a room with a large picture window that faced the pool and the woods surrounding the back of his property. Harry lay on a hospital bed with metal rails, his upper half tilted at an angle. He had tubes in his nose and an IV still attached to his right hand. He looked tired and gave Drew and me a slight nod of his head, acknowledging us. I walked over to him and kissed his forehead, and then turned back to Terri and asked, "Are we able to visit with him in private?"

She checked her watch, tapped the top screen with the tip of a nail, and said she'd give us thirty minutes that he'd need his medication at that time. I handed her the soup and bread, and she said she'd warm it up when he wanted to eat.

"Grandpa," I whispered after she left the room. Drew sat on a club chair on the other side of the bed. The room felt dark, and the décor reminded me of something from the seventies with all the dark woods, and wainscoting that resembled the notorious paneling we all are familiar with, but this had a deeper grain pattern. Bookcases, from floor to ceiling, lined the largest wall in the room, and heavy leather furniture placed in two optional seating areas. I expected Hugh Heffner to walk out in his silk robe sporting a pipe. Grandpa smiled and lifted his left hand to my face.

"How do you feel? Are you hungry?" I asked.

He shook his head and said and in a hoarse voice, "I'm tired." I saw his chest rise and lower in rapid succession. Maybe he was just nervous, which made my nerves start firing even more. I glanced at Drew, who sat quietly, both arms resting on the smooth leather of the armrest, his eyes glued to what I was doing. Showered and dressed in light-colored shorts and a blue printed golf shirt, shaven and smelling like a million bucks, my eyes were fixed on him, and hadn't realized I was staring till he winked and broke my concentration. Immediately, I turned my attention back to Grandpa Ben.

I pulled a fabric roller chair, which looked like it came from a dining room set from the eighties, closer to Grandpa's bed, and sat down facing him. His eyes followed my every move. I wondered if he thought I looked different from what he remembered. I only thought that because my memory hadn't served me correctly. I remembered him as a smaller man with a rounder face. Lying here in this bed was a man with a strong, broad jaw who stood at least three inches taller than I had remembered. Obviously, my memory had become distorted with so many years in between.

As the years have passed, the clarity of my memories of Grandpa Ben has inevitably begun to blur. The detailed images of his face, the subtle creases of his smile, and the twinkle in his eye have faded, replaced by abstract impressions and fragments of recollections. No longer can I vividly recall the specifics of his appearance; I was so young when he disappeared. What kind of details can a ten-year-old remember anyway? It's as if I'm looking at him through a glass smeared with the patina of time. However, even these fragmented images are treasured, serving as a silent testament to a past that was once rich with his presence.

"Grandpa," I said, touching his warm, veiny hand. "Is it okay to ask you a question? About our past?" His lips stayed in a straight line, but his eyes shut tightly. I waited for him to open them. I could see he was hurting, but we all were. I kept swallowing to keep the tears at bay.

There wasn't time to fall apart and start over. I was on a crucial timer.

I pulled up a picture of the necklace on my phone and showed it to him. "Is this Grandma?" I observed his weary gray eyes staring at my phone. And then he nodded, but he didn't look back at me till I placed the phone on my lap. "You were sad about losing her a long time ago, weren't you? Is that why you ran away?"

My mother used to tell us, with such enthusiasm, stories about Grandpa and Grandma. She mentioned numerous times how Grandpa Ben's love for Grandma was an unspoken legend within our family. It sounded like a fairly-tale to Rachel and me as she spoke of their devotion and adoration that could outshine the most passionate love stories. Grandpa was utterly smitten by Grandma from the moment they first crossed paths, a starry-eyed young man enchanted by a vivacious and spirited girl. Grandpa Ben would often wake up before sunrise to prepare breakfast for Grandma, meticulously arranging her favorite fruits and brewing the perfect cup of coffee. He would remember the little things: the way she liked her eggs sunny-side up, the precise amount of sugar and cream in her coffee, and her favorite flowers—daylilies--that brightened her day. Even after Grandma passed, Mom said that Grandpa Ben would sometimes make two cups of coffee before realizing she wasn't sitting at the table any longer, that his enduring love for her was the only thing on his mind.

I wanted a marriage like that so badly as a young girl. I wanted to be like Grandpa and Grandma. My desire for a love like that had me daydreaming for the right man at a very young age. Rachel was the one that said she could wait, that she was going to have fun before falling in love. I felt for sure she had it backward.

Despite the heartbreak of losing her, he continued to carry her in his heart, a flame that never flickered out. I came to the conclusion that that's what pulled him away from us all. He couldn't live with the memories, so he disappeared without a trace to live a life of secrets, hidden from anyone that could be that constant reminder of who he'd lost in the first place.

It made me uneasy to watch him trying to adjust himself in his bed. I wasn't sure if he needed the restroom, or if he was in pain. He never said, regardless of my attempt to ask. Maybe I needed to call Terri back into the room. When I looked down, I noticed the drainage bag, so it wasn't that. He seemed uncomfortable, his troubled look somehow inflicting blame my way, and now I felt guilt for causing this. He pointed to the button that raised the top part of the bed, and I pushed it till he gestured for me to stop. I still didn't understand why he wouldn't talk. He mostly pointed and whispered.

"I'm sorry," he finally said, his voice more than a whisper this time. I saw Drew's eyebrows lift at hearing his voice.

"Grandpa, listen. Do not apologize. Please." I held his hand in mine and looked directly into his sunken eyes. "Let's make this a happy occasion. It doesn't matter anymore why or how. Now that we've found one another again let's make the best of everything we've got right in front of us." I said, spilling out what words and sentences fell together. I hadn't rehearsed anything because when I tried, it didn't sound right, and I felt like I was trying to impute shame. So, I dismissed it.

I thought I'd need to tell him how sad we all were after he left and how much we missed him, but I got the sense that hearing those sentiments would hurt him too much. Maybe later, when he's healthier and stronger, can we express our emotions about him leaving. My parents were going to be here soon, and I prayed he'd be up and walking around soon, like the first time I jogged around this neighborhood and saw him with so much more strength in his body than what was evident at the moment.

"I brought you chicken soup and some biscuits. Terri said she'd get it for you when you were hungry. Are you hungry now?" That brought a big smile, and my heart soared with joy. He shook his head and grabbed my hand.

"I missed you," he said, tears dripping into the deep crevices on his face. Mine poured out like water from a faucet, and I didn't bother wiping them away. I just placed my head on his side, paying sole attention to his breathing, the heat from his body, and the clicking of the machine next to his bed. The smell alone wasn't so pleasant, but he was surrounded by hospital equipment and medicinal drugs. I figured once he's in his own bed and this hospital equipment is removed, I'd help with the cleaning and burn some tropical-scented candles to freshen up the rooms, removing the evidence of the hospital impediments.

Terri walked in, poking that same finger at her watch. "I'm sorry, but time is up. Harry needs to eat something and take his medicine. You're welcome to come back tomorrow." I moved out of the way so she could put the temp monitor on his forehead.

Drew stood and walked over to me and smiled at Grandpa Ben, patting his hand. While Terri pushed over a sliding table toward his bed, he said to Drew, "Take care of her."

Drew pulled me into a strong side hug, responding with, "There's no doubt I will. We'll see you tomorrow, Harry." That name rolled right off Drew's tongue as if my calling him Grandpa Ben was just a kid's memory for me. He was Harry to everyone but me.

In the five minutes it took to drive back to my place, I wondered if Grandpa Ben had any concerns about Devin and if he even crossed his mind now that we'd connected.

CHAPTER 28

Wednesday, September 16th

My mother's release from rehab was approved. A simultaneous sigh of relief as my father told me the good news. The three of us—Dad, Rachel, and I—agreed to keep the news of locating her father to ourselves until we all had a fair amount of time to be together in person. The idea to overwhelm her as soon as she stepped past the threshold of the rehabilitation center would likely cause her to fall three steps back just from the shock of it all. Disbelief was powerful, and an olive branch to emotional relief could be found again inside a bottle. Our union on this decision made it much easier to shelf such amazing news, knowing there was a time and a place for everything, including the news of finding your father alive after twenty-five years.

Their flights were booked, and they'd be arriving in Tampa next Wednesday, September 23rd. Rachel, her husband, Pete, and their two girls, —Lindsay and Lexi— were also coming to stay, so the six of them would be waking up in my new house that they'd only seen in pictures. They were aware of the time and effort it took to design my sweet beach home, although Rachel glossed over most details I unveiled when we were together. My gut told me she'd change her tune once she walked through my door. I couldn't describe in words the excitement of having my family staying for a few days. The sheer pleasure of this visit welled up inside like a spring in full bloom. With my hands overlapped on my chest and my head lowered, I silently thanked God for these miracles he's brought to me and my family. When was the last time I felt this grateful?

The last time all of us stayed under one roof was the weekend following Jack's funeral. I had stayed with Luke and Cassie, and the twins, in their hotel suite in Minneapolis. Being alone would have been detrimental after such a devastating loss. I knew they were right. By the time the funeral was over, barely able to hear and respond to another "I'm so sorry for your loss" sentiment, that I became zombie-like and shut down. "We want to be here for you, Rave. Please don't ask to be alone right now." Cassie had begged, and thankfully I was too exhausted to argue. They'd seen me at my worst; emotionally and physically so drained, Cassie had to help me get dressed for the funeral, so her begging turned into a blessing.

Before Cassie and Luke flew back to Florida, they had arranged with my parents and Rachel to at least urge, if not demand, that I spend the weekend with them in Austin. And I'm glad I did. Although, with all guarded emotions flung to the Spring winds, my mother and I imbibed in a love-hate relationship with a few bottles of wine while watching a movie that Saturday night. And then, Sunday, with Rachel and her family, we enjoyed pitchers of margaritas and Godfather's pizza that Dad and Pete had picked up. In my parent's backyard, the girls had decorated the picnic table with a tulip-embroidered tablecloth they found in one of the cabinets in the hallway of my parent's house. It had belonged to my grandmother, and when my mother noticed which one it was, she bit her lip and looked as if she was about to have them put it back, but instead smiled as she delicately ran her fingers over the bright red string outlining the shape of a tulip. I watched her bottom lip tremble and realized that the pain of losing my grandma and now Jack would never go away.

Despite our sorrow, it was a comfortable seventy-five-degree day in May, and my nieces were thrilled to have a pizza picnic with their grandparents and Aunt Raven. I relished in their sweet smiles with each cheesy bite of pizza they popped into their mouths. This wasn't the time or place to cry about the people who were missing from the table.

Rachel, Dad, and I decided it would be best to reveal the good news to Mom about Grandpa Ben once they arrived and were settled in, and we sensed she was steady enough to accept such an astonishing announcement. It was staggering for me when I learned the truth. I could only imagine how my mother was going to react.

"Are you serious, Rave? Harry's your grandpa?" Cassie asked, shock woven through her words. I told her what I had learned over the last few weeks about who the real Harry Fishmen was. "How did you find this out?"

"In the hospital. He told me in the hospital Labor Day weekend, Cass. He remembered the cufflinks Rachel and I had given him. You know, the ones in the box? I showed them to him, and he said our names."

"I sure do, but I'm confused." She let out an audible sigh, and I could tell this hit her like a load of bricks dropped on her like it did me. "I don't understand. How did you know he was in the hospital…I'm dying here, Rave. Spit it out." Her voice rose an octave, and then I heard her slurp her tea.

"I wasn't trying to be stingy or insensitive to you, Cass. I needed to make sure it was the truth before I blabbed to anyone else. I didn't even tell Drew or Trey right away." I breathed in slowly, a layer of guilt covering me like a wet blanket. I'm sure, if the tables were turned, I'd feel this same way. "Forgive me?"

"Oh, gosh, Raven McKade, of course! I love you, my dear friend, and I'm so happy for you! I love that you're finally here in Florida, but you're still too damn far away. I wish I could give you a hug and celebrate with you."

"We can on Saturday when you're here to help me with my first catering job."

She paused before saying, "So…that means you've made up with Drew? The last you told me you refused to see him and didn't care if you ever saw him again. Something like that anyway." I heard more of a disciplinary than an inquisitive tone in her voice.

"Well, I lied."

"I guess so. Anything else I should know?" I caught a snide interjection in her question, which made me smile. This was the motherly part of Cassie coming out.

"We've made up. I'll tell you the rest in person."

"Deal."

As much as I valued my personal relationships, it became apparent to me that, for the moment, they had to be put on the back burner. The impending reunion with Grandpa Ben was not just another family gathering—it was a moment of monumental significance, a moment that held the power to mend hearts and heal decades-old wounds. For all of us, this reunion was a priority, a beacon of hope and joy amid the turmoil that life had thrown our way. It was an occasion that deserved our complete and undivided attention. A moment that couldn't be overshadowed by personal matters.

Drew honored me by stepping back and allowing my family the space and time to reconvene with our long-lost family member. I've appreciated the immense patience he's shown me through all of this, especially in relation to Devin. The blame I directed at him for what happened to me on that fateful Sunday had now simmered, and the angst and apprehension associating myself with him seemed to flitter away like leaves off a tree blowing in the wind. And that was a comforting feeling. At this juncture, bringing our family together was what mattered most. And Drew understood without question.

He willingly gave me my space. He knew that the timing of his party and it being my first catering job was an added load of stress on top of my family visiting. Plus, learning the amazing fact that this very house I bought held secrets to the disappearance of my grandfather. It takes time to process such facts.

"Take all the time you need, Miss Raven McKade. Whenever you're ready, I'll be here." Drew had tucked a note in my mailbox the morning after we reignited the inevitable spark that still burned between us. I tingled just thinking about it. Yesterday, when Drew walked over with a dozen roses. I nearly dropped to my knees, my heart melting at such kindness. I had been vehemently focused on the steps for preparing my hors d' oeuvres for his party when the doorbell rang. Fumbling out of the dining room chair, I continued scratching a few more notes down as my feet inherently stepped toward the door. My jaw dropped along with the pen in of my hand when I opened the door. The aroma of fresh-cut roses blasted my senses and sent my heart fluttering but not as much as the man holding them. Drew came by, strictly to confirm the last of the details for his party. But before he grabbed the handle to the front door, he caressed my lips with a kiss that sent me skyward. He teased me in the worst way, but I liked it.

Grandpa Ben had been slowly improving till yesterday when I got a call from Terri. Apparently, through the night, his breathing stopped for a short minute, and the gentleman in charge of the midnight shift had to call the EMTs to the house. He didn't have to be taken in; they stabilized him right there, but the diagnosis was a small stroke. His speech and memory were debilitated for a few hours, but eventually, his vitals returned to normal range after increasing his oxygen levels that he'd remain on till further notice.

I was so beside myself with this bit of news. All I could think about was my mother coming to visit and be reunited with her father. We needed him strong and healthy. I begged for Grandpa Ben to heal, that his strength and vitality be returned. I felt so desperate. I had hoped Grandpa Ben would be up and dancing like Fred Astaire by the time my parents would arrive.

I loved watching Grandpa Ben eat what I cooked for him, especially the roasted vegetables and wild rice dishes. It was comical hearing him use the word "yum" after every bite. I made a raspberry and pear compote to drizzle over my homemade vanilla ice cream for a soothing dessert. At first, his mouth puckered. I grinned and told him, "There's very little sugar in this, so it will taste tart until you get used to it." His facial features had slightly drooped on his left side, but he could tease me by flashing me a pouty look and then quickly changing it to a sideways smile with an exaggerated eye roll. I even made a pasta dish with bits of SPAM in it. I didn't care for it, but he gave me two thumbs up. It felt like a simple game we played when I came to visit.

Drew also joined me a few days ago when I brought a homemade pizza with Alfredo sauce, chicken sausage, and spinach. It turned out to be a fun time. Between mouthfuls and shared smiles, and a few giggles, Grandpa Ben opened up a bit as he broke the comfortable silence with a question. His voice, despite his situation, still held the familiar timbre of concern and care. I was mid-bite when he asked, "Where's your mother?"

I sucked in a gasp but kept chewing as if it didn't faze me. Sweat trickled down my back. They had to keep the room cool and dry for him, so I wore a sweater during my visits, but right now, as the heat rose in my body, I removed it. I met his eyes, brimming with anticipation, and responded with a hopeful tone, "She's in Minnesota and doing wonderfully." I just fibbed, but it would be a mistake to tell him what truth I knew. "She'll be here next week to see you!" The words hung in the air, a promise of a reunion that I had been waiting for.

I watched his hand holding the pizza slice stop in midair as I observed him processing what I said. I set my plate down, waiting for what was to come next. I looked at Drew, who kept chewing, not seeming to be bothered about this. There was no reason for him to understand. I was just thankful he was here with me. I leaned toward my grandpa and said, "Does it bother you to see her? Should we wait till another time?"

Oh, God, I was hoping not. Inside, my head spun like a wound-up vintage spinning top with awful thoughts that maybe this shouldn't happen just yet. Then when? I was torn. His eyes, once clouded with hesitation, had now opened wider, reflecting a decision made after careful contemplation. His voice, frail yet firm, carried the acceptance that I'd hoped to hear. "It would be great to see Elaine again," he said, and then my heart stopped. My eyes darted at Drew, who looked confused, and then back at my grandfather.

Betsy was my mother's name, not Elaine. Elaine was my grandmother's name.

He recognized his mistake and mouthed *Sorry.* "I know what you meant, Grandpa," I replied softly as I laid my hand on his arm. His chin met his chest, and I watched a single tear rush over the deep grooves of his cheek. My shoulders trembled as I pushed back the tears welling up in my eyes. It hurt me to see my grandpa riddled with shame and pain. Drew walked over and sat next to Grandpa on the other side. I reached for Drew's hand across my grandpa's legs, and then we clasped hands with Grandpa Ben and sat in silence for a moment, the three of us looking at one another. I could tell Drew was anxious; his hands were lined with perspiration. I'm sure he felt out of place, so I squeezed his hand in a way that made him look at me. I smiled and silently mouthed *thank you.*

"Drew, would you mind checking to see if I have any more wild rice in my fridge?" He took the cue with flying colors. He clasped his other hand over Grandpa Ben's and wished him well that he'd be back soon. After giving me a peck on the cheek, he quietly left, leaving me and my grandpa alone.

I looked directly into the weary gray eyes of my grandfather and asked him, "Would you like to see your daughter, Betsy?" I suddenly felt a quick sharp pain in my cheek from biting it so hard. My body was so tense the toes in my left foot were numb. I uncrossed my legs and sat up straighter in my chair, fervently trying to release my tension.

"Yes, please. Please bring my daughter here."

A silent 'thank you' slipped from my lips, a prayer of gratitude for granting this heartfelt wish. The words were silent, but the sentiment was loud—a silent plea transformed into a solemn hymn of appreciation. This news had infused a warmth in me that was difficult to contain, radiating in my smiles and brightening my steps.

My Grandpa was back.

CHAPTER 29

Saturday, September 19th

"Okay, everyone, smile!" As soon as the five clicks sounded off, they all relaxed their picture poses as I walked over to the island to retrieve the camera and tripod. Violet followed me.

"Raven, what's your favorite word?" Violet rephrased her question after she saw the funny look on my face. "I mean, today. What would you say your favorite word of the day is?" I had to admit, with not having the experience as a mother with teenagers, I wondered if this was some kind of new game the kids were all playing now.

"Um…how about friends?" I watched her expression fade.

"No! Party! It's a party because that's what we're doing today. You know, Dad's party? Afterwards, we're going to have a party ourselves in the pool. Dad said." Her hazel eyes glistened with excitement. "Thanks so much for letting me help you cater my dad's party," she added, giving me a quick hug and a peck on my cheek.

I smiled as I watched her rejoin the group that stood around my dining table going over last-minute details and instructions in our service for Drew's vendor party. Cassie, Deidra and I wore black Bermuda shorts with a simple white V-neck tee. Violet and Felicia had on short shorts that only tiny young girls could get away with, although I overheard Cassie giving them the motherly spiel about shorts that barely cover your "you-know-what" and why boys like them. Their serious visage quickly softened, whispering in each other's ears once Cassie's attention turned to Deidra, who had a question. Because Phoebe had made the cast in her school play Mama Mia, she wasn't able to help us, which made Violet sad, but I was happy she had another friend that was able to help out.

Before we all needed to pack up and head over to Drew's house, I showed everyone the picture of us standing in line against the backdrop of my island. Clad in our matching black and white attire and striped cocktail aprons, we looked like a group of ladies ready for business. Felicia and Violet wore bright red baseball caps, while Cassie, Deidra, and I wore red headbands. Deidra's glossy red lipstick lit up the photo second in line to our toothy white smiles. This was definitely frame-worthy.

"Is Drew ready for his *magnificos servidores*?" Deidra asked as we walked out the front door, our arms loaded with platters and boxes. I had the backdoor lifted on my Escalade, so it was easy to slide in what was left to bring over. Luke and Phoenix had already taken over a trunk full. Originally, Luke was going to stay back and work on their yard with Phoenix's help, but Drew begged him to reconsider. According to Cassie, it didn't take much. Hanging out by a gorgeous pool, drink in hand, hob-knobbing with a group of people Drew caters to? "He had dollar signs lighting up his eyes after he hung up with Drew," Cassie said. I could tell she was delighted he was along but had wished Phoebe could have been part of this party, being my first catering job.

"There will be another," I said with more confidence than I'd felt in weeks.

"*Claro!*" replied Violet with certainty.

"You know Spanish?" I gave Violet an appraising elbow bump to her arm.

"*Claro!* Of Course…it's almost as important as learning English living in Florida.

"The twins are taking Spanish and Italian," Cassie added and then planted a friendly slap to my shoulder. I guess I was the only one in the dark about these facts. Again, something I'd be dealing with if I was a mother.

We were all set. Violet and Felicia were in charge of getting drink orders. With only three choices--red wine, white wine, and bourbon neat—it was easy for the young girls to understand. Cassie poured and helped the young girls serve while Deidra helped me assemble the first round of hors d'oeuvres. One tray of each--salmon tartare on cucumbers, roasted grape crostini's with rosemary, and prosciutto-wrapped pear with arugula—was served by the five of us on bright silver serving trays as we carefully shuffled through the crowd without spilling their drinks or dumping our trays. I told everyone it was detrimental to watch for flinging arms or quick turns of the clients while they excitedly talked among themselves. I learned it while hosting parties at my remodeling store and watching the caterers and how they delicately maneuvered through the crowd, especially my crowd of laborers; carpet and wood installers, sheet-rockers, and tile layers. They could become a little rambunctious after a few drinks standing around in a circle telling their stories.

"Oh my God, did you see that guy almost swung his arm in my face!" Violet exclaimed to Felicia as they walked back to load up their trays with more of the salmon on cucumber bites. "You were right, Raven, and thank God I saved my tray." I filled her tray, nodding in amusement at her near-miss experience. It was adorable. Felicia's hand was glued to her throat while Violet told her story.

"I'm going inside to get more bottles of wine. Those two ladies over there talking with Drew wanted a third glass," Cassie said, pointing a darting thumb in front of her as she faced me. "Drew said it was good."

"Oh, exceptions for the ladies, huh?" I said in jest.

"I guess so." Cassie displayed a playful grin as she slipped inside.

I could hear Deidra's girlish giggle all the way across the pool. She was delivering a tray of prosciutto and arugula bites and must have gotten caught up in a conversation. Trey was beside her and three other men who dressed, like most of the other guests, for a comfortable hot day, but the ironed creases in their tailored shorts and short-sleeved button-up shirts lit up with dollar signs. I could only imagine what they spent on their hairstylist. The few ladies in attendance had on summer dresses that simply smelled expensive. I wasn't surprised at the echelon of guests at Drew's party. In fact, it was a given. We're talking about Drew Hampton of Hampton Pools—the Harvey Specter doppelganger.

By 7:30, the small bites were gone except for the platter I hid inside Drew's fridge. I specifically made extra for the rest of us after the guests left. I knew we'd be hungry. "The bar is closed," Drew kindly announced to the few remaining guests. There were over a hundred, and by the time they had all left, the only signs that a party had occurred were the dirty white linen tablecloths that Violet and Felicia had rolled up in a heap for the dry cleaners and a few stray napkins fluttering around on the ground.

Drew grabbed a drink and sat with the rest of us tired servers in the corner of his patio next to the sliding doors. The air had cooled down, and the sun was a dynamic orange glow in the distance. Drew lit three large citronella candles in tall hurricane pillars that stood on two-foot pedestals surrounding us. The winds were picking up, and we could hear the Gulf waters splashing against the property rock ledge.

"This was my best party yet," Drew directed at the group, a pleasing note in his voice. "No one got crazy. No one fell in the pool, and I see the helium balloons are still intact. Not like a few years ago."

"That was just last year, Dad," Violet corrected. Drew thought for a moment and then nodded his head.

"You're right, that's when your mother showed up to get you, chewing me out in front of the CEO of Aquatic Motions." He drank from his glass before he added with hesitation, "That's why I was a little worried…"

"Dad, it was so much fun, and Raven is the best!" She punched her hands in an air-high-five at me, which I returned.

Drew turned directly at me with a raised glass, which everyone followed, including the kids, with their sodas or whatever they found left in the cooler. "And the "Rave reviews" on the food were non-stop. All thanks to you, Raven McKade. Your first catering job deserves an A+." They all clapped after taking a sip and setting their drinks down.

"Thank you to you ladies for being such…wonderful sous chefs and fabulous servers." I inhaled to steady myself. "The food…looked better than the pictures. I really appreciated your attention to detail." I tried covering up my sappy broken words by splashing another gulp of wine in my mouth. My emotions were bombarding me like a tsunami wave, and I didn't know why. Drew's gaze stayed locked on me, so I blew him a kiss.

Drew walked me over to the other side of the patio, closer to his outdoor kitchen, and motioned me to sit on one of the bar seats. He opened the tiny under-counter wine cooler and pulled out a bottle of Mailly Brut reserve champagne, and popped the cork so quick I hadn't realized he'd already removed the metal caging. After pouring only two glasses, I wondered about the rest, but when I looked back, Cassie and Deidra were jovially chatting on the edge of the pool, their feet soaking in the water. Lights illuminated the bottom of the pool. The three kids were involved in a game of volleyball, and Luke and Trey were bellied up at the other makeshift bar we used for the party earlier.

I turned my attention back to Drew, who leaned over the bar and planted a gentle kiss on my lips. "Here's to Raven Mckade, entrepreneur and extraordinaire and creator of Food & Wine Club with Raven, soon to be aired on local television. To a successful beginning and a lucrative future." My eyes shot open with shock as we toasted with a clink of our crystal champagne flutes.

"What did you just say?" I said after allowing the fizzy liquid stream down my throat. "Television?"

"Why not? I know people." The sound of his voice and the gleam in his eyes melted my heart more and more as I listened to him rattle off this game plan he had for me and my cooking videos. I heard bits and pieces, but I honestly couldn't keep my attention on the subject any longer. It was as if the walls were collapsing, and the loosened boulders pounded against what little fighting resistance I had left in me. Drew hadn't a clue as to what was going on inside my head and my heart, not a clue as to how he was affecting me this very moment, and I cherished the very essence of it.

As dawn broke, I looked out the window at a painting of the sky in hues of pink and orange. I was in the shelter of Drew's bedroom. Last night, after everyone left, Drew and I found ourselves with a bottomless champagne bottle and desires that swooped us up the elevator to the third floor. Our hands roamed freely, tracing the familiar and yet unknown contours of each other's bodies. Every sigh, every touch was an exploration, a tender dance that was as exhilarating as it was intimate. Every caress was a wordless confession, and each kiss was a promise. Our bodies intertwined in a language older than time, something I never thought I'd experience after Jack, which was another reason I said no to Drew walking me home and exploring this seductive dance further in my bedroom. With the photo tucked in the drawer near the bed, I had second thoughts after Drew stayed last week. I'd somehow need to make amends with this shame I kept holding onto. It wasn't right, but my heartstrings tugged at just the notion of us being together in this room while his picture remains close by. Something has to change soon, or I'd be twirling in the tornado cloud forever.

If it hadn't been for Violet talking me into reconsidering the catering job, I wouldn't have fallen into the inviting arms of a man who promises he will never stop loving me and will never turn against me. He poured his heart out as we connected in a way only two lovers could, and I found myself constantly in awe with every word he spoke of his desire to be with me.

And that kind of generosity, that kind of genuine kindness, always brought tears to my eyes. It was as if Drew had a special gift for touching people's hearts, and I felt profoundly grateful to be on the receiving end.

How hard is it to accept this man, and why did I fight it?

CHAPTER 30

Wednesday, September 23rd

A long-stretch limo pulled up at the end of my driveway. Drew offered to have my family picked up from the airport via a limo instead of our two vehicles. When Carly called me to say they passed through the gate, I watched from the window. Without having to drive to the airport, it gave me time to tidy up with the last details scribbled on my notes. I made sure my refrigerator was organized, and the bathroom necessities were replenished. I also wondered about having alcohol out in the open and decided to store it all behind the solid doors in my closet. Out of sight, out of mind. I hadn't inquired about any rules regarding Mom and the continuing recovery process once she returned home. But if I had to guess, it would be detrimental at any time.

"Are you sure you want me here right now? Shouldn't I give you some time to be alone with your family…to catch up first before you introduce me?" Drew was visibly anxious.

"If you weren't here to support me through all of this, I'd be hunting you down and dragging you here." I lifted up on my tiptoes and wrapped my arms around his neck. Just the smell of him calmed me.

After we parted, he placed a hand on my heart. "I think you're in aerobic mode." I could feel my heart racing all morning. I felt like I'd been in aerobic mode since I moved in. I had a sad thought of sipping a glass of wine while I got myself and the house ready, but how could I rely on such a notion when that's exactly what my mother did to override her anxiety. Disgusted with that thought, I, instead, made a large iced hibiscus tea and poured it in a wine glass.

"I guess my tea didn't calm me down enough."

"Maybe this will," Drew's silky voice against my ear brought goosebumps, but his lingering kiss on my neck and then my lips, quashed the tension that had riddled my body.

Drew and I stood on the top step while the limo driver opened the suicide doors to let everyone out. My dad appeared first, with Pete close behind. The rest followed, with my mother the last to step out. As I approached with open arms, my surprise was Rachel grabbing me first in a hug I had never felt from her before. It felt sincere and inviting, not forced or cold. She looked at me, tears already pooling in her eyes, and said, "Raven, this is absolutely beautiful! Your house is a real beach house. No more pine decorations for you." She lightly poked my shoulders as we both laughed at the many memories of pinecones and birch logs placed around my home in Minnesota.

The rest of the family scattered around the yard, checking out my landscape options in between hugs and hello's. I was surprised at the affectionate gestures they all had toward me. Yes, we hugged and said the normal pleasantries to one another when meeting up, but this seemed over the top mushy. Even my nieces leaned in for a peck on my cheek.

Drew took care of the limo driver as they all assembled around the front door waiting for me to usher them in. But, first, I needed to snatch my mother away from my nieces, Lindsay and Lexi, who were engrossed with the birds of paradise blooms, snapping all kinds of pictures on their cell phones and asking their grandmother why the grass felt so different on their sandaled feet. As Drew walked back to my group of family members, my father approached him with a solid handshake, and they chatted while I pulled Mom to the side. I waved the rest to go in with their luggage if they wanted.

"Mom, how are you doing? You look so rested, and your skin…" I touched her face, her eyes squinting from the sun, so I turned her back to the sun and peered into her bluish-gray eyes. Instantly, I saw the resemblance to those of the man just down the street; Benjamin Pierce III, my mother's father. Our plan tonight, over dinner, was to announce the news to my mom that her father was found and lives just a few blocks away. And if that is deciphered without a breakdown, I'd tell her that this very house was the first house he had built in this development. But not before I had a private conversation with my dad and Rachel, making sure we agreed on her state of mind and strength to be able to process this astonishing news. As I observed my mother's smile, her graying hair, now cut and layered, and her fitted new dress in garden colors, I refused to think back on the day I left and the condition she was in. It was heartbreaking to think about seeing the woman standing in front of me now. In front of me was a woman that radiated hope and new beginnings. The clarity in her eyes was the biggest transformation.

We held each other in a hug for so long, the heat forming between our bonded bodies was becoming uncomfortable for both of us. "It's too hot to hug out here," she said, wiping her neck with the lightweight sweater she had hanging over her tote on the ground next to her. "It was freezing in the airport and in the limo, but out here…by the way, who ordered us a limo? That's got to be ungodly expensive. We could have taken a cab or something." She picked up her bag from the ground as I gestured for all to get inside. I didn't want anyone passing out from the heat.

It took everyone a while to get situated in their rooms. Sounds of drawers and closet doors opening and shutting, my dad's voice light and airy as he asked my mother how she's holding up if she'd like a nap before dinner. Lexi and Lindsay came running out to the living room with their mini-computers in hand, screaming with excitement about being in Florida and what seat they're going to sit in. "Thanks, Aunt Raven. Wow! These are cool chairs!" I told Drew to pour them each a glass of Root Beer.

Rachel walked out to the kitchen and asked if I needed help. She looked over at Drew and the girls for an observant moment and then I felt her whisper breath near my ear, "God, is he a shoo-in for that dude on *Suits* or what?" Drew glanced at us but quickly turned his attention back to the girls who were telling him to look at what they were pointing at on their computer screens.

I busted out laughing but slapped my hand over my mouth. Rachel gave me a funny look. "I know he does. He's Harvey Specter's doppelganger for sure, and I've told him that."

"No way, you have? Does he know who it is?" Sometimes Rachel's naivete made you scratch your head, scrambling for a response.

I changed the subject for more relevant reasons. "Tell me the truth, is Mom strong enough to take the news? Do you think she'll be to handle it?" I asked Rachel looking directly into her eyes. She had a habit of blurting out an answer without thinking first, and even Pete agreed that her eyes were a tell-all.

"Before we boarded, Dad mentioned he had butterflies all night long about Mom seeing her father again." I had Rachel mixing up a vegetable dip. I thought a few munchies would be good while we hung out together before dinner later on.

"So, does that mean Mom is good to go?"

"The conversation I had with Mom over the phone when they let her out…what day is today? Wednesday? I guess it was Sunday. She said she couldn't wait to get down here to see you and that she's finally in her right mind, if that makes sense," Rachel replied, an obvious hesitation in her tone.

"We should talk with Dad then," I said more as a statement than a question.

"Yes, totally agree."

Dad came around the corner from down the hall changed from a dress shirt and khakis to shorts and a striped short-sleeved button-up. "Your mother is going to rest a little bit before we all gather for dinner." I looked at the clock. It was close to three o'clock. We planned on dinner at five.

"Is she going to be able to handle the news?" I said with a hint of impatience. I'd been dreaming about this moment for days now and was dying inside for it to all come together finally.

My dad rubbed his forehead, and I stood with my fingers wrapped so tightly behind my back they started to ache. Rachel finished laying the vegetables haphazardly on the plate with dividers and looked up at the two of us. "What do you think, Dad?"

"I think she's going to be able to handle it. Let's see when she wakes from her nap. Do you have any herbal tea? Lemon or ginger by chance?" My dad gazed around at all the cabinets, raising his eyebrows.

"I know. I've never had this many cabinets in a kitchen in my life," I said, a proud laugh escaping my throat. Rachel looked around without interest which didn't surprise me. A long time ago, she told me her tiny kitchen was all she needed. I replied to Dad, "Of course, I have tea. I have all those choices."

I could barely hold myself together through dinner. My anxiousness and anticipation of what was coming next overrode my interest in the small talk happening around the table. I was deeply involved with thoughts of Grandpa Ben and how he was doing today. I never received a text from Terri updating me on his condition. She was fully aware that my family was coming and wanted to visit with "Harry" before the weekend was over, and they had to head back to Minnesota. I was told it should be just fine and that Thursday or Friday would be great after his afternoon rest, that she'd text when he was up and ready for a visit. It's all I thought about during our dinner.

I owed Drew my life for being so congenial and helpful to my family. Rachel and I prepped the red snapper and shrimp for Drew to grill. My father joined him for the fifteen minutes it took to cook it all up. My mother and Rachel chopped the broccoli, cauliflower, and carrots while I made the sauces. Earlier, I made a potato salad and wild rice side dish. Lindsay and Lexi were picky eaters, according to Rachel, so I also made homemade cherry popsicles to bribe them with just in case they weren't going to eat any fish or vegetables. The rice and potato salad were a must for this Minnesota clan.

While the girls set the table, I took a hiatus into my closet and slugged down a few gulps of wine. I hated myself for it, but my nerves were about to fizzle into a fiery storm if I didn't do something to calm the burning itch. Plus, I saw my dad and Drew sipping a beer while they were outside and justified that if my dad could indulge, then why couldn't I? Something I hadn't asked about earlier when the three of us chatted quietly about telling Mom the terrific news. I primed myself in the mirror before rejoining my family. A wave of heat passed through my veins after downing three glugs of red wine, so I spritzed on a coconut-scented body spray down my cleavage and around my neck. I applied a swipe of pink lip gloss and adjusted a few locks of hair around my face. As I leaned in closer to the mirror, the tiny red lines in the white of my eyes just weren't going away; stress-pure stress. And I'm not even forty yet.

After dinner, my father and I walked out to the garage to dump the garbage. He suggested I give him a tour of my yard. "Do you think we could all go for a walk? It seems much nicer than it was when you first arrived." I hoped my dad would say yes. Then I could nonchalantly pass by Grandpa Ben's and point out where we all were going tomorrow, and then when we'd arrive back home, we could tell Mom the good news. I still hadn't heard from Terri, though, so it made me nervous as to why. Maybe it was simple; she hadn't received my text so I'd send another text later on just to verify our plans for tomorrow.

"Yes, that would be a lovely idea," my father said with an encouraging lilt in his voice.

Twenty minutes later with full stomachs, we scampered out the door. My nieces led the way and asked questions about everything and anything regarding Florida. To them, it seemed like a different planet compared to Minnesota. I heard them bragging to a friend on their cell phone. I guess Rachel and Pete gave into their rule of no phones till they were fifteen. I never thought that would happen.

"Isn't this wonderful?" I said to my mom, my arm hooked in hers. The men were walking ahead with Lindsay and Lexi while Rachel and I stayed next to Mom.

"It sure is, Raven. You've made yourself a wonderful home." She walked slowly, breathing in the air deeply through her nose, the setting sun bouncing off the water between the houses to our right. We had over an hour till sunset and planned on seeing the view from Drew's house on our way back. "Do you know who originally built your home? I'm only asking because you showed me pictures of it being gutted. I take it you didn't care for the other person's design."

My heart skipped a beat. I was shocked she'd ask such a question when I remember her being more buzzed up than sober when I did show her pictures. "Um…yes, I do." Rachel threw me a warning glance. "The original builder was the man who bought this development, and my house was the first one he built."

"Oh, so it was outdated. I see," my mother replied assuredly. There was no need for correction or to expound on her statement. I saw a pinched smile on Rachel's face, and knew I was safe at the moment, even though I was busting at the seams to tell her the truth.

We were a few houses past Drew's when my father approached me and motioned for Rachel and my mother to join the others up ahead. My mom gave him a funny look but then smiled, holding her hand on his arm while he lightly kissed her temple. It made me feel giddy inside to see this loving connection between my parents. I couldn't remember the last time I had seen true affection between them.

"What's up, Dad?"

"I'm thinking this would be a good time to broach the subject of Benjamin." His eyes were wide with anticipation. I knew exactly how he felt.

"It's not going to send her over the edge with it being a traveling day and all?"

"I believe this to be the icing on the cake."

"I love how you've phrased that because when we get to Drew's, I've a homemade cheesecake waiting just for you. Oh, and Drew. It's his favorite too. And a carrot cake. Mom and Rachel's favorite." I posed a wrinkled frustrated look at him. "I forgot to make Pete's favorite; chocolate brownies. Ughhh…He's going to be hurt." And then we let out a quiet belly laugh because we both knew Pete eats anything, especially desserts.

Dad and I waved the group back toward us, most had questionable expressions, except for the young girls, who seemed to be engrossed in their own little world. We unintentionally made a small circle around Mom which made her face crinkle with concern. "Mom, we have some good news."

"Fantastic news!" Rachel burst out.

"We found your father, our Grandpa Ben, Mom." I waited for her response, but we got nothing but a blank stare. I tried looking to see if her chest was moving, that she was breathing in and out like the rest of us with such excitement.

Slowly, while her body stayed still, her eyes shifted to her right, directly at Dad. "Is this true? Is this why you were talking with Raven?" I was becoming nervous watching how stiff her body was. She wasn't moving a muscle. I glanced at Pete and Rachel. Drew stood behind them. All three of them stiff with anticipation.

"Mom, are you alright?"

"Of course, I'm alright. Why wouldn't I be?" I sighed in relief. I could see everyone else dropping their shoulders as if they were attached to their ears. "Where is he?"

My father wrapped his arms around my mother as they walked in the direction I told them to go. Emotionally, I was on top of the world in love with my life at this very moment. The three of us couples walked with our arms around our partners in silence as we headed toward Grandpa Ben's house. Elation filled the air around us, and I could feel in my soul how wonderful it was going to be when we visited him tomorrow. My father was relaying the message to my mother that it was too late tonight and that he needed his rest for our visit tomorrow.

We were about a block and a half from Grandpa's house, and an ambulance cruised by. No sound, just flashing lights. They pulled into the driveway; Grandpa Ben's driveway. I was delirious. I snapped myself out of Drew's hold and ran toward the house. I barely made the steps before an EMT held me back from going any further. I yelled for Terri, who instantly appeared, shock written all over her face, as was mine. Placing her hands in mine, she stared into my eyes that were dripping with tears. My parents stood behind me, and we all watched while they brought out a stretcher, a sheet draped over the body.

I turned to Terri, horror bulging in my eyes, and I said, "What happened? He can't be gone! He can't be gone..nooooo!!!" She pulled me into a tight hold, telling my parents to please not go anywhere. They needed to stay right here with me.

I fell to the ground, screaming and frantically crying out for Grandpa Ben. My family surrounded me as I pounded the ground in anger, my mother knelt beside me rubbing my back. Drew and Pete asked Terri questions that I couldn't decipher, the blood was pounding in my ears and my heart was frantically beating like horse hooves on pavement.

"Mr. and Mrs. McKade, I assume? I'm sorry to tell you Harry has passed away. It happened less than a half hour ago. I'm so sorry," Terri said. She put a hand on my shoulder. My legs were too weak to stand. My father helped me up, but I wobbled like a wet noodle. I noticed my mother had her palm over her mouth, standing like a statue staring at the front door of Grandpa's house. I'm sure she did not understand hearing the name Harry. Dad, with a shaky voice, calmly talked with Terri about some immediate details concerning Harry.

Dad and Rachel told Mom the full story of how I found him. I sat to the side and watched in horror my mother's stoic reaction. I don't think she could process what my father and Rachel were telling her. I didn't know what to think about any of this. I was devastated that my mother never got to be reunited with her father.

After learning the truth about Harry, now Benjamin Pierce III, Terri asked if she could come by the next day to talk with us.

We were all huddled around the breakfast nook, except my nieces. Drew had picked them up a few hours earlier so they could have fun in his pool with Violet while we visited with Terry. She handed me a legal-sized envelope. Inside was a note and the items I had originally put in an envelope in his mailbox—the locket necklace and the newspaper article. According to Terri, I was to read this note in front of my mother, my father, and my sister, per Benjamin.

The note read:

My lovely granddaughter Raven. The day I heard the name of the person who purchased the house at 2028 Pelican Drive, I knew it had to be my granddaughter from Minnesota. There is no other Raven McKade. When I found this out and learned who you were, I watched your cooking videos and saw your store, Raven's Remodeling, online. I was made aware of these wonderful things by the person that has since crudely violated you. I cannot tell you how sorry I am and how sorry that I entrusted him to keep you at a distance from me. I was scared to death of you finding out about me, and as your contractor tore more walls out, I was devastated at the thought of you finding the items I specifically buried in those walls for reasons you now know. I was afraid of your reaction to me and where I ended up. I only hope that you can get through this knowing I have loved you and your sister and my daughters so much that it has broken my heart further to know your innocent angel heart has forgiven me for the wretched selfish acts I committed as a father and a grandfather during your lives.

I have willed to you, Raven Elaine McKade, every item and possession I own under the names.

Harry Joseph Fishmen and Benjamin Alfred Pierce III.

Take the keys you found and open the box buried in the shed in the backyard. There you will find pieces of jewelry that belonged to your grandmother, gifts your precious grandmother had given me, and $1Million in cash.

This will not redeem me of my cowardly sins, but please understand it's all I have for my atonement.

Pete and Drew dug up the box the next day while my father, Rachel, and I comforted Mom. She was dreadfully shocked, barely spoke for twenty-four hours, but listened intently to me explaining how I came about this information and what Grandpa Ben had told me in the hospital. I watched how her body slumped with sadness, knowing how close she had come to touching her long-lost father after all these years. She drank cups upon cups of chamomile tea during their duration here at my house. My father never left her side. We all seemed to be in a catatonic state for a good reason. There wasn't any fighting or shouting, just quiet moments filled with memory here and there. I planned on flying to Minnesota for a few weeks to be with my family as we needed to figure out some details regarding what he had left me in the will. I wanted to be close to them and make sure we could get back to a normal routine, knowing that we'd fully forgiven Benjamin Pierce III and that there wasn't a need to wonder anymore.

Since their flight back home was on Monday, Rachel and I made funeral arrangements for Grandpa on Sunday, the 27th of September. We all attended, including Drew, Trey, and Deidra. My family and I gazed at him peacefully, lying in the casket, noting the many changes that occurred from the pictures embedded in our minds from the past. I wanted this to be a private ceremony since Harry Fishmen was the resident the rest of the neighborhood was familiar with. I knew Frankie, as HOA president, would set up and conduct a memorial for him at the clubhouse. I didn't involve myself with the neighborhood service. Harry Fishmen wasn't a part of me, and it was best that the neighboring residents saw it that way.

My heart broke knowing my dad and Rachel never had a chance to be reunited with Grandpa Ben while he was alive, but my heart completely fell apart watching my mother's dream of finding her father completely disappear. All she could do was touch her lips and place those same fingers on his lips before we closed the casket for good.

Made in the USA
Monee, IL
15 February 2024

53594380R00164